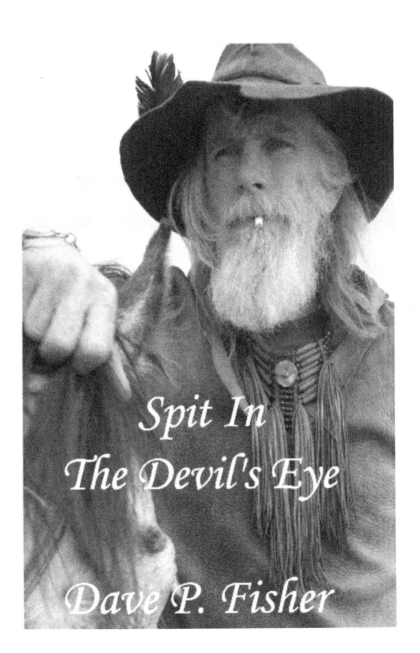

Spit In
The Devil's Eye

Dave P. Fisher

Cover Art:
Michelle Crocker

http://mlcdesigns4you.weebly.com/

Publisher's Note:

This is a work of fiction. All names, characters, places, and
events are the work of the author's imagination.

Any resemblance to real persons, places, or events is
coincidental.

Solstice Publishing - www.solsticepublishing.com

Spit in the Devil's Eye
by
Dave P. Fisher

Spit in the Devil's Eye

Chapter One

The young man was rushed along the dock between two burly Dock Watchmen. The ragged thin shirt he wore did nothing to prevent their dirty fingernails from digging to the bone of his upper arms where little muscle existed. He could smell the rum and stink on them that rose even above that of the cast-off bed pots and rotting sea waste of the Liverpool harbor.

The night hid their work as the watchmen opened a heavy wooden door and threw the young man forward. His cry of pain as he fell to the stone floor was covered by the slamming and bolting of the door. He lay still as the shoes of the men shuffled around him on the damp stone floor.

The two men latched onto his arms, lifted him, and threw him down into a wooden chair with one short leg. His long hair hung over his eyes as he waited for what would happen next. He was frightened. Even after eight years of surviving on the docks and streets, stealing, robbing, and killing, he was always frightened.

A cold laugh sounded from across the table he sat beside. "Well, well, if it's not Jules Drake. We haven't had you in the Bridewell in, oh, two or three weeks."

Jules slowly parted the dirty blonde hair that hung over his eyes and looked into the cynical face of the man he knew only as Mutton, as the boys liked to call the head of the Dock Watch. He stared at the white mutton chop sideburns that gave him his name. The most frightening aspect of Mutton was his little malicious eyes that enjoyed inflicting fear and pain.

Mutton went on, "We know you killed that little rat Morgan last evening. Stuck a shiv in his back *six times*. My, such anger. I don't care about the little wharf rat, but I had special uses for him and now I no longer have that."

"I never did," Jules choked out the words.

A heavy hand slammed across his ear sending him

5

flying back to the stone floor. He winced in pain, covering the ear with his hand. He pulled the hand away to find it bloody. The watchmen threw him back in the chair.

Mutton grinned, "You interrupted me. That is quite rude. How old are you, Drake?"

Jules' eyes flicked back and forth to the men around him. "Seventeen, sir, I think."

"Very good, the right age. I have a position for you, Drake."

Jules looked across the table at Mutton without answering.

Mutton glanced at one of the Watchmen, "Tell Robby we have one for him, the usual price."

Mutton returned his pig-like eyes to Jules. "I had your mother again last night. Did you know she is using opium now? Yes, I introduced her to that delicacy of the Orient and now she will do anything for me."

"She cast me out when a mere child, why should I care about the whore?"

"Why indeed?"

The comment returned Jules' thinking to his prostitute mother who kept a crib in an alley off the docks. She had kicked him out in a drunken fit when he was eight because he had a fruitless night picking pockets for her. The fact there was a gale blowing that night and no one was out made no difference.

He had learned the hard way how to cut a purse and pick a pocket. The first time he tried he was six and clumsily picked a shilling from a sailor's pocket and was caught. The beating he received still made his ears ring and only served to fester his hatred for all living beings. He made sure he was never caught again.

At ten, he killed another street waif for the coins he had collected from a cut purse. A year later he killed a merchant with a brick for the coins in his pouch. That was the first time he met Mutton and received a beating from his watchmen as he sat by and smiled. After that he was often dragged into the Bridewell for questioning.

He had killed Morgan. The gang leader had robbed him of his take for the last time. When Morgan had turned around to laugh he stuck the knife in him and kept sticking it in over and over. Morgan's gang saw the deed and gave chase, but he got away. The Watch was surely tipped off by the little squealers. He would kill them as well.

"You say you have a position for me, sir?" Jules asked.

"You are going to sea, Drake. First Mate Robinson of the Clipper ship *Montague* will be here for you shortly. She's a privateer owned by Lord Montague, a fine sleek vessel and you are to have a post on 'er."

Jules had often looked out to sea and wondered where the ships went as they sailed over the horizon. If nothing else, it was a way out of Liverpool.

"I shall be glad for the opportunity, sir." Jules hated Mutton with every ounce of his will, but knew that a submissive nature would take him further and more safely than a belligerent one.

Mutton rolled back his head and laughed loud and hearty. He looked back at Jules, "You have no idea."

A half hour passed in silence as Mutton and two watchmen passed a bottle of rum between them. They were well on their way to being drunk when the door opened and the watchman who had left walked in with a man dressed in seaman togs following him.

Jules took in the seaman. He was short but stout, heavily muscled with a thick neck. His black hair was tied back in a greasy tail and a short cropped beard covered most of his face. As with Mutton, this man had cold, cruel eyes that looked on all he saw with a sense of contempt and loathing.

"Ah, First Mate Robinson," Mutton slurred, "a pleasure to see you again."

Robinson glared at Mutton and then shifted his hard gaze to Jules. "Is this what you have for me?"

"Yes, a stout lad for your crew."

"He's a puny scarecrow, a white gilled weakling. I'd be better off with a girl than this little worm."

Mutton grinned slyly, "But I understand you lost a couple of crewmen on this last voyage. Doesn't Lord Montague demand a full crew?"

Robinson glanced toward Mutton with hate-filled eyes. "They went overboard."

"Jumped ship did they?"

"They went overboard," Robinson held his glare on Mutton.

Mutton smiled, knowing Robinson had a tendency to throw those he didn't like overboard while at sea. He took another pull from the bottle. "Put him to work scrubbing decks, that should put some muscle on him. Maybe put him in the kitchen."

"It's called a galley, yuh bloody dimwit."

Robinson looked Jules over. "Why is his ear bleeding?"

"He slipped on the damp floor."

"I don't want damaged goods. If they're damaged, it'll be by our doin'."

Mutton smirked, "Of course."

Robinson scowled, "I'll take him." He pulled a leather pouch from the pocket sewn to the outside of his pants. He opened it and removed several coins. He tossed the pouch on the table. "I don't pay full price for damaged goods."

Mutton waved a hand in the air in a gesture indicating he accepted the price.

Robinson grabbed Jules by the arm and lifted him out of the chair. "Come on scarecrow. You got a name?"

"Jules Drake, sir."

Together they walked out of the Bridewell without

another word to the watchmen. Once outside Robinson grabbed Jules by the throat with a huge hairy fist. With his other hand he pulled out a knife. "I can hit a moving target at a hundred paces so don't think of runnin'."

Jules' eyes grew large, he shook his head.

Robinson let go of him. "Follow me."

Jules walked a step behind the seaman as enmity swelled in his chest. He knew he had been yanked from a bad situation into a worse one. Although matters were out of his hands at present that didn't mean they had to stay that way. His mind was scheming. All the while he put up a false front of complacent acceptance. He would turn this to his advantage in the end.

Crossing the gangplank to the ship's deck a man stepped up to them and tapped his fingers to his forehead. "Mr. Robinson."

"Mr. Watts, this scarecrow is Drake. He will be swabbing decks under your watchful eye."

"Aye, sir. I'll be watchin' this one all right."

Robinson half turned toward Jules. "This is Bosun Watts, he deals out the work orders and the discipline on this ship. You will address him at all times as Mr. Watts. Understood?"

"Yes, Mr. Robinson."

Robinson walked off with Jules glaring daggers into his back. He looked back at Watts, who was smiling at him with a look that reminded him of a cat toying with a mouse before he killed it.

"Here's the word Drake, disobey one of my orders and you'll be kissin' the wooden lady. Disobey a second time, go to loafin', or steal from the galley and you'll be dancin' at the gratin's, you understand?"

Jules had no idea what the man was talking about. "Yes, Mr. Watts."

"Good." Watts looked up at the night sky, "It's a fine moonlit night we have here, just right for scrubbin' the decks so she's shinin' like a new penny in the mornin'. Mops and brushes are yonder. Get to work."

Jules worked through the night, falling asleep behind a coil of rope just before dawn. As the crew was assembled on deck he was found. Watts kicked him hard in the ribs. "Sleepin' on the job are yuh? Well, it's kissin' the wooden lady for you today."

Watts snapped an order, "Crane, Shoats, to the mast with him."

The two sailors dragged Jules to the mast, where his arms were stretched around the pole and shackled to the far side with his face against the rough wood of the mast.

Watts moved to where he could look in Jules' face. "The lads are obliged to kick your butt every time they pass. Have a nice day, Drake."

Jules' bitterness deepened through the day as heat, thirst, and hunger took their toll on his body. The seamen made it a point to walk by and kick his buttocks until he was numb from the shoulders down. At nightfall he was released and left to lay on the deck as his fevered mind twisted ever more to a state of loathing and planning on how he would kill Watts.

The ship was bound for Hong Kong. It was a long voyage around the Horn and up into the Pacific Ocean. Jules stayed out of trouble for three months until he caught a sailor stealing a lime from his hidden store. He stuck his knife into the man who wailed out in pain. For his part he found out what "dancing at the gratings" meant when he was shackled to the mast again and flogged repeatedly by Watts with a cat-o'-nine tails. He would murder Watts if it was the last thing he ever did.

As the months melted one into the other, Jules grew in strength and muscle from his labors. As his muscles grew, so did his yearning for a life where he was the master of his fate and any who opposed him would die. Still, for all his desires and bitterness, he harbored fear down in his heart. If he had the advantage he would kill, if not he would find a way to accomplish his goals without risk to himself.

The day arrived when the *Montague* dropped her moorings in the sea outside a Hong Kong harbor. Longboats were launched for the men to take a short shore leave by the captain's orders, much to the liking of the men. Jules had plotted for this day and placed himself in the same boat as Watts.

Pulling the boat alongside the dock the men climbed out. Jules walked up to Watts and put his hand on the bosun's back. "I would like to share a bottle with you, Mr. Watts. We have had our difficulties you and I, yet I know I was to fault. Come share a bottle with me."

Watts smiled, "Well, don't mind if I do. Why, you're not such a bad sort after all Drake, you'll make a seaman yet."

Jules smiled, "It's thanking you I'll be. Let's go have that bottle."

Jules stole two bottles of rum, giving one to Watts. Together they made their way down the street drinking. Jules pretended to be drinking, but was spitting the rum out, whereas Watts was guzzling it until staggering drunk.

Passing a dark, sinister-looking alley, Jules pointed down the cluttered pathway. "I say Mr. Watts, what is that?"

Watts tried to focus his eyes on the object Jules was pointing at. "What?" he slurred.

Jules gave Watts a slight push on the back. "Let's go have a see."

As Watts stumbled ahead, Jules slid his knife from the sheath.

Watts staggered into the alley, "What do yuh see? I don't see nothin'."

Jules growled savagely as he reached around Watts' neck and viciously sliced his throat to the spine.

Watts gurgled as he fell to his knees and then onto

his face.

Jules watched him with satisfaction. "I see that, you scurvy dog." He wiped the knife on the dead man's shirt, cut his coin purse out from inside his pants, and walked away from the body and the Montague.

The sea was not to his liking and he had no desire to remain in Hong Kong, where every minute he risked a knock on the skull and finding himself shanghaied onto a foreign vessel with a First Mate or Bosun that would make Watts look like a blessed saint. Avoiding the dives where shanghaiing crimps operated, he kept his head down, mouth shut, and ears open. He wanted out of the Orient and that would mean back to the sea again. He needed a ship to sign on to, but not one of British registry.

As he hurried along the docks, he passed a group of seaman sitting on dockside crates talking of the Oregon Land. Still carrying his bottle of rum he stepped up to the men. They looked him over, observing his sea-weathered face, calloused hands, and most importantly the bottle.

Jules smiled and handed the bottle to the nearest man who gladly accepted. "Gentlemen, I have signed off my ship and wish to leave these heathen yellow Chinee and this wretched land. I heard you speak of this Oregon Land. Tell me more."

The seaman that had the bottle passed it along. "'Tis a fair land on the east coast of the Pacific." He pointed eastward. "Inland it runs to mountains and wilderness, Rupert's Land it's called there. Goes for the Lord only knows how far, forever from the look of it."

"Who controls it?"

The seaman laughed, "The British hold it, the Americans want it, but it controls itself."

Another man spoke up, "Aye, the savages is what controls it."

Jules narrowed his eyes, "Savages?"

"Aye, the land is crawlin' with red heathen savages

that'll cut your heart out and eat yuh."

"Ah, that's only tales," the first man scoffed. "You've never gone in further than the harbor."

"The savages we trades with at Grays Harbor look fierce enough for me to believe it," he argued back.

A third chipped in, "It's a land of wealth. Gold just laying on the ground for the picking. Furs enough to cloak every royal in the world. It's a rich land I tell you, rich and no one to tell you otherwise or put out a hand to stop you."

The second man laughed as he took the bottle. "Surely, providin' the savages don't eat yuh."

Jules had heard enough. This Oregon, filled with wealth and no one to control your deeds or actions, was to his liking. As to the savages, if he could survive the docks of Liverpool, the savages would be nothing.

"This is a place I must see," Jules smiled at the group. "Is there a ship bound for it?"

The first man jabbed a thumb over his shoulder to the ship behind the group. "We are bound for Fort Vancouver and Grays Harbor on the Columbia. Sail with tomorrow's tide. See First Mate Closson and sign on."

"What country is the origin of your ship?"

"She's Dutch, but we sail to the pleasure of the Captain and his backers. Pick up silks and teas in China and furs from Oregon. We've men of all walks on board. We've a Britisher or two like yourself."

Jules thanked the men and proceeded to board the ship. A land of wealth, gold, furs, and no control. He knew enough to keep out of trouble on the ship and when he reached the other side he would be gone like a flash of gunpowder, inland and beyond.

Chapter Two

Reaching the shore of North America the ship slipped cautiously through the dangerous channel at Cape Disappointment, the deceptive mouth of the Columbia River, surrounded by shallow sand spits and the wreckage of ships. As the Montague tightened her lines, Jules again jumped ship and made his way inland. He wanted as much distance between him and the sea as possible.

He had been told of a Hudson Bay Company outpost called Fort Vancouver where he might find further help or at least information. He was in a strange place and had no idea where to go to find the vast treasures the land held for him.

He made his way to the fort that stood on the north shore of the river. Jules approached the British company with caution, worried that his jumping ship and killing the bosun in Hong Kong had reached their attention. The last thing he wanted was to be shipped back to England in chains to be hung.

He entered the company store to find a man behind a counter who could easily have passed for a shop merchant in any Liverpool establishment. The store man looked him over taking in the cut of his seaman's clothes. This was not the first man he had seen who left the ships for the deep woods.

Jules approached him with a false smile. "Greetings friend."

The man nodded as a response. "Are you joining the expedition or outfitting for yourself?" he asked coolly. The Bay did not like competition and he was told not to sell to independent trappers.

Jules raised his eyebrows as the idea of joining an expedition was one he had not considered, but now sounded like an answer to his concerns. "Yes, the expedition; however, I am sorry to say that I know little of

14

the work, but I've a strong back and good hands and can lend myself to any task." Work was the last thing he wanted, yet he would do what was needed to get what he desired.

The store man gave him a slight smile, "You wouldn't be the first. I see by your togs that you're a seaman."

"Aye," Jules replied. He shifted his eyes side-to-side and then looked at the man behind the counter. "What might Hudson Bay's feelings be in regards to maritime law?"

The man snorted, "We care nothing for the sea except to ship out our pelts."

"So, the laws of the King are not enforced here?"

"We enforce the laws of our own choosing."

Jules smiled. "Where do I sign on?"

"Right here." The man pulled a book from under the counter and laid it on the table. "Can you write?"

"Not a dot, sir."

"Tell me your name and I'll write it and you can put your X beside it."

"Jubal Smithe."

The man wrote the name and had Jules put an X beside the false name.

"Where is it we are bound?" Jules asked.

"*You* are bound, I will be here. You will be venturing deep into the wilderness of Prince Rupert's Land to trade with the savages."

Jules walked out of the store with a company issued rifle, powder, and ball. He had no idea how to load or shoot the rifle. An older, experienced member of the party was loafing outside the store and recognized the confused look and the seaman's clothes.

"I was a seaman once myself," the man said as Jules walked past him."

"I am no longer," Jules replied.

"Going on the expedition?"

"Aye." He lifted the gun and leather sack of powder and ball, "I have no idea how to use these."

The old man chuckled, "Not the first seaman who didn't. Come on then, I'll teach you."

The expedition set off into the wilderness bound for the Rocky Mountain House, hundreds of miles inland where the Company traded with the North Piegan tribe for furs. The further from the sea he got the better it suited him, although he had much to learn about this new life.

What he lacked in woods skill he made up for with a calculating mind. His criminal nature could foresee opportunities to advance himself without worry of legal retribution. He was quickly learning what was of value in this new country and how he could get his hands on it.

The expedition was guided by a Kainai Blood Indian named Cree Killer. The dark-skinned man, dressed in buckskins and a beaver hat, was quiet and solitary in his mood. The Hudson Bay men commonly referred to all the Indians of Cree Killer's tribe as Blackfeet even though they were made up of Piegan, Kainai Bloods, and Siksika Blackfeet tribes.

En route the expedition traded for furs with trappers, both white and Indian Though the Company was opposed to independent white trappers they were eager to take their pelts at a reduced price. In the process they collected several bundles of packed pelts even before reaching Rocky Mountain House. The rich, prime furs of beaver, fox, and marten made Jules' eyes gleam with greed as he calculated their value.

Jules made it a point to speak with Cree Killer at every opportunity. He knew it would be to his benefit to attach himself to a native who knew where the wealth was to be found and who could afford him protection from the other Indians. He managed to make friends with the quiet man, who would patiently answer his questions, and by observing the Indian, learn from him.

Months in the wilderness further toughened Jules' body while he soaked in everything he could about the land and people. By the time the party reached their destination, Jules was as adept at the wilderness life as any in the group. The freedom was the greatest attractor for him; no Dock Watch, no flogging bosuns, no laws.

The party was a short distance from Rocky Mountain House when they were stopped by a trapper on the verge of lunacy. "Stop!" he cried out to the party leader. "There's pox yonder. *Pox,* I tell you," he shouted louder. "The Indians are dying by the hundreds, it's worth your life to go further. Run! Run away!" With that warning the man dashed into the woods.

The men of the expedition panicked and turned around, intending to return to Fort Vancouver before anyone could spread the horrid smallpox to them. Jules had seen many die from diseases, so the warning did not worry him. He had heard of the dread pox disease, but had never witnessed it. He had no desire to go back toward the sea. He wanted to stay in the wilderness and collect its wealth.

Venturing closer to the population surrounding Rocky Mountain House, Jules saw some of those infected. He had never seen anything like it. Horrified by the massive scabs and disfigured faces of the pox victims, Jules realized the value in moving on quickly. Which way was the question.

Anxious to see if his village had been infected. Cree Killer left the company and headed south. With Cree Killer's venture south Jules saw his chance to stay in the wilderness. He asked if he could accompany the guide and was allowed to join him. Together they set off on foot.

Reaching Cree Killer's home village they found the disease there as well. His wife had died, as had all his children with the exception of his eldest daughter, Hurit, who had somehow evaded the disease. The young woman was also caring for Badger, the three-year-old son of Cree Killer's dead brother. Cree Killer gathered his daughter and nephew and set off south hoping to find the Siksika and southern Piegan free of the disease.

Reaching the first village of Siksika Blackfeet, they found that the disease had struck there as well. Avoiding the village they continued south, eventually crossing over the border from Rupert's Land to the American side and into the nation of the South Piegan. The disease had not reached these people.

It was a common practice for members of all four tribes to move from one group to another. Unlike their northern relatives, the South Piegan did not tolerate the intrusion of any white man into their country. They killed white trappers and explorers with a vengeance.

At the entrance to the village several armed warriors stopped the group. They recognized Cree Killer, his daughter, and Badger as their own. They saw full well that Jules was white. "He does not come in," the leader spoke in Piegan.

"He is my friend," Cree Killer said.

"We do not tolerate white men here. You can stay, he does not."

On the journey south Hurit had become attracted to Jules. He had lied often about his warrior prowess. Not being accustomed to liars, he was believed by father and daughter. Jules foresaw a way in with the tribe if he married Hurit while Cree Killer saw it as gaining a strong warrior for a son and so encouraged the relationship. In their tradition the woman was allowed to accept or reject the man's attentions and Hurit had shown herself willing to accept Jules'.

"It is different to the north," Cree Killer argued. "We have made friends with the whites. This one, Jules, has found acceptance in my daughter's eyes."

The warriors scowled at Jules. Why a woman of their blood would want a white man was beyond their understanding, yet she was allowed to choose. The warriors put their heads together and discussed the matter.

The leader nodded with obvious reluctance, "He can stay since he is your friend and chosen by your daughter." The warrior then glared at Jules, "We will be watching you and if you are a liar like a Cree we will kill you." With that they turned and walked away speaking in low tones to each other.

***

Jules' attraction to the girl was a combination of lust and opportunity, but not love. She was near his age as best he could tell and he could do worse. He had learned that the wedding custom required that the father of the girl demand the prospective suitor to prove his courage and pay a tribute to him for his daughter, and a gift was also to be given to the woman.

He realized the spot he was in. Should he refuse to wed Hurit, the warriors—who were allowing him to stay on that point alone—would kill him. He had no choice but to see it through. Along the way, he had learned what was of value to the Indians and the traits they respected, so he ventured out to find the appropriate tribute.

Carrying his rifle as he wandered about wondering what he should do, he spied a lone trapper with two horses and a pack of furs. Maneuvering to a position where he could shoot the trapper in the back from a safe distance, he murdered the man and scalped him. Pillaging through the wealth he had just secured, Jules was overjoyed with this new life.

The trapper had a new Hawken rifle, powder, ball, and gold coins, all of which he kept. Sorting through the furs he kept the best pelts for himself. Catching up the horses he returned to the village with the horses and furs and prominently displaying the fresh scalp tied to his belt.

Keeping one horse for himself, he gave the remaining furs, some of the trapper's camp gear, and his old rifle to Cree Killer. The second horse he gave to Hurit as a gift, knowing that he would later claim the horse, thus giving him two. With the exchange he and Hurit were married.

Over the fire that night Jules lied to the warriors and to Cree Killer. Standing up, Jules thumped his chest with one fist while holding up the scalp clenched in the other. "I am a warrior," he boasted. "I am fit to be with you. I challenged this trapper to a fight to the death for his furs and horses. He was foolish enough to accept. In no time I had killed him."

As with Cree Killer and Hurit, the Piegan were not accustomed to liars, so the men of the village accepted Jules' story as truth. The act of killing and scalping the white trapper in such a manner and taking his possessions raised him up in the eyes of the warrior societies. He had counted several coup in one fight and for this he was invited to accompany the next war party to raid the neighboring Gros Ventre tribe.

Three days later the war party set out. The idea of direct fighting terrified Jules, but he was a master of manipulation. When the war party jumped a hunting party of Gros Ventre he charged around on his horse, but let the other warriors take the brunt of the fight.

He saw a young Gros Ventre hunter take an arrow and crawl off into the brush to hide. He followed the wounded man. Finding him helpless, he killed him and pulled the arrow out throwing it away. He then took the scalp.

Before the fight was over he caught a loose Gros Ventre horse. When the war party assembled again he boasted, "See, I have killed a Gros Ventre dog and taken his horse."

The war party returned to the village with the

members displaying their scalps and captured weapons. Jules led his captured horse and boastfully displayed the scalp.

The war party questioned among themselves who had actually seen Jules kill the Gros Ventre and take his horse. None had. The warrior who had put the arrow in the hunter who had escaped furrowed his brow in thought. "I shot one that crawled into the trees where Jules said he killed his man. I wonder if it was not that one?"

They began to suspect that Jules had not done as he claimed. In the future they would be watching to catch him taking honors not due him.

Sensing that the warriors were on to his falsehoods, Jules began to gather friends who fell under his charismatic nature, drawing likeminded men to him. Little by little, he intended to form his own war party and be the leader. He was patient enough to develop his plans.

Ten months after Jules took Hurit for his wife, she gave birth to a son. On that day, Jules had been on a raid with his carefully cultivated war party. They returned to the village drunk on whiskey taken from trappers they had killed.

Jules looked in his lodge to see Hurit lying on the bed of elk skins and furs holding a newborn baby boy. Jules shouted out to the men who had rode with him, "I have a son! My woman has given me a son!"

Several of the men staggered up to him and slapped him on the back as a congratulations. "What will you name him?" one asked.

Jules blinked his eyes as he thought, then he grinned drunkenly and laughed, "I will call him Buckingham Palace Drake."

The men looked at him confused. "What is a Buckingham Palace?" the same man asked.

Jules laughed, "Why don't you know? It's where the bloody King of England lives."

The men shook their heads and walked away having no idea what Jules was talking about.

Hurit had continued to care for Badger as her own child. He was five when Buckingham was born. Jules had proven to be a worthless provider for his family. On occasion he brought in meat, but more often he was off raiding. If not for Cree Killer, Hurit and the children would have starved.

Cree Killer knew he had made a grave mistake in trusting Jules. His drunkenness, inappropriate raiding and not providing for his family brought grief and shame on Cree Killer. Those who had opposed Jules' entry into the tribe would cluck their tongues at Cree Killer and mocked his former support of the man who had shown himself to be a liar.

Due to her understanding of herbs and plants for healing, as well as having magically evaded the smallpox, Hurit was considered by many in the tribe to be a Medicine Woman who was obviously favored by the gods. In addition, her good virtue also allowed her to serve as the Medicine Lodge Woman, the one who prepared the buffalo tongues and said the prayers for the purification ceremonies. Being the husband of Hurit the Medicine Woman was the only factor that kept the others from killing Jules.

Hurit's position as a Medicine Woman and the respect it afforded her drew the ire of Dirt Eater, a despised self-appointed Shaman. He was so named due to his habit of driving himself into a false religious frenzy, rolling on the ground and eating dirt. Such actions were considered a violation against the Piegan god, Ground Man.

Dirt Eater was distrusted and disliked by all who looked on Hurit with respect. To Cree Killer's disgust, Dirt Eater and Jules became tight friends. That Jules would be friends with a man who hated his wife, a respected woman of the village, was disgraceful and earned Cree Killer additional scorn and mockery.

Chapter Three

As the years passed, Jules became ever more bloodthirsty, to the point of being considered insane. The white settlers moving west were Jules' preferred target. Most were easterners who did not have fighting skills and were easily killed. Their wagons offered much in goods and wealth. Jules and his followers murdered the men, torturing the ones they did not kill outright. The women were molested and then murdered.

Jules' attacks on the immigrants did not concern the village leaders. They had no love for the white invaders. His perceived insanity; however, was a potential threat to all members of the village. With his party running their own raids and acting separately from tribal interests, Jules was dangerous and his behavior needed to be addressed.

An assembly of the elders convened for the purpose of discussing Jules and what to do with him. Cree Killer, though an elder, was not allowed to participate since he was the one responsible for bringing him into the tribe.

"We should kill him," was one member's opening statement.

The chief of the council shook his head. "He is the husband of the Medicine Woman, we cannot kill him."

"He is insane. He violates our laws, the Braves should take him out and kill him."

Several voices echoed approval of turning Jules over to the tribe's law enforcers.

"He is possessed of evil spirits," a shaman said loud enough to silence the group. "If you kill the husband of Hurit, the Medicine Woman, you will release his evil spirits upon us. We must not kill him."

As fearless as the Piegan were, they were terrified of evil spirits and avoided anyone they considered possessed with them. To kill a brave man transferred the dead man's power to oneself. To kill one with evil spirits gave the slayer those.

"What are we to do with him then?"

"Hope he is killed by someone not among us who will take his evil," the shaman responded.

"But he only kills worthless white men and woman. Who is to kill him?"

"Even a weasel can kill if he sinks his teeth into the throat of a larger animal."

The chief held up his hand. "Do not argue. It is settled, we cannot kill him unless we wish to inflict his evil spirits on us."

The lodge flap opened and Dirt Eater entered. He lifted his nose in the air, "I was not called to this assembly, why?"

"Because it does not concern you, liar," the chief snapped out.

Dirt Eater had appointed himself the religious leader of Jules' band and proclaimed him to be on a holy mission to kill white people. The fact that Jules was white did not factor into the false shaman's vision.

"You talk of killing the holy Jules, I overheard you," Dirt Eater said in a threatening tone. "If you do, I will call a curse down on you."

The shaman in the assembly waved a hand at Dirt Eater. "Jules is not holy, he is as evil as you are, false one. Get out or I will call down a curse on *you*." He looked at those nearest to Dirt Eater, "Throw him out."

Two men stood. Dirt Eater raised his hands in the air, "Do not defile me, I am holy."

The men took ahold of him and shoved him back out of the lodge.

The man who argued for Jules' death looked at the others. "One is as crazy as the other. Is it any wonder Dirt Eater and Jules are friends? We must purge their evil from us."

The shaman looked at the speaker, "How?"

The man looked perplexed. "I do not know."

"Then, be silent if you have no answer to the problem. You are like a raven squawking."

"We must have no contact with him." the chief said. "Tell all to avoid Jules. Bring no harm on him, but do not associate with him. He is not to participate in any religious ceremonies as he will defile them."

The chief's words were final. They could not kill Jules, much to the disappointment of those who wanted that solution, but he was to be shunned.

The word spread quickly around the village that the council's decision regarding Jules was that he was possessed of evil spirits. He was not to be harmed, yet he was to be shunned and forbidden from participating in any tribal functions of a religious nature.

Jules' son, Buckingham, had avoided his father ever since he had been taken on his first raid with their party five years before. Raised in an environment of warriors, he was accustomed to death, yet the cowardly manner in which his father and the others went about it disgusted him. He believed what the elders were saying about his father being possessed of evil spirits as there was dark evil in him.

Twenty summers had passed since Buckingham's birth. He had inherited his father's blonde hair, but his mother's features and darker skin. His hair and whiskers made him stand out; however, his courage and mother's blood caused him to be readily accepted by the warriors.

He and Badger grew up together as brothers. Badger became a War Chief and Buckingham rode with him exclusively. They fought skirmishes against the Shoshone, Flatheads, Nez Perce, Gros Ventre, Crow, and Sioux. He had garnered a significant collection of coups and horses. The fact that his father was despised was not held against Buckingham. He was considered a courageous and trustworthy warrior.

Buckingham loved his grandfather and was a firm

supporter of his honor in the tribe. Any time something disparaging was said against Cree Killer, Buckingham was quick to come to his grandfather's defense. It became known to never saying anything bad about Cree Killer in front of Buckingham or Badger unless the person wanted to face the wrath of the young warriors.

Both young men were angry when they learned that Cree Killer had been barred from the council meeting regarding Jules. The fact he was blamed for Jules' lies and wretched actions was unacceptable. Buckingham and Badger both let their thoughts be known to the chief, who listened to them and then said he understood; however, he could not control the thoughts of others. The two walked away angry at the pathetic answer. Badger returned to his lodge with his wife and family. Buckingham joined a group of his friends.

Dirt Eater sat with Jules at his fire watching the twitching cheeks and narrowing eyes of the man. "You are disturbed by the decree of the council," Dirt Eater announced.

Jules seethed between his teeth, "As if I care for the mumblings of old pieces of dried buffalo dung. I have no need of them."

Hurit was working about the lodge. Dirt Eater followed her with eyes filled with contempt and jealousy. Hurit gave sidelong glances at her husband and Dirt Eater, but said nothing to them as she went about her work. She rarely spoke to her husband and hoped in her heart that he would be killed one day so she would be free of him. She despised Dirt Eater as much as she knew he did her. If the gods were good, both would soon die.

"I told them you are on a holy quest," Dirt Eater said in a haughty tone.

Jules snorted a laugh and gave the false shaman a look of scorn. He hated Dirt Eater as much as he hated everyone else, but he was useful.

He needed something on which to focus his anger and his favorite target was Buckingham, knowing the boy despised him. Jealous of his son and the respect he had with the tribe burned in Jules. He sought to disgrace him and drag down his reputation.

"I am hated with all of my coups and victories," Jules said with a sneer, "while my son, with his pathetic few trophies, is praised. I am sick of hearing the praises about my weakling son."

Hurit cast a quick look of anger toward Jules. He caught the look and curled his lip up at her, "Stay to your work squaw or take a beating."

Hurit stood up straight and glowered at him, "Do and there will be no stopping my sons Badger and Buckingham from killing you."

Jules smiled evilly, "I cannot be killed, the word of the council."

"Do not trust your safety to hiding behind your evil or me. There is an end to all patience."

"Shut up!"

Dirt Eater scowled at Hurit, "Jules is a greater warrior than your son. Jules should be praised, not him."

Hurit turned her back to Dirt Eater showing her contempt for him.

Jules stared into the fire with his eyes narrowed. "I need to show them how weak he is."

"He is too cowardly to ride with your brave warriors," Dirt Eater said with a mollifying tone.

Jules began to grin, "I will make him ride with us in defiance of the council. Then, his name will be down in the filth with mine."

Dirt Eater chuckled, "Destroy him in the eyes of the others. Your party is despised and he will be as well if he rides with you."

Jules looked up from the fire and glared at him, "Shut up. You talk too much."

Jules left the fire and walked across the camp to the group where Buckingham was speaking with his friends. As a group the men stopped talking and looked at Jules with reservation. Several involuntarily took a step back to avoid his evil spirits from jumping onto them.

Still angry over his grandfather's treatment Buckingham demanded, "What do you want?"

"For you to ride with my party to fight the Shoshone."

A scornful laugh escaped Buckingham's lips, "*You* fight the Shoshone? You are a killer of rabbits, frightened men and women. I am not interested."

"Then you *are* a coward," Jules said with feigned disappointment. "I told the others you were not."

Buckingham stiffened at the insult, glaring his hatred at Jules.

"I bet my warriors that you would ride with us. They said you were too cowardly. It appears I lose the bet."

Buckingham felt the eyes of the other young men on him. He was trapped in a no-win decision. If he refused to go along the word would spread among the young warriors that he was too cowardly to ride against the Shoshone. If he went along, in the eyes of the elders, he would be defying the command to shun Jules and lowering himself to that level.

He knew the minds of his young peers. In their youth and inexperience they considered valor of more importance than obeying council decisions. He did not want to go anywhere with Jules or his wretched party. He sought a way out.

"I cannot defy the rule of the council," Buckingham said. "You are to be ignored."

Jules smirked. "Such a cowardly excuse for a way out." He pointed to the two eagle feathers in his son's hair. "Best turn those in for white ptarmigan feathers."

Buckingham clenched his jaw while balling his fists

until the knuckles showed white through the dark skin. He knew his friends were watching, waiting for his answer.

Jules saw the struggle in his son's eyes. His own eyes glowed with menace as he delivered the fatal blow. "The word shall spread quickly that you are too frightened to ride against the weak Shoshone. Too bad I spawned a coward."

Buckingham's temper snapped. "I will ride with you and count more coup than all of your cowardly woman killers."

Jules grinned with satisfaction at having accomplished his maneuver. "Maybe you are not such a coward after all. We leave shortly."

Two days out from the village, Buckingham knew he had made a mistake in being taunted into joining this party of drunken cowards. He had been baited like a beaver and fell into the trap. They stumbled onto a hunting party of Shoshone and Jules led the party in a hasty escape away from their ancient enemy who had laughed at their retreat.

Buckingham was disgusted with the cowardice shown by his father's party. Now he was truly stuck with them. If he rode back alone the Shoshone would kill him. They continued to ride south in search of a trail it was said had a great number of white man's wagons following it.

Buckingham refused to attack any wagons with woman or children. Jules had no such reservations as they attacked the helpless immigrants. Buckingham's loathing for his father deepened. He wanted to get as far away from these men as he could, but a lone Blood in Shoshone country had little chance of making it back alive.

Unknown to the party, reports regarding their attacks had reached the ears of the Army posted at Fort Bridger. The military's major purpose at the post was to protect immigrants on the Oregon Trail. Patrols were out in force to find the offending Indians and, in particular, to learn if the stories of the party being led by a white man were true.

Chapter Four

Jules passed a whiskey bottle to the man sitting next to him. He took a long pull on it and passed the bottle down to the next man. In this manner the bottle passed through a dozen hands before reaching Buckingham. He refused to take it, so it was handed past him to Jules.

Jules took a drink and sneered with drunken malice at Buckingham, "What's the matter great warrior, too good to drink with your old man and your friends?"

Buckingham glared at him; taking in the man's whiskey-dulled eyes, but did not respond.

Jules took another drink and again passed it down the line. He snorted, "I can't believe you are my son. You have no nerve."

The young man snapped at him, "My coups are many and they are against men with weapons, not terrified women and children. You kill unarmed men who cry for mercy and have no power to give by their deaths. You are not a warrior; you are not fit to sit with true warriors. That is why you ride with cowards like you. You are dog vomit."

Jules glared at him and then suddenly burst into laughter. "Dog vomit? I was raised in dog vomit, boy; can you expect less from me?"

The other men of the party laughed with him and made snide remarks about Buckingham, calling him an old woman.

The sun was setting with a cool May breeze blowing through the grove of aspen where they had hidden after the last attack. Buckingham got up and walked away from the group. He stared out toward the north and wished he had not ridden with these men. He knew it was a mistake when he did it. He would return home to the disgusted looks of the elders and he had heaped more disgrace on his grandfather. He had been a fool.

He made a fire away from the party and sat alone listening to the drunken voices behind him. As darkness crept in, the drinkers fell asleep leaving the night air finally quiet. Looking back over his shoulder at the lumps on the ground that were the drink sodden men and their smoldering fire, he shook his head. He wondered how he managed to get himself into things like this. He passed it off as poor judgment by allowing his pride to rule his decisions.

His grandfather had long ago become angry at his son-in-law. He was angry that such a sneaking coyote as Jules had wormed his way into his good graces, and that Jules had taken his daughter, whom he ignored and did not hunt for. He had defended the miserable white man to let him into the village and now he was looked on as a fool for being taken in by him. They were now stuck with him because of his marriage to Hurit.

Buckingham knew his father cared for nothing and no one except himself and killing. He and Badger were the ones who now hunted and provided for their mother. A boy had been born to his mother, his brother, but when the child was small he fell into the river and drowned. His mother wept for days. Jules cared not at all.

His hope was that the evil Englishman would be killed one day and rid them all of his presence. In fact, the whole party who followed him needed to be killed. There was no honor in any of them.

As his fire died down he rolled up in his blankets and went to sleep. He would have to make a decision tomorrow whether to stay or chance a lone ride back to the village through hostile Shoshone country. He doubted the party would return home any time soon and he did not want to remain with them any longer.

Morning broke clear and warm. Buckingham rolled out of his blankets and looked over to see the men still asleep from their drunkenness. They would be touchy and surly today. They would want to find a fight. One of these days they would find a fight they couldn't win.

He saw his father standing at the edge of the trees looking over the expanse of land and hills in front of him. It seemed the man could soak up liquor and wake up sober, not like the others who woke up sick and angry. Just seeing him was enough to set Buckingham's teeth on edge and set his ill mood for the day.

Jules walked over to him. "Sorry about the spat we had last night. Too much drink." He laughed under his breath.

Buckingham did not answer or look at him as he began to roll his blankets.

Jules watched him, "You don't like me much, do you boy?"

Buckingham continued to ignore him as he stood up and pulled the picket pin holding his horse.

"Going somewhere?"

"Back to the village."

"You plan on riding through enemy country for a week alone?"

"It is better than being dishonored with you. I will take my chances."

"Suit yourself." Jules was about to say more when he spotted a lone wagon moving along the trail below them. His face broke into a smile as he turned and ran back to where the others were sleeping.

Jules began to viciously kick the men as he shouted at them, "Get up you lazy louts, there's a wagon down there, move."

The men groaned as they woke. They cursed in Piegan and tried to stand. It took several attempts for a few of them as they stumbled and crashed into the sod. Buckingham watched with disgust. He then turned to study the wagon. There was a man driving and a woman in a big sun bonnet sitting on the seat next to him.

He made a decision right then. The last thing he would do before leaving this group was to spoil their attack on those people. He had no love for the whites and deeply resented their invasion into his people's land, but he was also a warrior of honor, and there was no honor or power in killing a woman. Besides, seeing the cowards molest a terrified woman sickened him.

Jules was mounted and angrily cursing at the men to hurry. They picked up their weapons and mounted their horses following him down the hill toward the wagon. As the party drew closer to the wagon, the man and woman on the seat driving the four-mule-team seemed not to notice them. Buckingham followed them down.

When the party was fifty yards from the wagon, Buckingham broke his horse into a gallop toward the wagon. He shouted at the people on the seat in an attempt to raise their attention warning them of the attack.

Jules cursed and kicked his horse into a gallop in an effort to stop his son's warning. The party reached the wagon at the same time Buckingham did. They were all shocked to see the woman in the sun bonnet look up, raise a revolver, and shoot the closest attacker. It was a man dressed like a woman.

With the shot the wagon stopped and men in blue uniforms jumped out of the back of the wagon. Jules shoved one of his groggy renegades off his horse and into the man on the wagon seat, upsetting his aim. Buckingham found himself between Jules and the soldiers coming out of the wagon. Jules swung his rifle, striking Buckingham in the head and then shoved him off his horse and into the men coming out of the wagon. As the soldiers jumped to avoid the falling man, Jules dropped low on his horse and galloped away from the fight.

The soldiers recovered and killed every Indian in the party. In the Indians' hungover condition it was a quick and simple matter. Shots were fired at the fleeing man without scoring a hit as Jules escaped into the trees. There were no mounted soldiers who could give chase; however the trap had been a success.

A Sergeant kicked at the Indians on the ground, checking to be sure they were dead. He poked the toe of his boot into Buckingham's ribs as he lay on his back, unconscious, behind the wagon. The man wearing the bonnet and dress came off the wagon pulling the dress off to reveal his uniform under it. He threw the dress up on the wagon seat. He walked over to where the Sergeant studied the unconscious man who was on his back.

"This one's alive," the Sergeant commented.

"Strange thing is, Sergeant, I could have sworn he was shouting a warning to us before these others reached us."

The Sergeant nodded his head, "I heard that as well. Odd, very odd." He pushed Buckingham's head to the side and glanced up at the men around him. "You ever see a blonde haired Indian with chin whiskers? He's wearing Indian clothes, but that's a white man's face under all that sun-browned skin."

"Half breed?" the soldier ventured the question.

"Likely. Let's take him back to the fort and let the Lieutenant and Captain decide what to do with him."

They picked Buckingham up and put him on the floor of the wagon. The soldiers climbed back into the wagon and the driver turned the team around and headed back for Fort Bridger.

Buckingham woke up on a hard cold floor. His head throbbed with pounding pain. He raised a shaky hand to the place his head hurt the most only to find that a cloth had been wrapped around his head. He tried to remember what had happened. He recalled seeing the men in blue clothes, his father closing in on him, and then nothing.

A man in a blue uniform with stripes on his sleeves stood outside the bars looking at him. "The doctor patched up your head."

Buckingham turned his eyes up to look at the man standing over him and saw bars between them. "Where am I?" he asked in Piegan.

The man only stared at him. He then asked the question in English.

"You're in a guardhouse cell at Fort Bridger."

"Am I a captive?"

"Aye, you are that."

The Sergeant than shouted across the room, his voice thick with Irish brogue, "Corporal, tell the Lieutenant and Captain that our prisoner is awake."

Buckingham forced himself to sit up. He was dizzy and his head pounded with accelerating pain. He groaned and put his hands over his face.

"Want some water?

"Yes."

The Sergeant filled a dipper from a bucket and handed it through the bars to him. Buckingham drank and began to feel better. He handed the dipper back.

The Lieutenant and Captain came in the door and stood next to the Sergeant. The Captain spoke first. "I am Captain James. We want to ask you a few questions before we hang you."

Buckingham stared at him. He was aware of the white man's method for killing those they considered bad, or enemies. "That gives me little reason to answer your questions," he replied with a grimace of pain.

"What is your name?"

"Buckingham Palace Drake."

The Captain frowned, "Buckingham Palace?"

Buckingham looked at him.

"Don't you get smart with me. Tell me your name!"

"I did tell you my name; it is not my fault if you do not like it."

"Your name is Buckingham Palace Drake? Like

where the King and Queen of England live?"

"I have heard my father speak the word England, but I know nothing of it. I do not know King and Queen of England. Whose tribe is he in?"

The Captain stared at him as his face began to turn red with anger.

The Lieutenant put his hand on the Captain's arm. "Sir, I believe he is telling the truth. That may well be his name and being raised Indian he would have no idea who the King and Queen of England are."

James glanced at the Lieutenant and back at Buckingham. "Is your father a white man?"

"Yes, an English man. My mother is a Blood."

"Blood?"

"The Kainai tribe."

"He is Blackfeet," the Lieutenant interjected.

"Blackfeet." James looked at Buckingham, "I understand that the Blackfeet are the most vicious Indians in the West."

"Our enemies fear us."

"You are a vicious Blackfeet then?"

"The whites call us that, only the Siksika are Blackfeet. I am a Kainai Blood."

"You speak of whites as if they were a foreign race, aren't you half white?"

"My father is white, but he is a coward and I do not claim his side. I am a Blood."

"Fine, I don't really care, nor am I interested in Blackfeet genealogy."

The Lieutenant could see that the conversation was stalemated. He asked, "Is your father the one who hit you and used you as a shield to escape?"

Buckingham stared at him; things were starting to make sense. "He escaped?"

"Yes, he fled like a coward."

"I am sure he did. I remember now, he hit me. He

gave me to you so he could run away."

The Lieutenant nodded, "That is what my Sergeant told me."

"Did the others escape?"

"No, they were all killed, only the white man escaped."

"Good, they all needed to die."

"Why is that?"

"They were men without honor, killing women and children. I am not one of them."

"You were with them though!" James snapped.

"My mistake. I made a poor decision when I rode with them."

The Lieutenant asked, "Did you try to warn the wagon of the attack?"

"Yes, I was not going to let them kill another woman." He then gave a small smile. "The woman was a man. He was a brave man though, a warrior. In my tribe a man who is a coward is made to dress as a woman and sit with the women. Your custom is strange to see a warrior dressed as a woman."

The Lieutenant laughed, "The trooper was in disguise."

Buckingham looked at him blankly as the term meant nothing to him. He said no more.

The Lieutenant whispered to James, "Come outside with me, I want to discuss something."

The two officers left the room and stepped outside. "What is it, Lieutenant?"

"We are leaving here in a few days for the war in the east. I'm to head up the special task force to operate behind enemy lines and need to recruit men for it."

The Captain eyed him warily. "Yes, I am aware of that. Get on with it, I have more to ask the prisoner."

"I need men that can fight and kill without orders. They are suicide missions for the most part and the men face probable death. That man in there would be perfect for such a job."

"Are you *insane*?" James snapped. "Trust a redskin in the United States Army? He would have his whole unit scalped in an hour and escape."

"I do not believe so, sir. He is a Blackfeet; they have no qualms about killing an enemy. Show him what a Confederate soldier looks like, tell him he's the enemy, and let him kill."

James frowned, "I don't know."

"Do you really want to hang a man who can fight like that? A man we can use in wartime? And, he did try to help us."

James thought on it for a minute.

The Lieutenant added, "If you think he's a threat to *us,* imagine what he would do to the Rebels."

James looked at him, "You already recruited the Frenchman from the noose, are you trying to build a unit of criminals or are you playing missionary?"

"I am looking for men who can take on dangerous missions that most men would never consider doing. Western men accustomed to hard living, fighting, and killing to survive will do that, especially if it's a choice between that and hanging."

James huffed, "All right, let's put it to him and see what he says."

The officers reentered the room. They looked at Buckingham who was still sitting on the floor with his legs crossed in front of him. "We have an offer for you, Buckingham," James said.

Buckingham looked in his eyes. "I am listening."

"Would you be willing to go to war for your country?"

"What country? You mean for the Blackfeet country?"

"*No,*" James shouted. "For the United States of

America!"

Buckingham only stared at him; it was another term that meant nothing to him.

Once again the Lieutenant stepped in. "The country we are all living in is called the United States of America. We have been attacked by part of our own country and are at war with them. That would be as if the Siksika attacked the Kainai. We need warriors like you to fight with us."

"I see. What if I choose not to fight for the white man?"

"Then you will be hung as a criminal," James spit out.

Buckingham paused in thought.

"There will be many coups and honors," the Lieutenant added.

Buckingham's eyes lit up. "Then, I will do it."

"Good. We will be leaving for the war in a few days. You will go with us."

Buckingham nodded. "I will go with you." He stood up and grimaced at the pain in his head. "Do I have to stay in here?"

"No." The Lieutenant gestured toward the Sergeant. "Open the door."

The Sergeant immediately complied.

Buckingham walked out and faced the two uniformed officers. James said, "You will go with Lieutenant Parker and he will get you set up." With that James turned and headed for the door. He stopped and turned around. "Lieutenant, I expect you to educate Mr. Drake on the history and geography of the United States. I expect him to be fully informed of his place and duties when we reach the Potomac."

"Yes, sir, I will see to it."

The Lieutenant turned to look at Buckingham. "I am Lieutenant Parker. First off we will need to have your hair cut and dress you like a soldier."

"Will I wear blue clothes like you?"

"Yes, and I suggest we shorten your name to Buck. You can't go around calling yourself Buckingham Palace."

"Why?"

"I will explain all that to you in time, from now on your name is simply Buck Drake and you are in the United States Army."

The Sergeant watched Parker and Buck walk out together. He had been in the army since his youth and was now in his forties. He had seen a lot of good and bad men go. He saw Buck Drake as both. He grinned and spoke under his breath, "Those Rebels won't know what hit 'em."

Chapter Five

Buckingham was adjusting to the shorter version of his name. He still didn't see why his name was a problem for the soldiers, but then everything his people did was considered a problem to the white man. The past two days had been spent in fort-wide preparations for all the military personnel to leave the fort. He wondered if he had made a mistake in agreeing to fight in the white man's war. Maybe he should escape and return to the village.

He considered flight and then realized he was still a captive and being watched day and night. Any attempt to run would only get him a bullet in the back or, if caught, hung. Neither prospect was preferable to simply going along to the war. He learned the man with the stripes on his sleeves was called a sergeant, and seemed to be equal to a war chief in the Blackfeet world. The man was friendly to him and treated him fairly.

The other soldiers looked on him with suspicion and anger. They didn't like the idea of having an Indian in their midst, even if he was half white. He was given a wooden bunk in the barracks that was at the end of the row of bunks. The bunk next to his was vacant as no man wanted to sleep next to a savage who would likely scalp him in the night.

Buck ignored them and went about the jobs assigned to him without complaint. The blue uniform they had told him to wear was rough and uncomfortable. They told him to throw away his buckskins, but he had secretly hidden them in his blanket roll.

Walking past an open window in the barracks, the Irish Sergeant overheard several men talking about killing Buck. He stopped and stepped in the door to the shock of the enlisted soldiers. He looked them over. "What are you doing loafing in here?"

"Just getting some things, Sergeant Duffy," one of

the men stammered out.

"Get back to work. Oh, and I'd forget about your little plot to kill Trooper Drake. He's a skilled fightin' man who would have the lot of you gutted, skinned, and hung out before you could say boo. Oh, and if you should succeed, you'd all be hung for murder. Now get your lazy butts out of here!"

The soldiers dashed out of the barracks without a word of reply. The plot died, but not the hatred directed toward Buck.

On the third day after the supplies for the trip were loaded into wagons, the cavalry mounted up and the long trek east began. The first night out the men were given tents with two men assigned to a tent. No one wanted to partner with the "redskin."

Buck realized he might never see his village or mountains again. He again regretted the day he had joined the party with his father. He was being taken by force from his people and country and put in with white men who hated him and who he, in turn, hated. It was all because of his cowardly father who had not fought for the party, but instead sacrificed them all to save his own life. The deep hatred he felt for Jules Drake sat like a hot ember in his stomach.

Buck was handed a tent and told to pitch it. He looked at the canvas and stick bundle in his hands and walked to a spot away from the other men who were setting up their tents. He watched them and then looked at his bundle. It made no sense to him. He threw the tent on the ground and walked away from it.

He was sitting on the ground with his back to the other soldiers when he heard footsteps coming up behind him. He turned his head to see who it was. A white man older than himself stood behind him holding the canvas and stick bundle. The man had freshly trimmed brown hair and a short beard. He was weather-tanned and he looked like a warrior, not like the other soldiers with skin like a fawn's belly, but more like the trappers he had known and fought at times.

"These things are a pain to put up," the man said. "You have to know the trick."

Buck scowled at the tent. "I do not want it."

The man began to unfold the canvas and separate the sticks from it. "Beats sleeping in the rain though."

Buck studied the man who also wore a blue uniform. "You do not look like the others."

The man didn't look up from untangling the tent as he snorted his contempt. "I ain't one of them pink-cheeked momma's boys."

Buck glared in the direction where the other soldiers were busy setting up their tents. "They are children who never counted a single coup."

The man again snorted his contempt. "They ain't like you and me, Buck."

"You know my name?"

"Yup. Duffy told me who you were."

"Who is Duffy?"

"Sergeant Duffy." The man placed three fingers across his upper arm to indicate Duffy's stripes. "War chief."

Buck nodded his head in understanding.

"An Irishman. They come pretty tough, the ones I've known anyway."

Buck stood up and helped the man finish erecting the little tent. The man then put his hand out to Buck, "Renard Ravenel. Just call me Raven, it's easier and you don't sprain your tongue saying it."

Buck shook his hand. "My name is Buckingham Palace Drake, but the chief, Parker, did not like it and told me to change it to Buck."

"That's because Buckingham Palace is a great big fancy lodge in England clear across the ocean from here.

Going into the white man's world packing that name would have them laughing at you. It would be like a man in your village being named, Great Big Lodge Where the Chief of The Gros Ventre Lives."

Buck stared at him for a second. "Are the whites at war with the Buckingham Palace tribe?"

"Not anymore, but we did have a couple of fights with them and kicked them out of our hunting grounds."

Buck considered that. "Maybe the chief, Parker, was right. Buck is better than such a name. My father named me that."

"Guess he was having a laugh at your expense, partner. Hope you don't mind my sharing a lodge with you." He pointed at the dirty, saggy canvas tent and grinned. "No warrior's lodge is it?"

"Are you not afraid like the others that I will kill you in the night?"

"You're a Blood. You face your enemies, you don't kill them in their sleep. No power in such a killing."

Buck liked the man. "We will share the little lodge then."

"Besides," Raven added, "I couldn't stomach being stuck in a tent with one of them momma's boys. He might wake up crying in the night and expect me to nurse him. I'd have to cut his throat."

Buck laughed. "You are a trapper?"

"Was. Beaver played out, too many greenhorns moving in. Country's gone lame. It won't be long before the whole thing is overrun with pilgrims clear to the Pacific Ocean." He pointed at himself and then Buck. "Our way of life is gone beaver, partner."

Buck nodded, "We have killed the whites and they only keep coming. There is no end to them."

"You got that right. Wait until you get back east. You can't throw a rock without hitting a pilgrim. Plumb loaded with them, it is. These blue uniforms will be all over the west in a few years, mark my words."

Buck was silent for a minute before speaking again. "Why are you going to the white man's war?"

Raven laughed, "Well, I had no choice, sorta like you. Seems I killed one of their soldier boys in a fight that he started, just because I took his payroll on a turn of cards. Lieutenant Parker gave me a choice to join this special unit of his and fight for the Union or get hung. Well, my mother never raised no foolish children. I took up his offer."

The two sat and talked about the country and fights they had been in. A bell rang out signaling the men to come to the mess wagon for supper. They both got up and walked to where the soldiers were lining up.

Buck and Raven fell into the back of the line. As they moved forward, two young soldiers pushed into the line ahead of Buck shoving him back against Raven. "Back of the line, redskin," one of the soldiers growled.

Raven reached in front of Buck and tapped the soldier on the shoulder. When the man turned around Raven punched him hard in the face knocking him to the ground. The soldier's friend spun around to jump Raven. His attack was aborted mid-move by Buck kicking his legs out from under him, causing him to fall over his friend.

Duffy came on the run to the scene. "What happened here?" he demanded.

The other soldiers in line immediately faced forward and remained silent. Duffy looked at Buck and then Raven. Raven shrugged, "These little boys come a-runnin' all excited for supper and one of them tripped and the other fell over him. They took a nasty fall."

Duffy looked down at the two young soldiers as they struggled to stand up. The one Raven had hit had a cut under his left eye that was quickly swelling shut. Duffy studied the damage on the soldier's face. "It almost looks like he fell on a fist."

"Like I said," Raven repeated, "he took a nasty fall,

maybe hit a rock. Guess he should be more careful where he runs, don't you think?"

Duffy nodded, "Guess so." He gave Raven a knowing look. He then looked at the two soldiers, "Get in the back of the line where you belong."

The two immediately complied. Duffy shouted at the line, "Line forms at the rear gentlemen. Let's have a nice orderly meal and save your fighting for Johnny Reb." He walked away from the line.

Buck and Raven moved up with the line. Two of the younger soldiers ahead of them turned around to look accusingly at Raven and Buck. "What are you momma's boys looking at?" Raven snapped at them. They both quickly turned around and faced forward.

The cook was dishing up plates of stew and dropping a biscuit on each plate. When Buck and Raven reached him he grinned at them. He was a gray haired man in his fifties who had seen a lot of military life. "I liked that, that was slick," was all he said as he dropped an extra biscuit on each of their plates.

They moved off carrying their plates. Raven had handed a tin cup of coffee to Buck. They sat down by their tent. Buck stared tentatively into the cup of black, hot liquid.

"That's coffee," Raven told him. "Elixir of the gods. Try it."

Buck took a sip, and then another. He grinned. "I do not know if our gods drink this, but I like it." He continued to drink between bites of the stew and biscuits.

They had finished eating when Lieutenant Parker walked up to them. They stood up and faced him. "I happened to be watching the chow line when those boys had their accident."

Raven looked him in the eyes. "They were out of line and no one is calling my partner a *redskin*, so you might want to pass that along to the kids."

Parker stifled a grin. "They have already been told to behave themselves. I didn't come here to make an issue over a kid getting a black eye he had coming. I was impressed by the way the two of you worked that together; I like to see fighting men working together. When we reach the Potomac and I organize the unit I want the two of you teamed up together on all assignments."

Raven grinned, "Suits me. I was hoping I wouldn't get stuck with one of these wet-behind-the-ears kids."

"I assure you there will be no wet-behind-the-ears kids in this unit. Every man in it has, shall we say, acquired skills at fighting."

"Will we have to wear these uniforms?"

"Only until we reach our headquarters and then I don't want to see any of my men in a blue uniform. It's a bit difficult to work in secret behind enemy lines wearing a Union uniform." He grinned, "You might get noticed."

Parker then looked at Buck. "How does that set with you, Mr. Drake?"

Buck nodded, "I would like to fight beside my friend."

"Good. Now, Buck come along with me, it's time to start your lessons in American history."

Buck walked away with Parker to begin his indoctrination into the white man's world.

An hour later Buck came walking back to the tent. Raven was sitting on the ground reading a book by the final light of the day. He looked up at Buck, "Get educated?"

"Educated?"

"Taught, learned, it's called educated."

"Oh, yes. I learned that the white man came to this land from other lands across the ocean. That they took what belonged to others and pushed them out or killed them."

Raven grinned at Buck. "Sorta like the Sioux pushed out the Comanche and the Blackfeet pushed out the Shoshone and took their lands? The Navajo killed a whole tribe of peaceful farmer Indians and took their land. It's not just white men."

Buck thought on that and then looked back at Raven. "You are right. All men fight and take over land. The white man is now pushing us; they will take what we have taken."

"Pretty soon the white man will sweep west like a flooded river. The Blackfeet can't stop the white man any more than the Shoshone could stop the Blackfeet."

"Parker said that the Rebels are trying to take part of the white man's land and that is what they are fighting over."

"Actually, the south wants to secede from the United States of America and form their own Confederate States. To split the country in half. It would be like if the Bloods decided they hated the Piegan and wanted to be separate from them, and the Piegan said no, the Bloods had to stay with them so the two tribes fought to see who would get their way."

"But the Bloods and Piegan do not hate each other."

"It's not the best comparison, but it's the general idea of why the North and South are fighting."

Buck shrugged, "It is battle that is important, not why. To gain honors and coups is what makes life good. I can count coup on a Rebel as well as a Shoshone."

"Except," Raven broke in, "they don't want us just counting touches on the enemy, they want the enemy soldiers killed dead. Our coups will only be counted on those we kill."

"Do we scalp them to prove the coup?"

"I don't think the officers would appreciate the scalps, best leave them to the dead. We'll just add up our coups and boast of them in camp."

Buck grinned, "I think I will like this white man's war."

Raven looked back down at the book in his hands.

"Sure beats the hell outta hangin'."

Chapter Six

The wagons continued east for several weeks with Buck continuing to take his evening lessons from Parker. All in the company were weary of travel. The soldiers were too worn out to worry about Buck as a threat, yet neither did they make friends with him. There was nothing more said to him to initiate a fight. The fact that Sergeant Duffy threatened to make any man who started a, fight walk the entire way to the railhead curtailed the expression of their prejudices.

The railhead that extended furthest into the west was at St. Joseph, Missouri; however, Rebels had seized the city and torn down the United States flag, replacing it with the Stars and Bars. Union troops from Iowa were marching down to retake the city and protect this important railhead. Until the city was secured, the eastbound Union soldiers were diverted to the railhead in Iowa City for transportation to the eastern war front.

As the wagons drew nearer to Iowa City, Buck was coming to fully understand what Raven had been telling him about the number of white people spreading west. He had never seen so many people in one place. It was becoming clearer by the day how they could easily overwhelm the Indian and push him aside like a grizzly bear throwing over a log for the ants that lay under it.

The wagons pulled up to the depot at Iowa City and the men were ordered into a marching line. Buck and Raven were not military trained so they brought up the rear as the men moved in formation to load onto the troop train. The depot was filled with blue uniforms and officers studying the men as they marched along.

A Major eyed Buck and Raven with distaste as they moved along at a normal walk. He shouted at them, "Who taught you men how to march?"

Raven looked at him with a steady gaze that showed

he was not intimidated by the insignia on the man's coat. "The Blackfeet, Crow, and Sioux. They keep a man on his toes."

The Major began to bluster at the improper military response. Before he could say more, Lieutenant Parker rushed up to the Major and saluted. "Excuse my men sir, they are recruits for secret missions. They are western men and not trained soldiers."

The Major looked at Parker with displeasure. "And how do you expect us to win a war with men like these?"

"Very quickly, sir." He saluted and departed to rejoin his company.

Buck's eyes grew wide as he looked at the huge locomotive spewing steam and smoke from above and below it. He jumped when the shrill whistle cut through the din of marching feet and officers shouting commands. He had never seen such a thing and wasn't sure what he was supposed to do with it.

Raven saw the look on his friend's face when he jumped at the whistle. "It's a train," he said matter-of-factly. "We get inside these cars here and ride."

Buck gaped at the train. He saw the men ahead of them climbing up the steps and disappearing inside the beast. He followed Raven, took the two steps up and looked down the narrow aisle with pairs of seats filling each side. The men moved to the back slipping into the vacant seats as they reached them. They followed the soldiers ahead of them. Raven slid into the next open set of seats and up against the window. Buck sat down nervously beside him.

Once the train was filled the whistle blew two shrill blasts indicating that it was leaving the platform. The train suddenly lurched into movement. Buck jumped in his seat and looked anxiously around him. None of the other men seemed upset the thing they were in was moving. He glanced over at Raven who was looking out the window and watching the depot and people disappear as they rolled forward. Buck stared out the window in awe as the train picked up speed and the scenery outside began to slide ever faster past them.

After the first hour Buck relaxed realizing that there was no danger in the train. He began to enjoy the ride as it was much smoother and faster than a wagon. The further east they went the heavier the population density grew. Buck was amazed at the buildings and swarms of people when the train made stops in Chicago and Pittsburg. The train ran continuously for two days stopping only to take on more fuel and water and to allow the men to eat. It finally arrived at the Union staging ground on the Potomac River.

The men were ordered off the train by Sergeant Duffy who snapped orders at them to move along. The soldiers moved smartly at his barked commands. Buck and Raven were the last off the train.

Duffy stopped them. "You two are to report directly to Lieutenant Parker. Come with me."

Duffy started off at a brisk walk with Buck and Raven following him. Duffy stopped at a building with a number of windows in it and a set of heavy double doors. He opened the doors and went inside.

Parker was standing in a room talking with other uniformed men. He looked up at the three men as they entered. "Thank you, Sergeant. Take the men to the last room down the hall."

Duffy nodded and walked down the hall to an open door. "In here, men."

Raven looked at Duffy, "Are you leaving or staying here?"

"I'll be marching south with my company in the morning."

Raven put out his hand, "Thanks, and may the luck of the Irish be with you."

Duffy shook his hand. "You be careful out there."

"I always am. I'll buy you a drink when this little

ruckus is over."

"Irish whiskey, and I'll be holdin' you to it."

Duffy shook hands with Buck. "A bit of a shock, isn't it?"

Over the weeks Buck had not spoken his native language so his English was improving and less stilted as he began to sound like the other men. "I'm learning much."

"Well, don't kill all the Rebs, save a few for the rest of us."

Buck smiled, "Maybe one or two."

Duffy turned on his heels and walked away down the hall. Buck and Raven walked through the open door to see several other uniformed men sitting in chairs around the room. The men were hard eyed and seasoned. Raven thought back on Parker's comment that there would be no wet-behind-the-ears kids in this group. He was right; this was a gathering of tough men. They sat down without anyone in the room speaking.

A few minutes later six more uniformed men entered the room followed by Lieutenant Parker and a tall, heavily muscled Sergeant Major. The six men took seats. The men in the room all sat stone faced, their eyes on the Lieutenant and Sergeant. Parker looked them over while the Sergeant stood a step behind him with his hands clasped behind his back.

Parker began to address the group. "I am going to be frank and direct with you men. There are no blushing maidens in this room or wet-behind-the-ears kids, as some have put it. You men are here for a specific reason. You are men who have fighting experience and, to be perfectly blunt, the ability to kill. Some of you have volunteered; some of you have been spared the hangman's noose by agreeing to fight in this unit." He looked at no one in particular when he said it.

"Your job is to kill Rebs and undermine their resources. You will not be in uniform; you will be in civilian clothes. You will work behind enemy lines and raise as much hell as you can for them. You will kill them, blow up their ammunition stores, trains, bridges, and what have you. You will spend the next week learning how to do this. You will learn what we want you to do. You will be provided with an Army Colt revolver and a knife. There will be a range practice; however, I am sure you know what to do with them.

"You are soldiers, not civilians, not renegades; do not forget that for a moment. You may operate in civilian attire, but you are United States Army. You are under orders at all times. Any man violating his orders had better have a *very* good reason for doing so and then convince me of it. Any man deliberately violating orders, to the detriment of his fellow soldiers, will be shot.

"This is not a free-for-all for those of you who think that because no officer is directly controlling you that you are autonomous to commit criminal acts. Let me make this very clear and I will only say it once so you'd better hear it. Any man found to be harming civilians, looting, pillaging, or molesting women will be shot. Deserters will be shot. If criminal activity or escape are in your thoughts, forget them."

One man with a cocky expression on his face leaned back in his chair and remarked, "How are you going to *really* know what I do out there? If I see something I want, who's to stop me?" The man folded his arms across his chest and smirked insolently at Parker. It was obvious to everyone in the room that the man was testing Parker.

Parker did not reply but only jerked his head toward the man. Freeman stepped out from behind Parker, crossed the room on heavy boots and grabbed the offending man by the front of his shirt, yanking him roughly out of the chair.

"Take him back to the guardhouse Sergeant and reinstate his execution order," Parker said calmly.

The man shouted out in protest and curses as

Freeman dragged him out of the room. The slamming of the outside door ended the screaming. Parker looked the men over. "Anyone else?"

Parker paused for several seconds. No one moved in the silent room. He continued, "To answer that fool's question, there will be many officers in the field constantly passing on a chain of information, so we will know if you have committed any of these atrocities. If you desert we will find you, make no mistake about that.

"You will take your orders directly from me or Sergeant Major Freeman, who happens to be busy at the moment. You will not take an order from any other officer that has not been sent through one of us. If we need to pass an order to you in the field, the message will be relayed through a field officer and be prefaced with the phrase, 'This order is from Lieutenant Parker' or 'Sergeant Freeman.' All officers in the field will know about your duties. If you need to eat or need medical attention from a unit in the field you will give the officer in charge this code, 'I am Parker Freeman.' They will all know what that means and take you in.

"The chances of your being killed in action are very high, I won't sugar coat the fact. Your assignments are incredibly dangerous. If you survive to the end of the war, it will be due to your skills and instincts. If you are careless and stupid, you will surely die.

"You will be paid more than the average soldier; your pay will be twenty dollars a month and be put in an account in your name. I strongly suggest you give us a next of kin to send it to in the event you are killed. You will be given one month's wage in advance to buy what you need in the field. I suggest you make it last, you will need it. Do not drink it up.

"Which brings up another point: any man caught drunk on duty, and you will always be on duty, will be arrested and imprisoned. There will be absolutely no tolerance for breaking any of the rules I have mentioned. The lives of many are dependent on you. We are at war and there is no time for putting up with idiocies. Now, with that said, who here wishes to leave, or return to the guardhouse if that be the case?"

No one moved or spoke.

Parker paused and then nodded his head. "You will operate in pairs. If you have a partner here with you that you would like to team up with let me know. If not, at the end of the training week we will pair you up according to your compatibility to each other. Meet here at six o'clock tomorrow morning. Do not make Sergeant Major Freeman come looking for you. You have already witnessed that Sergeant Major Freeman plays rough. That is all for today. You are dismissed."

Chapter Seven

Six o'clock found fifteen men filing into the room where Lieutenant Parker and Sergeant Major Freeman stood waiting for them. The men sat down quietly, the example set the day before by Freeman dragging the man away to his execution having quelled any further belligerence.

Parker stood up and nodded his approval. "Very good, men, I see you have all returned. You are a dedicated and courageous group."

The first day was spent with Parker and Freeman taking turns telling the men about the cause of the war and how the enemy would operate. Battle tactics were explained and what they would need to do to work their way into enemy controlled territory without detection.

It was clear to the men that Lieutenant Parker was no West Point dandy who had only studied the theory of war. He was a man in his forties with an amiable nature, yet a hard no-nonsense attitude toward their task. Freeman, also a man in his forties, never smiled. He took his work seriously and saw nothing funny in war and teaching men to kill. Both men were battle hardened, having earned their ranks in the war with Mexico.

The second day began the field work. The men were taught to use dynamite and blasting powder and how to place it for maximum damage. The fifteen men were, for the most part, loners who had come to the unit each for his own reasons. As the men became more acquainted with each other there arrived a common understanding that none of them were afraid of the others. They were men who had lived danger-filled lives and fear did not have a place there.

By the third day the men began to speak a bit to each other and pairings emerged between men who felt they could work together and trust each other. The group had begun with sixteen, an even number to make up eight pairs; however, the arrest and removal of the one left a man out. The man practiced the lessons being taught as a single unit; he neither sought out a partner nor expected one.

Buck and Raven sat at the noon meal with the lone man sitting silently across from them. Raven studied him. The man was shorter than he was, yet built like a bull, with a heavily muscled torso and a face that had seen its share of fights. Raven reached his hand across the table to him, "Renard Ravenel, Raven to my friends," he said matter-of-factly.

The man looked up from his plate to the extended hand and then gripped it. "Kai Maddock." His voice was heavily accented.

Raven smiled, "You look like a man who has seen his share of the rougher side of life."

"I'm no stranger to hard work or to fightin'," he grinned.

Raven jabbed a thumb toward Buck, "My partner, Buck Drake."

Kai reached his hand across the table and shook Buck's hand. "Glad to make your acquaintance." He looked intensely at Buck, beyond the short blonde hair. "You're part red man?"

Buck nodded, "My mother is a Blood. My father was an English man."

Kai nodded, "I've got nothin' agin the red man, but I surely despise the English."

Buck grinned, "I do too."

Kai grinned back, "Hate your father, do you?"

Buck nodded.

"I'm a Welshman. The English look down on us, but then we are happy to return the favor."

"What are you going to do for a partner?" Raven asked between bites.

Kai shrugged. "A man should be able to handle his own fights."

"Can't argue with you there. I don't think Buck

would mind if you threw in with us though."

Buck nodded in agreement, "Sure, work with us."

Kai looked from Buck to Raven with a twinkle of humor in his eyes. "Can you stand a Welshman in your midst?"

Raven laughed, "A Frenchman and a half breed, we're not exactly popular ourselves."

Kai laughed in return. "Then, it's a partnership."

"Are you from Wales?" Raven asked.

"Aye, I was a coal miner and broke my back for the company and had nothin' to show for it. I worked my way across the sea to America for a better opportunity. I made my way to West Virginia to mine coal. Then, the war broke out and I thought it my duty, and honor bound I am, to fight for my new country. I heard some of the boys talkin' of this unit, they were sayin' it was suicide and they'd have naught of it. I thinks to myself, Kai Maddock that's just the spot for you. 'Tis a little more adventurous for men with real red blood in the veins. How about you?"

Raven grinned, "Lieutenant Parker was generous enough to offer me a place with them back at Fort Bridger."

"So, you know the Lieutenant then?"

"In a way."

Kai spooned stew into his mouth as he watched Raven. He smiled, "Sounds like there's a story behind that."

"I, umm, killed one of his troopers in a fight."

"Imagine that, and here I was thinkin' you were a proper choirboy singin' like an angel in the church."

"Not quite. It wasn't my fault though."

"It never is," Kai grinned.

"I had four tens and he had three fours. He didn't like that too much, seeing how he had his whole payday on the table. He pulled a knife and I shot him."

"Isn't there a sayin' in America about not bringin' a knife to a gunfight?"

"They put me in the guardhouse and started making the noose. Parker showed up and made me an offer, fight or hang. I'm here, so you know which idea appealed to me the most."

Kai finished his stew and looked at Buck. "Since we're all tellin' our tales, what's yours my Blood friend?"

Buck frowned. "My father was a renegade. I was foolish enough to go along with his party on a raid. They attacked a wagon that had soldiers hiding in it. My father hit me with his rifle and shoved me into the soldiers so he could run away. They were going to hang me until Lieutenant Parker made me the same offer. Here I am."

"So your own father fed you to the soldiers so he could escape? No wonder you hate the yellow coward."

"When the war is over I am going to find him and kill him."

"Sounds like a reasonable course of action, under the circumstances."

The meal ended with a command shouted across the room for all men to return to their units. The three filed out and returned to the room where the training continued for the rest of the day. At the end of the session the men were walking out when Parker stopped Raven, Buck, and Kai. "I noticed today that Mr. Maddock seems to be on your team."

"He joined up with Buck and me," Raven answered.

Parker thought for a second, "Good. I have some special assignments that actually require more than two men. I didn't want to join two teams when I only needed three men. I didn't really want to lose a team needed in the field. The three of you are perfect for what I have in mind."

"And what might that be?" Raven asked.

"The Rebels have taken Richmond as their headquarters. That's a little too close to Washington for us not to challenge them. We want them to know that it isn't going to be a comfortable place to be. I want their communication lines interfered with and their munitions stores and railroads blown up. In general, I want you to tear apart their efforts to coordinate a fight from Richmond."

"Sounds dangerous," Kai said.

"Very," Parker answered. "If you get out alive it will be a miracle."

Kai grinned, "Sounds like my kind of odds."

"When do we start?" Raven added.

Buck grinned, "The coup count will be something to boast about."

Parker looked at each of them and then burst out laughing. "What a group! If you survive this, I'll see to it you all get medals."

"Do they give medals for insanity?" Raven laughed.

"Sometimes. I often wonder if there isn't a fine line between courage and insanity."

"Being dropped on your head as an infant might have something to do with it," Kai put in with a wry grin.

"Go on," Parker said shaking his head and laughing. "Hit the mess tent before it's all gone."

Parker watched the three men walk out the door. Under different circumstances they were men he would have liked to have for friends, but he knew better. You didn't make friends in a war. Friends get killed and it leaves a hole in you. He learned that lesson the hard way when he was a young infantryman. He hoped to see the three together at the end of the war, yet he doubted that all three would come out alive.

The week of training ended with each team meeting privately with Parker and Freeman. It was their idea that if each team was ignorant of the activities of the others, should they be captured they would not be able to give information out on the others. Buck, Raven, and Kai were the last to meet with their leaders.

They all sat down together. "I'm sure you have questions," Parker began.

Raven grinned, "Yeah, which way to the fighting?"

Parker grinned back. "You'll get your fill, I promise you that."

"We're ready," Kai put in. "What do you want us to do first?"

"You will each be given a horse that does not have a U.S. brand on it or a military saddle. You will make your way down toward Richmond, to the last camp of our forces before the enemy line; it is under the command of Major Graham. You will leave the horses at the camp and set out on foot under the cover of darkness.

"The Rebels have telegraph lines that must be cut in as many places as possible. One cut can be repaired quickly, a hundred takes more time and right now the side with the most time has the advantage over the other. You will get your munitions from Major Graham; he is my contact in that particular camp. He knows to give you whatever you need. Ride there and ask for him and only him. He will know where the enemy has established munitions stores and about the railroad running fresh supplies to them."

"How long do we stay around there?" Buck asked. "The longer we are there the more likely we are to be captured."

"You will do as much damage as you can in a three-day period. Stay at it as much as safely possible especially at night. Destroy their munitions, sabotage the tracks and water tanks for the train, set fires. In general keep them running around in circles. After that, return to Graham's camp for further orders."

"What if we are stopped and questioned?" Kai asked.

"You are merely civilians trying to get out of the war zone and are heading west. If they ask why you have Yankee revolvers, say you took them off dead soldiers."

They all fell silent for a moment and then Parker

stood up and extended his hand to each of them. "Pray this war is over quickly." They shook hands all around and left the building.

The three men wore the revolvers and knives. A revolver was new to Buck. He had never handled or fired one before he was given this one. He quickly decided that he liked the short gun. It was not accurate at long range like a rifle, but he could move it around fast and shoot in close quarters.

Collecting the horses, they mounted up and rode south for Major Graham's camp. They rode through camps where thousands of blue uniformed men waited for orders to march into battle. There were uncountable young faces among them that reflected the fear brought on by what they were about to do.

The sounds of cannon and rifle fire came on the wind from places distant to them. It was all well and good for young men to talk of glory and bravery in battle while sitting in the safety of the town square, it was quite another to have the reality of it inundate your every sense.

They were three days on the road, asking along the way for Major Graham's camp and were steadily directed southward. Asking for the last time, they were told Graham's was the next camp down.

Reaching the camp, the three men were confronted by a uniformed sentry who barely seemed old enough to shave. Blue uniformed and holding a bayoneted rifle in both hands in front of him, he stood his ground.

"Halt!" the young man shouted.

The men stopped at the command.

"This is an Army camp," the sentry spoke in a command voice. "Civilians are not allowed to go further."

"We're not civilians," Raven answered. "We are to report to Major Graham."

The sentry refused to move as he eyed them suspiciously. "My orders are that no one except uniformed men are allowed to pass."

"That's all well and good, but we're not civilians."

"You don't pass; if you try I will shoot you."

Raven sighed in exasperation. "Come on boy, get out of the way."

The young sentry aimed his rifle at them. "You had better go, now."

Kai leaned forward in his saddle, "Son, do you really want to go against the orders of a Lieutenant and a Major and bring the wrath of a Sergeant Major big enough to hunt bears with a switch down on yuh?"

The young man shifted nervously back and forth from one foot to the other, yet kept his rifle pointed at Raven. "You don't pass," he said stubbornly.

"Can we talk to someone else?" Buck asked.

"No."

"I'm about to take that gun away from you and shove it down your throat," Buck snapped angrily.

"Try it." He shifted the rifle to point at Buck.

At that moment a Sergeant Major walked up to them. He looked at the sentry as he stood ready to fire at Buck. He then looked the three men over. "What is going on here, soldier?"

"Civilians, Sergeant, they insist on passing through. They say they are army and have to report to Major Graham, but I don't believe them."

The Sergeant looked at the men, "I am directly affiliated with Major Graham, state your business."

"I am Parker Freeman," Raven said.

The Sergeant nodded at the recognition of the code words. "It's okay, sentry, we have been expecting them."

The young soldier lowered his gun looking sheepish and embarrassed.

"Come with me," the Sergeant called to the three men.

Kai spoke to the embarrassed young man, "You did

fine, lad. You did your job."

The soldier nodded meekly, "Yes, sir."

As Buck passed the soldier he spoke in a low voice to him, "You won't kill many Rebels if you don't cock your hammer before trying to shoot them."

The young man looked at his rifle and realized that he had been pointing the hammer-down ineffective weapon at the men. He felt even more foolish as the men passed him following the Sergeant.

They rode through the camp up to a house that had been abandoned and taken over as the headquarters for the camp. They dismounted and walked in the door behind the Sergeant.

He stepped into a room where a gray haired, stern faced man sat behind a desk. The Sergeant snapped a salute. "The men from Lieutenant Parker, sir."

The Major stood up and returned the salute. "Thank you, Sergeant."

The Major shook hands with each of the men. "I have your orders from Lieutenant Parker. You have a difficult assignment ahead of you. Come with me to the map room and I will show you how the city is laid out and what my scouts have found the enemy strengths to be."

They followed the Major into another room with the Sergeant Major tailing behind them. The room they entered held several officers looking over maps and discussing their situation and prospective moves. A large map was pinned to a wall. The Major began to point at the lines and marks. Buck, being unable to read would have to rely on Raven to explain what he had learned.

"We had a munitions store in the city when it was still under federal control. When the Confederates took the city, they thought they had a gold mine of munitions to use against us. We surprised them, however, by burning the place down after getting out all we could. They have since filled another building with munitions that have been moved in by train from further south. That building is here," he pointed at a spot on the map.

"The railroad is one hundred percent Confederate controlled and bringing in supplies from the south without interruption. We want that rail line interrupted permanently. The munitions house and the rail are your primary targets. Blow the house and then the train if it is there; if it isn't blow as much track as possible. Destruction is what we want to achieve here."

"Parker said he wanted us in there no more than three days," Kai commented.

"Yes, three days and then get back here. By then the enemy will have troops out in force to find you."

"We'll go in tonight," Raven said.

Buck turned his head to look at the Sergeant Major standing only inches behind him and listening intently. He didn't like the feeling. The man paid him no mind as he studied the map where the Major was pointing. Buck growled at the Sergeant, "If you want to stand in my pocket let me know."

The Sergeant looked at him with a scowl and took a step back. Buck returned the scowl and then turned his attention back to the Major and the map.

The Major looked at Buck, "Is there an issue here?"

"Not anymore," Buck answered.

"Please pay attention then."

Buck nodded his compliance.

"At the least fulfill your primary mission if you can't do anything else," the Major continued. "The munitions and rail must be destroyed, the munitions tonight first off. If you can do more over the three days do it, but if it means capture or death don't. Having you captured or dead will do us little good. We need you alive and operating, so no foolish heroics."

"We'll get it done," Raven answered.

"Good. Any questions?"

The three men shook their heads.

"You are dismissed. I expect to see you back here in three days."

"We'll be here," Kai responded with a serious expression.

The three walked out of the room while the Major and Sergeant remained where they were. Buck looked back at the Sergeant and their eyes met with a challenging glare.

"What was that all about?" Raven asked Buck.

"I don't like him."

"Who?"

"That Sergeant."

"What was he doing, getting a little too friendly?" Kai remarked with a grin.

"I sensed there was a little hostility between you two," Raven put in. "Maybe he just doesn't like half breeds, it's not an uncommon prejudice you know."

"He reminded me of crows that sit in the trees waiting for the wolves to finish eating on a buffalo so they can swoop down on the carcass."

They walked out of the house and stood outside in the fading light of the day. They watched the activity of the bustling camp. "What are you thinking, Buck?" Raven asked without looking at him.

"I think we should wait until the third day to blow the munitions."

"But the Major said first thing tonight," Kai argued.

"We might find a war party waiting for us tonight if we do."

Raven turned to look his partner in the face. "You think that Sergeant is a spy?"

"I think we need to find out by watching the munitions building before going into it. If I'm right, we can blow up the rails farther down the track while they are all waiting for us at the house."

Raven and Kai exchanged glances. "We *were* told

to make our own decisions in the field," Kai said. "If our friend here thinks this is a trap we should give him the benefit of listening. We can blow up the munitions another night."

"Did anyone catch his name?" Raven looked from one to the other.

Just then a Captain who had been in the map room walked out. Raven stopped him. "Excuse me, sir."

The Captain recognized them from the map room and stopped.

"What is the name of the Sergeant Major who was in the room with us?"

"That would be Nelson."

"Has he been here long, sir?"

"Two weeks, maybe. You should know him, he arrived with orders from Lieutenant Parker to directly aid Major Graham with your mission."

"Thank you, sir." The Captain nodded and moved along.

Raven looked at his partners. "I sure never saw him around."

Kai shook his head. "We would have at least seen him moving about the camp or in the mess tent."

Buck looked at them, "Only one Sergeant works with Parker and that's Freeman."

Raven nodded. "Parker would never give that information to anyone else. This Nelson is lying."

Kai looked at each of them. "That means the enemy knows about our unit. How else would Nelson know who Parker was?"

Raven scowled. "That also means whatever Graham knows Nelson knows."

Kai grinned, "We can use that to our advantage though and throw a wrench in their gears. Let's give that building a good study and then go blow up a railroad."

Chapter Eight

The three men waited until darkness had fully descended and then began their walk into Richmond with knapsacks filled with three days' dry rations and uncapped dynamite on their backs. The night was humid with the July heat holding strong. Clouds drifted across the sky covering the half moon and threatening to rain. Heat lightning knifed silently on the horizon.

It was an hour later when they spotted the first gray uniforms. The Rebels had total control from that point on and everywhere they looked were tents and moving Confederate soldiers. The three lay down on a low hill and watched the patterns of the enemy.

"We don't want to follow the roads or any route where they would expect us," Raven whispered.

Buck agreed. "If Nelson did set a trap for us, and I'm pretty sure he did, they will be expecting us to walk right into it."

Kai whispered, "That's right, he knows we were ordered to hit the munitions building first thing tonight."

Buck replied, "He has no idea we're on to him though. We need to go cross country and around the city. Raven, do you know where the building is?"

"I recall it from the map, but it'll take a bit to figure out where it actually is on the ground."

Kai pointed to a cluster of buildings showing lights in the windows. "From what I remember from the map, it has to be that way."

Buck pointed in the opposite direction, "Then we go that way, wrap around, and come in behind it."

They set off in the direction Buck had indicated. Several times they had to lie down flat in sheltered places to hide from Rebel soldiers or patrols. Sentries were posted along the roads and on the main streets of the city. They had several hours of pure darkness to figure it out and they intended to move slowly and scout out the city and enemy positions before doing anything.

Another hour and they were on the opposite side of the city and within sight of the house where the munitions were stored. They moved in close enough to make out the guards around the building. They lay on the grass under a trio of huge old oak trees and watched in silence.

There were the usual guards they expected to be there. Several guards stood stationary around the building while others walked a route around it. It was heavily guarded as a matter of course.

Kai shifted closer to Raven and put his head close to his. "About what we expected for guards. I don't see any extras though."

Raven watched the movement of the men. He had survived in Indian country half his life and knew that nothing was ever as it appeared. He looked for things beyond the obvious. "You won't," he whispered.

Buck's eyes were searching every inch of the area around the building, but not in the immediate vicinity of it. He ignored the obvious guards out in the open, as they were expected to be there. A trap would have men hidden where they were not expected to be. It was the way the Crow set up an ambush. There were the obvious riders in the party, the bait that would draw the attackers out, but it was the hidden ones who would kill you. He looked for that pattern here.

He finally found what he was looking for. A match flared in the trees fifty paces from the building. No doubt it was a hidden soldier bored enough to carelessly strike a match to light a smoke. Once he had located the man, he narrowed his eyes and studied around him and made out the forms of others in various places surrounding the building out the same distance as the smoker.

Buck crawled next to Raven. "Did you see the match?"

"I saw it. I'm seeing a bunch of them all around the

place now. Good thinking war chief, it is a trap."

"These whites don't know it, but that's an old Crow trap. It's nothing new. We use it too."

Kai was staring out into the night, not seeing what the others had. Raven moved his head toward him and explained what he and Buck had seen. He pointed out where the hidden soldiers were.

"You see a movement," Raven whispered, "and then focus on it and pretty soon a body part—arm, leg, or head--takes shape and then you can see the man. You keep looking for that type of thing and pretty soon you see a whole herd of them."

Kai nodded. "Ah, I see 'em now. I've something to learn from you mountain men. What now?"

"We head down the tracks, a mile out of the city and start blowing track."

They slipped down off the hill where they had been for the last two hours and made their way south to the tracks.

Keeping out of sight, they moved away from the city area where the Rebels were concentrated. Patrols were active throughout so there was no hurrying or careless movement. Coming onto the tracks they stopped and looked around. Save for the sound of frogs and crickets the night was quiet.

"No one is out there," Buck spoke low as they looked over the tracks.

"How can you be sure?" Kai asked.

"If there were men out there the crickets and frogs would stop."

Kai nodded silently in the dark.

The three quickly worked their way south along the tracks. Reaching a point that looked right, they began capping dynamite and placing it tightly under the rails. They placed charges on both tracks spaced out at fifty yards per charge, enough to destroy two to three hundred yards of track. At the end of the charged section Raven tied a stick of dynamite to one of the legs of the water tower.

They returned to the beginning of the charges. Fuses had been cut so the longest were set first and the shortest last so they could get the last ones lit before the first charges blew. Matches flared in the dark as did the sparkling fuse as it burned. The three hurried along lighting fuses as they moved southward. The first charge blew as they were lighting the stick on the tank leg. They ran for the cover of a grove of trees where they had agreed to hide.

They reached the trees as the blasts exploded one after another rocking the night into ground-shaking concussion and fire. As the sound faded away it was followed by the raining patter of bits of wood and steel falling back to the earth. Then, the unmistakable sound of creaking wood followed by a booming crash mixed with the splashing and sloshing of hundreds of gallons of water.

Raven grinned, "Perfect."

They ran further into the woods and waited for the sounds of rushing horses and shouting men that were certain to come next. It took a quarter of an hour, but they came by the dozens. The burning ties illuminated the Confederate soldiers as they scurried about putting out the fires as best they could. In the dim light given off by the dancing flames, they could see the splintered ties and twisted steel.

"That should shut it down for a while," Kai chuckled.

Buck spoke low to the others, "Let's make our way back to the munitions building and see if that drew the extra men off."

"Thought we were going to wait until the third night," Raven questioned Buck's idea.

"That's what we first thought, but now they know we are here, right?"

"Yeah."

"We didn't follow the plan to blow the building the way Nelson expected us to. They have to know now that we discovered their trap. Keeping the extra guards on the building is pointless anymore so they will pull them off to look for us by the tracks."

Kai broke in, "So, now is the time to blow the munitions building while they are all at the tracks."

"Yes. If we wait, they will double the guard on the building tomorrow."

Raven grinned, "Man, you are one good war chief. Let's go."

As they hurried back toward the city Kai explained, "I've set a lot of explosive charges in minin'; there is always a chain reaction if charges come in contact with each other. Even if we can throw a couple sticks of dynamite through the windows, the explosions will cause a chain reaction and the whole place will go up in fire."

Raven nodded, "Sounds like a good plan."

The three men hurried through the darkness in a more direct route to the munitions building. To the west and south they could hear the shouting and commotion as the camps flared into action in response to the explosions.

They made it back to the hill with the three oak trees. Soldiers were running in all directions as officers shouted orders. "They're having fits," Raven laughed.

Priming several sticks of dynamite they held them in their hands. "In and out fast," Raven instructed. "They won't notice us in the confusion. Run in, throw the sticks and meet back here and then we hightail it for the woods."

They began to get up from their crouched positions when several soldiers ran by closely, causing them to flop back on their bellies. Kai grabbed Raven's arm, "Uniforms. If we can get into gray coats and hats we won't be noticed at all. We will look like the rest of 'em runnin' around."

Buck pointed at three Rebels approaching the hill, "Like those three gray coats and hats."

"Aye, those three will work."

Picking up heavy branches that had fallen from the oak trees they waited for the Rebels to pass. They quickly fell in behind the gray coats and rushed toward their backs. One of the Rebels turned around just as the heavy oak branches crashed into their heads sending them into tumbling falls. They lay still while their coats and hats were pulled off.

Raven, Buck, and Kai put on the gray outer coats and caps. They didn't fit exactly, but they would do the trick. They headed toward the munitions building. When they got close enough to get a good look at the building they could see that the windows were boarded over from the inside. It was the reflection of the glass that had fooled them into thinking they were normal windows. The building was made of impenetrable stone, but it was the windows they had hoped to break through.

Raven cursed. "So much for that plan."

"We need to throw the dynamite in the door then," Kai said quickly.

"What do you think we should do, knock and ask to come in?" Raven's tone was frustrated.

"No, we need another diversion. Me and Buck will go down there, kill the guard at the door, open it and throw the sticks in. While we're doin' that, you will be doin' other things."

Raven's eyes showed his understanding. "Like blowing up other things?"

"Aye."

Buck snapped, "We can't keep standing here, let's go."

Kai stepped out quickly with Buck, running toward the building like they were part of the scurrying Rebel army. Reaching the door they found the guard steadfastly holding his position. Without slowing, Buck pulled his gun, shoved the barrel into the man's belly, and fired. The sound of the shot was muffled in the man's shirt. The man fell where he had stood with the dull sound of the shot being lost in the explosion that Raven had caused by throwing a stick of dynamite into a large tent.

The tent went up in fire and smoke, drawing the attention of the surrounding soldiers. Kai and Buck hunkered down low over the dead soldier and twisted and turned the handle on the door. Just as they were pushing the door open an officer stopped and looked at them.

"What are you men doing there?" he commanded.

Buck called out to him, "Sir, this man has been shot."

The officer hurried over to the door and bent over them. As he bent, Buck shoved his knife directly into the officer's heart. The man's eyes popped open wide at the impact. He made a squeaking sound and fell over the body of the soldier.

Kai pushed the door open, struck a match on his thumb, lit the twisted fuses of the triple stick bundle and tossed it in the door. Raven's second explosion sounded from a different location. Kai and Buck bolted into the night. The explosion sounded behind them slightly muffled by the heavy stone walls of the building. Within seconds the chain reaction started within the building's walls as the roof blew into the sky, raining burning wood and tar down on the Rebels.

The three men met back on the oak tree hill and then kept running for the safety of the woods. The night behind them was lit up with fire. The smoke made eerie shapes against the flickering light of the fires. They reached the woods and moved deeper in until they came to a brushy gulley. Sliding down the side of the hill, they got to the bottom splashing into a small rivulet of water moving down the hill. Dropping to the ground they dug for air breathing heavily from the run.

After several minutes they had regained their breath

and sat up sweating profusely from their exertions in the humid summer air.

Raven chuckled, "Now I know what John Colter felt like when he was running from your people, Buck."

Buck grinned. "The story is told often of the white trapper who outran our best runners. It angered them, but they respected him for it. He was a warrior."

"Except we didn't have any Blackfeet chasing us."

"No," Kai laughed lightly, "just half the Confederate army."

They all laughed.

"I'd say that went well," Raven said with a grin.

They dug into their packs to find the paper-wrapped biscuits and dried meat they had brought from the camp. The biscuits were reduced to crumbles, but to hungry men they were a feast. Drinking from the creek and eating, they sat and listened in the darkness. The distant sounds of crackling fire and excited voices drifted on the breeze.

Raven looked around. "I'd say this is a pretty good hiding place for us."

"Depends on what it looks like in the light," Buck answered. "Right now it looks good though."

Kai glanced from Raven to Buck. "They were expectin' us."

"That they were," Raven nodded. "You called it, Buck."

"I didn't like Nelson."

"So, what do we do about it?" Kai asked.

Buck answered, "We tell Graham when we get back."

"What if he's one of them?" Kai argued. "Maybe him and Nelson are workin' together."

Raven frowned at the thought. "We need to get a wire off to Parker and let him handle it from his end. Graham might simply be an idiot and Nelson wormed his way into his inner circle."

"No one was supposed to know about us except commanding officers," Buck spit out angrily. "Why is this fool giving our codes and assignments to an unknown Sergeant?"

"Good question," Kai agreed.

Raven put in, "It's a big war and the information that is supposed to be confined to a certain few is more than likely to spill over to a lot of people who shouldn't have it. We'll just have to be sure and not trust anyone outside of Parker or Freeman and be wary of what other officers say was passed on to them from Parker. If we had followed Parker's orders to the letter, and Graham had compromised those orders by letting Nelson know about them, we'd all be dead now."

Buck looked at Raven while he talked and then agreed. "From now on we make our own decisions out here."

"Agreed," Raven and Kai said at the same time.

The early morning hours had turned cool and they were happy for the gray coats they wore. The adrenalin surges the men had been operating under were wearing off, leaving them exhausted and sleepy.

"Until we know this is a safe place to hide we will have to take turns keeping watch," Buck said

"Agreed," Raven said. "One hour shifts for the rest of the night and then we'll see what the morning brings."

"I'll take first watch," Buck volunteered.

"I'll take second and then wake Kai."

Raven and Kai lay down on the ground and fell directly to sleep. Buck listened into the night for anything that didn't sound right. It was quiet except for frogs in the creek.

Buck sat and wondered about the changes that had taken over his life in the last two months. Battle was battle, whether here against the Rebs or in the mountains against other tribes. The tactics were the same so he applied them here with success. What was different was the environment he was now in. He was quickly falling into the ways of the people around him.

He knew he had already changed a good bit due to what he was learning, even his speech was becoming more like his friends. He was a long way from his village, people, and mountains. He knew that his life was headed in other directions. Even if he returned to the village he would always remember what he saw here and know that their time was limited.

His thinking drifted to his father and he frowned as he recalled the cowardly things the man had done. He wondered if the scoundrel had the nerve to return to the village after getting his entire party wiped out. He hoped that he was killed along the way or just kept riding; either would be better for his mother and grandfather.

He knew that he would go back to the village when this war was over and, if Jules was there, he would announce to the entire village what the coward had done and then kill him. He would redeem his grandfather's honor and right the wrong Jules had done to him at the same time.

Chapter Nine

Daylight was filling the Virginia woods as Kai woke up and looked around him. The sky was a dull blue, the threat of rain having passed. It was already growing humid and hot. Raven was sitting in a pose of concentration at the bottom of the gulley. He appeared to be listening to something. Buck had stood two watches and was asleep.

Kai slipped quietly up beside Raven. "Do you hear something?"

Raven shook his head. "Thought I did, but I don't hear it now. Probably some animal running in the dry leaves."

Kai jabbed a thumb toward Buck, "Nerves of steel that one. No fear in him. He shot that guard without a second's hesitation and when that officer challenged us I thought we were dead. But, what's Buck do? He goes and calls him over. I thought he was daft and then he sticks that knife right into the man's heart. Then, he tells me to hurry and throw the dynamite in the door. I'll admit I was shakin' a bit, not him though. Ice water in his veins, that one has."

"You have to remember," Raven replied, "he's a Blood. The Blackfeet are the deadliest Indians in the west, they have no fear of anything. Because of it, they're also the most hated by whites and other Indians alike. Buck's been in war parties since he was a kid. Killing in battle is just part of what they do. Blackfeet make great, loyal friends, but wretched enemies."

Buck opened his eyes and lay silently letting his senses take in everything around him. Once satisfied that the immediate area was safe, he sat up. He looked over at Raven and Kai and asked, "Have you looked over the top yet?"

Raven shook his head, "Not yet. I thought I heard movement up there so I've stayed low. Whatever it was seems to be gone now."

The three moved in a crouch up the wall of the gully. Lying on their bellies they peeked over the top at the land around them. They were in the first part of bigger woods that ran behind them and to their right and left. Brush and trees surrounded them.

They could see buildings and houses in the distance marking the beginning of the city. In one direction smoke continued to curl up from what they figured was the remnant of the munitions building. In another, smoke continued to rise from the burning creosote-soaked railroad ties. In the distance a locomotive blew a long, shrill whistle coupled with the sound of screeching brakes.

Raven grinned, "Guess he ran out of track. We need to blow up some more of it miles out of town. They can still transfer the goods from the train to the city in wagons."

Buck paused in thought, "Wouldn't it be easier if we blew up the train?"

Raven held the grin, "Oh, I like that idea. Let's see what kind of a plan we can come up with while we hide out today."

"We need a better hiding place," Kai said.

Raven looked around. "These woods and this gulley are pretty dense, we could stay right here for the couple of days left."

Buck shook his head, "Too open if they come looking." He gestured toward the scarred walls of the gulley and the litter of grass and branches caught up in the brush several feet above the gully's floor. "This floods when the heavy rains come. We can follow the stream up and see if there is a place where the water washed out a cave under one of these big trees."

They moved back down the hill and headed up the stream, staying in the bottom of the gully. Fighting their way through brambles and brush, they came on a huge oak hanging over the edge of the gully. Its giant gnarled roots had been deeply undercut by years of flood waters forming a cave several feet back into the bank.

"There." Buck pointed. "We can cut brush to hide the front of the entrance and get back inside it out of sight. I don't think anyone would want to fight their way up this gulley so we should be safe here."

They set to work digging the soft dirt out of the cave with their knives and sticks to make it big enough to sit up in. Once satisfied with the enlarged space the entrance was then disguised with cut brush.

The three men crawled into the cave and sat back against the dirt walls. "Cozy," Raven grinned.

"If you're a bear," Kai chuckled.

"Or a gopher," Buck laughed.

"Oh, I don't know," Raven mused, "a settee over there, a few embroidered pillows . . ."

"Some light," Kai cut him off with a laugh.

"Well, sure if you're going to be picky."

"I understand white men like their comforts, but we should probably decide what we're going to do about that train," Buck said good naturedly.

Raven looked at Kai and shook his head, "There's one in every crowd."

"And here I thought we were on a holiday," Kai grinned.

"Okay," Raven agreed, "business before decorating. They can't move that train forward; it'll take weeks to repair the track, if they can at all. They might try backing it all the way to wherever it came from, but I doubt it."

"We should blow it tonight, then," Kai said.

Raven shook his head, "It will be heavily guarded."

Buck agreed. "Nelson knows it was us who blew the track, the train will be buried in gray coats."

Kai argued, "Granted, it will be guarded, but what if they *do* decide to back it up? We'll lose it."

"We can blow the track behind it so it can't go anywhere," Buck said.

Kai shook his head, "If we're going to do that we might as well blow the train. Track can be repaired, but once the train is gone it's gone."

"Let's do this," Raven began. "Come dark we sneak down to the train and see what's going on. I think we should watch it tonight and see what they are doing. See how the guards are set and spot any weakness in their defenses. Then, we blow the train tomorrow night."

"If nothing happens tonight they will think we are gone and maybe lower their guard tomorrow night," Buck said.

Kai nodded, "A nice parting gift on our way out."

"Okay," Raven said, "tonight we play spy."

With the plan agreed on, they settled back to wait. Raven pulled a small book out of his pack and leaned toward the cave's entrance where there was light enough to read.

"Smart man," Kai gestured at the book. "I wish I had brought something to read. I may go mad starin' at these dirt walls for a whole day."

Raven replied, "One of the habits I brought West with me."

"You seem a learned man, Raven."

"I come from a well-to-do family in St. Louis. My grandfather was from France where he killed a friend of King Louis in a duel. They were going to throw him in the dungeon so he signed on a ship and headed for the Acadian Peninsula.

"He eventually drifted down into Connecticut where he fought in the revolt against England. He was highly educated, and so was my father, who went to St. Louis when the country began opening up. He became a successful businessman dealing in furs and ended up involved in politics. I was sent to school and even spent a year at a university."

"How did a high-born, university educated man like

you end up trappin' beaver?"

"I wasn't really cut out for the life of a city man. Ever since I was a boy I saw those expeditions and free trappers coming in with loads of fur and enough tales to make a young man green with envy. My studies began to slip when I spent more time with the trappers than my teachers. My father knew I had the itch to go west. He finally told me to go and get it out of my system and then come back when I was ready to make something of myself. That was almost twenty years ago and I never went back." He laughed, "And here I am hiding in a hole."

Kai laughed, "So, you did make something of yourself after all."

"Yeah, a squirrel."

Kai's smile faded. "My father died in a Welsh coal mine collapse. My mother taught us to read and write, she said we'd never get out of the mines or break free of the British if we were lacking education. I left the old country alone, yet educated. I've come further than my brothers who stayed and I intend to go further yet. Providin' I survive this war."

Buck remained silent as he listened to the men talk of education. His people had a spoken language, but there was no written word or reading of it. From what he was seeing and hearing all around him now, he knew that if he didn't learn what the white man learned he would forever be behind them.

He knew that white missionaries had come west to educate the Indians. He could see now that if his people didn't learn the things the missionaries taught, they were destined to be forever ground under the heels of the white man. Unfortunately, his ancestors were more interested in scalping missionaries than learning from them. When this was over he needed to go back and tell them that. He knew his people were proud and would never willingly follow the ways of the white man; however, in time they would have no choice as it would be thrust upon them.

It was a hard thing for him to admit to his weaknesses, and being unable to read and write in a changing world was a weakness he must overcome. He swallowed his pride.

"Raven, could you teach me to read and write?"

Raven looked up at him, "Certainly."

"We both can help you," Kai volunteered. "It will give us something to do while we wait."

The lessons began with the simple alphabet and letters scratched into the dirt with twigs. The lessons occupied the day until night began to fall over the woods casting the gully in shadow. When full darkness came, the men put on the gray coats they had taken the night before, and slipped out of the cave headed for the tracks to find the train.

Staying to the darkness well back from the tracks, they walked until they heard the sounds of talking and moving men. They got down on their hands and knees sneaking toward the tracks until they could see the shutdown locomotive and the cars behind it. A small amount of work had been done on the torn ties and twisted rails directly in front of the train; however, it was obvious the work was going to be labor intensive and take weeks to repair.

An added benefit to the explosions was the destruction of the telegraph lines along the track. The poles had either been blown apart or burned down resulting in a massive tangle of broken telegraph wire for a distance further than the blown track and ties. There would be no messages on that line for a while.

Five armed guards were posted to each side of the train and another up in the cab of the locomotive. The three men lay in the field silently watching the activity. What interested them was the routine the guards followed and when they were relieved.

An hour had passed when they heard men coming up the tracks. An officer on horseback was followed by eleven men on foot. Each incoming man replaced a guard as the officer was heard speaking to the men and then he turned his horse and headed back with the off duty guards following him.

The new guards held to their specific stations and stared out into the night. As time passed, the guards grew restless and bored. They leaned against the cars, squatted down, lit pipes, and paid little attention to their surroundings. They were men not accustomed to war and its threats.

Four hours passed and then the guard was again changed in the same manner. Because of the early hour, this set of guards was even less alert than the previous set had been. Some even fell asleep. The three spies noted that the changing of the guard was on a four-hour rotation.

As the hours ticked by the guards grew sleepy and lethargic. The relief guards had yet to arrive when the sun cracked a slight glow over the eastern sky. The trio of spies headed back for the gully under the cover of the pre-dawn darkness.

They slept for half the day and awoke to the sounds of horses moving through the trees above them. Buck was the first to hear the sounds of brush scraping saddle leather, the grunts of horses, and a man coughing. He put his hand on Raven who had already awakened. He then woke Kai. They listened as the riders moved along the ridge above them.

One of the riders was heard to say, "I'm not riding down that gulley through all that brush and brambles, crim-a-ney, a rabbit wouldn't go through there let alone a man."

The second man answered, "There's Yankee spies about, the Major wants them found. That means search everywhere."

The two riders stopped above the cave. "Fine, you

can go down into that mess. My old coon hound wouldn't go in there, but you go right on ahead and please your ownself."

The second voice came back, "Guess I'm smarter'n a coon hound."

The horses moved on. The three lay quiet and unmoving for another hour before deciding the searchers had passed.

"Guess they're still looking for us," Raven whispered.

"Well, they can search forever after tonight and find nothing," Kai whispered back.

"Wish we had some food left," Raven commented.

"We could line up at the Rebel's Mess tent," Kai suggested.

"I'm not that hungry."

They lay on the ground of the cave listening for a long while. Hearing nothing more, they sat up and made plans for the night to finish off the train. They would slip up on the guards during the early morning watch when the men were the least attentive to their duty. Buck, who was the most silent, would kill the guard in the cab and set dynamite in it. Then, Raven and Kai would toss sticks under the cars and blow them along with the guards. They would then make their escape straight back to Graham's camp.

They took an inventory of their remaining dynamite. Among them they had twelve sticks left, enough to finish the job. The remainder of the day was spent in lessons for Buck, which took their minds off their growling stomachs. They remained in the cave until they knew the second watch had been set at the train. Putting on the gray coats they headed for the train.

Arriving at the train, they lay as they had before and watched the guards grow restless. While waiting they capped and fused the last of their dynamite. The guard was changed at the same time and manner as the night before. They waited for sleep and boredom to overtake the replacement guards.

The half-moon suddenly disappeared and a cool breeze began to blow against the sticky humid night. A low rumbling began to grow in the distance, heralding an on-coming thunderstorm. The storm would be a helpful aid for the night's work. The rumbling grew louder and the air cooler as the minutes ticked off. Thirty minutes after the first rumble of thunder it began to rain, five minutes later the rain was coming down in a torrent accented by flashing lightning and booming thunder.

The guards began to grumble and curse at the storm. They pulled their collars up around their ears and eyes and hunkered down under the cars to escape the driving rain. The rain continued to pound down as the guards began to slip into sleep under the cars.

Raven whispered, "We'll never get a match to light in this."

Buck reached into the pocket of the Confederate coat and pulled out a silver-tone box.

"What's that?" Raven asked.

Buck shrugged and handed it to Raven. "I don't know what this is."

Raven opened the box to find a slim cigar in it. "Oh, this is perfect," he grinned.

"What is it? Buck asked.

"A match that won't go out," Kai answered.

Raven cut the cigar in half and gave a piece to Kai. Buck watched as they lit the cigar pieces.

"We touch the burning end to the fuse," Raven explained. "You can strike a match up in the cab of the locomotive, but we can't in the rain."

Buck nodded his understanding and slipped into the night. He snuck silently toward the front of the locomotive. He moved like a cat keeping low to the ground. The rain and thunder covered his movement as he crept up beside the locomotive.

The guards were under the train cars with coat collars flipped up around their ears and their heads pulled down into them like turtles, which limited their field of view. Their hearing was cut off by the solid pattering of rain on the ground and the frequent rumbles of thunder.

Buck put a foot up on the step and looked into the cab. The guard was huddled in the corner with his coat pulled up tight and holding his rifle in front of him like a flagpole. Snoring was coming out of the coat.

The guard only felt for an instant the blade that ended his military career. Buck slipped the knapsack off his back and pulled out his share of the dynamite, three sticks tied together with the fuses twisted into one. He pushed the sticks under the boiler controls and struck a match. The wet lucifer match crumbled in his fingers. He cursed as he stared at the wet matchstick in his hand. He quickly dug into the dead soldier's pockets and found a pipe with dry matches. He hunkered over the match as it flared and ignited the fuse that began to sputter and burn down toward the sticks. He quickly jumped down from the cab and ran.

The soldier closest to him saw the movement and crab walked out from under the train. "Who goes there?" he shouted. When no answer came back to him, he climbed up the steps of the locomotive. He looked in at the same time the dynamite ignited.

The locomotive blew apart from the inside out taking the tender car and three guards with it. Raven and Kai moved in quickly tossing the last of the dynamite under the cars. The explosions rocked the ground and sent wood and steel debris fifty feet into the air and farther out to the sides. The iron wheels of two of the cars where shifted off the tracks.

The night was lit by the fire, revealing the entire train in shambles and splinters with only the iron wheels remaining intact. None of the guards remained alive. Once satisfied with the destruction, the three men began running north.

Chapter Ten

The heavy rain continued through the early morning hours as the three men moved steadily northward. Several times they had to take cover to hide from Rebel patrols. The rain storm was a mixed blessing, it made for a wet, miserable night, yet on the other hand, it made it harder for the Rebels to find them.

It was full daylight when they approached the Union controlled line. They threw the gray coats away before coming in contact with any Federal troops. It was still raining and their shirts were quickly soaked through; however, the air had turned humid keeping them from being cold.

It was mid-morning when they reached the outskirts of a small Maryland town where Union soldiers were gathering and awaiting orders. The rain had stopped leaving muddy conditions around the town. The residents going about their daily affairs eyed the wet and mud splattered men with suspicion. The war was at their doorstep, but as of yet they had not experienced it firsthand.

The three men ignored the looks as they walked along the street. Raven pointed up at the telegraph wires. "That reminds me we need to send a message to Parker about Nelson before we reach Graham's camp."

They walked on until they came to a telegraph office. Raven went inside as Buck and Kai waited outside letting the sun that was burning through the clouds dry their clothes.

The telegrapher stared at Raven. To him this disheveled, dirty specimen looked like a deserter or a criminal on the run. He was trying to think of how to notify the nearest Union soldier.

Raven picked up a pencil and wrote out his message. He pushed the paper across the counter toward the man. "I need this wire sent to the Army of the Potomac headquarters immediately."

The man didn't look at the paper. "You don't look like a man who has capitol business."

Raven was exhausted, half-starved, and in a foul mood. He snapped angrily, "I'm a Federal soldier and, yes, I do have business with my commanding officer in Washington. Now, send the wire!"

The telegrapher took a step back and then read the message Raven had written out. *Lt. Parker, Mission accomplished. Sgt. Nelson is spy in Graham camp. Need you to deal with it. Ravenel.*

The telegrapher looked up at Raven and then quickly began tapping out the message. Raven watched him until he was content that the message had been sent in full. "Give me the paper," Raven demanded.

The man pushed the paper cautiously toward Raven, "That will be fifty cents, sir."

"Bill the army," Raven growled as he shredded the paper and dropped it in a cuspidor by the door. He then walked out.

They made their way to an encampment of Union soldiers. They walked up to the Corporal standing sentry, "Who is your commanding officer?" Raven asked.

"Colonel Sherman," the Corporal answered.

"Tell him Parker Freeman is here."

The young Corporal narrowed his eyes at Raven. "Is this some kind of joke?"

Raven glared at the young man, "Tell him and tell him *now!*"

The look in Raven's eyes told the sentry he was not joking. The Corporal stopped a passing Private and told him to take the message to the Colonel. The Private ran off and quickly returned asking the men to follow him.

They followed the soldier to a large tent where the Colonel had his temporary headquarters set up. Colonel Sherman looked up and studied them from his chair as they entered the open doorway of the tent. "You are Parker's men?"

"Yes, sir," Raven answered.

"What can I do for you?"

"We are on our way back to Major Graham's camp and could use some dry clothes and a hot meal."

"Of course." the Colonel gestured to the Private who had brought them in. "Take these men to the Quartermaster for clothes and get them fed."

The soldier saluted, "Yes, sir." He turned his attention to the three men, "Please come with me."

As they turned to go the Colonel stopped them. "My scouts tell me that over the last couple of nights the main Rebel munitions dump, a rail train, and half a mile of telegraph and track in Richmond were destroyed."

Raven grinned in spite of his fatigue, "Yes, sir we heard the same thing."

The Colonel smiled, "Good work, men."

The three followed the soldier out. They were given Union pants, shirts, and coats that they would leave behind on their next trip into enemy territory, but for now the clothes were clean and dry. They were then guided to the Mess tent where the soldier told the cook that they were supposed to be fed.

The cooks were in the process of getting the noon meal cooked. The cook in charge was clearly in a sour mood. He frowned and curtly nodded his compliance. The three men sat down at a table setting their bundles of wet civilian clothes beside them. The cook yelled at them, "This isn't a restaurant you want it you get up here and get it."

Kai glanced at Raven, "Friendly, now isn't he?"

The men got up and wearily dragged their feet to the long stretch of tables where the cook carelessly tossed plates of food down. He glared at them and growled, "What's makes you so special?"

Raven matched the cook's scowl, "What makes you so special you have to know?"

"Because it's my Mess, and I don't like feeding men out of ordered meal times." He then turned his angry eyes on Buck and studied him for a second. "What are you, an *Indian*?"

Buck held the man's eyes with his own steady gaze. "Half."

"A *breed* then," the cook huffed like he had looked at something disgusting.

Buck stayed as he was. "You ever been scalped by an Indian?"

"Is that a threat?"

"A question."

"Is there a problem here?" A commanding voice came from behind them.

The cook stiffened and stared past the men. "No, sir."

"It certainly sounds like *you* are having one."

The men turned to see Colonel Sherman coming up behind them. "Do you have an issue with obeying my order, Sergeant? I can very quickly make it Private and then send you out to the front with a rifle instead of a spoon."

The cook's cheek twitched nervously, "No, sir."

"Give me a cup of coffee and be quick about it. Give these men cups as well . . . politely."

The cook instantly obeyed and carefully placed four filled cups on the table.

The Colonel held a steady hard eye on the cook. "This is not a high society Washington restaurant filled with politicians and rich debutantes, this is an army camp destined for war. You will feed men when they need to be fed and if that remains a problem I can certainly have you transferred."

The cook stammered, "Yes, sir, I understand, sir."

"Good. I am glad we had this amiable little talk." The colonel looked the three men over. "You look a bit drier. Sit with me, I want to get some information from you."

The men hesitated.

"It is all right, I understand your orders. I wired Lieutenant Parker that you were here and he wired back." He showed them the telegram. "I have orders for you from Lieutenant Parker."

The men recognized the coded term and walked to a table with the Colonel. Sitting down in a huddled group the Colonel began. "Parker received your wire in regards to the spy. He wants you to proceed directly to Graham's camp. Sergeant Freeman will be taking the train down and will meet you there. We will furnish you with horses to speed your way."

The men nodded their understanding.

"What can you tell me about Richmond? Graham's camp and mine will be the first to march in. We are going to strike in Manassas. What can we expect?"

"You can expect serious opposition," Raven explained. "There are hundreds of Rebel troops in the city alone, not counting the outlying areas. We put the main track and supply train out of order, but that's only temporary I'm sure. Hitting them now would probably be the best chance to win a fight."

"They also lost their main munitions stores," Kai added.

Sherman looked stern. "We need to push them all the way back to Montgomery, to their original headquarters, and corral them in the deep south and finish this quickly."

Buck spoke for the first time, "They did not seem very organized. They were easily put into a panic that their officers were having a hard time controlling. My guess is they are green soldiers and not battle tested."

"So are most of mine. This should be interesting." The Colonel then studied Buck. "I overheard the conversation that you are half Indian. Which tribe?"

"Bloods, Blackfeet as the whites know us."

"I'm not familiar with the tribe. Good in the woods for covert operations?"

Buck shrugged, "We move pretty good in the woods."

"Blackfeet are warriors," Raven broke in. "I have spent the past twenty years in the West. Blackfeet are fearless fighters and you won't even know they are there until you're dead."

"I've only been around this man a short time, but I swear he would walk right up to the devil himself and spit in his eye," Kai added.

Sherman glanced at Kai. "I'll keep that in mind if this war goes longer than anticipated." He turned his attention back to Buck, "What is your name?"

"Buck Drake, sir."

The Colonel finished his coffee and stood up. "If you men need anything just use my name, Colonel William Sherman." On that parting comment, he walked out of the tent leaving the men sitting and eating.

The next day the three men rode into Major Graham's camp. The soldiers were organizing for the march into Virginia. Stopping their horses in front of the headquarters building they had left several days before, they dismounted and entered the house.

Walking up the short hallway, they looked in Graham's office to see Sergeant Freeman standing there talking to Graham. The Major was sitting behind his desk looking like he had been kicked in the stomach.

Freeman turned around to look at the three men. His face reflected no warmth or greeting only the stoic expression of a soldier who had hardened his emotions. "Your mission was successful I am told," Freeman said matter-of-factly.

The three men all nodded in unison. "They were expecting us though," Raven said in a matching tone.

"Yes, it seems our Sergeant Nelson has flown the coop."

Kai frowned, "That's not good."

Freeman looked at him coolly, "You have a gift for understatement, Mr. Maddock."

Buck asked, "How much does he know about our operation?"

Freeman's unfriendly expression grew even more so as he turned his head and glared at Graham. "Too much. Major Graham and I have been discussing the matter. It seems Nelson was taken into the inner circle where he *did not belong*." He raised his voice on the last three words.

Graham stiffened in his chair. "Watch how you address me Sergeant Freeman, I am a Major. I do not care if you are representing the General Staff."

Freeman turned his cold angry eyes on Graham as he spoke to the three men. "I have come with orders directly from General McDowell that Major Graham is to be replaced immediately and report directly to the General Staff at the Army of the Potomac headquarters to explain his actions. I doubt he will be returning to a command position."

Graham's eyes opened wide as his mouth dropped open. "I am to do what?"

"You are to report to headquarters immediately, sir."

"I am relieved of my command?"

"Yes, sir."

"Who is to relieve me?"

"General McDowell will be here presently."

Graham wiped his hand across his forehead and blanched white. His career was over and he knew it. He might even face charges and be dishonorably discharged.

He had been a fool to believe Nelson, if that even was his true name, taking his word without verifying the information he bore.

Freeman gestured toward the door. The men walked out of the room and to the outside of the building.

"What happened out there?" Freeman asked.

"First off, Buck was suspicious of Nelson," Raven explained. "He didn't seem right and he paid too much attention to the plan for our operation, which he shouldn't even have been privy to in the first place. After we talked it over we decided to be careful just in case he was a spy. We checked out the munitions building and found it surrounded by hidden Rebs. The regular guards were posted as expected, but the hidden soldiers could only mean one thing."

"A trap," Freeman muttered.

"So, we blew the tracks to draw them off and then blew the munitions."

Freeman cracked a rare fleeting smile, "Good thinking."

"How compromised are we?" Raven asked.

"Severely. The codes, the operations, everything."

"*Wonderful*," Raven spit out angrily.

Freeman scowled. "Men are in the field not knowing this and we can only hope the word passes to them before it is too late."

Buck looked at Freeman, "Maybe we can find Nelson and kill him before he talks too much."

"If you can, sure, but good luck finding a needle in a haystack."

"We have an advantage not everyone else has; we know what he looks like."

"If you can find him then kill him, but I'm sure the information has been well disseminated throughout the Confederate ranks by now."

"We'll keep an eye out for him anyway," Kai put in.

Freeman watched the troops moving in preparation for the upcoming assault. His face was a picture of concern and uncertainty.

"What's on your mind, Sergeant?" Raven asked.

Freeman shook his head, "I have a bad feeling about this assault. The troops are green as willow trees and McDowell is a politician, a desk man. He is as green as these troops. There are others more capable of command. I fear it will be a rout and our first true assault will end in defeat."

"Colonel Sherman seems capable," Kai said.

"He may be the only one; at least he was in the Mexican War for a bit." Freeman signed heavily, "Enough of that. The Confederate forces are heavily reinforcing Virginia even as we speak with the intention of storming Washington. Your job from here is to work your way into the enemy strongholds and destroy what you can. Break down their communications and destroy their supplies wherever possible. It may be like swatting a dinosaur with a penny dreadful, but we need every advantage we can get."

"How do we resupply?" Kai asked.

"As best you can from the enemy. As we make inroads against the Rebel forces there will be Union camps to resupply from. Until then, it will be up to you to be inventive."

Chapter Eleven

Sergeant Freeman's concerns were not unfounded. The battle of Manassas was fought at Bull Run and the Union forces were soundly defeated and driven back into Maryland. General McDowell proved to be an incompetent leader, while Colonel Sherman was the only officer to make a significant impact against the Confederate forces. Even at that, the battle was lost.

The war dragged into the next year with only minor skirmishes. The battles began in earnest in February. The Confederate Army of Northern Virginia, led by General Robert E. Lee, pushed northward while the Union forces fought the Rebels on their home ground attacking their southern fortifications. Both sides won and lost battles with neither force giving in nor making progress against the other. There appeared to be no quick end to the war as had been hoped for.

Raven, Buck, and Kai worked at cutting telegraph lines and causing destruction by night and hiding by day. They stole food and explosives wherever they could. It was a meager existence filled with frayed nerves, hunger, and miserable conditions that forged the three men into a friendship to last the ages.

Buck learned that a white man's war was not about coups, stolen weapons, and captured horses. It boiled down to whichever side killed the most soldiers from the other side won. The death toll he saw made the battles and victories of his youth seem like nothing. His people could never stand up against forces like these or this type of warfare.

On occasion, when they moved out of enemy territory to a friendly camp, they received orders from Parker through the field officers. The greatest threat to the Union still lay in Lee's forces occupying Virginia. Their orders were to work in Virginia thwarting Lee as best they could. There were other Parker teams operating in the area. Once in a while they would meet and exchange information.

It was in the cold and snow of December that President Lincoln made a bold move against the Rebels. Northern morale was flagging and his leadership severely questioned. The President needed a victory. He ordered his forces to attack the Confederate stronghold at Fredericksburg. Lincoln replaced General McClellan with General Burnside to lead the attack, but it was a change that would prove costly.

Raven, Buck, and Kai worked their way into Fredericksburg and began disrupting supply lines and communications.

Gray uniforms were like ants on a hill as the three men hid in a cluster of trees cloaked by the night. There was a trace of snow on the ground and they were wet and shivering. Raven whispered to Buck through chattering teeth, "I think I'm beginning to hate this war."

Buck didn't answer. His life with the Bloods in the Rocky Mountains had been one hardship after another. They endured the bitter mountain cold. Hunger was common in the winter when the buffalo meat ran out and game was hard to reach in the deep snow. It was not an easy life. Where he found himself now was not any more miserable than that life had been.

Rebel soldiers were on the move all around them. Their target was a tent filled with food supplies. They wanted to steal some for themselves and then destroy the rest. The distance from the trees to the tent was a scant hundred yards, but it was filled with gray uniforms. It would be like crawling through a field of poisonous snakes expecting to not be bitten.

Buck whispered to Raven, "I will go around and cause a disturbance, you and Kai go to the tent."

Raven nodded and Buck disappeared into the night.

Kai shook his head, "I don't know how he just disappears like that."

The sound of footfalls in the frozen crust of snow stopped behind them. A voice commanded, "You, on the ground, what are you doing?"

Raven and Kai turned their heads slowly to see three Rebel soldiers standing over them with bayoneted rifles pointed at them.

"Get up!" the voice commanded.

Raven cursed under his breath and hoped Buck was seeing this and would get them out.

Raven and Kai got up, their legs and arms stiff from the cold and wet. They held their hands out in front of them. One of the three Rebels was an officer who quickly took their revolvers and knives. He looked at the guns, "Yankee Colts. Looks like we got us a couple of Yankee spies here."

The men with the officer held their rifles on Raven and Kai. "Bring them," the officer ordered. "We will let Captain Rollins deal with them."

The soldiers jabbed the bayonet points into them as Raven and Kai followed the officer with their hands on their heads. They walked across an open area toward a large tent that was glowing from the lantern light inside of it. The officer pulled the tent flap back while the soldiers held their prisoners outside of it.

"Captain Rollins," the officer called out. "We have just captured two Yankee spies. Would you like to have them?"

A voice came from inside the tent. "Very much so, bring them into the light."

The officer stepped aside and gestured for his men to push the prisoners inside. Raven and Kai looked at the man in the tent and immediately recognized him as the man who had passed himself off as Sergeant Nelson.

Raven looked at him, "Well, if isn't Sergeant

Nelson."

"Captain Rollins, actually," he said with a smile. "You boys have been very busy haven't you? I was concerned about you three more than the others, especially the Indian, who I don't see with you."

"He was killed a while back."

"Is that so?"

"Yeah, Indians aren't used to handling dynamite and he held onto it a bit too long."

"And you expect me to believe that?"

Raven shrugged, "It's a war, men die. We weren't expected to even live this long."

"True, your life expectancy was not given the greatest of odds. It seems your work has accomplished little as the Confederacy does seem to have the Yankee army on the run."

Rollins looked past them to the officer behind them. "Lieutenant, send your men on their way and you stay here with me."

The Lieutenant turned and gestured for the two soldiers to leave. He then stepped into the tent and closed the flap.

Rollins pulled two wooden chairs out into the middle of the tent. "You men look frozen and hungry, please have a seat."

Raven and Kai sat down facing the rear of the tent. They were trying to control their shivering without success. A small stove was kicking warming heat out into the space that felt good to them.

"So, this is how your revered Yankee leaders treat their men?" Rollins began. "You are ill dressed, ill fed, and ill-treated. Should you choose to trade sides I will see you fed, properly clothed, and treated with the respect due to you."

Raven looked up at him, "I've seen your soldiers freezing and hungry too. They didn't seem all that excited to be in your illustrious Army of the Confederacy."

Rollins frowned and looked at the other officer. "Tie their hands behind them."

The Lieutenant picked up two pieces of thin rope from the floor where they had been cut and dropped from some supply boxes. He tied the men's hands around the back of their chairs.

Rollins looked down at them and shook his head. "I made you an attractive offer."

Raven shrugged, "Wasn't all that attractive."

"How about you?" Rollins looked at Kai.

Kai smiled at him, "I guess I wasn't listening, what was the offer?"

"Very well," Rollins said with a sigh. "My scouts tell me that the Union is planning to attack us here in Fredericksburg. What can you tell me about it?"

Raven gave him a blank look and then said in the Blackfeet tongue, "I do not understand the white man's words."

Rollins looked coldly at him. "Cute."

Kai broke in, "You were in our camp, you know we are told nothing except to blow things up. The Generals don't discuss plans with the likes of us."

"True, but men do talk and conversations are overheard and I am sure you know more than you should. So, be cooperative and tell me what you know."

Kai simply looked at him and smiled, "I know I'm hungry, how about a sandwich?"

Rollins slapped Kai soundly across the face, the smacking sound was loud in the confined space. Kai's head snapped sharply to the right as a red hand print appeared on his half frozen face.

"Please, stay to the subject."

"Okay." Kai stretched his jaw. "You can skip the sandwich if it's that much trouble."

Rollins struck him again. "Battle plans?"

"To kick your cracker butts all the way back to Alabama."

Rollins struck him again drawing blood from Kai's lips. He then turned his attention to Raven. "What do you have to say? And English, please."

Raven looked at him and said in English, "I'll skip the sandwich if it makes you that mad. I'll just have coffee. Got any cookies?"

Rollins slapped Raven. "Battle plans?"

Looking bemused in spite of his split lips Kai answered, "I told you the plan is to kick your sorry gray butts back to where you came from."

Rollins punched Kai with a closed fist making his nose bleed down over his split lips.

"This is getting us nowhere," Rollins growled. "Take them out and shoot them. If we can't get information out of them we can at least stop them from causing any further problems."

A sudden explosion rocked the night close to the tent. Rollins snarled, "Now *what?*"

The zipping sound of quickly splitting canvas emanated from the rear of the tent. Rollins and the Lieutenant turned as Buck stepped through the split canvas knife in hand. Buck pointed his Colt at Rollins and pulled the trigger. The bullet took him squarely in the forehead. As fast as he could thumb back the hammer, he shot the Lieutenant in the back of the head as he turned to escape.

Buck ran around the chairs and swung the razor sharp edge of the knife down the backs of each chair slicing cleanly through the ropes. The men jumped up and burst through the split canvas with Buck directly behind them. They ran as hard as they could into the night as shouts rose up behind them. Pursuit was quick as shots were fired at them, the bullets whistling by like angry hornets. The soldiers gave chase to the fleeing men.

Stopping for a second to catch their breath, Raven

said through gasping breaths, "We need guns."

Kai grabbed up a handful of snow and pressed it against his bleeding lips and nose. He threw down the bloody snow. "Here come a couple dozen, I'm sure they can spare us one." He pushed another handful of snow against his nose and lips as they resumed their escape.

They ran hard, out distancing their pursuers in the darkness. They ran down a darkened street of the town and ducked into an alley between two buildings. After a few minutes they could hear running feet on the street outside the alley. The soldiers ran past and kept going. The three men hunkered down in the alley and caught their breath.

Raven clapped Buck on the shoulder, "I owe you my life."

"As do I," Kai added. "He was about to take us out and shoot us."

"We aren't out of here yet," Buck answered. "Thank me when we're actually out of here."

"Aye, but it's far better odds than we had back there."

Buck stood up and peeked out of the alley. "I don't see anyone, let's go."

They continued to move through the town to the opposite side and out into an open expanse of fields. The night sky was cloud covered, creating intense darkness. With no moon or starlight it would be difficult for their pursuers to see them. They walked on in a westerly direction for another hour before turning to the northeast and the Potomac River.

Before them was a small house standing like a black square against the darkness. They stopped and peered hard at it. No light shown from inside, but then it was late, the occupants could be asleep. They stole closer to see a stable behind the house, at least it offered shelter. They reached the stable to find it empty of livestock.

"What do you think?" Kai asked. "Abandoned?"

"Appears to be so," Raven answered. "A lot of people got out before they were crushed between the two armies."

"Should we try the house?"

"There is no smoke coming from the stovepipe," Buck pointed out. "On a cold night like this they would have a fire."

Kai nodded. "You've got a point there."

Buck snuck up to the house and stepped up on the wood pile at the rear wall and placed his hand gingerly on the stovepipe. "Ice cold," he said to the others. "There's no one in there."

Raven pushed at the door and it opened. The house consisted solely of a single room, empty and cold. A bed, striped of blankets, was on the far end. A potbellied stove was the only other household item present. "It's empty. We can at least make a fire and get warm."

The three entered the house and closed the door behind them. A pile of wood with shavings lay beside the cold stove. Raven quickly began to build a fire in the iron stove.

As the fire caught the flames cast enough light in the room to look about. Kai found a candle on the floor and lit it as he and Buck searched for any remaining food. They found a small amount of beans in a cloth sack hanging from a rafter that had been overlooked and kept safe from vermin. A sealed tin of beef was under the bed likely missed by the owner who had fled.

Taking the candle Kai made a check of the outside and found a wooden bucket and discarded empty food tins. Buck took the bucket and walked to a creek behind the house. Slamming the bucket down on the ice to break through he dipped the bucket into the water and filled it. When he returned to the house the fire was going with the stove door left open to throw some light into the dark room.

The beans were divided equally into the three

largest tins with water and put on the stove to boil.

The men sat in close to the stove appreciating the warmth it cast off. Raven shivered, "I was wondering if I'd ever get warm again."

Buck grinned at him, "Some trapper you are, can't take a little cold."

Raven laughed, "I've slept in the snow plenty of nights, that's why I don't like being cold in my old age."

Buck taunted him good naturedly, "Yes, you are so old, eighty winters at least."

"Well, not that many."

"What do you say," Kai asked. "Should we stay here a day or two?"

"We could kill a deer," Buck said. "And rest up and eat."

Raven nodded, "We'd have to keep a sharp eye out for Rebs though, but yeah, I could use a rest where it's warm. You're the only one with a gun Buck, or a knife for that matter. I hope you have some reloads for it."

"A few." He then remembered to reload the two chambers he had fired.

"That was some shooting," Raven smiled.

Raven put his hand out to Buck. "I won't be forgetting this partner, one day I hope I can do something as big for you."

Buck shook his hand.

Kai then shook Buck's hand. "Aye, I owe you; anytime you need something you just give a shout."

"You would have done the same for me."

Both men nodded in agreement.

The warmth began to lull them to sleep; they dozed as the beans boiled. Once they had cooked, Buck cut open the beef tin with his knife and dumped the meat into the beans and let it get hot. Taking turns carving makeshift spoons out of pieces of firewood with Buck's knife they each took a can. They then locked the door, banked the fire, and fell asleep.

They awoke to the fire being out and the room cold. The cold winter sun had brought light in through the windows, but no warmth. The three men got up off the floor stiff from the cold. Raven started a new fire.

Buck opened the backdoor and looked out over the fields. The land had been plowed and then abandoned. The frozen weeds across the field were evidence the owner had left before putting in seed. On the far side of the field, several deer grazed on the frozen grass.

Buck snuck out and circled the plowed field using the leafless trees and brush for cover. Working his way into pistol range he killed a young deer with a single shot.

The men were gathered around the stove's warmth with venison steaks cooking directly on the stovetop when they heard movement outside. Raven went to the window, looked out and cursed. In a low voice he called back, "Rebs, three of them."

Kai made a face. "Only three and no others? Isn't that unusual?"

"Not if they're deserters," Raven replied. "They'll want to kill us for whatever we might have."

"Which is nothin'."

"They don't know that. They see the smoke; they're coming to the door."

"Do they have guns?" Buck asked.

"Yeah."

"You need guns." Buck pulled his Colt and held it down at his side as he walked past Raven and opened the door.

The three gray coated deserters were temporarily taken aback at the door's sudden opening in their faces. Making a belated effort to raise their rifles Buck brought the Colt up. With three rolling shots coming one on top of the other, he killed all three.

He walked out to the bodies with Raven and Kai

coming behind him. They stripped the dead men of their coats and the belts with pouches holding ball and powder loads and knives. One had a Navy revolver that Buck handed to Raven. Two of the rebels had knapsacks that they also kept.

They drug the bodies to the stable and dumped hay over them.

"We'd better cook up as much of that venison as we can carry and get out of here," Raven said as he looked across the field. "The Confederate army takes a dim view of deserters and might be on their trail right now."

The three headed back into the house and went through the knapsacks. There was some food and more powder and ball. Buck kept a watch out the window as Buck and Kai cut and cooked as much of the venison as they could. Stuffing the cooked meat in the sacks they put on the gray coats, slung the packs on their backs, and with a sigh of regret left the warmth of the little house and bowed their heads into the cold wind.

They traveled another two days until they reached the Potomac River. Throwing off the gray coats they crossed over a bridge and into the safety of the Union side. Coming to a Union camp they identified themselves to the officer in command and sat down to a hot meal.

Raven sent a telegram to Lieutenant Parker that read *Found Capt. Rollins, alias Sgt. Nelson. Died of lead poisoning. Ravenel.*

Chapter Twelve

The attack on the Confederate stronghold at Fredericksburg ended badly. The attack was poorly executed resulting in another severe Union defeat and the deaths of more than twelve hundred Union soldiers and many times more wounded.

After losing both battles at Bull Run and now Fredericksburg, it was becoming clear the Confederate hold on Virginia was not to be shaken loose. The best they could hope for at this point was to keep the Rebels on the Virginia side of the Potomac River and Chesapeake Bay.

The Army of the Potomac formed a line between Virginia and Maryland that protected the capital while the Union Generals and politicians tried to work out their problems. The greatest obstacle blocking a Union victory in Virginia was Robert E. Lee and his Army of Northern Virginia. Lee was a brilliant strategist and was determined not to be budged from Virginia.

Union General Joseph Hooker had been an outspoken critic regarding the leadership and tactics employed in the Fredericksburg defeat. He was credited with the victory at the Battle of Williamsburg, as well as being instrumental in the crucial victory at Antietam three months prior. The judgment and views of General Hooker bore weight. He was given command of the Army of the Potomac.

Lieutenant Parker, now promoted to Captain, made the rounds of the Maryland camps, meeting with his remaining teams whenever they came in from behind enemy lines. Some of his men had been killed. He met with Raven, Buck, and Kai where they were taking a much needed break in General Hooker's camp.

The three men reported to the building where Parker was borrowing an office. Parker stood up as the men entered and shook their hands all around.

"Good to see you again, Lieutenant," Raven smiled.

"Actually, it's Captain now. Please have seats and let's talk."

As they sat down Parker began to explain the position the Union forces were in. "We have won a few victories, Antietam the most important. Had Lee broken through, there would have been no stopping his march directly into Washington. On the other hand, every time we attack the Rebels in Virginia we get our heads handed to us."

"Are we winnin' though?" Kai asked.

"We haven't lost yet, let's put it that way. The war is being fought on two levels, defensively and offensively. Defensively, the Army of the Potomac is protecting the Capitol. Presently the Army is under the command of General Hooker, but the officers in charge change as often as a senator's wife changes her gowns. Offensively, General Grant leads the Army of the Tennessee in an effort to defeat the South at its source. Both theaters of battle have won and lost at about the same rate."

"In other words," Raven broke in, "the Rebs are a lot stronger than Washington has led us to believe."

"We are under orders to tell the men in the field that we are always victorious."

Buck looked at Parker, "That must be a little hard to sell when the men see the losses."

Parker nodded, "Indeed. Politicians like to believe that everyone is foolish and naive enough to believe everything they are told. In the large cities, where people only read about the war, that is true more than not, people believe anything they hear or read especially if it is in a newspaper. On the battle front no one is fooled. We are not victorious, not yet anyway.

"I did receive your wire in regards to Sergeant Nelson. I am interested in hearing about your discovery of his being Confederate Captain Rollins. The information he took with him has resulted in the deaths of six of my men. They fell into traps like the one that had been planned for you. Graham has much to answer for in his stupidity."

Raven explained the circumstances of their capture in Fredericksburg. He told of Rollins' offer to them to switch sides and their resulting death sentence for refusing. He then told of how Buck rescued them, their escape, and encountering the Rebel deserters.

Parker looked at Buck, "I have applied to Washington for medals to be awarded to all of you for your service to the United States and for bravery. I will also apply for another for you, Mr. Drake, for heroism in saving your fellow soldiers."

Buck shrugged, "I don't need a medal, I was only helping my friends."

"A modest man, I can appreciate that, but, Mr. Drake, war is what makes or breaks men. It divides those with steel backbones from those with mush for a spine."

"It is the way of the Bloods to fight. We do not allow cowards to ride in battle or on raids. A man who is a coward is made to dress like a woman and sit and work with the women. He is not allowed in the warrior societies or to hunt. The women look down on him and none want him for a husband. He has no place in either group. It discourages cowardice."

Parker laughed heartily. "I wonder how that would work for dealing with our deserters and cowards."

They sat in silence for a full minute before Parker spoke again. "I wish I could tell you men that the war was almost over and you could go back about your business."

Buck looked him in the eyes, "But you're an honorable man."

"Yes, so I won't lie to you. You may be doing this for a long time yet."

Raven looked at his friends. "We'd just be fighting someone else out West if we weren't doing it here."

Kai agreed. "And not being paid so handsomely for it either."

Parker laughed out loud. "Come on, I could use a cup of coffee."

The men walked out headed for the Mess tent. Entering the tent they poured coffee from the huge army sized pots. Sitting down at a table they continued to talk. Buck was watching the men coming and going when he spotted two Sergeants walking in carrying rifles like he had never seen before. There were two barrels on the rifle one over the other and the action was shiny brass colored with a lever underneath surrounding the trigger.

The others looked at him as he got up from the table and walked to where the two Sergeants had sat down. Buck stood over the two men, they looked up at him with questioning eyes. Buck pointed to the rifle of the Sergeant nearest to him, "Your rifles caught my attention."

One of the Sergeants nodded, "They're Henrys."

"How do they work?"

The Sergeant dug into his pocket and pulled out several copper colored cartridges. "With these. They're cartridges, no more powder and ball. By God, man, this rifle can shoot . . . *sixteen* shots before reloading."

The Sergeant placed the rifle butt down on the floor. He pointed at the spring tang and the bottom tube under the barrel, "She's already loaded to the teeth, but what you do is this here do-dad lets you lift the spring in the magazine here.

"She'll open up and you drop the cartridges, bullet end up, down the tube here." He brought the rifle up off the floor. "You pull this lever down and back, it cocks the hammer at the same time it shoves a cartridge up into the chamber and you're ready to shoot. Every time you pull the lever down it kicks the spent shell out the top here and pushes a new cartridge in under the hammer and you're ready to shoot again."

The second Sergeant added, "If every Union soldier had one of these we'd have Johnny Reb beat to dog meat inside a week."

"You have to buy your own though," the first Sergeant said. "The fatheads in Washington don't want to waste their party money on rifles to win this accursed war."

The second Sergeant added, "Costs twenty dollars for one, but it just might keep you alive."

Buck nodded. "What happens if the Rebs get ahold of them?"

"That's the beauty of it, they're only made in Connecticut, so's the ammunition. Even if a Reb got one he could never get the ammunition. The company is very careful who they sell them to. We're the only ones who can get them and the cartridges."

Buck turned to see Raven, Kai, and Parker step up beside him. The two Sergeants immediately stood and saluted Parker who saluted back.

"Henry rifles," Parker commented. "We could win the war with those."

"That's what we were just talking about, sir," the second Sergeant said.

Buck asked, "Where did you get them?"

"A gun shop up in Baltimore had a bunch of them. Said he was selling them only to Union soldiers. The ammunition too."

"How much?" Raven asked.

"Twenty dollars and the ammunition is a dollar for fifty cartridges."

"A whole month's wage for the rifle and another for enough ammunition to last," Kai shook his head.

Raven looked at Kai, "And what exactly are you doing with the money piling up in your account?"

Kai chuckled knowing his comment was foolish. "Savin' it for my old age?"

"You might not see old age at the rate we're going.

Have one of those in your hands and you might live to tell your grandchildren about it."

Parker finished the coffee in his cup. "Think I'll take a ride up Baltimore way. Would you men like to come with me and pick yourselves up one of these?"

"Yes, sir," all three answered at once.

Buck thanked the Sergeants for the information about the rifles.

"Good luck to you," the first Sergeant said as the four moved away from their table.

***

It was the end of April when the Union forces led by General Hooker prepared to launch another attack into Virginia, this time at Chancellorsville. They had Lee outnumbered two-to-one and expected a sound victory. Raven, Buck, and Kai stole their way into Virginia to scout out the forces. They found the Confederate army undersupplied, weary, hungry, and scattered. They reported directly to General Hooker and it was the kind of news he wanted to hear.

The Army of the Potomac maneuvered around to pin Lee's weakened Army of Northern Virginia between massive Union forces. Raven, Buck, and Kai worked their way back into Chancellorsville and dug in making ready for Hooker's army. With the battle on, they would wreak havoc with the enemy's weakened supply lines.

Confederate leaders Lee, Stuart, and Jackson routed the Union forces through the area known as the Wilderness when Hooker mentally collapsed under the pressure of the battle. The Army of the Potomac, suffering heavy loses and splintered into disorganized groups, was in full retreat back to Maryland when the tide of the war changed for the three friends.

The three were moving back as fast as they could toward the safety of the Union side of the river. They came across a splintered group of Union soldiers in the brush and trees surrounded and being shot to pieces by a greater number of Rebels. Buck, Raven, and Kai moved in separate directions around the besieged soldiers and began to pick off the Rebels one at a time with the Henrys they now carried. They continued to move and shift positions, all the while depleting the Rebel numbers.

The surrounded Union soldiers took heart and renewed their efforts to fight.

Their battle raged on for close to an hour before the last Rebel fell. The three moved in quickly to the now safe soldiers. The Lieutenant, who was the last remaining officer, looked around confused and then stared at the three men. "Who are you?"

"Parker's men," Raven answered.

The Lieutenant knew about Parker's "behind the lines" men. "Where is the rest of the army?"

Raven grinned, "We're it."

"No," the Lieutenant shook his head, "there were hundreds of shots fired at the enemy."

Raven held up his Henry. "Three of these *are* an army, Lieutenant."

The Lieutenant laughed, "By God, I will have to tell this one around. Maybe it will help us get better arms."

Once back in Maryland the soldiers spread the story of how three of Parker's men had shot it out with the Rebs to save them. The stories related that the three killed over a hundred Rebs; however, when the three compared notes later they could only account for having shot thirty-two Rebs altogether.

Two months later General Grant won a decisive victory at Vicksburg, Mississippi, after a six-week siege of the city.

In June, Lee marched his Northern Virginia army into Pennsylvania. Riding high on their Chancellorsville victory, and the need to strike fast after Vicksburg, Lee's intention was to again move toward Washington from the north and take Philadelphia in the process. Such a victory would demoralize the northerners and force the politicians in Washington to surrender.

Parker called all his men in for a meeting in General Meade's camp. He bitterly explained to them that his unit had been disbanded. The politicians believed that the men in his service were needed on the front lines more than they were needed behind the lines. Their work was considered by the politicians, who had yet to hear a single shot, to be too little and too ineffective. They would be reassigned to other units.

Parker dismissed the men, but held Raven, Buck, and Kai back. "I need to talk with you three separately from the others." Parker spoke in a tone reflecting his unhappiness with the change. "Your actions in the Wilderness have made it to the highest ranks. You are all to be awarded medals when things calm down enough to give them to you," he sighed, "which could be years from now."

The three waited for what Parker was going to say that required a private meeting.

"Your marksmanship is not to be wasted; you are all assigned duty as snipers. You will not charge across fields, but rather find a vantage point and shoot Rebs, officers in particular. Mr. Ravenel, you and Mr. Maddock are to remain with General Meade's forces. We will be moving up to Pennsylvania into the area of Gettysburg where it looks like we will be meeting Lee's army."

The words fell hard on the men. "What about Buck?" Kai asked in a voice reflecting his shock.

"General Meade wanted all three of you; however, Sherman, who is now a General in the south, is working closely with General Grant." Parker looked at Buck, "General Sherman remembered you, Mr. Drake, and when he heard about what you three did he sent specific orders that you are to be sent to him and Grant as a sharpshooter. I'm sorry to break up your team, but you are all to go immediately."

The three friends looked at each other in silence. Raven spit out, "This ain't right."

"No, it's not," Parker replied. "But it is the nature of war."

Raven met Buck's eyes, "We've been through hell together my friend, and I still owe you for that night in Fredericksburg." He put his hand out to Buck, "See you after the war."

Buck shook his hand. "If not, look for me back in the Rocky Mountains."

Raven grinned, "Where we almost got hung together."

Buck matched the grin, "Almost, but we got to come here instead because it's more fun."

Kai put out his hand to Buck, but was unable to speak for the lump in his throat. He finally managed to say, "Be safe and thanks. I will find you after the war and we'll have a drink and laugh about it all."

"We'll do that."

Parker broke in, "Mr. Drake, there is a company heading down to reinforce Grant and Sherman, they are leaving in the morning. You will leave with them and report directly to General Sherman." He shook Buck's hand.

Parker turned to Raven and Kai. "We leave for Pennsylvania immediately."

With a last look at Buck and a final head nod, the two men walked away with Parker.

Buck joined the company headed south. He talked to no one and stayed to himself. He was coming to understand why Sergeant Freeman was the way he was, cold, emotionless, and friendless. 'You don't make friends during a war,' he had overheard the big Sergeant say. He now knew why.

Arriving at General Sherman's camp the General

welcomed him and told him what he wanted. Simply put, he was to deplete the Rebel forces one soldier at a time. Killing a Confederate officer was more important than dropping an infantryman. If he could take only one target, and there was an officer present, that officer was his target. He would also see to it that Buck had all the ammunition he would need for the Henry.

Word came down to them about the fight at Gettysburg. Lee had been driven back out of Pennsylvania. The Union forces had won, but at a horrible cost in lives. Buck wondered about his friends since they were headed for that fight the day they were split up. He wondered if they had survived or if they were among the stiff bodies scattered across the fields.

Grant and Sherman continued to pound the south, winning victories and squeezing the life and heart out of the southern rebellion. It was in 1864, almost a year after Gettysburg, that Sherman fought his way across the South, burning Atlanta and other cities along the way in a sixty-mile-wide swath. Sherman's attitude was that if the Rebels wanted a war that bad, he would show them the misery that came with that decision.

Buck had no idea how many men he killed. Pretty soon it was only gray in the rifle sights and it never seemed to end. The clear blue skies of the Rocky Mountain country, the snowcapped mountains, and clear streams seemed only a dream he once had in a night. All about him was death and destruction, the smell of burning, and fouled streams. He wondered if there was such a place as the pristine Rockies or had he only imagined it.

The war slowly began to turn in favor of the Union. Victories were being won in the north. Petersburg was taken and then Richmond fell to Union forces. After so many demoralizing defeats in Virginia, the Army of the Potomac had Lee on the run until he found himself and his army surrounded by General Grant at the battle of

Appomattox. Here Lee decided it was better to surrender to Grant than have his men face total annihilation. They came together at the Appomattox courthouse and the war began to shut down.

Sherman continued to put down the last of the southern effort until General Johnston surrendered at the Battle of Bentonville. Confederate President Jefferson Davis was outraged at Johnston's surrender, still believing they could win the war. He had not personally joined the bloodied Confederate troops on the front line and starved with them. Three weeks later Davis was arrested by Federal troops and jailed. The war was ended.

It was at Bentonville that Buck pulled the trigger on the last gray uniform. The war was over and he wondered what they would want him to do now, but they wanted nothing more from him as the Army mustered him and the other men out. He was given a horse with a McClellan saddle, and sent on his way. .

He rode north through the battle-torn countryside in search of his friends. He rode where their camps had been; saw the burned ruins of Richmond, and the field at Gettysburg. He questioned all who might know, but the month-long search for his friends proved futile. Where Parker had ended up he had no idea and no one seemed to know who Parker even was. He was forced to accept the inevitable, that they had all been killed and their bodies lost with the thousands of others.

With the money he had removed from his account and a heavy heart, he turned the horse west and headed back to his people and the mountain country he had once lived in. He wanted to see if it had been a dream or if it really did exist in something other than his mind. Much had changed in him since that day he rode out of the village.

Chapter Thirteen

Buck still wore the shirt, pants, and boots the army had issued to him. He asked for and received a blue wool army coat when he left Maryland, as it was raining and he had nothing to wear that was warm. The Colt and knife he had to give back. The battle and weather beaten officer's slouch hat, minus the gold band, that he wore was a remnant left on a battlefield.

Except for the horse, the money in his pocket, and the Henry in his saddle scabbard, he was riding out from the east with nothing more than he came into it with. The buckskin shirt and pants he had concealed in his bedroll when he left Fort Bridger were gone, along with the bedroll. Things simply got lost in a war.

His ride west was a solemn one. As the days stretched into weeks he left behind the sorrow of losing his friends, but remembered that they had been his friends and that was worth something. They were dead and he had to accept that.

His thinking was filled with the sights and sounds of the east; it was a complete contrast to the western country. The knowledge that all of the never-ending commotion and uncountable people would be headed toward the Rocky Mountains, now that the dust of the war was settling, made him sick inside. The thought that the western land he loved would all be like that one day was a nightmare.

The white man waged war much differently than the Indian. The white man believed in total destruction of the enemy, not in the hit-and-run skirmishes that the Indian enjoyed. For the Indian, leaving his enemy alive meant you could count coup on him again in a later fight. It was important to the future of battles and coups not to kill all your enemies, only some.

Should the whites choose to launch their kind of

warfare against the Indian, the latter would soon be wiped out. They would end up in the same shape as the defeated, battered and starved southerners he had seen. The thought was unsettling, even frightening if Sherman did to the Indian what he did to the South. He knew what the future held for him and his people and he would never be the same again. It planted a bitter seed in his heart.

With that bitterness, the thought of his father was resurrected. It had been years since the man betrayed him and the others. Those who rode with him were no better than he was, but they were betrayed all the same so the cowardly dog could save himself at their expense. He had thought rarely of Jules Drake over the last years as the war preoccupied his thinking wholly. Now, he was returning and the oath he had made to kill him fired anew.

He wondered what manner of lie Jules had told the village when he returned with his entire party wiped out. He would surely lie about his heroism, that they had been outnumbered by the white soldiers and only he survived. The elders would know he was lying and those that said he had an evil spirit in him would have their confirmation. Badger certainly would know he was lying and might even call him on it. Badger might kill him. He hoped not, for he wanted that privilege for himself.

Yes, he would ride into the village to the surprise of all. His mother and grandfather, who thought him dead, would embrace their lost son. He would then stand before the village and tell out loud Jules' betrayal and challenge him to fight. In front of all he would kill the father he loathed.

Summer was high when he reached the Red River of the North. He rode into a small Minnesota town and looked for a place to eat. He was trail weary and dirty, his hair long.

The town was occupied by farmers and business people who had not been affected by the war except for the families that had sons who had joined the Union army. The town had not experienced the rumble of cannons, the endless reports of rifle fire, and the hideous screams of wounded men. Their farms were growing and beautiful, their houses not smoldering ruins, their fields not torn to pieces by war.

The people on the streets eyed him in two extremes, with admiration for he wore the coat of a soldier who had won the bitter war or with disdain for his unkempt appearance. He ignored them equally. He had been careful with his money and had enough for meals or to buy food with. He chose a clean looking saloon that offered meals. He had no interest in drink though.

The saloon was as neat and orderly on the inside as it was on the outside. The floor was swept and mopped clean, the bar and tables wiped down. He walked in carrying the Henry as he did not trust to leave it on the horse. He sat down at a table and waited.

The man behind the bar called out to him, "If you're looking for the lunch, go through that door right there. Cafe's on the other side of the wall."

Buck nodded to him and stood up.

The man called out to him again, "You from the war?"

Buck nodded.

"Where you headed?"

"Rocky Mountains. Headwaters of the Missouri."

"Oh, Montana Territory."

Buck gave him a blank look, "What is Montana Territory?"

"Brand new Territory, just established last year. They took a bit out of the Washington Territory and big chunk out of Dakota and made a whole new Territory, likely be a state one day. They're finding gold out that way too. Virginia City, Helena, all the way to California. Boom towns sprouting up fast as daisies."

"Gold makes men go crazy."

"It does that. You should see some of them that come through here. Slicked up like Sunday-go-to-meeting, never been out of the city in their lives. Likely the Sioux will kill them before they get across Dakota."

"The Sioux are always looking for a fight."

"The Santee did some killing up this way, but the army whipped them good and stuck them on a reservation. Army will be heading west now that the war's over. It will soon be safe to travel that country as there'll be forts all over the place."

"Sounds like much has changed since I left."

How long has that been?"

Buck shrugged, "Four years?"

"You fought the whole war? My God man, step up to the bar and let me buy you a drink."

Buck waved his hand, "No, just a meal."

"Okay, well you go right on through that door and set yourself down. Tell the gal that Mort said it's on the house."

"Thank you."

Buck began to walk to the open doorway that separated the two sides of the room. Two men sat at a table looking him over with taunting grins and troublemaking in their eyes. One of the men spoke with a smirk in his voice, "Nice rifle you got there. I could use me a gun like that."

"Then get a job and buy one," Buck answered coldly.

"Headwaters of the Missouri? That's Injun country, stinkin' Blackfeet all over the place."

Buck looked at the man with a growing expression of annoyance.

The man narrowed his eyes at Buck, "In fact you look kinda like one of 'em."

Anger flared up in Buck's eyes. "That's because I *am* one of them."

126

"Never seen a blonde injun before. You ain't full blood injun, half maybe? You wouldn't be a *breed*, now would yuh?" Both men laughed. "You must be powerful ignorant not to know there's a Montana Territory. Are you ignorant, breed?"

That fact that the man was picking a fight was plain. Buck was too tired to fight.

"I'm only looking to eat and ride on."

The talker wouldn't let it go. "So, you've been in the war, huh? I'm thinking you wasn't, they'd never let a *breed* in the army. I'm thinking you just killed a soldier and took that coat like the Sioux have been doing all over this country."

Buck held down his anger and attempted to walk on, but the troublemaker stood up to block his path. "Sorry, no breeds allowed in the café."

Buck locked a cold hard eye on the troublemaker's eyes. "I've lost count of how many men I've killed, one more won't mean a thing to me. You don't know anything about what the army does or doesn't do, since you're a yellow-bellied coward who sat out the war drinking and talking tough. Now, you're getting on my nerves, so you can either get out of my way or I'll walk over you."

The man's face grew red with anger, "You called me a coward?"

"A yellow-bellied coward to be exact."

The man reached for a pistol that was tucked into his waistband. Buck swung the butt of the Henry up hard and fast catching the man in the solar plexus. The man fell to his knees with a woof of escaping air. At the same time Buck spun the rifle around thumbing back the hammer as he did, ending the move with the bore pointing in the second man's face. He said nothing as he stood there holding the rifle on the man.

The second man had begun to jump out of his chair when the bore of the .44 made him decide it was wiser to sit back down. The man he had hit rolled over on his back groaning as he gripped both hands over his mid-section. Buck stepped on his stomach causing him to yelp in pain as he walked over him and through the open doorway.

Several people in the two rooms had witnessed the exchange. It was only a matter of minutes before a man with a badge on his chest walked through the saloon door. The man was fiftyish, gray haired, yet lean and muscled. His face was a picture of a frontier man with no tolerance for nonsense. He walked up to the barman. "I got a report of a fight in here."

The barman shook his head, "No fight. Those two over at that table tried to hoorah a man returning from the war and got what they had coming."

"Where's the man from the war now?"

The barman pointed toward the doorway, "Eating."

The marshal walked toward the two men at the table. The one that had been hit was back in his chair leaning over the table with a sick look on his face. The marshal eyed the men and recognized drinking troublemakers when he saw them. He stopped at the table, "Get out of town. I don't abide troublemakers in my town. I'll be back in five minutes and this table had better be empty."

The man that had been hit protested, "I want him arrested for hitting me."

The second man joined his partners protest, "We were just sitting here and that *breed* attacked us. Typical for a stinkin' injun."

The marshal looked at the men with an uncaring expression. "You just wasted one of those five minutes." He walked into the café.

He walked up to Buck who was silently eating his meal with the Henry across his knees the bore pointed toward the saloon door. "I don't abide fighting in my town."

Buck did not look up, "Then, you should keep the troublemakers out of your town."

"They've been given their walking papers. Finish your meal and then ride on."

"I intended to."

The marshal looked at Buck for another second. "Been in the war?"

"Yeah."

"My brother went out with the Minnesota volunteers. He hasn't come home yet."

"A lot of men won't come home."

"What did you do in the war?"

"Killed Rebs."

The marshal nodded, "Take your time, son."

He walked back through the door to the saloon and saw the two men walking across the room. The one who had been hit looked back at the marshal, "Since you ain't gonna do something about that breed, we will."

"I'd suggest you stay as far away from that man as you can. That's one dangerous fellow and it won't be him who's feeding the buzzards." He glanced at a clock standing in the corner its long pendulum arm swinging silently back and forth, "Your time's up and you're still in my town."

"We're goin'." They went out the door and mounted their horses.

The marshal walked back into the café and up to Buck. "Best watch yourself; those two are going to lay for you."

Buck continued to eat. "Likely. Figured I'd have to kill them before I was done anyway." He then glanced up at the marshal, "Don't worry, it won't be in your town."

"They rode west. There's a lot of open country out there so what you do is up to you."

Buck continued to look at him for a second longer. "Thanks."

The marshal nodded and walked out of the room.

He stopped when Buck said, "Hope your brother comes home."

The marshal looked at Buck. "Yeah, me too." He continued out the door.

Finishing his meal, Buck headed out to the street. He stood with his horse between him and the street surveying his surroundings. Seeing nothing that worried him he stepped into the saddle. He rode out of town, crossed the river on the ferry, and kept riding. The road gave way to a wagon-rutted trail as it left the town and any resemblance to law and order behind.

The trail left by the two troublemakers was lost in the clutter of hoof prints and wagon tracks. They were dressed like they belonged in the wild country and would know where they were going. Buck rode alert and attentive to the country around him for possible spots to be ambushed from.

A pair of horse trails cut off the wagon ruts and through the long grass toward a pine covered knoll a couple hundred yards from the trail. The trail was fresh, the grass newly crushed down with shod horse tracks in the sod. The troublemakers had left only a short time before him so it was a safe bet the trail was theirs. He studied the way the trail went and was convinced that the men would shoot at him from the knoll.

It would be a long shot, but they might be good marksmen, it didn't pay to assume they weren't. He moved his horse back down the trail. As he did, a herd of deer came bouncing and running toward him from the direction the trail led. That was all the proof he needed, the two men had spooked the deer out of their beds on their way to the knoll.

Making a wide circle around to the backside of the knoll, he left his horse tied to a tree and made his way closer on foot. He slipped ghost-like through the trees, coming to a place above the knoll with a clear view down on it. He sat down and searched for movement. A flicker of movement caught his eye; he focused on it and made out the shape of a horse. He then spotted the second horse. He got up and crept along the hill, eyes searching the knoll until he found the two men. They had rifles and were watching the wagon trail below them.

The man Buck had hit was on his hands and knees intently peering through the trees. Buck raised the Henry and shot the man in his up raised rear end. The man lurched forward landing hard on his face with a scream of shock and agony.

At the rifle report and impact the second man threw himself sideways away from his partner. He lay on the ground frozen in place staring in horror at his partner as he convulsed on the ground kicking and screaming.

Buck shouted down to the man. "You men are mighty troublesome. Your friend there is going to have some problems so I suggest you take him back to that town and get him to a doctor. Likely need a wagon; he won't be riding anytime soon."

The man stared up the hill where the unseen voice had emanated from. His panicked eyes searched for the man he knew was the one from the saloon. He fervently hoped the next bullet wasn't for him.

Buck stood up so the man could see him. "Next time I shoot to kill, so don't come for me again." He then slipped back into the trees and returned to his horse.

He rode back to the wagon ruts and continued riding west.

He continued to ride across the Dakota country. This was Sioux country, he had been hearing all along the way how the Sioux were attacking and killing anyone who dared to cross their land. In his discussions with Raven, he learned that the Laramie Treaty of 1851 designated this land to them.

The treaty had not included the Blackfeet tribes so he had known nothing of it. Raven had said that the army had broken the treaty almost immediately after signing it. It was apparent that the gold hunters and immigrants, feeling free to cross their land, angered the Sioux. They reacted as the Sioux always did--they killed.

The majority of the wagons and gold seekers were following the Oregon Trail further south and out of the Sioux country. It was the land of the Cheyenne, Arapahoe, and Shoshones that the Oregon Trail crossed. They were tribes that were more tolerant of the white intrusion, but it would only be a matter of time before they got fed up as well and took up arms against them. Buck understood these tribes thought they could stop the immigrant flow, but they had no idea what lay to their east.

Several yards off the trail lay a dead horse with a pair of Sioux arrows sticking out of the hide and bones not eaten by the scavengers. The stock saddle still on the remains of the horse said it had belonged to a white man. He pulled up and studied the horse and the vicinity around it. An arrow lying on the ground and a few scattered bones left by the same scavengers was what remained of the rider.

Buck looked at the saddle. Except for some grime from the rotting horse and being sun dried it appeared to be in pretty good shape. Taking a careful look around he studied the terrain for Sioux. Seeing none he quickly dismounted, tucked the reins to his horse under his belt and pulled the saddle cinch loose on the dead horse.

With some yanking and effort he pulled the stirrup out from under the dead horse. The saddle was in good shape except for the smell and dried leather. He had been riding the McClellan saddle and didn't care for it. A scrubbing at the next stream and a little animal fat rubbed into the dried leather and the saddle would be good as new.

The saddle had a pair of saddlebags on it. The bag that had been on top of the horse was empty; no doubt the

Sioux had taken whatever was in it. The right side of the saddle that had been under the eight hundred pound horse had an empty rifle scabbard. The rider probably had the rifle out and the Sioux got it. When he opened the saddlebag from that side he found a hundred rounds of .44 ammunition in it.

He studied the country around him again and then quickly stripped off the McClellan and put the other saddle on his horse. Ripping up chunks of sod he cleaned the grime off the saddle fenders and skirt. Scraping the dirt out of the scabbard he was about to slide the Henry into it, but then changed his mind and decided to ride with it in his hands. He remounted and rode on.

The miles that followed were marked by burned wagons, dead livestock, and dug up mounds surrounded by scattered bones that likely had been graves. The Sioux had been active in patrolling their country and this trail; however, he had yet to see a war party.

As the day waned he saw ahead a line of trees that indicated a stream course. He rode toward it. He wanted to give the saddle a good cleaning and rest for the night. It would have to be fireless camp for the night, but he didn't need a fire to sleep. Drawing closer, a plume of smoke suddenly rose up out of the trees. He abruptly pulled the horse to a stop and studied the spot. His first thought was a Sioux war party camp.

He reined the horse toward a small rise where he could look down on the stream. Through the smoke he could make out the dirty white canvas top of a wagon. He rode on to the wagon. As he closed the distance he made out a man in eastern dress sitting at the fire. Across from him was a woman with a small boy and girl of five or six years of age. Buck shook his head and grumbled about pilgrims. A four hitch of mules were staked out in the grass too far from the camp.

He approached the camp and shouted, "Hello, the

camp, a man's riding in."

He rode in cautiously as the man rose to his feet and looked at him. The woman was stirring a spoon in a pot. She looked up at him with a frightened expression. The two children gaped with curiosity. The man spoke out to him, "Can we help you?"

Buck pulled the horse up and studied the group. "You know that you're in Sioux country don't you?"

The man nodded. "We had heard such, but have not seen any savages."

"You won't see them, but they'll see you and right now the Sioux are real unhappy about trespassers on their land."

"Trespassers? This is United States of America land; we have a right to be here."

"Not according to the Sioux. They don't read the papers, and don't much care about the United States of America or what it figures to own. They hunted this country since the Old Man put it together."

The man looked at him confused, "What old man?"

"*The* Old Man, the Great Spirit, God. Sioux figure it's theirs because it always has been. Where are you headed anyway?"

"The Montana gold fields."

"You have to go through a couple hundred miles of Sioux country to get there, you won't make it."

"Why not?"

Buck's irritation was growing at the man's nonchalance and ignorance. He snapped, "Because some Sioux warrior will have your scalp on his lance before you get there and I don't even want to say what they'll do to your woman and youngsters."

The man stiffened angrily, "There is no need to scare my family with such talk."

"Dammit man, *those Sioux of something to be scared of.*"

"I can defend my family."

"With what?"

"I have a rifle."

"You ever kill a man with it?"

The man shifted nervously. "Well, no, just deer and such."

"What kind of gun is it?"

"A Springfield."

"A *muzzleloader*," Buck spit out. "One shot against twenty in a war party. Mister, you're a fool to drag your family out here. You need to turn around and head back to Minnesota or at least head south into that Nebraska country where the Indians are either peaceful or on reservations."

Trying to present a tough face he asked with a cocky tone, "Why are you riding out here alone then, if it is so dangerous?"

"Because, I know what I'm doing. I grew up fighting the Sioux and every other tribe too."

"The Sioux don't scare you then?"

"They worry me, they worry me a lot."

The woman turned her eyes to her husband with fear etched on her face. "Please, Robert, please can we go back? I am very afraid."

"There is nothing to be afraid of, he is simply trying to impress us."

"No, Robert, he is right. Did you not see the burned wagons and dead animals? Who did that if not the Indians? You know I did not want to do this in the first place. Please, take me and the children to safety and then you can go on to Montana or wherever you please."

"No," the man shouted. "We are going to the gold fields and become rich and . . ."

"Dead," Buck finished the sentence.

The man bristled angrily, his pride wounded. "You have worn out your welcome, sir. Please leave us."

Buck shrugged, "Suit yourself, it's not my scalp or

family." He kicked the horse and splashed across the stream away from the camp.

He glanced back and the woman was crying. He shouted back, "Best get them mules in closer or you'll be pulling that wagon yourself." He muttered under his breath, "You stupid pilgrim."

He rode downstream from the family. He couldn't help thinking of the woman and children. The man was a prideful fool and deserved whatever he got. The woman was smart, she wanted to go back, except that millstone of a husband around her neck was keeping her out in the kill area. He feared for the woman, knowing full well what her lot would be. He thought of what Jules would do to her and the bile of hatred for the man boiled up.

He made most of a mile before stopping. He stripped the saddle off the horse and washed it down in the stream. It looked better and smelled better as well. He tied the horse with a long rope to let him graze and sat down in the trees watching him. He chewed on a chunk of dried beef and washed it down with water. If any Sioux were around they had already spotted that fire and would be closing in. He didn't want to hang in too close to them, but he felt a nagging need to because of the helpless woman and children.

He cussed himself for a fool thinking about that family. He wanted to get home. He was anxious to confront his father and make him pay for his betrayal. Now, he felt he should do something for the woman and children. He'd end up with his own hair lifted if he tagged along with them. Besides, he would end up shooting that fool Robert himself if he had to be around him. The pilgrim was just too stupid to live.

He wrapped his blanket around him and fell asleep sitting up with the Henry across his knees. He woke up every hour and looked to the horse for any indication that they were not alone. The horse remained undisturbed all night.

Morning broke with the summer sun turning the prairie hot at first light. He had decided on a compromise. Since he was heading the same way as the wagon he'd shadow them just in case. He had no intention of going into their camp, still, in this way, he could keep an eye on them.

Chapter Fourteen

Buck rode back to where the people had camped. They were gone with the wagon, the tracks showing where they had crossed the stream and continued west. Buck grumbled about the man being a stubborn fool.

He moved off to the south and then turned west paralleling the route the wagon would take. He topped a rise and took a quick look to the north and spotted the wagon rocking along painfully slow a quarter mile away. He jumped the horse off the rise to prevent skylining himself for too long. He put the sun to his back and continued riding with the Henry between his belt buckle and the saddle's pommel, eyes ever searching as he rode along.

He knew they would encounter a Sioux hunting or war party eventually, it was only a matter of time. They might not be in this area right now, which would lead Robert into a false sense of security believing he was right, but they would be along. Four mules, a woman, and a wagonload of treasures was too much to pass up, and only one man to deal with to get it.

The sun moved up his back, shortening the shadow he and his horse cast out in front of them. At straight up noon he stopped at a creek and let the horse drink. He refilled his canteen and stretched his legs leading the horse for a short walk. He figured Robert was running on pure luck, except luck was a very poor companion as it had the bad habit of dropping out of sight when you needed it most.

The sun was halfway between high noon and the western horizon, the afternoon heat intense, when he heard the first shots pop dully in the distance. It was hard to tell where they came from, his first guess was the wagon. He reined the horse to the north and galloped for the trail the wagon would be on.

As he closed the distance between him and where

he supposed the wagon to be he heard the last shot. Topping out on a rise the unmistakable sound of Sioux warriors howling and shouting with excitement drifted to him. A few seconds later allowed him to see the war party swarming over the wagon. He swung the horse down into a gulley and then broke up out of it less than a hundred yards from the halted wagon.

One of the lead mules was down in the harness. A man lay on the ground not moving. Eight mounted Sioux rode around the wagon slapping the canvas while they laughed and shouted. He could hear the woman screaming inside the canvas cover as the party enjoyed the sport of taunting her. They were so preoccupied with their game they failed to see him.

Jerking the horse to a sliding stop, Buck swung the Henry up and shot the closest Indian off his horse. Levering in another cartridge he killed a second one before they figured out where he was. In that time he killed a third. The remaining five charged at him forgetting the wagon. He killed a fourth.

Buck coolly sat on his horse levering in cartridges and firing at the oncoming Indians. It was only slightly harder than picking off Rebs since they were horseback, but not difficult. The horse he rode was from the war and had long since learned to ignore the sound of gunfire. With a fifth Sioux dropping from his horse, the other three spread out to come at him from different angles.

Buck kicked his horse into an instant gallop directly at the Indian in front of him. The heavy bodied warhorse slammed into the lighter Sioux mustang. Horse and rider went down. Buck jerked the horse's head around and fired a shot directly into the prone man.

The two last members of the party came back together, stopped and stared at Buck. They spoke toward each other. He knew they were thinking he was crazy or possessed of a spirit that could not be killed. They feared both.

Buck pounded his chest and shouted at the top of his lungs in the spattering of Sioux he knew. "I am a Kanai Blood, I do not fear the Sioux dog eaters. I will hang your scalps on my horse's bridle, carry them into battle, and tell all what women the Sioux dog eaters are."

He saw that these two were young and armed only with bows. Those who had the muzzle loading rifles were lying in the grass. To prove his point he charged at them shouting curses and insults. They turned and rode away from the crazy man at a hard gallop. Buck pulled his horse up and watched them disappear into a draw.

Buck rode back to the wagon. The woman was still inside of it, he could hear her shushing the crying children between reciting prayers and sobbing. He called out toward the canvas cover, "Ma'am, it's Buck Drake, the man who was in your camp last night."

The woman's voice stopped as he heard shuffling sounds from inside the canvas. The woman tentatively stuck her head out of the split in the back of the wagon cover and looked around. Her hair was pulled down in frayed strands framing a face contorted with fear. Her dust coated skin was etched in muddy rivulets from crying. She stared at him for several seconds. "Are they gone?" she whispered with a choking sob.

"Yes, ma'am. I'm afraid your man is dead though."

The woman let out a wail of loss and agony at the words. Wiping her face with a dirty hand she asked, "Where is he?"

Buck pointed to the front of the wagon. "Yonder."

The woman climbed out of the wagon instructing the children to stay put. She walked around to where her husband lay in the grass. He had been shot at least once and had a half dozen arrows in him. She fell to her knees and wept with sobbing, lung wrenching howls and cries.

Buck sat on his horse and watched her in silence.

He looked at the back of the wagon and saw two little faces staring at him. He looked back at them saying nothing. He then turned his attention back at the woman. "I'll bury him if you have a shovel."

The woman did not answer. Buck scanned the country around him while she wept over her dead husband for several more minutes. She finally stood up. Wiping her face with her hands she simply said, "Yes, thank you."

The woman climbed back in the wagon with the children. Buck could hear her explaining to them what had happened. They cried and moaned like lost souls.

Buck dug a grave a short ways from the wagon. The dry sandy sod made for easy and quick digging. Reaching an acceptable depth he dragged the dead man to the grave and rolled him into it. Shoveling the dirt back in he packed it down and put the shovel back in its place on the side of the wagon.

He called to the back of the wagon, "What do you want to do now, ma'am?"

The woman parted the canvas tying the two sides up and open. She stared out to the prairie past Buck. "I do not know what to do. We sold everything to come out here. It was a foolish undertaking and now I have nowhere to go." The woman wrung her hands together as her face twisted in grief, she wailed, "I do not know what to do."

"Do you have any money?"

The woman gaped at him with shock and fear.

"I'm not going to rob you," his tone reflected his irritation by the look she gave him. "I can get you to a town. If you have money you can get by. You can sell these mules and the wagon for a good bit too."

She nodded, "Yes, I have some."

"Can you drive this team?"

"Yes."

"There's a town back on the Red River I passed through. I can take you back there and leave you off. They seemed like decent folks and likely will help you and the youngsters out."

"I have family in Wisconsin," she replied. "If we can get back to Minnesota I am sure they will help us."

Buck nodded. He stepped down from the horse and cut the dead mule loose from the harness. He led the team around until they faced east back down the trail they had drove over. "You get on up there and drive this rig and I'll ride alongside."

The woman nodded and climbed up on the seat from inside the wagon. Taking up the reins she snapped them over the three mules and the wagon lurched forward. One of the children asked where they were going. The woman answered, "Home, we're going back home."

No words were exchanged throughout the day. Silence was preferable to Buck and the woman was still in shock. They moved steadily on until the sun went down. They stopped west of the stream where they had camped the night before. Buck unhitched the mules and staked them close to the camp as the woman made supper over a small fire that was put out as soon as the food was cooked.

Buck ate with the silent family. The woman put the children to bed in the wagon and climbed back out. She stared up at the stars. "I never wanted to come out here."

Buck sat with his back against his saddle. He remained silent to let the woman get her thoughts out and clear her troubled mind.

"Robert heard the stories about men getting rich on gold. We had a nice little store, nice house, we were happy . . . and then he got this fool idea to go west." She paused continuing to search the stars. "I never wanted this."

She then looked at Buck. "You are obviously a man of this country. Was Robert right or wrong to want to come west?"

"That's not for me to say, ma'am. A man's business is his own."

"Eve, my name is Eve. Would you have brought a town woman and two small children out here?"

"I'm half Blood, I was born in this country, I understand it. A man who doesn't won't make it."

"I will take that as a no. Blood? What is that?"

"Blackfeet. Indian as the whites call us."

Eve looked at him with great curiosity. "If you are half Indian how come you killed other Indians? Do you not all stick together?"

Buck smiled and shook his head. "Indians have been fighting Indians since time began. Indians live for battle. We fight, take over another's hunting grounds, and then fight someone else. The Sioux are good at fighting other Indians. They are enemies with the Crow, Shoshone, and we Blackfeet especially hate the Sioux."

"What strange people."

"Not really. I just spent four years killing men because they wanted to have their own country and not be part of the United States. They were all white men, yet they killed each other. I killed men simply because they wore a gray uniform and I wore a blue one. Brothers killed brothers and tore the country to pieces. Compared to that, what the Indian does is pretty mild."

Eve pondered that. "Yes, I see your point. We are not Indians, why did they attack us then?"

"You are trespassers. It's a little complicated for easterners to understand or maybe it's just too simple. It boils down to the Laramie Treaty of 1851, when the United States Government promised the Sioux that no white man would pass through their lands or take it from them. The treaty was broken before the ink was dry. The Sioux are angry at the betrayal and, to their way of thinking, the only way to counter that is to kill every white person that comes here."

"I am not sure I understand, since this is all part of the United States."

"Sioux, and for that matter most tribes, don't recognize the United States as having power over them or the right to take what they have. You could compare it to someone coming into your Wisconsin store and telling you to get out because they wanted it and were taking it over. How would you react?"

Eve stared into the night. "We have no business out here then, do we?"

Buck shrugged, "Times change. The country is expanding west and will continue to. You have a right to come west if you're strong enough to survive it. The west is a good example of the saying, 'only the strong will survive'."

"Robert wasn't strong enough, was he?"

"I didn't know your husband, I can't say."

"I know he wasn't." She looked back at Buck. "I never did thank you for coming to our rescue. I was certain we were all dead. I was too terrified to even think of anything except protecting my children."

"I decided I'd best shadow you until your man came to his senses and turned back. Sorry about your loss."

"How long will it take for us to reach the town?"

"Day after tomorrow. The wagon is slower than a man on horseback."

Eve nodded. "I am very tired." She turned and climbed up into the back of the wagon disappearing behind the canvas.

Buck listened to the mules and his horse cropping grass. Looking at the wagon he shook his head and muttered, "Fool of a pilgrim."

Getting up he threw his bedroll down by the animals and laid down looking up at the sky. He lay there listening to the night. Crickets echoed through the darkness and a pack of hunting wolves called to each other. He drifted into sleep as a coyote yipped across the stream.

***

Two days later they reached the town on the Red River. Buck had not paid attention to the name of it on his last pass through. The sign on the outskirts identified it as *Breckenridge*. He rode up to the city marshal's office and stepped off the horse as Eve pulled the mules to a stop behind him.

Buck went in the office to find the marshal sitting at his desk working on some writing. The marshal looked up. "You came back? You must have liked that café food."

Buck jerked his thumb over his shoulder, "Got a woman and youngsters out here. I found them out in the wild country this side of the Missouri, they were attacked by Sioux."

The marshal jumped up. "Let me see them." He walked past Buck to the door.

Eve was still on the wagon seat looking haggard and drawn out. The marshal looked up at her.

"Her man was killed," Buck explained. "They need a place to go."

The marshal nodded his understanding. He pointed at the white church at the end of the street. "Ma'am, you go right on down to the church and ask for Reverend Drew. He and his wife will help you out."

Eve nodded and then looked down at Buck. "Thank you again, Mr. Drake."

Buck tipped his hat to her. "Yes, ma'am."

She snapped the reins and moved the wagon toward the church.

The marshal turned his attention to Buck. "Another easterner that bit off too much?"

"A *fool* who bit off too much. I warned them to go back, but her man was prideful and insisted on going to Montana to get rich on gold."

The marshal shook his head, "Gold kills more men than war."

"Probably."

"Are you heading back out?"

"I'm heading for my home and figure to get there someday if I don't run into anymore pilgrims trying to get themselves killed."

"How did you get them away from the Indians?"

"Killed six and the last two ran off."

The marshal stared at him. "You're a skilled man."

"It's a dangerous country and no place for the weak."

"By the way, those boys you had the run-in with limped back to town. One had a chunk of lead up his backside."

"That's what happens when you're careless where you point your gun."

The marshal chuckled. "I'm going to head on over to the church and see what I can do to help that woman. I'd say be careful, but I think it's the other fellow that needs to be careful." He turned and walked away.

Buck called after him, "She said she's from Wisconsin and wants to go home." He mounted his horse and grumbled, "I might get home one of these days."

Chapter Fifteen

The day Buck rode out of Breckenridge he took his own advice and crossed the Missouri at Yankton and rode west through Nebraska and the Dakota Territory below Crow country. He didn't swing north until he reached the Rockies, where he followed the eastern slope up through Yellowstone and on to the Teton River where he had last seen his village.

The blue army coat served him well while he rode through country where white men had settled. Towns were popping up wherever the Indian threat had been eliminated. The people he met recognized he was a soldier and accorded him a certain amount of respect. Once he began to enter Blackfeet country he kept the coat tied behind his saddle. A Blackfeet war party might see the coat, shoot first, and then see who was in the coat.

He was within ten miles of the place he had left the village that day he made the ill-fated decision to ride with Jules. He could no longer stomach acknowledging the wretch as his father and refused to think of him as anything other than Jules. He knew the villages moved when necessary and it might be long gone from the former location. He was following the Teton upstream when a party of Blackfeet warriors came galloping at him.

He stopped his horse and watched them come on. He knew his people were notional and often as curious as they were aggressive. He figured if he simply sat still watching them like a fool they would check him out before killing him.

He had called it right as the party of a dozen warriors surrounded him and stopped. They stared at him and talked among themselves in their tongue as to why he sat staring at them like he was crazy. To their way of thinking, anyone dressed in white man's clothes should have fled. They concluded that he was blind, deaf, and crazy.

The last time Buck had spoken his native language was the day he was arrested by the army; however, it was coming back to him as if he had never left it. In their own tongue Buck replied, "I am not blind, deaf, or crazy."

They looked at him with surprise.

"I am Buckingham Palace, grandson of Cree Killer, and son of Hurit, the Medicine Woman." He recognized the leader of the group, a war chief named Short Leg. "I know Short Leg as well, I have ridden with him."

Short Leg looked surprised.

One of the warriors said, "We are from their village. Cree Killer is a chief."

Short Leg stared at Buck harder. "I do know you, the son of the Medicine Woman. You were the one with yellow hair. You were a young man when you rode away and never returned. Your mother wept and offered many prayers at the Medicine Lodge for you to return."

"I am alive. I was captured by the white soldiers and made to fight in their war many miles away to the east where the white men all live."

The warriors nodded their heads in acknowledgement.

"You rode with the evil Jules that day you left. Your grandfather was displeased."

Buck cringed at the reminder. "I was a fool that day. I was young and let Jules trick my pride into riding with them. I am ashamed of that day."

Short Leg nodded, "Well said."

Buck went on, "Badger, my brother, is he still alive?"

Short leg nodded, "He is and lives with great honor in the village. He is among The Comrades society and a ranking member of the Braves. His coups cannot be counted there are so many. His lodge skins have no room left to add his honors."

Buck knew that The Comrades were the controlling society of all the bands of the nation and the Braves were the policeman with that society. Buck smiled, "That sounds like Badger."

"Come with us, we will take you home. Your mother will weep tears of happiness that her son has returned."

"Is Jules in the village?"

"Jules is dead."

Buck felt a pang of anger shoot through him. He felt cheated in being denied the opportunity to kill the betraying snake. "Are you sure he is dead? Maybe he just never came back."

Short Leg thought on that for a moment. "It is possible he is not dead. He and his band of stinking dogs never returned, we believed them all to be dead like you."

Hope sprang back up in Buck, maybe Jules was still alive. He would find him if he was. "I will tell everyone in the meeting space what cowardice Jules showed in battle and how he got all of his party killed by the soldiers. They were truly stinking dogs, but he betrayed them all the same."

Short Leg and the others nodded. "We would like to hear that story," Short Leg remarked.

The party turned their horses around and rode back to the village with Buck in their midst. He took in the grandeur of the country around him. He was finally home and there really was a place like this filled with mountains and clean streams. He had not imagined or dreamed it. The war was behind him and the Rocky Mountain sky was bluer and the mountains higher than he had remembered them.

Short Leg's party was talking among themselves as they rode into the village. Short Leg announced in a loud voice that Buckingham Palace had escaped his capture from the white soldiers. All members of the village came out to see what the commotion was about. The party led

Buck to the lodge of his mother and moved aside to watch what would happen.

Buck looked the lodge over as he dismounted. This was not the lodge his mother had lived in with Jules. Jules had not painted his glory and manhood on the buffalo hide walls as the Blackfeet warriors did. His was the only lodge with nothing on it. This lodge was covered with scenes of horses, fights, and coups. This was the lodge of a warrior; why was his mother living in it?

Hurit stuck her head out of the lodge doorway and looked up. Her eyes widened in disbelief as she focused on her long lost son. Recognition filled her eyes and she hurriedly scrambled out of the lodge and embraced her son. "You are alive, you are alive!" she called out as tears ran down her cheeks.

The other women gathered around and smiled to see the joy their friend was filled with at the return of her son. Men wandered up and patted Buck on the shoulder in welcome as they remembered him as an up and coming warrior. Now he was older and had the look of experience in his eyes.

A small girl of perhaps three years came out of the lodge and gripped onto Hurit's legs as she stared up at Buck. He Who Fights, a man he remembered as a noted war chief, walked up to the lodge and patted Buck on the shoulder. "Welcome back, my wife has offered prayers for your return."

Buck stared at the man and then at his mother. Hurit suddenly understood her son's confusion. "Your father is dead."

Hurit gestured toward the man with her. "When your father did not return, He Who Fights became my husband. He has been a good husband." She then lifted the little girl, "This is your sister, Nuttah, daughter of He Who Fights."

Buck smiled at the child; her name meant *My Heart*

in their language. The child reached out and touched Buck's face. She giggled pulling on his short beard. She had never seen a man with hair on his face.

Buck laughed and took the child from his mother and held her up at arm's length. "She is a beautiful child." He then gave her back.

Hurit suddenly looked concerned, "We thought Jules died with you, but you have returned. Is he not dead?"

Buck frowned; he could not take his long anticipated revenge on Jules by shaming him and then killing him in front of the village. "I do not know if he is dead. He betrayed his party to the white soldiers and they were all killed. He hit me in the head with his gun and pushed me into the soldiers so he could escape. He ran away like the coward he always was and the soldiers captured me."

The men and woman listening were silent. The men who had distrusted Jules nodded their heads in agreement. "It is good that he is gone," said an aged war chief. "We do not allow white men in our country and should never have in our village."

Buck glared at the man, "I will not hear evil spoken of my grandfather."

The old chief raised his hand, "Peace, Buckingham Palace. Your grandfather was long ago forgiven for his mistake and has honor in the village."

"I have heard he is now a chief."

"He is, and wiser for his mistake."

Buck smiled and nodded his approval to the old man. He continued with his telling. "Jules ran from a small party of Shoshone who laughed and mocked his retreat."

The warriors made sounds of disgust at the idea of being mocked by what they considered a weak enemy.

"That was before he betrayed us," Buck added. "It was my shame to have ridden with the stinking dogs that day. I was taunted by Jules' evil spirit and in my foolish youth let my pride sweep me into his dung. If he is dead, I am angry that I cannot kill him. I had planned to shame him before the village and then challenge him to fight. If he lives, one day I will find the slinking coyote and kill him."

The men listening all nodded and muttered in agreement to Buck's vow.

Cree Killer walked slowly up to Buck as those assembled parted to allow him access to his grandson. "The coward is my shame. I was angry that you had rode with him, but I cannot condemn you for the same mistake I made."

Buck embraced his grandfather and then stepped back looking in his wrinkled face. "He was his own shame, Grandfather, not yours. You were kind to him and he repaid your kindness with evil. If you were shamed before the village would they have made you a chief?"

A warrior spoke out from the group, "Chief Cree Killer is not shamed in my eyes."

A round of affirming comments went through the group agreeing with the warrior.

"See, Grandfather, you are respected. The shame is on the evil one and only on him."

Cree Killer said with a smile, "You are my pride and honor, grandson. I am pleased to see you have returned safely to us. We all believed you were dead."

"I am happy to be back with my people. I have much to tell you about the white men, their villages, and what we can expect from them."

"Good, we will want to know everything you learned."

Badger suddenly burst through the crowd. He let out a bear growl and grabbed Buck up in a strong embrace. "My brother! You do not walk among the ghosts and spirits after all."

Buck threw his arms around Badger and squeezed him in return each trying to see who could crush the ribs of the other first.

Badger let go and stepped back. "You are stronger. I am glad to see you remember your brother."

Buck grinned at him, "I remember you shot me in the rear end with an arrow thinking it was a deer."

"Oh, we were children then, and it was only a rabbit hunting arrowhead. Besides, you should not have been in the bushes doing your business when we were hunting."

The surrounding men laughed and the women giggled behind their hands.

"Come and tell us about the many summers you were away." Badger led Buck to the central meeting area with the men all following. More men and women drifted in from other parts of the village to the meeting place to hear what Buck had to say. They all sat down on the ground as Buck remained standing in front of them.

He retold how Jules ran from the Shoshone, which caused grumblings among the men. He related how he was captured by the soldiers and given the choice of going east to fight in their war or to be hung. Heads nodded in agreement that it was better to fight, even if it were for the white man, than to be hung like a haunch of deer meat.

He then related how the war progressed and how the white men were killing each other and burning the villages and homes. He couldn't resist telling of his part and how many coups he had counted and scalps he could have taken except the white chiefs did not allow scalping Johnny Rebs. This caused the men to grumble again at such a waste of scalps.

Buck was quick to explain that there were so many Johnny Rebs, and the fact that the white men wanted them all killed, that a warrior could not help but count many coups. It did not make him a greater warrior than the men in the village because they did not have as many opportunities to count coup as a soldier in the white man's war. He did this so the honored warriors in the village didn't feel he was trying to be bigger than them.

He compared the killing in the war to how many rabbits, deer, and buffalo each Blackfeet hunter present had killed in his lifetime. Add all together and that was how many men were killed in the war. The men were amazed at such a number of dead men.

Walking Crane, a sub-chief, stood up on his long skinny legs that earned him his name and asked, "If you compare the whites to rabbits, deer, and buffalo and we know there are as many of these as stars in the sky, then how many white men are there?"

Buck held up both of his hands fingers spread and clenched them into a fist with each hand making the known symbol representing one hundred. He did this several times and then said, "I could do this all day and it would not come close to how many white men there are across the big rivers to the east."

A collective gasp went through the group.

He Who Fights asked, "Will they continue to come toward us?"

Buck nodded, "They already are coming and the soldiers will follow them."

"We have seen their wagons and their people on the Medicine Road to the south, but when they come into our land we attack them so they stay on the Medicine Road. I think they will stay down there."

"For now," Buck answered. "The whites call it the Oregon Trail and it is to Oregon and California far to the west that they go, past the land of the Nez Perce, but they will one day stop and stay in our country here.

"They have already had fights with the Sioux in the land of the many lakes. The whites have already broken the treaty they signed with the Sioux, Cheyenne, Arapahoe, and Crow. They will have to fight through them first before they can get to us."

"Our enemies," He Who Fights spit out. "Old

women, dog eaters, the white soldiers will go through them like a herd of sick rabbits. We are not so weak; when the whites and their soldiers come here we will beat them so badly they will never return."

An elder chief came to his feet and looked at He Who Fights. "We are not as strong as we once were. I am north Piegan from up in Rupert's Land. We were a powerful nation until the putrid Rupert soldiers gave us the wagon load of poisoned blankets that caused the people to have the white blister sickness and most died. It spread through us, and through the Kainai, and the Siksika, you here were spared. It destroyed us as a power. There are few of us left where once you could not count all the people. Do not underestimate the cunning and treachery of the white man. We are fighters, but even the grizzly can be tricked and killed."

He Who Fights bowed his head slightly in respect. "I will listen to your wisdom, Bighorn Chief, and be careful.

"I am not saying to fear the white man," Bighorn Chief was quick to clarify. "Only watch his treachery and trust him not at all, especially their soldiers."

He Who Fights agreed, he was a man who did not trust white men and was disquieted to learn how many of them there actually were. His father had often told the story of how the first white men they ever saw came up the river in their boats and killed two young boys who they had accused of stealing. His father hated the white man and collected a good number of trapper scalps.

Swift Runner spoke out, "I believe it is in our best interest to make peace with the whites."

A young warrior shouted out, "We should kill all white men. That is my thought, steal their horses and take their hair."

"You are young and wild, Angry All The Time," Swift Runner chided the young warrior. "Actions such as you speak of so recklessly will get us all killed."

Angry All The Time glared at his elder, but did not respond.

"I do not agree with Angry All The Time's rashness," Bighorn Chief broke in. "But, Swift Runner would you have us lick their shoes like a dog?"

Swift Runner stiffened at the insult. "Making peace and living in peace is not licking shoes. I am a warrior who wishes for peace."

Bighorn Chief huffed his disapproval and sat back down.

Swift Runner turned his attention to Buck. "You have seen the white man, what do you say, Buckingham Palace?"

Buck thought before speaking. It was a fine line they walked. The ancient drive to fight, the hatred they had for the whites ignited when the Corps of Discovery killed the Blackfeet boys, and the need to realize that they were no longer the power they once had been were bond to clash. The whites had begun the treachery with the deliberate distribution of small pox infected blankets to the North Piegan. The people had reason to be angry and fight, they also needed to survive and that required coming to grips with the changing west. How could he bridge the two sides?

"The soldiers *will* come," Buck began slowly. "Their forts will dot the land like beaver lodges and each will be filled with hundreds of soldiers. One fort can hold as many soldiers as we have warriors and there will be many forts. I saw what happened when the gray coats chose to break away from the blue coats of the United States. As I have said, the killing was large. It is the white soldiers' way to kill everyone they think of as an enemy. Many of them don't care if they kill warriors, woman, or children. Some of their leaders say the only good enemy is a dead one."

"That is not an answer," Angry All The Time spit

out venomously.

Buck glared at him, "No, it is not. I don't have an answer, I can only say what I have seen and know. I tell you and then it is up to the wisdom of the chiefs and elders to decide what is best for the people." Pausing for a second he added, "*Wisdom* is needed here, Angry All The Time, something you do not have."

Angry All The Time jumped to his feet, clenched his fists, and stomped away. He had been humiliated and his pride stepped on twice and that was enough. The furious youth stormed out of the gathering.

Cree Killer spoke out, "And that is why leadership is left to the experienced and old." He stood up and faced the assembled. "My grandson has seen what none of us have. It would be wise to listen to him and allow his council to be entered in with the leaders when decisions are made."

A voice sounded from beyond the assembled men, "I do not agree!" They all turned to watch the man walking toward Buck from the far side of the gathering space. He walked with his head high and his eyes half closed. He put on a theatrical performance as he made his way through the gathered group. Men shifted over to let him pass while snickers and laughter followed him. The man reached the place where Buck stood, stopped and struck a mystic-like pose in front of him.

Buck snorted, "Nice show, Dirt Eater. Let's see you go into your act and roll around on the ground eating dirt, I always liked that part."

Lifting his head, Dirt Eater looked down his eagle-beaked nose at Buck and opened his eyes a bit wider. "You have brought an evil spirit into this gathering. Your council is corrupt."

"And you have embarrassed us by rolling in the dirt like a lice ridden dog and acting like a Digger Indian eating bugs and dirt."

Dirt Eater continued to hold his theatrical pose. "You are responsible for your father's death. He was a brave and holy man."

Buck huffed in disgust, "He was a coward and a devil. I don't recall our religion holding up devils and evil spirits as holy men. My father might be dead, I hope he is not because I want to kill him myself, but if he is, he has not gone to the Old Man in the hunting grounds. He has gone to the evil one under the earth."

Dirt Eater ignored Buck's comments and continued on. "I foresaw a great victory for the party of Jules. Your corruption in the party doomed them to defeat and death."

"I saw them run from the Shoshone. I saw their great victories in the murder of children and the rape of women. I saw their power as they killed terrified white men who sat like frozen rabbits before the fox. Your *holy* party was killed by soldiers who were not afraid of them and Jules ran like a beaten dog with his tail jammed up against his belly. Do not tell me about what you foresaw, you fraud. You are not a shaman, you are not a holy man, you are a devil. Be gone from me before I cut you open from crotch to chin."

A look of fear flashed across Dirt Eaters eyes and then he turned and walked away as if he were walking on bird eggs trying not to crush them. Behind him the men laughed and watched him as they made circling motions with their forefingers around the side of their heads.

Bighorn Chief stood up to leave. He winked at Buck and gave him a grin, "We should end all serious meetings with something to laugh at."

Buck's expression remained serious. "Dirt Eater will do us great harm one day."

The old man nodded, "Yes, but one day you will open him up like gutting a deer. Your paths shall cross a final time, as you and your father's will. I have dreamed it, Buckingham Palace."

Chapter Sixteen

The summer ended with a village buffalo hunt. A good number of buffalo were needed to supply enough meat to feed the people through the long, bitter mountain winter. Even with that storage of meat, they would run out if the winter lingered longer than usual as had happened many times in the past.

When the snows lay deep in the high mountains, and the rivers and streams froze solid from bank to bank, the game would move down onto the prairies miles from the mountain villages. The snow was too deep, and the distance too far, to follow the game and only the wolves enjoyed the bounty of winter-killed elk, deer, and buffalo.

In the years of long winters, rabbits had to provide the bulk of the meat after the buffalo meat ran out. Rabbits were plentiful in the snow before spring broke through and the big game migrated back to the mountains; however, a scrawny rabbit was next to nothing in an empty belly.

The hunt was critical for their survival and required planning. A man could hunt buffalo for his family anytime he wished except during the period when preparations for the big hunt were in progress. The buffalo hunt for winter meat was organized for the greatest number of kills. Should any man hunt during this period, and as a result scare the chosen herd away, he was seized by the Braves and beaten, his weapons were then taken from him.

The hunt was directed by the Hunt Chief who was responsible for all hunters involved knowing their part. The closest herd was located and the men were mounted on their buffalo horses. The horses were chosen for their courage and sturdy nature in galloping directly up to a buffalo running at full speed. Should the horse shy or panic at a critical moment the rider could be killed.

Short Leg was chief of this year's hunt as he had been in years past. When he was a young man he had a horse that panicked as he closed in on one of the shaggy beasts. The horse went down and Short Leg was rolled under the great hooves of the buffalo. His leg was smashed and it healed poorly, leaving him with a right leg shorter than the left and thus earning him his name as he walked lopsided about the camp.

The day of the hunt broke clear and hot. Everyone was ready in the village as they awaited the scouts for the final report on the herd. With a flourish of excited voices and running horses, the scouts rode in to inform Short Leg that the herd they had previously located along the river was still there and only a short ride from the village.

The women had travois hitched to their horses and their knives and tools for the butchering were bundled in deerskin cases. The hunters had brought their extra buffalo horses, which were gathered into a herd that was watched over and controlled by boys too young for the hunt. With all in readiness the hunters set out behind the scouts with the women following.

Angry All The Time was banned from the hunt as he was considered mentally unstable and a danger to the other hunters. On the last hunt, he did not follow orders and caused the herd to stampede prematurely resulting in the death of a man. His actions brought the punishment of The Comrades on him: he was beaten by Badger and his weapons seized. The public beating and ban brought shame on the prideful young man. His ensuing bitterness was directed toward the other hunters and in particular, Badger. The animosity between the two men was evident.

Short Leg and the scouts rode to the top of a bluff to look down on the herd. There were hundreds of animals moving slowly along as they grazed on the drying summer grass. The plan for attack was set and the men returned to the hunting party. Buck was mounted on one of his brother's buffalo horses.

The party was to split into two groups and approach

the animals from the rear and left side. The idea was to force the buffalo to run in a circle so the animals could be killed in one area and not chased cross country leaving dead buffalo scattered over a long distance. The closer the animals fell to each other the quicker and easier the butchering would be. The tactic would only work if each hunter did his part correctly. For that reason inexperienced hunters and those who couldn't work with the group were not allowed on this critical hunt.

The hunt split into the two parties and set out. Approaching the herd slowly the leaders of each group watched the bluff where a sentinel would signal by waving a blanket when the groups were set. The parties fell into position, the blanket waved, and both parties charged against the herd.

Several buffalo were killed before the herd broke and ran. The hunters continued to ride against the herd pushing them into a milling circle as they lanced and shot arrows into the animals. A few of the hunters had Hawken rifles that they had taken from slain trappers. Buck was the only one with a repeating rifle, which he used with good effect.

The dust churned up from the hundreds of running buffalo was caught on the wind. The brown cloud rose high into the sky and for a mile in every direction. The buffalo could be contained in the milling circle for only a short period of time before, through their sheer numbers and strength, they broke free of the hunters and charged in a straight line across the prairie. At that point the hunters broke off the chase.

As the dust blew away and settled, dozens of brown lumps could be seen scattered within an ever-widening circle. The hunters rode among the dead animals making certain they were all dead before the women approached them. An occasional shot sounded or a lance thrust finished a wounded animal.

The hunters regrouped to boast on their prowess as hunters and to marvel at Buck's repeating rifle, or as they called it, the 'many shoots gun.' He answered a steady stream of questions in regards to the gun and was made to tell of the kills he had made with it in the white man's war.

The women now entered the field riding the horses that each dragged a travois along behind. Wolves, coyotes, and fox could be seen trotting cautiously into the kill area. Ravens and magpies flew in to boldly settle on the dead animals while eagles and vultures began to circle.

Arriving at the dead animals, the woman broke out their butchering tools and began to skin and gut. Between slashes and cuts with their knives, the women chased the bravest and foolhardiest of the scavengers away with shouts and waving blades. A woman could often be seen jumping at and waving a skinning knife at a coyote or fox that ventured in too close.

As they worked, the women tossed pieces of meat out to the birds and animals to give them something to steal off with and keep them away from the main body of meat. A coyote would dart in, grab up a chunk of tossed meat and run, only to be attacked by a wolf and have the prize taken from him. The sounds of snarling and fighting canines surrounded the working women.

With the women working, the hunters turned from the field and headed back to the camp. They had done their part, from here out it was women's work and they had no part in it. Buck thought of what he had learned about white women in the east and knew they would never do what these women were doing.

To his people this was how it had always been and neither man nor woman thought the gender duties unfair or unusual. In fact, the women took great pride in the mastery of their skills. They would have thought a man who helped do women's work had something wrong with his manhood and was not a good choice for a husband.

For the next several weeks, the village was a beehive of activity. Countless numbers of wooden racks held strips of buffalo meat drying in the sun. Buffalo hides were stretched and pegged out all around the camp drying into leather for clothing, blankets, as well as for lodge floor and wall coverings. The women, in between their cooking and sewing duties, continued to work the hides with wooden paddles to break the skin fibers down so the leather would dry soft.

Chasing birds and scavengers away from the meat and hides were jobs given to the children to perform. The young boys and girls saw this as an important function for the benefit of all and took their duties with all seriousness and not as child's play. A child neglecting his or her duties was taken to task by their mother and made to feel shamed by their actions. No child, especially the boys, wished to be shamed, so there were few occurrences of neglected duties.

Buck had been living in the lodge of He Who Fights, with his mother and sister. The Blackfeet had a close family society and he was not unwelcome in the lodge; however, he was growing restless. The time he spent in the white man's world had changed him and he knew there was more to life than the village. As much as he loved his people, he now needed more than what they offered.

Being sent to the war showed him what the future held and he couldn't get that out of his mind. Before, his life had revolved around the village as it did even now for his family and friends, but, for him, it couldn't be that way any longer. Maybe his experiences had spoiled him for the village life, or maybe it had opened his eyes to the bigger picture of the expanding west. Then again, maybe he was meant to know all this so one day he could help them through the change. Maybe, the Old Man had a plan.

He decided to head up into the Bitterroot country to trap for the winter. It was still early enough to build a small cabin to live and trap from. Most of the country had been stripped clean of beaver, but not the mountains controlled by the Blackfeet. Few trappers had ventured into the area, and of those that did, few came back out as the Blackfeet killed them when found. He should be able to take at least two packs of prime fur from that country.

He needed to head down to Fort Benton to buy traps and outfit himself for the winter. At the end of the winter he would return to Fort Benton and sell his fur, then head out to see what he could find.

He told his mother and friends that he would be leaving in the morning for Fort Benton and then back up into the mountains to trap for the winter. People moved from village to village and camp to camp as the mood struck. There were north and south Piegan, Siksika, and Kainai mixed in all the villages. Parting was not sorrowful it was simply the way they lived.

Come morning, Buck left the Teton River village headed east for the fort. He rode his old army horse and led a blue roan pack horse his brother had given him. When he thanked Badger for the generous gift of the horse his brother explained that he had taken it from a white trapper who he caught stealing a beaver from his trap. He could always get another.

Buck still had most of the army pay he had left the east with. He had spent little of it coming across the country and had enough to outfit himself for the winter trapping. He'd get what he needed and then head back up the Marias River to the headwaters.

The further east he rode, the more evidence he saw of the white man's presence in the area. Towns were springing up, whether temporary tent cities thrown up around a gold strike or permanent structures at an important river crossing. The country was filling up.

This was Gros Ventre country and they had always shown friendliness to the whites. The Blackfeet were still set against the whites and the army had yet to push with any great force against them. In spite of his feelings to move on from the village life, he still felt a sense of pride in being part of a people as formidable as the Blackfeet.

Fort Benton stretched along the bank of the Missouri River amid a cluttered landscape. The last time he had been to this fort, which served as the westernmost fur trading post of Auguste Chouteau, it was only that, a fur trading post set strategically on the river. It was not a military compound. Now, it was almost a city with steamboat traffic moving up and down the river.

The structures and walls of the fort itself were made from mud bricks that were now crumbling. Newer buildings were growing up around the walls strangling the deteriorating fort. The loud, hoarse call of steamboat whistles was carried on wind. The fort had become a river port bustling with commerce and immigrants heading into the Montana goldfields.

He was riding toward the fort when a company of cavalry rode out of the fort grounds. He was surprised to see that the army now occupied the fort and he remembered Raven's prediction of the forts and army moving west. It didn't take more than a quick look to see that inside the fort was now military and the old trading post gone.

Buck rode through the town looking around, confused. He had expected a simple trip into the post store and out. Now, there were stores for everything except for what he wanted. Wandering among the clamor of moving people and wagons he finally stopped a fur and leather clad frontiersman and asked if the old trading post still existed.

The man explained that the post had moved out of the walls and directed him to its new location. He followed the directions and found the trading store on the outskirts of the expanding growth. He tied his horses to a hitchrail in front of the store and went inside.

There were several men dressed in miners garb buying supplies. Buck was wearing the army pants;

however, he had exchanged the wool army shirt for one of beaded elk skin that his mother had made for him. Around his neck he wore a decorated bone necklace, combined with his dark skin he looked more Indian than white.

He walked up to the counter carrying the Henry. On the left side of his belt with the handle facing forward was a sheathed knife of Jim Bowie's design. A couple of the men in the store studied the rifle as the Henry had yet to become a prominent firearm in the western end of the Territory.

Buck looked the store over as the sixtyish, gray bearded store man moved to a place in front of him. Buck laid a list on the counter. "Do you have all of these?"

The man read the list and nodded, "Yup." He then looked Buck over with an appraising eye, "You payin' cash or gold? I don't give no credit."

Buck nodded his understanding, "Cash money."

"Good, I can use cash money. With gold I have to sell it to get my money and hope the assayer has a fair scale."

Buck studied a rack of rifles behind the counter and several revolvers lying on the shelf in front of them. One of the revolvers caught his eye.

"What kind of revolver is that? Looks pretty stout."

The store man looked at what Buck was referring to, picked up the gun, and set it down on the counter for Buck to look at. "Remington 1858," he explained. ".44 caliber, most prefer it over the Army Colt. You can even get an extra cylinder so you can have a second loaded and primed."

The store man picked up the revolver and demonstrated by removing the cylinder and then snapping it back in. "Just that easy. Shoot one up and you can snap in a second and be back in business. Comes in mighty handy when Indians are honin' down on yuh."

"How much?"

"With an extra cylinder, twenty dollars. American

dollars, none of that Confederate outhouse wipe them Johnny Rebs keep tryin' to pass off on me."

"You have a holster and belt to go with it?"

"Yup. Ball, powder, and caps too."

"I'll take it and enough ball and caps for a hundred shots."

"That'll make it forty dollars."

"How much for everything, traps and all?"

While the store man was gathering and tallying the lot Buck loaded the Remington, buckled on the belt and dropped the gun in his holster.

The man grinned, "Don't waste much time, do yuh?"

"An empty gun is worthless weight."

"Sixty-five dollars in all."

Buck peeled off the bills and laid them on the counter.

A man standing behind Buck and watching him commented to his partner, "Must be a millionaire."

Buck turned his head and looked at him. "What's it to you?"

The man glared at him, "You don't see that kinda cash money around these parts, unless it's been robbed."

"It's none of your business, but it's what's left of my army pay. Happy, nosy girl?"

The man bristled at the insult, but said no more. His partner went out of the store.

The store man watched the exchange and then asked, "Where you plan to trap? Most everything around this country's been pretty well trapped out."

Ordinarily Buck wouldn't have answered the question, but the old man had been decent to him and besides he'd be back and a friend would always be good to have. "Upper Marias, into the Bitterroots."

"Marias!" the man behind Buck almost shouted it out. "No one traps up there mister, that's Blackfoot country, everyone knows that, unless they're a pilgrim. Them red devils will have your hair before you get two miles in. They got my brother up there."

Buck turned fully around and glared at the man, getting tired of his busybody nature. "Maybe your brother should have stayed where he belonged and not went trespassing into another man's land."

The man returned Buck's glare. "What the . . ., you sound like one of 'em!" He studied Buck with a disdainful eye, "Fact is you *look* like one of 'em."

Buck held the man's eyes for another second. "I am one of 'em."

Just then the man's partner came back in the store. "Hey," he shouted at Buck. "You own that bay horse with the mousy roan next to it."

Buck shifted his attention to the second man, "What if I do?"

The second man looked at his partner, "Del, it's your brother's roan."

Del's head snapped around to look at his partner, "What?"

"This pilgrim's pack horse is Buddy's roan."

Del ran across the room and out the door to look at the horse. Buck knew what was coming next and figured it would be rude to mess up the old man's store. He was starting to get the picture that this Buddy was the fur thief Badger killed.

The man whirled around to face Buck, "That's my brother's horse, the one he was ridin' when the Blackfeet killed him. How'd you get it?"

Buck shrugged, "My brother. Seems the man who was riding it was stealing from his traps and everyone who lives in this country knows that's a killing offense." He gave Del a steady gaze, "Unless they're pilgrims or robbers."

Del knew the comment was throwing his own

words back in his face. He didn't like it.

Del's partner sneered and gestured toward Buck, "Maybe him and his bastard redskin brother killed Buddy. He admitted to being one of 'em. I think we should give him a little of his own Blackfoot treatment and find out."

The two men moved toward Buck in a rush. Swinging the Henry up fast and hard to the right he caught Del's partner in the eye with the barrel. The man slammed his hands over his eyes and screamed as fell to the ground. Del drew a knife as he charged in, holding the knife at belly height.

Holding the Henry in his left hand Buck was unable to bring the bore around on Del's close in rush. In one fluid movement he reached across his body and pulled the Bowie out from the sheath. He swung the heavy blade up and under Del's knife, slamming the razor edge against the incoming knife and the man's hand. With a shriek of pain Del dropped the knife and fell to his knees clamping his good hand over the other trying to stop the flow of blood. His two smaller fingers lay in the dirt with the knife.

Buck wiped the blade off on Del's back as he knelt whimpering on the ground. "Don't call my brother a bastard," Buck said calmly.

Buck turned around to see the store man watching from the doorway. "Figured that was coming and I didn't want to mess up your store."

"Well, I appreciate that, I surely do," the old man replied. "You know I came into this country in twenty-five, trapped with Sublette and knew everyone who was anyone in the fur trade. I've seen your like; you ain't no pilgrim, son." He studied Buck for a silent second, "Blackfoot, huh?"

"Half, Blood. I grew up in the village on the Teton."

"Fierce they are and Bloods are the worst. I was always a little scared of them and shied away from that country. Plenty of trapping among the Snakes, Big Bellies, and Crows, didn't need to push my luck with the Blackfeet."

The two men got up from the ground and staggered away. The old man watched them unmoved and unconcerned. "Army took over the fort last year. They don't like fights and I'd bet a prime beaver pelt to a mule marble that they're going to run to mother on you. Unless you want to end up in the guardhouse, you'd best be heading out."

Showing little concern for the warning Buck shrugged. "I didn't know the army had taken over here."

"Yeah, American Fur Company sold out to them. Figure the army wants it since this here's on the west border of Sioux country and Red Cloud's on the war path."

Buck started packing his supplies on the roan. "What's the story with Red Cloud?"

"He's irate over the whites stomping all over his best hunting grounds. Talk is the Cheyenne behind Dull Knife, and Arapahoe behind Black Bear, have joined ranks with him."

"I'm surprised it took the Cheyenne and Arapahoe this long to get mad about it."

"Wasn't all that much to get mad about when it was just some trappers. Then, some fool found gold and men started pouring in like free day at Sadie's whorehouse. To top it off, some General or Colonel or something name of Carrington started building a series of forts up Charlie Goodnight's Bozeman Trail."

Buck snorted, "Right through everyone's front yard, yeah, that would do it. A friend once predicted that the army would have forts all over this country. Looks like he was right."

Buck threw the canvas tarp over the load and tied it down. "Had a run in with some Sioux a while back, got a pilgrim woman and her youngsters back to Minnesota after her man went to looking like a Sioux arrow factory.

Figured they were on the warpath over that broken Laramie treaty."

"That's part of it."

"I guess building forts would sort of cancel out the treaty all by itself."

"Yeah, Army figures they can take on the lot of 'em. Personally, I think they're biting off a big chew that they're likely to choke on."

"I was in the war and believe me the army has the manpower and better weapons to do it. We beat the Rebel army and there was a lot more of them than Indians. The Sioux have been my people's enemy forever and I'm fine with Red Cloud getting his head handed to him."

The old man nodded, "He might, or Red Cloud might just hand over a couple of army heads. He's a mighty sharp ol' bird. So's Rain In The Face, and that young buck war chief, Crazy Horse."

"I'll give them that, but they've been asking for it for a long time. Stomping on everyone like they were supposed to be the only ones on earth."

The old man grinned, "Sounds like the Blackfeet. Made a lot of enemies they have."

Buck shrugged but made no comment.

"Mind you though, it's the Sioux today, Blackfeet tomorrow. Think on it."

Buck toed the stirrup and mounted the bay. "They have no reason to push my people out of the mountains. There's no gold or farmland to be had up in the high country."

"The Blackfeet have been a thorn in the white man's side ever since Lewis and Clark's expedition."

Buck looked at him, "Meaning?"

"What do most folks do with a thorn when it's stuck in their hide? What happened up in Canada with the blankets?"

Buck frowned at the thought. "Yeah, it's something

to think on." He reined his horse around and headed out of town.

Chapter Seventeen

The May sun reflected with blinding effect off the remaining snow as Buck made his way out of the mountains. The snow still lay deep above the timberline, but was quickly melting in the lower elevations. Streams were running at full bank from the melting snow.

Green grass and wildflowers filled the lower mountain meadows. Elk cows had calves clinging to their sides and deer hid their spotted fawns in the long grass. As in all nature, spring was a time of rebirth, even so, death hung continuously at the fringes. Wolves and mountain lions stalked the mountain meadows in search of a calf or fawn whose inattentive mother wandered too far away.

Grizzlies were coming out of hibernation hungry and sporting foul moods. Sows had cubs ambling clumsily along as they searched for food to replenish the six-month fast that took fat bodies and rendered them down to a mass of shedding, sagging fur. The great bears sought out deer and elk carcasses from those animals that had not survived the snow and cold. They dug for ground squirrels and ate vegetation, constantly hungry for anything.

The roan pack horse carried two full packs of fur. The trapping had been good and each bundle held the pelts of several different animals. Buck had used the traps for beaver, otter, and wolves while building dozens of deadfalls and setting snares for fox, mink, and marten.

He intended to first make his way to the Teton River and visit his family and friends before heading down to Fort Benton. He wanted to see how well or poorly they had faired through the winter. Winter saw the villages break up into smaller groups of twenty to thirty lodges with each moving well apart from the others to make winter survival easier. In the spring the groups would come back together to form the main village. Winters were a hard time and it was during the below zero nights that those who were going to die did so, especially if the food had run low.

He had thought long and hard about that last conversation he had with the old trapper at the store. The future was always an unknown entity; however, the one thing he knew for certain was that the mass of white people was pushing ever farther westward. Change was coming and he needed to help his people to understand that. Going to war against the white soldiers would write a death sentence to the tribe as a whole.

He had figured the Sioux were angry over the broken treaty, but over time the problem had grown beyond that. To make the Cheyenne and Arapahoe join their forces with the Sioux, an unusual show of unity, indicated the immensity of the effort to stop the white advancement. He wondered how many other tribes would join them. He knew the Crow would never join with the Sioux; there had been too much animosity between the two nations to ever let them get along.

The three nations together would put up a fight, that was for sure. They would win a few battles, but they didn't have the kind of power the army had. He had seen what Sherman did in his march to the sea, leaving a sixty mile-wide wake of death and destruction behind him. Like the Confederacy, the Indians would win one here and there, but in the end lose the war and everything with it.

The only advantage the warring Indians had over the southerners was that they could pick up and move at the drop of a hat. They didn't have farms and homes full of possessions to bog them down in one spot where they could be easily crushed. The Indian had a huge open country to maneuver in and trying to pin them down in it might be a task the army had not anticipated. Atlanta, Georgia was not the Dakota and Montana plains. Red Cloud might hand over a few heads at that.

The Teton River village was again filled with racks of drying buffalo and pegged-out hides. The tribe had completed the spring hunt and spirits were high as everyone now had a full belly. His friends came out to meet him and compliment him on his fine catch of furs. Backs were slapped all around.

Riding up to the lodge of He Who Fights, he found his mother sitting in front of the buffalo hide lodge working on an elk skin. She came to her feet and embraced him. Nuttah was sitting next to her mother imitating what she did with a piece of hide. She squealed and embraced his legs shouting, "Brother."

He Who Fights came up from his horse herd and welcomed Buck into his lodge. "Will you stay long, Buckingham Palace?"

"A short time," Buck answered. "I will be going down to Fort Benton to sell my pelts and then going on east. Red Cloud is making war on the whites and I am interested in seeing what is going on."

He Who Fights nodded, "I do not like the Sioux or Red Cloud. I do not like the army seizers either. Who will you fight with?"

"Maybe, nobody. If I have to choose, I would probably scout for the army against our old enemy."

"It would be a difficult choice for me."

"Let's hope you never have to make it."

"Unpack your horses and put them with my horses. Stay and eat with us and be with us a few suns at least."

Buck nodded as he began to pull the rope hitch from the roan. "How did everyone come through the winter?"

"No one died except one old woman. We had enough meat."

"Did Bighorn Chief and Swift Runner go the Marias River camp this year?"

"As they always do. Your grandfather went with them. He is tired and has let a younger man take his place as chief. We watch over him as he has always refused to take a new wife. He does not want us to treat him like a child so he goes with Swift Runner and stays in his own lodge. He is back now. Make sure you visit him."

"I will see him. Are Bighorn Chief and Swift Runner still angry with each other? They were trading some angry words before I left."

"They do not speak. Bighorn Chief still thinks Swift Runner is foolish to trust anything the whites would promise. Swift Runner thinks Bighorn Chief is blinded by his stubbornness and wrong about the whites. We will see who is right as time goes on."

"Yes, we will. What does my grandfather think?"

He Who Fights shrugged, "He says he is old and ready to return to the Old Man and doesn't care about it."

"He has seen much and still feels that he has been shamed. He knows our life is changing and it cannot be stopped. I can understand why he doesn't care."

Buck was bent over placing the second fur pack on the ground when something heavy landed on his back. Buck went down rolling and sprang up on his feet with the Remington in his hand. He looked to see Badger grinning at him.

"You are getting careless, brother," Badger taunted Buck. "I could have had your scalp."

"I heard you coming," Buck came back at him. "You made as much noise as a love-sick bull buffalo. You are the one getting careless."

Badger laughed. "I think we are both lying."

Buck holstered the gun. "I think you're right." The brothers then embraced.

Badger pointed at Buck's hip, "I see you have one of the white man's short guns."

"Yes, they come in pretty handy in the white man's world. Speaking of, I met the man whose brother you killed. The one that had the roan horse you gave me. He tried to kill me because of it."

Badger looked Buck up and down, "You don't look

dead. I guess he did not succeed."

"He got to meet my Bowie intimately."

With a shrug Badger grinned, "I told you I killed a trapper for that horse, what did you expect taking him among the whites?"

"You knew where I was going with that horse, you old woman."

"I knew it would give you a chance to count a coup. You haven't had one in a long time."

"Well, I got two."

Badger held his hands up and spread his arms out, "See! What are you complaining about?"

He Who Fights grinned and broke in, "All right, children, you have argued enough. I can find women's work for you both if you have nothing to do."

Hurit grinned and held the elk skin up to Buck, "Here, you can sew this and then make food. Badger, go and scrape the buffalo hides."

Badger grabbed Buck by the arm, "Next they will have us wearing women's clothes. I think we should go take your horses to the herd." Together they hurried away leading the horses.

Husband and wife looked at each other and laughed.

Badger and Buck slowed their hurried walk and began to laugh. "Why not stay with us?" Badger asked.

Buck looked up and pointed at an eagle circling on the wind drafts in the blue sky above them. "Why doesn't he stay in one place?"

"You are restless, Buckingham."

"I am that. The war I was in changed me. It was not like any fight we ever had with the Shoshone or Gros Ventre." Buck paused as his mind ran quickly over the scenes of the war years. "It was total destruction, thousands dead, and I still don't understand what all the fighting was about, except that the south wanted to break away from the north."

"We fight for honor and hunting grounds," Badger said. "Is that not the same?"

Buck shook his head, "Not at all. You can't even imagine what it was like and I hope you will never see it."

The pair sobered as they continued to walk, leading the horses. They reached the herd and let the horses go on their own into it.

Buck watched the horses as they walked away. "It made me restless, made me want to see what else is out there."

"Where will you go?"

Buck looked up into the sky, "East, north, south."

Badger put his hand on Buck's shoulder and gave him a feigned expression of concern. "You should seek the wise counsel of Dirt Eater. He will give you direction."

Buck slowly turned his head and gave Badger an incredulous look.

"What? You do not find the words and the . . ." Badger struck a pose with his nose in the air and eyes closed as he minced an effeminate couple of steps, "holy walk of Dirt Eater enlightening?" Badger stopped and tried to look at Buck seriously while fighting down a laugh.

"You do that quite well, the walk that is; maybe you *should* wear women's clothes."

"You avoided the question."

"I think Dirt Eater is crazy and evil. He supported Jules and his renegades and even prayed for them. He claimed they were holy men. He is as evil as my father."

Badger turned serious. "You believe he is a threat to the safety of the village?"

Buck nodded. "The Braves should watch him. Maybe not today, but one day he will do us harm. He hates me and will do something to get back at me for humiliating him at the meeting."

"He has not the courage to fight you."

"It won't be me; it will be someone who can't fight

back. He is a coward." Buck stopped talking and stared hard at the ground.

"What is it? You look like you just thought of something."

"Just something Bighorn Chief said to me last summer. I hadn't thought about it until you brought up Dirt Eater. He said I would one day gut Dirt Eater like a deer and I would again cross paths with my father. He said he had dreamed it."

"But your father is dead."

Buck looked up and locked eyes with his brother, "Is he?"

Chapter Eighteen

Buck rode into Fort Benton with his pelts. Pulling up at the post store he untied the fur packs from the roan's packsaddle and carried them inside the store. The old trapper turned storekeeper was behind the counter and cast an approving eye over the collection of furs. Buck laid the furs on the wooden floor.

The old man came out from behind the counter and started sorting through the pelts separating the different animals. "You do nice work. You ain't no pilgrim so I won't play games with you and just quote you the fair market price. Beaver's not what it was in the rendezvous days, you know that of course."

Buck watched the old man's eyes as he calculated in his head what each pelt was worth. There were other men in the store watching curiously and listening in on their business. The old man looked at the observers and frowned. He took a piece of paper from the counter, wrote down a number and handed to Buck.

Buck read it and nodded.

"You want it in cash or trade?"

"Both."

Buck went about picking out the things he wanted and set them on the counter.

"Got some of them rimfire .44 cartridges for that Henry of yours. Been seeing a few of them rifles around now and figured I ought to carry some of that ammunition."

"Got four boxes?"

"Got plenty." He set four boxes on the counter. "That it?"

Buck looked it all over and nodded. The store man tallied up the cost and then opened an iron box and counted out some bills and coins. He laid the money on the counter. "That squares us."

Buck picked up the money and put it in his pocket.

"Say, you gotta name?" the old man asked.

Buck grinned, "Most folks do." He put his hand out to the old man, "Buck Drake."

The old man shook his hand, "Jake Cullen. Nice making your acquaintance. Where you headin' now?"

"South and west."

"Bound and determined to wade into that Sioux and Cheyenne foo-fer-ah down that way, aren't yuh?"

Buck chuckled, "Getting a little dull around here."

"Well, it won't be for long. Hear tell the army's fixin' to build a new fort right down from here on the Sun River and another further down toward Bozeman Pass."

"What's all that about?"

"Folks have been complaining that they're scared of the Blackfeet and want protection. Like I told you last summer, they'll be breathing down your folks' necks pretty quick."

Buck nodded as he gathered his things together. "Likely. Some of the elders are talking about it and some like Swift Runner want peace. Others don't want to give in."

"They'll all have to give in eventually."

Buck nodded again, "Likely."

Buck began to carry his purchases out and load them in the panniers hung over the sawbuck on the roan. Jake gave him a hand. "Say, that reminds me, seein' your roan there. A couple of them army boys come over here right after you left looking for who it was cut up those troublemakers. I told them it had been a fair fight; the losers started it and got what they asked for. The army boys figured that was good enough and left."

"Thanks."

"Yeah, those boys you cut up came back in once after that. The one, that Del, was sportin' only two fingers and a thumb on half a hand and the other had a patch over his eye."

"Know where they went?"

"One said something about Bozeman. That Del fella's partner is named Abe. They're cousins, last name of Yarrow."

"Probably never see them again." Buck finished tying down the load and then mounted his horse.

"You figure on ever headin' back this way again, Buck?"

"You never know where a man's paths will lead him. I just might."

Jake grinned, "Providin' your top knot ain't blowin' in the breeze off some Sioux's coup stick."

"If he can take it, then he deserves it." Bucked grinned as he shook hands with the old man and moved his horses out onto the road.

His route followed south on Graham Road toward the Big Belt Mountains. Breaking off the road, he continued on through the gap between the two Belt Mountain ranges. He crossed the Shields River and tapped into what was known as Bridger's Route through the Bighorn Mountains. He skirted Crow country without an incident.

By the time he cleared the Bighorns, August had laid its suffocating heat across the prairie. Creeks were drying up and the sparse grass was brown and brittle. He had learned by talking to others along the way that Fort Reno had been built on the Powder River north of long established Fort Laramie to protect travelers on the Bozeman Road.

Colonel Carrington's detail that Jake had spoken of had built Fort Reno and then Fort Phil Kearny north of it on Little Piney Creek. This one was smack in Red Cloud's front yard and he wasn't too happy about it. A third was going up to the north and west of it on the Bighorn River.

Buck was in Dull Knife's Cheyenne country and they were now part of the Red Cloud army. He didn't expect to be as lucky avoiding them as he had with the Crow. He felt it might be in his best interest to make for Fort Reno and find out what was going on before venturing into trouble. He left the Bridger route and headed east, cross-country toward the fort.

The country spread out flat and brown before him. Mounds of finely ground dirt covered with scurrying red ants rose up in between jagged chunks of red rocks protruding out of the hot sand. The sun beat down and smothered him like a heated blanket thrown over his head. The high country to the west got hot, but not like this. He put his hand on the leather-covered saddle horn and jerked it away, finding it hot as a stove top.

Reaching the crest of a low row of hills he could see the fort in the distance. A crooked green line of trees wound its way across the prairie on the far side of the fort marking the course of the Powder River. The fort was a simple square of upright logs, the inside walls lined with structures. He moved off the hill quickly to prevent being sky-lined to the Cheyenne and headed toward the fort.

Reaching the open gate he pulled up as a dozen blue uniformed cavrlymen rode out preceded by two Indian scouts. He nudged the horse forward jerking the rope attached to the roan's halter, who had taken the moment to fall into an exhausted heat-induced sleep. A pair of guards with Spencer rifles watched him as he rode into the compound. This was a place of safety for travelers and because of that he was not challenged by the guards.

He stopped next to one of the guards. "Who's in charge here?'

"That would be Captain Proctor," the guard answered.

"Where?"

The guard pointed to an adobe building across the compound, "Captain's headquarters."

"I see you have Indian scouts, what tribe? I don't

recognize them."

The soldier shrugged, "Heck if I know, all Indians look alike to me."

Buck nodded and moved his horse on. Low-slung log buildings with dirt and sod covered roofs made up the majority of the structures lining the inside walls of the compound. A few were made of sunbaked adobe including the Captain's headquarters.

He rode slowly through the busy compound until he reached the adobe the guard had pointed out. Stepping out of the saddle he wrapped the roan's lead rope around the saddle horn. The roan sighed, lowered its head and fell back to sleep.

Buck looked around at the men in blue uniforms who were ignoring him as they went about their duties. They all shared the same dull-eyed exhausted look brought on by the intense heat. A familiar voice carried across the yard as a man called for help from the medical staff.

Buck looked in the direction to see a uniformed man lying on the ground with a man bearing six stripes on each sleeve standing over him. Two men hurried out of another building and up to the prone soldier. They picked him up and carried the unconscious man back into the building.

The Sergeant then walked toward him and as he did Buck was struck with a memory of the man's face and walk. He was a few years older now and gray hair that had once been red stuck out from under his blue hat. As he walked by Buck, paying no attention to him, Buck spoke out, "What happened to him, melt in this heat?"

"Aye, sun stroke," he answered with an Irish brogue. "They're not used to it."

"Probably those *stupid* wool uniforms they have to wear. You'd think the army would figure out that men can't wear such as that out here in the summer."

The Sergeant glanced up at Buck with a frown and

continued on, ignoring the comment. He didn't like to hear anything that was not supportive of his chosen career and home. He suddenly stopped mid-step, turned and stared at Buck. "I know you."

Buck grinned, "I should hope so. Fort Bridger ring a bell? They were going to hang an Indian and a Frenchman."

The Sergeant's eyes suddenly filled with recognition, "Well, the saints preserve us if it ain't Buck Drake." He put his hand out and the two men shook hands. "I see you survived the war."

Buck laughed, "Looks like we both did. Good to see you again, Sergeant Duffy."

"Aye, but its barely you're seein' me after that affair. What about you? You don't look like you're in the army anymore?"

"No. I left the army behind in what was left of Georgia."

"Want to join up again?"

Buck shook his head, "Not a chance."

Duffy grinned, "All right, well, since you're not in the army anymore, my friends call me Tim."

"Okay, Tim, but if you're in the market for a scout I'd be interested."

"Might be. We've got some Omaha's scouting for us. I'll take you in to see Captain Proctor, he'd be the one to say yay or nay."

They began to walk when Duffy asked, "How did Ravenel come out?"

Buck shook his head, "Couldn't find him after the war. We got split up just before Gettysburg. We were working together in Hooker's command and then they made us sharp shooters and sent me down to Sherman. I have no idea if he made it or not. I searched for him after the war with no luck. I'm thinking he died at Gettysburg."

Duffy frowned at the memory. "I was there, my

God what a horror. I'm sorry to hear about Ravenel, he was a good sort and quite a fighter, for a Frenchmen."

Buck only nodded his head as Duffy opened the door in the adobe wall and they went in. The room was dimly lit and noticeably cooler than outside. Several men bearing officer insignia on their shirts were busy going about whatever officers did in a remote fort without any of the eastern niceties. At a desk sat a man pushing his fingers against his temples and looking like he was in pain.

Duffy walked up to the desk. "Captain Proctor, are you all right, sir?"

Proctor looked up at him through eyes that were only slits. "Cursed headache, Sergeant. Between the Indians and this heat, I'm about to lose my mind."

"Yes sir, it is hot. Say, Captain, could we stand to take on another scout? A former army man who has fought Indians and knows his business?"

Proctor shifted his pained gaze onto Buck and studied him. He took in the beaded elk skin shirt, and then scanned down to the store bought pants and the pistol on his hip. "You don't look like an Omaha or completely a white man either."

"I'm half Blood."

Proctor's humorless face scrunched up a bit tighter, "Half blood? If that's a medical joke I'm not in the mood for it."

"Bloods," Duffy broke in, "are a tribe of the Blackfeet. Kainai or Bloods are what they are called, sir."

"Oh. Sure, we can use all the help we can get. He's in your and Lieutenant Brighton's patrol. Take . . . umm, what's your name?"

"Buck Drake."

"Take Mr. Drake and get him settled in with the other scouts."

"Yes sir." Duffy turned to leave.

Buck said to the Captain, "The next time your men

go to the river for water have them strip a bunch of willow bark. Chew the inside lining of the bark."

"Thank you, Mr. Drake; however I am not a beaver."

"It kills headache pain. My people have used it for hundreds of years."

Buck began to walk out with Duffy when Proctor called after them. "Sergeant Duffy, send out a water detail and tell them to bring back willow bark. I'm willing to try anything at this point."

"Yes sir," Duffy answered with a grin.

Duffy stopped a twenty year old Corporal, "Corporal, Captain wants a water detail right away, go organize it. And, strip a goodly amount of willow bark and bring it to the Captain."

"Willow bark, Sergeant?"

"Did I say question the Captain or did I say to just get it?"

"Yes, Sergeant." The Corporal quickly left to organize the party.

Duffy shook his head, "Kids. Gotta question everything. Let's head over to the Mess and get a cup of coffee and I'll explain what is going on here."

They walked into a building with several long tables. Each table had a continuous split log bench seat running the full length of each side. The cook was standing beside a hot wood stove with sweat streaking down his face. He poured two cups from an army-size metal coffee pot and handed them to Duffy.

Duffy and Buck sat down opposite each other. "I hear tell that Red Cloud and Dull Knife have been on the war path," Buck said as he sipped at the coffee.

Duffy nodded. "The Sioux and Cheyenne are upset about the white men crossing their hunting grounds on the way to the gold fields."

"In violation of the Laramie Treaty."

Duffy frowned, "Aye."

"And, to top it off the army is building forts on the same ground."

Duffy again frowned, "The powers that be decided a series of forts needed to be built up the Bozeman Road to protect the travelers. They sent Colonel Carrington with seven hundred men and over two hundred and twenty wagons to Fort Laramie to start up the road building forts along the way. I came in with them.

"Our timing wasn't the best for our arrival at Fort Laramie. It seems that the Interior Department had gathered together some of the big chiefs, including Red Cloud himself, and Rain In The Face, for a peace talk. They were trying to get the Sioux to sell the land for the road and forts."

Buck shook his head, "And here comes the whole bunch of you to build forts on their land before they had said yes or no."

"Aye, all seven hundred of us, wagons and all. It was the worst possible timing and Carrington had no idea the negotiations were going on."

"How did the chiefs react to that?"

"Like turning a skunk loose at High Mass. Red Cloud was furious, he said that the army was already stealing the land before they had said yes or no to the deal. The chiefs all marched out declaring it an act of war and they've been on the warpath ever since."

Buck scowled, "And the politicians and army can't understand why the Sioux are fighting."

"Just as Carrington didn't know about the peace talks going on. I don't think Fort Laramie knew he was coming either. He had orders they hadn't heard anything about."

Buck huffed, "The right hand didn't know what the left hand was doing. That sounds about right. Has this fort had any fights?"

"We got here to Fort Reno and relieved the boys who had been stationed here all along and sent them back to Fort Laramie. There were no tears of regret in that bunch I'll tell you that.

"Right after we got here with Carrington, Dull Knife and his Cheyennes came to call on him. They made like they were against Red Cloud, but it was only a ruse. The next day they ran off a couple hundred of our horses."

Buck snorted, "These eastern boys had better learn to protect their horses or the cavalry will be infantry in short order."

"A couple of days later we had some wagons with soldiers and civilians come through here bound for Fort Phil Kearny. They were advised not to go on, but they had orders to be in Phil Kearny and pushed on. They got attacked at the Crazy Woman fork of the Powder.

"The party was kept pinned down until a column from Phil Kearny, heading here for supplies, stumbled onto them and fought the Indians off. It was pure luck. A Lieutenant and an enlisted man were killed. That's been it for fights so far."

"Sioux or Cheyenne?"

"The Omahas said it was both."

"Yeah, talk is they're plenty mad. My understanding is that Black Bear and his Arapaho have sided with Red Cloud and Dull Knife too."

Duffy frowned, "That's bad isn't it?"

"Well, let's put it this way. Bringing Red Cloud and Dull Knife together would be like putting Grant and Lee in the same room against a common enemy. Then, adding Black Bear into the mix would be like throwing Sherman or Stonewall Jackson in for good measure."

"We're in trouble aren't we?"

"I would say the army has its work cut out for them. These chiefs aren't the ignorant savages easterners and the army like to make them out to be. They're Generals in their own right. Our military leaders could well learn a lesson on battle tactics from these warrior Generals."

"You still want to stick around with all that against us?"

"Why not? There's no love lost between the Blackfeet and Sioux, and if the Cheyenne and Arapaho want to side in with them they can be my enemies too."

Duffy studied Buck for a long moment and then asked, "Since you're both Indian and white, and have fought Indians and white men, how do you feel about the situation?"

"Mixed feelings. I don't know what Washington has planned for this country, so from the Indian side I'm distrustful. This Laramie business shows that my distrust is not misplaced. I also know how the white soldier feels. He's here doing a job others have told him needs doing. He doesn't want to die with a Sioux arrow in his guts."

"And if it comes down to choosing a side?"

Buck looked directly at Duffy, "Against Red Cloud I'll be riding with the blue. If the army comes against my people, I'll be putting on war paint."

Chapter Nineteen

Fort Reno had a two-fold purpose, to serve as a place of safety for travelers following the old Bozeman Trail, which was being converted into the Bozeman Road, and as a supply point for Fort Phil Kearny. Fort Reno cavalry patrols made regular rounds of the area and escorted wagons. They did not directly seek out confrontations with the *hostiles*, as the Cheyenne, Arapaho, and Sioux were referred to as a whole. The army's presence here was meant for protection, not to garrison an attack force.

Buck had been a scout with Fort Reno for two weeks when he rode out with Lieutenant Brighton, Sergeant Duffy, and a twenty trooper escort to intercept a supply train from Fort Laramie and escort it to the fort. Two Omaha scouts had split out, one riding to the east and one to the west, to spot any ambushes that may have been set for them. Buck rode in advance of the column.

Three fast rifle shots rang out causing Brighton to bring the column to a halt with all eyes scanning for an attack. A war party suddenly burst out from a west side hollow between the hills.

There was no time to take cover or form a defensive line as Brighton and Duffy shouted orders for the men to hold the column line and fire from their saddles. Each trooper was armed with a repeating Spencer rifle. The first volley of trooper shots echoed hard off the hills filling the air with black powder smoke and clearing five Indian horses of their riders. Buck jerked his horse around.

A dozen warriors galloped around the front of the column to come up on their east flank. Intent on their direction and target, the Indians did not see the lone rider as they cut in between him and the troopers under fire. Buck's Henry was up and shouldered. He killed the first warrior before they realized their blunder. As they turned their heads to look he killed a second. The cluster of Indians broke and scattered.

A scattering of heavy rifle reports continued for another minute before silence came back over the prairie. Buck caught up to the column as Brighton and Duffy checked over the men and regrouped them. Two men had minor wounds.

The troopers had held their ground without fear. The men who replaced the original Fort Reno enlisted men were veterans of the war. They had faced enough enemy fire to stand up under it. Several of the troopers were what the Union referred to as "galvanized yankees"—they had been Confederate prisoners of war who joined the Union to fight out west. Like most Rebels, they were quick to fight and showed no fear.

Buck met up with the Omaha scout who had ridden to the east. The scout said he had killed one of the attackers as they fled past him. The one he had killed was Cheyenne. Buck and the scout looked over another dead Indian the retreating party had missed. He was Cheyenne as well. They reported that to Brighton.

"At least there weren't any Sioux mixed in," Brighton responded.

"The Sioux are fighting up north," the Omaha scout said. "The Sioux have said they will not come south of Crazy Woman and the army is not to go north of it."

Brighton nodded his acknowledgement and returned to the head of the patrol that Duffy had reorganized. The two wounded men were patched up, but refused to return to the fort indicating that they were perfectly capable of finishing the patrol. The Omaha scout who had ridden off to the west did not return.

Buck rode up next to Brighton, "I'd like to go find the scout who didn't come back. If he's wounded he'll need help, if he's dead, he's earned a proper burial."

Brighton nodded, "Go ahead and find him. Catch up

when you can." Brighton ordered the column on.

Buck waited until the column had passed. He looked to see the remaining Omaha scout sitting on his horse looking at him. "I want to find my brother," Buck said to him.

The Omaha continued to look at him. Among the Omaha scouts there had been a sense of distrust directed at Buck because he was Blackfeet, who were known to be enemies to whites and Indians alike. They were not sure what to make of him or if someone who was Blackfeet could be trusted. The Omaha were one of the first plains tribes to sign peace treaties with the whites. They had lived in peace with the white man and now scouted for his army.

"Why do you call Strong Tree your brother?"

"We all ride together, we all eat together, and we fight our common enemy together. That makes Strong Tree my brother."

"I thought the Blackfeet had no brothers except their own people."

Buck turned his horse. "I am going to find Strong Tree and bring him back so he can be wrapped in his blanket and buried with his weapons. I will not leave my brother to be eaten by the birds. You can ride with a Blood or go join the patrol." Buck kicked his horse and moved out to the west to find him.

He rode along sorting out the mixed horse tracks. The Cheyenne had run over the scout's trail, but Buck was able to pick out the tracks of Strong Tree's shod army horse. He soon found the scout lying dead with several arrows sticking out of him. There had been shots, but he had no bullet wounds, so it was he who had fired the shots before being killed. His rifle was gone, which was expected as the Cheyenne would not have left it, but it was those shots that saved them.

Buck stepped off his horse and up to the body. He broke off the arrows and picked the small man up in his arms. He was about to lay Strong Tree's body over his saddle when the second scout rode up to him leading a Cheyenne horse.

He stopped beside Buck. "There is blood back over there. Strong Tree killed one. Put our brother on his enemy's horse and he will be honored."

Buck carried the body to the horse and laid him over the blanket covered saddle. The scout watched and then stared at Buck again. He put his hand out to Buck. "I am Iron Horse, I once rode the train to Washington to meet the President. My people were impressed that I had no fear of the Iron Horse and called me so."

Buck shook his hand. "I have been to Washington as well. I fought in the great war."

Iron Horse nodded. "Let us take our brother back."

"You take him back and I will finish with the patrol as they will need one of us. When we get back, you and I will bury our brother."

Iron Horse nodded. He turned his horse and headed back to the road leading the horse bearing the body.

Buck mounted and turned in the opposite direction to rejoin the patrol.

***

The never-ending summer continued to wear the men down under the pressure of unrelenting heat and strangling dust. The water in the river became brackish and caused several men in the fort to become sick from drinking it. Hunters killed game, yet for the population of Fort Reno it was never enough. Supply trains came up from Fort Laramie on an irregular basis accompanied by soldiers and then met by Fort Reno soldiers and escorted in. Life in the frontier fort was rife with boredom, poor food, and exhaustion.

Regular patrols continued to make the rounds of the area. A few minor skirmishes were fought with the Cheyenne; however, most of the Cheyenne had moved north to join Red Cloud and concentrate their fight with the army in that pivotal area.

Immigrants made it as far as Fort Reno where they were advised not to go further north. Even though Forts Phil Kearney and C.F. Smith were along the Bozeman, the threat from Indians was too great to be controlled and safety could not be guaranteed. Some travelers turned back while others took alternate trails to the west.

October came in with a turning of the leaves along the river and the welcome coolness of autumn. The soldiers reveled in the relief as the heat diminished; however, autumn was a short season on the prairie and dove directly into winter. The misery of summer's heat was soon replaced with the misery of winter's ice, snow, and sub-zero temperatures.

Where the men had earlier sought out any speck of shade and cursed the relentless pounding of the summer sun, they now sought out the thawing heat of glowing wood stoves. Only a few months before the cooks had suffered working over hot stoves with outside temperatures topping one hundred degrees. Now, they were envied for their constant proximity to warmth.

Buck and the Omaha scouts were the only men to never complain about the weather. They were men who lived on the land and accepted all that nature threw at them as merely a part of the life they had always known. In their favor was the fact they were free to wear their own clothes and were not regulated to official army-issued clothing. In the summer they dressed cooler, in the winter they wrapped in buffalo coats.

The end of December found no Christmas cheer in Fort Reno. The men grew evermore sullen as they thought of their families preparing for the yuletide season while they sat in frozen misery on the God forsaken blizzard-swept plains of the wild country. The only break in the monotony were the patrols between blizzards and wood cutting along the frozen Powder River. Freezing on patrol was no better than freezing in the fort, but it was a change at least. Spirits were low and dove to a lower point two days before Christmas when a rider came into the fort.

A blizzard was driving fiercely across the prairie that day when John Phillips rode in through the gates frozen to the leather of his saddle. Bundled in a snow-covered buffalo coat, heavy clothes, and buffalo boots, the man made an eerie sight resembling the reputed snow monster of Tibet.

Phillips quickly told the men the tale of Captain Fetterman's demise at the hands of the hostiles. His entire command had been lured into a trap and wiped out. He was carrying a message from Colonel Carrington to Fort Laramie for reinforcements and also needed to reach the telegraph at Horseshoe Station to send the message east. Once fed and warmed, he set off again into the teeth of the storm.

The news of the army's greatest defeat thus far in Red Cloud's war sunk the soldiers' spirits deeper into the boots covering their frozen feet. They were convinced that they would never get back home and they would all die riddled with arrows in this frozen, desolate land.

Buck, Iron Horse, and the other scouts stayed to themselves in the scout's quarters. Christmas was something totally foreign to them and they could not understand the significance the soldiers put on it. The first Buck had heard of Christmas was from Raven and Kai. They had explained it to him, but it still held no particular significance for him.

The thought brought Buck's thinking around to his lost friends as he sat on the edge of his bunk. He wondered how and where his friends had died. It was likely at Gettysburg, though not for certain. There were so many battles after it that they could have died anywhere. He pictured their bodies lying in some farm field lost and unclaimed like so many others had been.

The thought disturbed him and he shook it from his head. A lot of men had died and his friends had only been two more. He was lucky to have survived and he could have easily been one of those bodies bloated and foul with crows squawking his epitaph.

Buck looked at Iron Horse and watched him deftly roll a cigarette. "What do you think about this Fetterman business?"

Iron Horse struck a match with his thumb nail and lit the cigarette. Throwing the spent match toward the wood pile beside the glowing red stove he shrugged. "The army chiefs take the Sioux too lightly. They believe that because Indians do not wear uniforms they cannot fight. I have no good feelings toward Red Cloud or his chiefs, or Dull Knife and his, but I know they are warriors."

Buck nodded his agreement. "I don't think Red Cloud took too well to that fort going up in his front yard."

"There will be more. My people saw it was useless to fight the white man. There are few of us and many of them, we would have been wiped out, so we made peace and they have left us alone. Red Cloud has not learned that yet."

"My people are like him,' Buck said. "They have always fought and will eventually have to learn that they are outnumbered."

Iron Horse finished his cigarette in silence and then tossed his cigarette butt at the stove. "The Blackfeet are warriors, but they have made too many enemies, it will be their ruin."

"We have some chiefs who are talking peace and accepting the white expansion. Others want to fight on."

Iron Horse nodded, "Fighting is good. You have to know when to stop fighting though. I once heard a man say that a wise man picks his fights. I think that is true."

Buck got up and poured a cup of coffee from the

blue pot on the stove top. The fluid rolled out steaming, black, and thick. It reminded him of the tar used in the east for streets. He stared silently into the cup for several seconds. "Sometimes a man has a fight thrust on him and he has no choice. I fought in the eastern war because I had no choice and once I was in it, I fought to stay alive and killed many enemies. Two good friends died there. I will choose my fights when I can. Still, if one is forced on me, I will kill again."

Iron Horse lay down and pulled his buffalo coat around him. "A man does what he must." In a second the Omaha was asleep.

Buck pulled on his buffalo coat and snugged his battered old hat down on his head. Picking up the coffee cup he left the room and stepped out into the cold. The snow had let up, yet the leaden gray sky promised more. The wind blew cold against his face chilling the skin above his short beard. Deep snow covered the surrounding hills but it had been tramped down to brown frozen mud and slush inside the fort. He sipped at the coffee as it quickly cooled in the below zero air.

Duffy came across the compound toward him. The Sergeant was dressed in a heavy wool uniform coat with the golden stripes on each shoulder. On his head was a heavy fur hat. Buck grinned at the Irishman as he got within speaking range. "Is that a regulation hat Sergeant Duffy?"

"Actually it is, Scout Drake." He laughed, "Formal today, aren't we?"

Buck only laughed.

"Merry Christmas to you, Buck."

Buck looked at him, "Is that today?"

"You don't know it's Christmas?"

Buck shrugged which barely moved his wooly black coat. "Blackfeet don't have Christmas."

"You're better off. The boys are mighty lonesome

for home today. Captain wants to honor the day, but he's got little to work with. It's a time for family togetherness where we come from and being away from family today is hard."

"The same kind of feeling was on the men this time of year during the war. It must be important."

"It depends on how you look at it. My family is away in Ireland and it's not a good time for them there with the oppression of the English and the plague. I'm better off here, even at Fort Reno, than there."

The two men stood in silence for another minute before Buck spoke again. "There must not be many soldiers left in Fort Phil Kearny after Fetterman's company got wiped out. Think they've got a chance?"

"They got a smattering of reinforcements back a month or so ago. Surely, not enough though. Reports are that they have been having almost daily skirmishes with the hostiles. Every wood cutting crew is attacked."

"The politicians in Washington are too busy pushing for higher seats in the re-forming government to care about lowly soldiers in the field."

Duffy smiled without humor, "You seem to have learned a bit about how the government works."

"I've kept my eyes and ears open. Raven knew the workings of the government and we talked a lot about it. The army Generals aren't any better than the politicians."

"Aye, there's the truth. I hate to speak ill of the army, it's been a good home and career to me, but we out here seem to have been forgotten in the rush for power."

"I'll bet Carrington has his hands full and they'll drop the whole Fetterman mess square in his lap. Never mind he had no support from his superiors, it'll be his fault."

"As I said before, I came in through Fort Laramie with the Colonel. Never spoke with him, but he seemed a man fit for the job. Sure, he's new to this country, but he was wise enough to understand the forces against him and he takes care of his men."

Buck took a drink from the cup and made a face. "This stuff is bad enough hot, it's downright evil when cold." He tossed the remains of the cup out onto the ground.

Duffy thought aloud as he stared out over the fort walls, "I wonder if Phillips made it?"

"Probably. I've heard enough about Phillips to know he's plenty tough. If the country swells up with troopers I guess he got through."

"You've heard that Sherman has been put in charge of the Western front?"

Buck shook his head, "No. I served under him in the war. He treated the Rebs fairly at the surrender."

"He wants a quick end to the Indian resistance. Killing them all if need be. Sheridan has been killing Indians down south and he has become Sherman's right hand man."

Buck held Duffy's eyes, "Sheridan?"

"Aye."

Buck cursed under his breath. "Sheridan believes in total destruction, like the burning of the Shenandoah Valley. Destroy the food sources, burn the homes, and the enemy will cave in, that's Sheridan's policy."

"Aye, *The Burning* they called it, and he's bringing that policy west."

Buck stared into his empty cup and the coffee residue turned to frozen crystals that reflected the feeling in his heart. "God help us all."

Chapter Twenty

Red Cloud's warriors settled into their camps for the winter after the Fetterman fight. They put their war away until spring knowing that the soldiers could do little during the deep snow and cold time. The same conditions also stopped the white wagons and trespassers. It would be time to resume the war when the weather was warm again.

In January, the officers at Fort Reno were shocked to see Colonel Carrington and his staff, consisting of several wagons and men, coming into the fort plowing through deep snow and sub-zero temperatures. Accompanying him were his wife, and the wife of Lieutenant Grummond, her husband having been killed with Fetterman. One of the wagons carried the Lieutenant's coffin as his wife was taking him back to Tennessee for burial. The coffin was brought inside where Captain Proctor assigned an honor guard to it.

As Buck had predicted, Colonel Carrington had been recalled. He was ordered to go first to Fort Caspar and then on to the western headquarters at Omaha. The men at the fort considered it a cruel trick to force the Colonel to leave the prairie in the dead of winter, proving to them how the commanding officers back east had no idea of the conditions soldiers on the frontier faced. Several of Carrington's party suffered frostbite requiring amputations and two of his men died at the fort from exposure. After a suitable rest the party moved on

Spring came to the prairie with a rush of melting snow and flooding streams. The Powder River burst over its banks flooding out onto the prairie, fortunately Fort Reno had been constructed on ground high enough to avoid the flood waters. Further north, Red Cloud picked up his war against Forts Phil Kearney and C.F. Smith again.

The combined forces of the Sioux, Cheyenne, and Arapaho nations proved to be more than the army had expected. The Indians effectively blockaded the Bozeman Road and stopped all supplies from coming into the forts. They refused to back down and Washington had to come to grips with the fact that Red Cloud and his allies were proving to be as formidable as the Army of Northern Virginia had been at the beginning of the war.

The politicians along with the military officers in command of the western front were forced to agree that a peace treaty needed to be made with the Indian forces. In the spring of 1868, they met again with Red Cloud and the leaders of his forces at Fort Laramie. This time there was no army of soldiers and wagons heading up the Bozeman Trail to build forts.

Washington saw this as an opportunity to drop back and reformulate a plan to oust the Indians once and for all. Give into them now and then come back at them later with a superior force and plan. The treaty was signed in the summer. The agreement included abandoning Forts Reno, Phil Kearney, and C.F. Smith and removing the military, sending them back east. The dust from the departing army was still in the air when Red Cloud burned Fort Phil Kearny to the ground.

***

With the closing of Fort Reno Buck departed the country bound for his home village on the Teton River. He rode west coursing through the Big Horns Mountains. He was able to shorten the distance by crossing through Crow country. The Crow were no longer a concern to travelers as they had befriended the army and served as scouts at Fort C.F. Smith against their ancient Sioux enemy.

Buck rode into the Teton River village to He Who Fights' lodge to find his mother hanging elk meat from the drying racks. Hurit turned at the approach of his horse and stared for a moment at her son before she hurried over to him. Buck dismounted and hugged his mother. Nuttah came out of the lodge and squealed with delight at seeing her brother. The growing girl jumped into Buck's arms and wrapped her arms around his neck in a choking hug.

"Nuttah," Hurit laughed. "Do not kill your brother by breaking his neck."

Buck laughed, "And I'm happy to see you too, Nuttah."

The girl let go and dropped back to the ground. Buck studied her, "You are becoming a fine looking woman. Have you picked out your warrior husband yet?"

Nuttah giggled, "I am only six summers, I will not have a husband for many more summers."

Buck pretended to look around the camp. "I see many young warriors lining up to bring your father horses."

"They are not. You are funny, Buckingham Palace."

Buck winked at her, "Believe me little one, they will be."

"Do you try to marry my daughter off so fast?"

Buck turned to see He Who Fights coming up from his horses. "You will double your horse herd when she is of age," Buck replied.

He Who Fights smiled, "A pleasant thought. It is good to see you again. How long will you stay this time?"

Buck shrugged, "How long does the eagle stay in one place?"

"Long enough to visit his family."

"I will stay the winter. Maybe go to the Marias camp with my grandfather."

"Father asks about you often," Hurit said.

"Then, I will go and see him." Buck walked toward his grandfather's lodge leading his two horses.

Stopping in front of Cree Killer's lodge Buck called out, "Grandfather, do you have room for a wandering elk calf?"

He heard movement inside the buffalo hide walls and then a head of gray hair looked out the doorway. Seeing his grandson standing and looking at him, the old man climbed stiffly out of the low entry and stood up. "The elk calf is welcome." He then broke into a smile and embraced Buck.

Buck looked around, "Do you have meat, grandfather?"

"Yes, my daughter's husband and Badger, have been generous to this old man and help me since I am getting too old to hunt."

"Can I put my horses with your herd?"

"It is no longer a herd, Buckingham Palace. Put your horses with mine and those wagging tongues will see my wealth increase and be silent about this old man."

"Do some speak ill of you grandfather?"

"Some. My shame you know."

"I have told you that you bear no shame. Good warriors have also said as much."

The old man nodded his head making the deep wrinkles on his face deepen. "If I could have killed him I would have redeemed my honor, but it was forbidden."

Buck knew it was futile to argue over the issue. "If he still lives, Grandfather, I will one day kill him for you and redeem your honor."

Cree Killer smiled showing his many missing teeth. "You are a good grandson. When I die, you and Badger are to have my horses and weapons."

"Let us not talk of your dying, Grandfather."

Cree Killer turned back toward the lodge entry. "Did you bring coffee?"

"Yes."

"Good. Put your horses away and make me some." The old man bent over and reentered the lodge.

Buck dropped his tack and pack off in front of the lodge and led the horses to join the two belonging to his grandfather. He walked back and threw his saddle and pack through the lodge doorway and followed them in. The area was dark except for the top smoke hole where the poles were tied together. A fire was burning low with smoke filtering up toward the light.

Buck moved his gear against the wall opposite his grandfather's bed. He dug out the coffee pot and coffee. Buck looked up, "Why don't you open a flap and let some air in? It is a beautiful day."

"I am cold. Old men get cold."

Buck nodded his acceptance of the reason. He added wood to the fire and poured water into the coffee pot from a buffalo skin bucket. Cree Killer watched his every move in silence. Buck put the pot on the fire and sat back.

The old man smiled, "I gather my own wood. It is woman's work, but I have no woman to gather wood for me, so it is that or be cold and eat raw meat."

Buck smiled in return. Pulling a piece of dried venison from his pack he offered it to his grandfather.

Cree Killer waved his hand at the meat, "I have no teeth to chew that with."

Buck looked across the fire at the old man, "I heard you are spending the winters with Swift Runner's village on the Marias."

"Yes, he is my friend. Bighorn Chief also shares that camp, the two of them do not speak to each other."

Buck tore a chunk off the meat and packed it into the side of his mouth with his tongue. "I guess they are still angry with each other."

Cree Killer nodded, "Bighorn Chief thinks Swift Runner licks the white man's shoes like a dog. Swift Runner is rightly insulted and has refused to speak to him. Bighorn Chief also protects Angry All The Time in his side of the camp. Swift Runner does not want the spoiled child in his side of the camp."

"I don't blame him; Angry All The Time is a troublemaker."

"He is and he has no respect for Swift Runner or any chief except Bighorn Chief. I do not like Angry All

The Time. Bighorn Chief is my friend, as is Swift Runner, and I do not take a side. I mind my own business."

"Swift Runner still wants peace?"

Cree Killer nodded, "And Bighorn Chief does not trust the whites and says he will go to Rupert's Land if the army comes here."

"They have army in Rupert's Land, too."

The old man shrugged, "Maybe there is no good place to go. I am happy that I am close to returning to the Old Man. Much has changed and I am glad I lived before it did."

The coffee began to boil out around the lid. Buck grabbed a rabbit skin and pulled the pot off the fire. He poured out two cups and handed one to his grandfather.

The old man smiled, "This is the only good thing the whites have brought us."

A voice came from outside, "I smell coffee. Grandfather, may I come in?"

"If you bring meat from your mother," Cree Killer replied.

"I will be right back." The sound of running feet could be heard going away.

"He is a good grandson, too."

Buck had never known a time when his grandfather had looked on Badger as his nephew, he had always called him grandson. "Yes, he is. He is also a good brother."

A few minutes passed before a head came in through the open entry way. Black hair with an eagle feather tied into it was followed by a buckskin clad body. Badger grinned at Buck, "Mother said you were here."

Buck smiled back at him, "It appears that way."

"Did you bring meat, Badger?"

Badger looked at the old man, "Yes, Grandfather." Picking up the cooking sticks Badger stabbed pieces of elk on the sharpened ends and pushed the opposite ends into the holes around the fire pit. The meat began to sizzle in the flames.

Badger sat down. "Where have you been this time?"

"Fort Reno. Scouting for the army who were fighting the Sioux and Cheyenne."

"I do not know where Fort Reno is."

Buck shook his head, "It doesn't matter. The army signed a treaty with Red Cloud and pulled the army out. Red Cloud made quick firewood out of the forts."

Cree Killers eyes lit up, "So, the army is gone?"

"No, Grandfather. They have only fallen back to the east to make new plans. They will return with a bigger army."

The old man frowned, "I had hoped."

Badger broke in, "There are still soldiers at Fort Benton, and now there is a new fort on the Sun River called Shaw, and another three days ride to the south called Ellis."

Buck nodded, "Only the soldiers on the Powder and Bighorn have left, the others remain."

Cree Killer sighed and repeated, "I had hoped."

Buck handed Badger a coffee cup, "That's my last one, don't lose it."

"How can I lose it?"

"You have your ways. Has the army shown any interest in bothering our people?"

"We have not had any fights with them. There are some scouts and interpreters at Fort Shaw who ride with the army chiefs and have been here to talk to us. The interpreters also talk for our people at Fort Benton."

"I have spoken with Jim Twist, he is a good one," Cree Killer said. "He speaks for us. His mother is Siksika, daughter of Chief Four Arrows. His father is a trapper, a white man, but a good one and he lives among the Siksika. Jim speaks for us to the army seizers."

Buck looked from his grandfather to Badger. "Jim Twist is an army scout and interpreter, I take it."

Badger nodded, "He seems to be a good man. He is

younger than you, but unlike you he has a good head for thinking."

Buck started to reply to his brother's quip when another voice called from outside the lodge, "Cree Killer, my friend, may I come in?"

"It is Swift Runner," Cree Killer said. "Yes, my old friend, come in and join me and my grandsons."

"Buckingham Palace has returned?"

"Yes. Come in and stop acting like a shy boy coming to a girl's father to ask for her."

Swift Runner crawled in through the open entry. "I am happy to see you Buckingham Palace. It has been a long time. I heard you went off to fight the Sioux, is that so?"

"It is. I was a scout for the army far to the east of here in Cheyenne land."

"See what I have," Swift Runner said proudly as he held out an official looking document.

Cree Killer looked at the paper. "What is that?"

"I was meeting with Agent Prater at Fort Benton and he gave me this. He said it says that those who are with me have safe passage from the army wherever we go." He handed it to Cree Killer.

Cree Killer took it and stared at it. "It is white man bird scratching."

"May I see it, Grandfather?" Buck held out his hand.

Cree Killer handed it to him. Buck read it over, struggling with some of the more complicated words; however, he could read enough of it to know that it was an official paper from Lieutenant Prater, the Indian Agent officer at Fort Benton. The document was guaranteeing that Swift Runner could move about and hunt without being challenged by the army.

"He gave me this too." Swift Runner pulled a medal out from inside his shirt that was hung around his neck. "It is a medal that shows we are peaceful to the whites."

Cree Killer nodded, "Very nice. Will they honor it?"

"I was promised."

Buck looked at Swift Runner's excited face and then tossed a glance at Badger who held a concerned expression. Their eyes met. They both knew that army promises meant very little where the Indian was concerned.

Buck remembered about Carrington coming into Fort Laramie with his fort building crew at the same time Red Cloud was there for a peace talk. He was worried that Swift Runner may be too trusting.

"That is good," Buck said, "but be cautious."

Swift Runner looked at him, "About what?"

"Trusting the army's promises, or any white man's, until he has proven that he can be trusted. They are large on breaking promises when it suits them."

"But, I was promised. I believe Agent Prater. I could see it in his eyes that he was truthful."

"Yes, he might be a trustworthy man, but there are others who are not. Do not be too trusting of others besides Agent Prater. Other army officers could do something bad that he is not aware of."

"I will be careful."

Buck frowned as he thought. Then he said, "I have learned disturbing news. Two army Generals that I knew in the big war in the east have been put in charge of the army in the west."

"What kind of men are they?" Cree Killer asked.

"Hard men, who showed no mercy in destroying the gray coat enemy. They burned lodges, villages, crops, and killed men. There was only smoke and death behind them."

They all watched Buck's face. "What does that mean?" Cree Killer asked.

Buck frowned, "That I am very worried for us."

Chapter Twenty-One

Buck stayed for several weeks with his grandfather and family in the village. As winter approached he helped the old man pack up his lodge and follow Swift Runner to their winter camp on the Marias River. Bighorn Chief was with the group. He spoke well to Buck and Cree Killer, while refusing to acknowledge Swift Runner's existence as he rode with them. Swift Runner responded by deliberately looking away from him.

The two chiefs were at impassable odds and accepted that neither would give in nor relent on his beliefs about the white man. There was also the fact that Bighorn Chief had insulted Swift Runner in front of the village by saying he licked the white man's shoes. The former had not apologized and the latter refused to forgive the insult.

Angry All The Time moved in company with Bighorn Chief keeping his small, disheveled lodge on the opposite side of the camp from Swift Runner. He had a few friends who shared his attitude, but no seasoned warrior wanted anything to do with him. No young woman wanted him as they feared his anger and apparent insanity.

Animosity was strong between Angry All The Time and Buck. Buck had humiliated him and the young man bore him a grudge for it. Buck disliked the young man intensely and did not hide the fact. He let it be known that if the youngster wanted to fight him, he was ready any time. Bighorn Chief ordered Angry All The Time to stay away from Buck and not to cause trouble if he wanted the old chief's protection.

It proved to be a mild winter with the worst of it passing without incident. The men were able to supplement the buffalo meat with deer and elk well into the winter before the animals migrated down to the flat prairie. The camp consisted mainly of women, children, and old men.

Twenty young men of fighting age followed Swift Runner and an equal number stayed to Bighorn Chief's side of the camp. Their political views were reflected by whom they chose for their chief.

The snow was thawing under the spring sun when Jim Twist rode into the Marias camp with an army officer. Twist greeted Swift Runner and Cree Killer. Twist and Buck studied each other. Buck saw that Jim Twist wasn't more than twenty years old, yet he had an old face that spoke of his experience in the mountain country. Twist spoke Piegan as well as he spoke English.

Twist explained to Swift Runner that the accompanying officer wanted to meet him because he was a friend to the white man and a peaceful man. He introduced Major William Shelton, commander at Fort Shaw. Shelton and Swift Runner shook hands.

Swift Runner asked them to come into his lodge for food. They agreed and entered the lodge with the chief. Buck stood with his grandfather and looked around the camp. He saw Bighorn Chief and Angry All The Time standing together glaring at the group. Bighorn Chief was saying something to the younger man and from his expression it wasn't anything good.

Buck walked with Cree Killer back to his lodge. "That was Jim Twist," Cree Killer said. "He is like you; his mother is of our people. Yet, unlike you his father is a good man."

Buck stiffened at the mention of his father, but did not respond. "Seems pretty young," he said in regards to Jim Twist.

Cree Killer smiled, "Were we not all young once? Did it make us any less warriors?"

Buck smiled. "I must have forgotten."

They went into the lodge and settled down around the fire. "Grandson, make this old man some coffee."

Buck filled the coffee pot with water, tossed in a

handful of ground coffee, and put it on the fire.

A short time had passed since Twist and Major Shelton rode into the camp. Buck and Cree Killer were drinking coffee when they heard the shuffling of hard boots outside the lodge. "Cree Killer, may I see you?" Jim Twist called out in Piegan.

The old man crawled across the floor, flipped back the covering entryway flap and looked out. He saw Twist standing with Shelton.

"May we come into your lodge? We would like to speak with your grandson."

"Yes, you are welcome." Cree Killer backed his head into the lodge and was soon followed by the two men. Buck and Cree Killer stood up to meet them.

Twist and Shelton greeted Cree Killer and then turned their attention to Buck.

Twist extended his hand to Buck. "I'm Jim Twist, chief scout and interpreter for Major Shelton at Fort Shaw."

Buck shook his hand, "Buck Drake."

Shelton stood by silently and watched.

Twist went on, "Swift Runner told us that you scouted out of Fort Reno."

"That's right, until they abandoned the forts on the Bozeman."

"That means you understand the Sioux."

"Do you have a point to all this?"

"Plain talk, Mr. Drake," Major Shelton broke in. "We are on the western edge of the Sioux-claimed territory. We are here to form a buffer between them and the local population, and to give aid in the event Red Cloud pushes his war toward us." Shelton hesitated for a moment and then added, "There are many who are afraid of the Blackfeet as well and we are here for that purpose too."

Buck studied Shelton for a moment before answering. His appearance was that of most army brass, a little haughty and superior. "My people have been fighting the Shoshone and Gros Ventre, not the whites, and it's been a long time since we've even done that."

"I don't believe you would deny that there is a history of Blackfeet killing white men."

"Not recently."

"And we'd like to keep it that way."

Buck nodded without comment.

"Mr. Twist is as fine a scout as we could hope to find and has helped us maintain peaceful relations with the Blackfeet. I could use another man of your experience and bloodlines to scout and interpret."

"Scout against who? I won't assist the army in going against my own people."

"That's understandable. Actually, I was thinking of your helping on our eastern flank, scouting for my patrols into the Sioux country. We also have Blackfeet coming to the fort for various reasons and they are coming into Fort Benton as well. There would be times your interpreting for us in those regards would be a valuable service. I want to maintain a state of nonviolence with the Blackfeet."

"I could do that," Buck agreed.

Shelton nodded stiffly, "Very good. When can you start?"

"Not until the camp moves back to the main village on the Teton. My grandfather will need my help. In a month or two I could come down."

"That is acceptable. I also understand you fought in the War Between the States."

"I did, from '61 to '65."

"The whole war. I did as well. Who did you serve under and what was your position?"

"I began under Lieutenant Parker in his special unit, and that was under several generals. Then, I was assigned to Sherman as a sharpshooter. I ended the war in his command at Bennett Place when Johnston surrendered."

"So, you were one of the behind-the-lines men who

cleared the way for the rest of us."

"I blew up a few things."

"Impressive. You may be interested in knowing that Parker is now a Lieutenant Colonel and in charge of a special investigations unit where federal law is concerned."

Buck smiled, happy that Parker was alive. "I wondered how he faired, if he had survived the war. The last I saw of him he was headed for Gettysburg. I'm happy to hear he's alive."

"He is that." Shelton looked at Twist. "Anything else, Mr. Twist?"

"Buck and I can get acquainted later when he comes to Fort Shaw."

The men all exchanged parting words as Twist and Shelton left the lodge. They mounted their horses and rode back down the river. Buck followed them out and watched as they disappeared in the distance.

Bighorn Chief walked up to Buck. "What did the seizers want?" His voice reflected his resentment of having one of the hated army officers in camp.

"They want me to scout for them against the Sioux."

The old chief nodded. "Our old enemy. you will count coup I am sure."

They stood silent for a minute before Bighorn Chief spoke again. "I am not so sure about Jim Twist. His mother is one of us, and he has lived among us, and yet he rides with the seizers. If it comes to war, whose side will he be on? Will he shoot us or help us?"

"I was once asked that question by an army friend. I told him if they fought the Sioux I would fight with the army, but if they fought my people, I would stand against them with my people."

Bighorn Chief smiled, "Well said."

"I believe Jim Twist wants to help us. He interprets for us to the army so there is no misunderstanding between us and them. We can use that kind of help."

The chief grunted, "We will see." With that he walked away.

***

A strong chinook wind melted the last of the mountain snow allowing the winter camps to rejoin the main village earlier than usual. The last week of April found Buck riding down the river toward Fort Shaw. He left his traps and winter gear with Badger, telling him he could use them if he didn't come back to trap the next winter.

He still rode the bay horse he had come west on. The horse was getting older, but the gelding was the best horse he had ever ridden and he wouldn't part with him. He led the roan with his pack.

Buck rode through the open gates of Fort Shaw and asked the guard on duty where he could find Jim Twist. The trooper directed him to a small structure across the compound that served as the scout quarters. Nudging the bay with his heels, Buck moved across the busy compound to the place he had been directed. Dismounting, he spun the roan's lead rope around the saddle horn and tied the bay's reins to a post and went in the room.

Two Gros Ventre scouts sat in chairs up against the wall smoking cigarettes. They wore buckskin pants and moccasins but army shirts and coats. The two stared hard at Buck. Jim Twist had told them he was coming and that he was half Blood. Their expressions turned into scowls as they spoke in their own tongue regarding the stench of a Blood in the room.

Buck understood and answered in Gros Ventre, "The stench you smell is the breath of a Big Belly blowing back in his face."

The two scouts continued to glare at him. One snarled, "My cousin's scalp hangs on a Piegan lance. I will have yours to replace his."

Buck gave the man a look of utter contempt. "If an old woman of the Gros Ventre worm-filled bellies can take my scalp I do not deserve to wear it."

The Gros Ventre jumped to his feet, threw down the cigarette, and took the three steps necessary to come nose-to-nose with Buck. The two glared into each other's eyes without blinking.

"Your breath smells like worms," Buck said in a calm tone.

Just then Jim Twist came out of his room. "What is this?" he snapped in Gros Ventre.

Buck and the scout didn't move or speak as their eyes were locked on each other's, testing the other's mettle.

"Jack!" Twist's voice cracked like a whip. "Sit down, that's an order."

Jack's eyes flicked toward Twist and then back to Buck. He slowly backed up and sat down. The two men's eyes remaining locked on each other showing that one had no fear of the other.

"There will be another time," Jack whispered. "I will look forward to it."

"And I will look behind at it and say you died a man," Buck responded.

A smile parted the lips on Jack's hard face as he burst out with a loud laugh. "I like him, Twist," he said in clear English.

Buck laughed with him.

"Twist said your name is Buck Drake."

"He didn't lie."

"Want to kill some Sioux, Buck?"

"Always."

Jack jerked a thumb at his friend sitting next to him, "This is Antelope Eater. We like to kill Sioux."

Buck grinned, "Who doesn't?"

Antelope Eater grinned with him as he sifted tobacco into a paper and rolled a cigarette. "My father would never believe I am riding with a Blood," Antelope Eater said with a laugh.

Twist was listening to the exchange with a relieved grin. "Well, now that we're all acquainted," he put out his hand to Buck, "glad to have you on."

Twist pointed at a bunk. "That's yours, go ahead and stow your gear. Captain Clarke wants to take a patrol out for a few days and scout the Sioux border. We'll be leaving within the hour."

Buck dropped his gear on the bunk. "Seen anything of the Sioux this far west?"

Twist shook his head. "Not for a while. We keep running into Crow hunting parties and they tell us that the Sioux are concentrated in the Bighorn River area and blockading the Bozeman Road."

"When I was down that way it seemed a priority to them to stop all white traffic from getting past the Black Hills. Probably won't see them over this way at all."

Twist jerked a thumb toward the Gros Ventre scouts. "I know, it's been a big disappointment to these boys."

Jack smiled, "Maybe this will be our lucky day. We can take several Sioux scalps."

Twist looked at Jack, "You know the United States Army does not allow its scouts to scalp the enemy killed in a fight."

Jack shook his head, "You whites are so backward. You don't understand what is important."

Buck studied Jack. It was clear by the way he spoke he had spent a lot of time around white soldiers. Jack was picking up their manner of speech, the same as he had.

"Yeah, well you go tell that to Shelton and Clarke and see what they say," Twist replied.

"I know what they will say. They will say what you said. It makes me sad."

"You can still count coup," Buck put in. "They

can't stop that."

"That is something," Jack agreed.

Twist looked out the window. "Column's getting together, let's get to it."

Buck quickly unpacked the roan, putting his gear inside the room. He turned the roan out with the cavalry mounts while the other scouts saddled up. Mounting together, the four scouts joined the forming column.

They moved up to the front where Captain Clarke sat posed and arrogant on his horse. Twist introduced Buck, "Captain, this is our new scout and interpreter, Buck Drake."

Clarke looked at Buck coldly, and then glanced at his horse, "Nice horse." He then looked at Twist, "Take us out, Mr. Twist."

Twist brought his horse around and moved forward with Buck as the Captain lifted his arm and waved the column to begin. They rode out of the fort with the jangling of metal on tack and the rhythmic drumming of a hundred shod hooves. The two Gros Ventre scouts brought up the rear.

Twist leaned toward Buck, "Nice, isn't he?"

Buck snorted, "He likes my horse anyway."

Twist laughed, "That's because he's part horse himself – the back end part."

Buck grinned, "I can see the family resemblance."

Twist barked out a laugh and took his horse out at a lope.

Buck moved up alongside of him. He liked the young man as the seeds of their friendship were planted.

Riding a quarter hour ahead of the patrol Twist stopped and dismounted to study a stretch of hilly land bordering the river. "Dull Knife used to set up a big camp over there," he pointed at the sage and brush studded sand.

Buck stepped off his horse and stood beside Twist as the young man surveyed the area through his field glasses. After several minutes of silence Twist lowered the glasses and shook his head. "Not a thing to show anyone had ever been there. I think they even packed up the rocks and took them along."

"That means they're not coming back – not to this spot anyway."

"No, they realize we know about this being their big camp. They'll find another."

Buck looked over the country, then commented, "We moved our village with the summer and winter."

"Yes, you always came back though."

"That's because we knew it was safe. If it wasn't a safe camp we wouldn't use it again. I'm sure Dull Knife is thinking the same thing." Buck paused. "But now with the military threat against us I think a lot of things will change and not for the better."

"I will do what I can for the Blackfeet," Twist promised. "I have the ear of some of the officers at Fort Benton who are working with our people."

Buck turned his eyes on Twist. The words 'our people' had caught his attention. He and Twist had the same blood which made them brothers, much the same as he and Badger. That moment was a defining one for Buck, from here on he would think of Jim Twist as his brother.

The two mounted back up and returned to the column to give their report to Clarke. The Captain, dust covered and in a foul mood, received the report with an unimpressed grunt.

Twist turned his horse and rode away with Buck again. Twist scowled, "He was hoping the Cheyenne would be there. He wants to kill Indians and it drives him crazy that we can't find him some."

Buck glanced at his friend, "That man is going to make some big trouble one of these days. I just hope you and me aren't in the middle of it."

The day wore on as the patrol covered the bleak

landscape. Buck and Twist wandered beyond the confines of the precision column scanning the country for any indication that the Cheyenne were gathering or lying in wait for them. They found nothing as they accepted the conclusion that the Cheyenne had all rode north to join Red Cloud.

***

The summer, made up of stifling heat and wind driven dust, was one endless flow of long daily patrols without a single incident with hostile Indians. Clarke's mood remained foul due to the lack of action that he craved. His hatred of Indians was taken out on the scouts in small ways leading them to hate the man more with each passing day.

In November, Lieutenant Prater requested that Buck be transferred to Fort Benton to work with him. The friendly Blackfeet from all three tribes were coming to Fort Benton on a regular basis and Buck's skills and relation to the people were needed.

The air was growing colder with storm clouds gathering for a late autumn snow when Buck rode out of Fort Shaw bound for Fort Benton thirty miles north. It was a ride that would change his life forever.

Chapter Twenty-Two

Through December and into January few Blackfeet left their winter camps to come down to Fort Benton. Winter camps were spread north and south across the face of the mountains. It was ninety miles to the fort from the Marias River camp and further from the Teton River camp. In the frigid temperatures and deep snow, it was not a trip worth taking for what little the fort could provide them.

The Gros Ventre, being closer to the fort and on more level terrain, came regularly to the fort seeking food and blankets. Prater made sure they got what they needed. At first the Gros Ventre didn't trust Buck due to his being Blackfeet. The more powerful Blackfeet had caused no end of misery for the smaller tribe and the hatred the Gros Ventre harbored for their enemy was plainly visible. In time they came to accept Buck's presence, if not totally trusting him.

January was a month that never saw the temperature rise above 30 degrees below zero. The Blackfeet stayed to their lodge fires, eating the dwindling buffalo from the autumn hunt. The young men in each winter camp were charged with hunting to provide as much meat as possible to carry the people through the remainder of the winter. Game was scarce, requiring the hunters to go far afield to kill whatever they could.

Buck was in his room at Fort Benton repairing some tack and keeping warm by the fire when his door suddenly burst open. He jumped up with a start grabbing for the revolver. A Private bundled in a heavy coat and hat stood gasping for breath in the open doorway. "Mr. Drake, Lieutenant Prater needs you to come to the Infirmary immediately."

"Why, what happened?"

"We just had a bunch of Blackfeet come into the fort. There's about fifty women and children and a few old men. They look real bad. The Lieutenant wants you right now."

"Tell him I'm on the way." Buck grabbed his coat and hat as he rushed out the door slamming it closed behind him. His boots struck hard on the frozen ground as he sprinted across the compound. He was scared. What could bring women and children, the whole camp, all the way to the fort in this weather? He knew it couldn't be anything good.

Nearing the infirmary Buck saw several Blackfeet women staggering toward the building wearing only their elk skin dresses. A few had a blanket or fur clutched around their shoulders. Panic rose up in Buck. He recognized a couple of the woman from Swift Runner's winter camp.

He ran into the open Infirmary door to see a cluster of women, old men, and a few older children lying on the floor. Several had new army blankets thrown over them. Prater was running around the room shouting directions to three soldiers while a physician called out directions to his staff. The fire in the stove had been stoked to the limit.

Lieutenant Prater shouted at Buck as he came in staring in alarm at the people scattered on the floor. "Buck, quick, give me a hand. They all have frostbite and some are completely frozen through. Get blankets on them."

Buck looked at the frozen faces and hands of the people. Most were close to death. There were no sounds from them except the moans and cries of pain and despair.

"What happened?" Buck shouted.

"I don't know," Prater snapped. "Aid first, questions second . . . move!"

Buck began shaking out blankets and wrapping them around the people sitting up and covering those lying down. Grabbing a blanket he made to throw it over an old man who was on the floor shivering, his paled skin covered with frostbite. With a start he saw it was his grandfather.

Throwing the blanket over the old man Buck knelt

down next to him. The old man shifted his eyes up to look at Buck. His face was frozen, but he was able to whisper. Buck put his ear down against his grandfather's lips. "Grandfather, what happened?"

"The soldiers came. They killed us."

"What soldiers?"

"Seizers. They killed us. Burned the village."

Buck ground his teeth together in rage. "Why?"

"They came for Angry All The Time. He killed white men. He was not in our camp. They killed us anyway. They left us without food or robes. I led the people here."

"Where were the young men?"

"Hunting."

Buck shouted out to Prater, "They were attacked by the army. Why? This was a village of old men and women and children."

Prater stood in momentary shock. "I will get to the bottom of it."

Cree Killer whispered for Buck. Buck put his head back down and listened. "Swift Runner showed his paper and medal. They shot him anyway." The old man fell silent again as he closed his eyes. Buck knew he was going to die; he was too old and too frozen. He could only look into the face of his grandfather.

The old man opened his eyes again. "Jim Twist was with them. I thought he was our friend." The old man gave a violent shiver and let out a long rattling breath and died.

Buck stared at the still face of his grandfather. With his mind numb he looked at the people around him. They had no robes or blankets and they had walked the 90 miles to the fort. He knew this had to be the remnant, there were over three hundred people in the Marias camp. The rest had to be dead for many of the little ones and old women could never have made it all the way.

A violent rage boiled up inside of him. His mind

centered on Jim Twist. He cursed the scout he had thought was his friend. He had betrayed them, betrayed their friendship and his trust. He cursed him for a traitor and a coward. Cursed him for leading an attack against woman and children. Twist would pay dearly for this.

Prater came over to Buck, "Do you know any these people?"

Buck spoke through clenched jaws, "They were part of my village." He looked down at the old man, "This is my grandfather."

"I'm sorry, Buck. I swear to you, I will go all the way to Washington, to the Bureau of Indian Affairs, to the President if necessary, and demand an accounting. I will demand the prosecution of those responsible. Do you know where their camp was?"

"On the Marias River, 90 miles from here."

"*Ninety miles!*" Prater exclaimed. "My God, they walked all this way, in this weather, without clothes? I want to know about this. Will you take me to the camp? I want to see for myself and make my report from personal observation."

Buck got up from the floor. "It will take two days to get there by horse, so dress warm."

Lieutenant Prater put individuals in charge of helping the people and the physician and went to saddle a horse and prepared to ride out with Buck.

Buck met the Lieutenant and they headed out of the fort. They followed the trail left by the people. It was marked not only by bloody tracks in the snow, but by the bodies of those who had died along the way. Prater took careful notes and counted the bodies.

Two days out, they came unto the remains of the camp. The sky was blue and the sun bright, yet offering no warmth. Snow fell from the trees making a loud hissing as it rained down on the pine and larch bows. Birds called back and forth among the trees. Save for those sounds the

224

land was as silent as the death in it.

The bodies of old men, women, and children riddled with bullets lay twisted in frozen grotesque shapes. The remains of those who had been trapped and burned under the falling hides of their lodges were accounted for. Prater remained stone silent as he took notes and observed the scene.

Buck walked around, his anger and rage simmering dangerously below the surface. A pair of dead and gutted deer were lying frozen on the ground. He called out to Prater, "The hunters came back and left again."

Buck found Swift Runner lying on his back with several bullet holes in his chest and body. In his frozen clutched hand, he found the corner of the paper the old chief was so certain would protect them. It had obviously been taken from him and thrown into the fire to hide the evidence. He looked under Swift Runner's shirt and found that the medal was also missing.

He snarled toward Prater, "They took the safe passage paper and medal from Swift Runner to hide the evidence."

Lieutenant Prater mounted his horse, "I have enough for my report and investigation. Nearly two hundred bodies in the camp and another fifty-four that died trying to get to the fort. I gave Swift Runner that safe passage paper. I want heads to roll on this one."

Buck snorted and gave an angry, cynical laugh. "They'll bury it and you know that as well as I do."

"Not if I can help it."

"It will be beyond your control, Lieutenant." He looked around, "We can't bury the bodies in the ice. The village will find them and bury them to our customs."

Buck mounted up and they left the camp.

A day from the fort, Buck told Prater to ride on in, that he was going down to Fort Shaw.

"Why are you going there?" Prater asked with a hint

of concern.

"Grandfather said that Jim Twist led the attack. I know Jim and I intend to find out what happened."

Prater looked appalled, "Jim Twist? I find it hard to believe that he would have a hand in this. He was always a friend to the Blackfeet."

"That's what I thought."

"And if you find out he did have a hand in this?"

Buck tossed a hard look at Prater as he turned his horse away from him. Kicking the bay into a lope, he left Lieutenant Prater staring after him. He knew exactly what he was going to do if Twist was part of this.

Buck rode in through the gates of Fort Shaw and directly up to the little structure the scouts lived in. He dismounted and charged for the door, shoving it open so it slammed hard against the wall. Jack and Antelope Eater were sitting in chairs by the fire and Twist was standing staring blankly out the window. They all jumped at the sound.

Buck stormed across the room. As Twist turned to look at him, Buck grabbed him by the front of his shirt and threw him against the wall. Moving in, he slammed his fist into Twist's face. Jack and Antelope Eater grabbed Buck by the arms and dragged him back away from Twist.

"*What in God's name happened, Twist?*" Buck screamed at him. "What did you murderers do up on the Marias? You traitor, I'll kill you."

Jack shouted in Buck's ear, "He didn't do it, Buck."

Buck stopped struggling and turned his head to look at Jack. He was breathing hard from his outburst and his eyes reflected his rage.

"He didn't do it," Jack repeated.

Twist slid his back down the wall until he was sitting on the floor and had his face buried in his hands. Sobs were coming out from behind his hands. Buck stared at him, suddenly feeling overcome with guilt for his actions. Jim was his friend, he should have let him explain.

Jack pulled over a chair, "Sit!" he commanded Buck.

Buck sat down, shivering from his cold ride and the fury that boiled in him. He took a deep breath, "Jim, what happened?"

The young scout took his hands away from his face, a darkening bruise was forming under his eye where Buck had hit him. Tears were in his eyes and rolling down his cheeks as sobs wracked his body.

Buck cringed at the damage he had done to his friend. The young scout's tears and anguished face made him suddenly realized just how young Jim was. He had seen so many that age die in the war, boys holding down a difficult job.

"Oh, God, Buck it was awful. I tried to stop them, I swear to God I tried. They were going to shoot me for trying."

Twist wiped at his eyes and sobbed.

Jack hunkered down next to Buck. "Angry All The Time and some of his friends stole some horses and killed three white men down by Fort Ellis. The army took out of Fort Ellis and came here. Some Indians had told them that Angry All The Time was in Bighorn Chief's camp up on the Marias. They forced Jim to go with them to show them where Bighorn Chief's camp was."

Twist looked up at Buck, "We reached Swift Runner's camp first. It was early in the morning. Major Bates was in charge and he was drunk, as were some of his officers. I told them they had the wrong camp that it was Swift Runner's camp and he was friendly to the whites. The drunken cur said he didn't care, that he had rode all this way in the cold to kill Indians and, by God, he was going to kill Indians.

"They surrounded the camp. Swift Runner came running out waving his safe passage paper. He was talking in Piegan and they didn't understand, he was saying that they were good Indians. Then someone shot him. I screamed at them that they had the wrong camp." Twist broke down in tears again.

He dug for a settling breath and whispered, "They just kept shooting and shooting. Bates told a Sergeant to shoot me if I said another word. He put his gun in my back. They shot everyone they could and tore down the lodges and set them on fire. Finally they rounded up the last of the people and took them prisoner. They took all the horses and burned every robe, blanket, and piece of food. The survivors just stood there.

"They got one of the horse boys to tell them that Bighorn Chief and Angry All The Time had taken some of the people and left their camp and made their own camp down river. Bates made me go with them again to find Bighorn Chief, leaving the survivors to make out on their own without food and warm clothes.

"We found Bighorn Chief's camp, but it was deserted. We tracked them up to the Canada border, where we had to turn back. I wanted to go back and help the people get to Fort Benton, but they made me go along with them back here, threatening to shoot me if I didn't. Bates told me to keep my mouth shut or he'd have me thrown in prison."

Filled with remorse for his violent actions Buck stared at him. "I'm sorry, Jim."

Twist nodded and sniffed, "I am too."

"Lieutenant Prater is starting an investigation, will you tell him all that?'

Twist nodded, "Yeah, I will."

Buck watched the young man for another minute. "My grandfather made it as far as the fort before he died. He said that you led the attack and that he thought you were their friend."

Twist gaped at Buck in horror. "They will all think

that now. I would never be able to explain why I was there."

"I believe you and I'll tell the people the truth of what happened."

Twist sniffed, "I can't ever face them again."

"They need you."

Twist dropped his head. "They don't need the likes of me. I'm sorry about your grandfather."

Buck left his chair and sat down beside Twist. He put his arm around the young man's shoulders. They sat together in silent misery. Finally Buck asked, "Who shot Swift Runner?"

"That Bates had a couple of no account riff-raff with him. Civilians that said they could guide him to Bighorn Chief. It was one of them who shot Swift Runner."

"What's his name?"

"Some weasel, name of Del Yarrow."

The name hit Buck like a slap in the face. "Did this Yarrow have a couple of fingers missing and his partner have an eye covered?"

Twist looked up at Buck surprised, "Yeah, how did you know?"

"Because I gave those to them up in Fort Benton a few years back."

"Who was the Sergeant who held the gun on you?"

"Jones. He seemed to be pretty chummy with the Yarrows."

"Where can I find the Yarrows?"

Twist stared up at Buck. "What are you going to do?"

Buck slid his arm off Twist. "Where are they?" Buck's frigid tone left no room for argument.

"Here at the fort. Jones is too."

"If Jones is out of Fort Ellis, why is he still here?"

"To make sure I don't talk. He was told to shoot me if I tried to make a report."

"Does Major Shelton know he's here?"

"I don't think so or he'd have booted him out. Clarke does, but he doesn't seem to care."

Buck scowled, "Knowing Clarke he's protecting them."

Jack broke in, "I saw them all together drinking whiskey down at the barn not long ago."

Buck got up from the floor, walked across the room and out the door.

Buck calmed his angry mind as he made his way to the barn. He knew the layout of the building. It had stalls for twenty-five horses for early morning patrols. The officer's horses were always stabled. In the front was a blacksmith shop. Hay was stored in the loft above the horses where it could be forked down to them. There was a large tack room holding all the saddles and bridles.

The blacksmith was not in the shop as Buck walked past it and into the run between the stalls. He stopped and listened for voices. He figured that if Jones was hiding from Shelton and drinking, he wouldn't be out in the open. A murmur of voices punctuated with an occasional drunken laugh drifted through the barn. He headed for the tack room.

The voices grew louder as he approached the tack room. The door was closed. He listened and could hear the voices plainly behind the door. Opening the door he stepped into the room and took a quick look around. Dozens of saddles were each set over a round pole protruding out of the wall in two neat rows facing each other. At the end of the rows, passing a bottle between them were the Yarrow cousins and a man in a Sergeant's coat.

The three men stopped and stared at Buck as he advanced toward them. The Yarrows recognized him as he drew closer. Del shouted out drunkenly, "Well, if it ain't the breed." Del jabbed his cousin with an elbow, "We cleaned some Blackfeet clocks, didn't we Abe?"

Abe was holding the bottle and looking nervously at Buck. He whispered, "Shut up, Del."

Del hissed and jerked the bottle from his cousin's hand and took a long drink. He let out a breath and sneered, "What, you're scared of some breed who killed my brother?"

Del held up his hand missing the two fingers, "I owe you, breed."

Jones was watching the exchange with a scowl, "Who's this fool?" He gestured toward Buck.

Del laughed, "We just shot up a bunch of his cousins."

Jones glared at Del, "Bates doesn't want that spread around, so shut up."

"Too late," Buck spoke in a cold voice. "Everyone knows and you're in the wrong fort. That makes you absent without leave, Jones, a deserter. Major Shelton will be happy to know that he has a deserter in his fort."

"I'm on an assignment."

"I know, to kill Jim Twist if he makes a report. How are you going to explain that to Shelton?"

Jones looked at Buck suspiciously. "That's a lie. How do you know who I am, anyway?"

"Like I said, everyone knows and I'm going to just beat the three of you to dog meat." He grabbed a wide leather billet off the wall above a saddle and slapped it hard against Del's shoulder knocking him to the ground.

Del rolled and pushed up off the ground with a curse and a knife in his hand. He clumsily lunged at Buck with the knife pointed at him. Buck side stepped it and hit Del across the back of the head with the heavy billet sprawling him unconscious on the packed dirt floor.

At the same moment that Del hit the floor, Jones jerked out his Colt. Buck drew the Remington from his hip and shot Jones in the heart from three feet away. In desperation, Abe drew his gun and pointed it at Buck. Buck swung the revolver and shot Abe between the eyes.

Buck could hear footsteps coming up behind him. He whirled around to see Jim Twist and Antelope Eater running into the room.

Twist stared momentarily at the bodies and then grabbed Buck and shoved him toward the tack room door. "Get out of here . . . go! We'll hold them off. They're coming, go!"

Buck hurried out of the tack room as Jack ran up leading his bay. "Get mounted," Jack yelled. "Go!"

Buck swung into the saddle and kicked the bay into a gallop, racing out of the barn and toward the open fort gates. He blew past the guards and into the open country headed west.

Captain Clarke ran into the barn with several armed troopers behind him. He hurried to the tack room, pushing past the scouts. He stared at the men on the floor then turned back toward the scouts. "What happened? I saw Drake blasting out of here like he was on fire. He did this, didn't he?"

Twist shrugged, "I see a whiskey bottle and two men with their guns out, there's a knife on the floor too. I'd say whoever it was did it in self-defense."

"Then, why did Drake run?" Clarke snapped.

"I have no idea."

"You stinking redskins all stick together. Well, I can fix that."

Major Shelton rushed in. "What happened?" he demanded.

Clarke pointed at the bodies, "Drake's doing."

"How do you know that?"

"I saw him galloping out of here guilty as sin. He murdered these men, I'm certain."

Shelton moved on into the tack room looking the scene over. He bent over the Sergeant. "Who is this? He isn't one of my men."

"He's from Fort Ellis," Twist spoke out. "Bates gave him orders to kill me if I made a report about the massacre."

Clarke snapped, "Don't listen to him, Major. He's lying to protect his friend."

Shelton frowned at Twist, "I don't believe that a Sergeant in the United States Army would be ordered to murder a scout to shut him up." His voice took on an angry tone, "I order you to tell me what you know about this!"

Twist glared at the Major who had just called him a liar. "I heard the shots. Like I told Captain Clarke, there's a whiskey bottle and they have their guns out. Captain Clarke knew these men were in here drinking and did nothing about it."

"Liar!" Clarke shouted at Twist. "I'll have you up on charges."

Shelton looked back at the bodies. "Captain Clarke, I want answers. Take a dozen men and go get Drake back here."

"Yes sir." Clarke pointed at a group of troopers standing by watching and snapped, "Mount up." He then cast an evil glare on Twist, "I'll be back for you."

The men hurried to obey the order. Clarke followed them. Within fifteen minutes the group was saddled and riding out of the fort.

"The physician came in and looked the bodies over. He slid his hand under Del Yarrow's coat feeling his back, "This one is alive."

"Get him to the Infirmary," Shelton ordered. "Maybe he can tell us something."

"I wouldn't believe him, sir," Twist said. "He was with the command that massacred the Blackfeet.

Shelton barked at Twist, "Revenge killing, is it?"

"What?"

"Drake, killing these men in revenge."

"I wouldn't say that as a fact."

"Why not?"

"Look, two of those men have guns out and there is a knife. There is a mostly empty whiskey bottle on the ground. If Buck murdered them, they wouldn't have weapons drawn would they?"

"That doesn't mean anything. Why did Drake run if it was self-defense? A man only runs when he is guilty."

"Because no one is going to believe a half breed, are they? You sure don't!"

Shelton ignored him. "I'll have the United States Territorial Marshal on this. I want Drake arrested for murder."

Twist glared at the Major. "You would condemn a man without knowing the facts? Clarke called me a liar and so have you. I'll tell you what Major, between what happened up on the Marias and now this, I've had about all the army I can stomach. I quit." He then jerked his saddle off the pole and carried it to his horse and saddled him.

Shelton walked out of the tack room as men carried Del Yarrow out on a stretcher. He stood in the alley between the horse stalls and watched them leave the barn. He looked at Twist as he rode up beside him and stopped.

Twist glared down at the Major. "Up on the mountain that dead Sergeant in there was told by Major Bates to kill me if I interfered with their slaughter of the Blackfeet. I don't care if you believe it or not. I intend to give my statement to Lieutenant Prater and everyone else who wants it. And no man calls me a liar. As far as I'm concerned you and the army can go to blazes." He kicked the horse in the ribs and rode out of the barn and then the fort.

Shelton looked at Jack and Antelope Eater, "What do you two know about this?"

Jack shrugged, "We're just stinking redskins, why should we know anything?" The two began to saddle their horses.

"Where are you going?" Shelton demanded.

Neither man looked at him as Jack answered in a flat tone, "Back to our village. We don't much like the blue coats anymore. Do your own scouting." They mounted and rode out the way Twist had gone.

Shelton stared after them, cursing under his breath he muttered, "*Indians!* Can't depend on them for anything."

Buck kept the bay running hard up into the mountains. The snow slowed him, but the powerful war horse surged on kicking up waves of snow with each hoof fall. The snow would leave an easy trail to follow and he held no illusions that they would not be hot on him. He stopped on a tree-covered hilltop to let the bay catch his breath. He looked down the way he had come and cursed. A line of blue uniforms was moving along his trail.

There was no way to lose them in the snow. His only chance was to halt the pursuit and send them back down the mountain to lick their wounds. He watched the column moving closer as he thought back on the sudden change of events.

He hadn't planned on shooting the Yarrows, and especially not the Sergeant. He was going to give them all a sound beating for their crimes and then turn Jones in as a deserter. He hadn't expected them to pull guns on him, which he should have had he been thinking clearly. They left him no choice but to shoot. It had been a poorly executed action on his part.

Twist and Antelope Eater were the first ones to appear, but they had not seen the fight. It would be his word against the army's and the army always protected its own. Del Yarrow was likely still alive and he'd lie through his teeth and they'd believe him because he was white.

No one would believe him; a jury would never take the word of a half-breed. Twist would be treated the same and Antelope Eater would be ignored, as Indians were not allowed in a courtroom or their testimony considered of value. His only hope was to get into Canada, but first he had to get the hounds off his trail.

Buck studied the terrain around him. The wind began to pick up making the air colder. His breath was blowing out in front of his face and steam was rising off the bay as the sweat froze on the animal's body. Looking up at the sky, he could see the lead gray overcast darkening for snow. Snow would cover his tracks.

He picked out a cluster of fir trees above him with their ice covered boughs scraping the ground. It would offer cover and a wind block while giving him a long view of his back trail. Riding up and around the trees he tied the bay behind them. Pulling the Henry from the scabbard he worked his way into the boughs and sat down to watch the trail.

He heard the jangle of tack drifting on the freezing wind before he saw the troopers. Captain Clarke was in the lead. He didn't need another killing, he only needed to discourage pursuit. As Clarke came into view, he sighted between the front legs of the Captain's horse. He hated to kill a good horse, but it was better than killing a man, even one he despised as much as Clarke. He squeezed off the shot and the horse went down hard spilling Clarke into the crusted snow.

Levering in another cartridge Buck shot the horse next in line. The rifle reports bounced hard off the mountains as the mounted troopers scattered. Clarke and the other horseless trooper took cover behind a pile of snow-covered rocks. It began to snow.

Several minutes passed and the troopers made no effort to come further up the trail. The snow was coming down harder. Buck fired two shots at Clarke's hiding spot to keep them down for a while longer and then slipped back through the boughs. He led his horse away into the growing snow storm.

The troopers waited in the falling snow not daring to move. A half hour passed before Clarke ventured to stand up without drawing fire. The blowing snow had cut the visibility down to a short distance. He walked back down the trail calling out to his command. "We are going back, we'll never find him in this storm."

As the troopers reassembled Clarke's angry expression never slackened. "We're just lucky he missed us and hit our horses instead," he growled to the men.

Clarke took over a trooper's horse and made him ride double as the other horseless trooper had to. They were chilled through and covered in snow when they rode back into the fort. Major Shelton, bundled in a warm coat and hat, stepped out of his office to meet them. He watched as the men riding double dismounted with the others.

Walking up to the Major Clarke shook his head, "We lost him in the storm. He did shoot at us though and we are very lucky. He hit my horse and the Corporal's. Fortunately for us, he is a poor shot."

Shelton had calmed down between the time of the shooting and now. He began to consider what Jim Twist had said and was putting the pieces together. Why was Sergeant Jones here? Why was he hiding and drinking with civilians? He wished he had handled the situation with more tact and gotten the full story. He cussed himself for handling it so poorly and running off the only men who could give him that story.

Coupling his thoughts and questions with Clarke's report he had to wonder. Drake had been a sharpshooter for General Sherman and he knew that those men always hit what they aimed at. Had Drake deliberately shot the horses when he could have easily killed every man in the detail?

"Captain Clarke, Drake was General Sherman's sharpshooter in the war. He hits what he aims at."

Clarke gave Shelton an incredulous look, "You mean he wanted to shoot our horses? I find that hard to believe. He's a filthy redskin, he was trying to kill us." Clarke began banging the snow off his coat. "Why would he shoot horses when he could shoot the pursuers?"

Shelton eyed Clarke with growing annoyance at his insubordinate tone. "Did it slow you down? Get you off his trail without inflicting casualties?"

Clarke scowled; he wanted to believe Drake had tried to kill them. It made it easier to fuel his hate of Indians and build his case against the scout. He had never liked the half breed and saw this as a chance to hang him.

Shelton went on, "Drake sniped off scores of Rebels. If his intention was to kill you, then you would all be lying up on that mountain dead."

Clarke stubbornly shook his head, "With all due respect Major, I was there. You were not."

Shelton scowled at him. "Go change your uniform and get back to your duties."

Shelton watched Clarke as he walked away. He then turned his eyes toward the mountains and stared into the swirling snow. He thought about what Jim Twist had said to him before he left. He had already wired the Territorial Marshal at the capital in Virginia City about finding Drake and bringing him in. His thinking was beginning to change as he said in a low voice, "Now, I have to wonder who really was at fault in that shooting."

Chapter Twenty-Three

The bay moved slowly through the fresh snow, throwing showers of the light powder with every step. Buck was satisfied that the snow had effectively covered his trail. He intended to go to the Teton River village first and speak to them about the massacre. He wouldn't stay long as he was now a hunted man and his presence in the village was a danger to them. He didn't want this Major Bates or Clarke killing the rest of his family looking for him.

Smoke from the lodges hung over the camp in the still, cold air. The long-haired horses in the main herd stood tight against each other for warmth. A cloud of concentrated frozen breath hung over the animals. The horse boys were bundled in furs and leather and going about their jobs with the horses. Outside of that the village was a silent picture of mid-winter inactivity.

Riding up to the lodge of He Who Fights, Buck stepped out of the saddle leaving the bay standing in place. He Who Fights stuck his head out of the entry door. "Buckingham Palace, come in, it is warmer in here than out there."

Buck ducked down and followed the man into the dim, smoky interior of the buffalo hide lodge. Hurit was quick to give her son an embrace, as did Nuttah. Hurit took a stick from the fire with a piece of hot meat on the end and handed it to him as he sat down. They looked at him as he took a bite from it.

"I cannot stay long. The soldiers are hunting me."

All eyes showed concern. "Why?" He Who Fights asked.

"Do you know what happened to Swift Runner's camp?"

"Yes. The horse boys and the hunters came back and told us. We brought back the bodies. The boys said the others walked to Fort Benton."

"Many did not make it and died on the trail. Some did make it in, most of them are frozen and will die too." He looked at his mother. "Grandfather led them to the fort. He told me what happened and then he died."

Hurit let out a wail of grief, "Oh, my father." She then wept.

Anger was evident on He Who Fights' face. "The seizers killed them. What kind of cowards shoot women and children and then leave the rest to die in the cold?"

"Lieutenant Prater is demanding an investigation. He is very angry."

"Prater has been good to our people. Many speak well of him. Why do the seizers hunt you?"

"I killed two, maybe three, of the men who killed Swift Runner."

He Who Fights nodded his approval of the action. "Good. We should kill them all. This is an act of war."

Buck shook his head, "There are too many soldiers."

He Who Fights scowled. He turned an angry eye on Buck. "The boys said Jim Twist was with them. He is a traitor to us and a coward. Should I ever see him again I will spit in his face and kill him."

"Jim Twist didn't do it."

"He was with the seizers and he even walked through the dead. He was seen!"

"Yes, he was there. Now, you must listen to what I say with open ears and I will trust you to tell the others the truth for me."

"I will listen. Go ahead."

"Angry All The Time and his friends stole some horses and killed three white men doing it. They hid in Bighorn Chief's camp. The army was told that Angry All The Time was there. They forced Jim Twist to go with them to show where Bighorn Chief's camp was. The army chief was drunk and so were his sub-chiefs. They came on

Swift Runner's camp first. Jim told them they had the wrong camp. The soldiers didn't care, they just wanted to kill Indians. Jim tried to stop them and the army chief told one of his sub-chiefs to kill Jim if he said anymore. I have seen Jim, he is sick with grief."

He Who Fights thought it over. "Then, Jim Twist did not take them to Swift Runner's camp?"

"No. They only came on it first."

"And Jim Twist tried to stop them?"

"Yes. They were going to shoot him for it. They went crazy killing and there was nothing he could do to stop them."

"The seizers must have been filled with hate to do such a thing."

"And full of whiskey."

"I will tell everyone the truth. If you see Jim Twist, tell him we do not blame him and we will welcome him again."

"Good. He will be happy to hear that."

"Did the seizers find Bighorn Chief?"

"No. They escaped to Rupert's Land."

"So, Angry All The Time is responsible for this slaughter. If he had not killed the white men, they would not have come looking, would they?"

"No. He stirred them up, they wanted revenge. If you want to kill anyone for this, kill Angry All The Time before he makes more trouble."

"But you said he has gone to Rupert's Land."

"If he returns here, kill him."

He Who Fights nodded. "Yes, if I ever see the putrid dung of a dog again I will kill him on the spot."

"You will spread the word about Jim Twist and let the people know who is responsible?"

"I will."

"Good." Buck got up. "I have to leave; if the soldiers find me here they will kill everyone in the village."

"Where will you go?"

"I have a cabin up on the headwaters of the Marias River where I trapped. I will go there and then when the snow melts in the high country, I will go into Rupert's Land. Badger knows the cabin."

Hurit's eyes were streaming tears as she listened to her son. "Your brother is out hunting. You will not wait to see your brother?"

"The longer I stay the more danger you are in. Tell him to come to the cabin. Also tell him the roan horse is at Fort Benton and he should go get it."

Hurit and Nuttah embraced Buck as they cried.

He Who Fights slapped him on the shoulder. "May the Old Man watch over you."

Buck turned abruptly and went out of the lodge. He stood in the cold clear air and listened. Ice cracked on the river, snow sifted down through the trees, branches snapped, and ravens squawked. He heard nothing else. Stepping into the saddle, he made his way north to the Marias River.

Reaching the cabin Buck studied the area around it. The snow and ice had broken down the brush giving him a clear field of view all around. He would need that to watch for his enemies who might find this place, he doubted they could, but anything was possible. He would need to plan for an escape if needed.

He pushed the door open and walked into the darkened cabin. He had cut window holes in the log walls and covered them with oilskin he had brought up from the fort. It offered a dull light to the interior.

Candles and matches wrapped in elk skin were on the table where he had left them. He stood two of the candles up in the wooden holders he had carved and lit them. The dried beans, hard tack, and jerked venison he had hung from the rafters to keep them away from vermin were still intact. He could at least eat.

He had been in the cabin for a month when the ice began to break and the snow thawed under a warming sun. He had stayed to the cabin and did not venture further than to shoot whatever game was close, which was mainly snowshoe hares and fool hens. He had eaten the last of the beans and hardtack. With the thaw and warming he might be able to kill a deer or elk.

He was standing outside the cabin taking in the warming sun. He had closed his eyes for a moment and when he opened them again Badger was sitting on the roan horse looking at him. Badger grinned. "You are getting so careless. If I had seizers chasing me, I would be more careful."

"I heard you coming half way down the river. I came out to meet you, but you move as slow as an old woman. I got bored waiting for you and fell asleep."

"Liar. You should go join the Cree or the seizers if you want to be a liar. They can teach you how to do it well."

Buck feigned a sad expression, "Now, you went and hurt my feelings."

Badger dismounted. "I doubt it. Have any coffee?"

"Ran out."

"Thought as much." Badger pulled a bundle from behind his saddle and handed it to Buck. "Here."

Buck took the bundle and opened it to find cloth sacks of coffee and beans. "Thanks. I was wondering how I was going to get some more food."

"Well, don't just stand there like a love struck girl, cook it up."

They went into the cabin and shut the door. Buck started with the coffee. "I take it you went to the fort."

Badger nodded, "Got your horse back."

"Your horse, Badger. Have any trouble getting it?"

"No, I had Jim Twist get it for me. I asked him what

was going on since the slaughter."

"How is Jim doing?"

"He is well. He is helping Prater. He acted shamed when I came up to him. I told him that you had spoken up for him and that we held no bad feelings against him."

"I'm sure that made him feel better."

"It did. He said Generals Sherman and Sheridan did a nice job of covering up for the slaughter."

Buck snorted with disgust, "I expected as much."

"Jim said they stopped the investigation that Prater started and turned the whole thing into a battle and victory for the army where two hundred Blackfeet warriors were killed."

Buck cursed under his breath. "What a pack of lies."

"We are talking about the liars of liars, the treaty breakers and killers of women and children. Do you think another lie is anything to them?"

Buck shook his head and went back to making the coffee. "Is Jim still scouting for the army?"

"No, he said that Clarke and Shelton both called him a liar when he told them the shooting was in self-defense. He told Shelton what he thought of the whole affair and him, and then he quit. He said Shelton called for the Territorial Marshal to hunt you down and arrest you for murder."

Buck cursed again. "The marshal will stay on it, where the army has other problems to deal with and might have given up."

"Jim said that Del Yarrow is alive and saying that you drew your gun to kill them. They tried to defend themselves, but you were ahead of them. Jim said he told them different and they said he was lying to protect you."

"That sounds about right."

"Who do you think the seizers are going to believe, two Indians speaking the truth or one white man lying?"

"I need to get into Canada. I have to go by way of the high country and it's still too snowed in to get my horse through. If I drop down to the lowlands and try to go across the border they'll have me."

"Leave your horse and snowshoe across the mountain."

"I can't leave my horse."

Badger laughed, "A true Blood, can't part with his horse to save his life."

Buck gave a weak grin, "Something like that. I want to show you something."

Buck pulled his bunk away from the wall and took out his knife. He poked the tip of it into the hard packed dirt that made up the cabin floor. He worked the knife around and lifted a four foot long hand cut slab of pine, leaving a four-by-one-foot hole in the floor. "If they catch me in here and take me away I will hide my knife, Remington, and Henry and ammunition in here. You come back and get them. You can have them. You already have your roan back."

"But, they will not believe you are without a gun and will tear up the place looking."

Buck picked up a well-worn Navy .36 caliber from the bunk. "I picked this old thing up a long time ago for a backup gun. I'll give this to them if they come. I hope I don't have to do any of this and can just get away."

Badger watched Buck fit the slab back in place. "I will remember."

"What will happen to you if they take you?"

Buck shrugged, "Hang me or send me to prison."

Badger frowned. "Let us hope you make it to Rupert's Land."

Badger stayed the night and then left the next morning promising to go back down to the fort and get more news for Buck. He would come back and if Buck wasn't there he would check the gun cache and if the guns were there he would know he had been taken. If Buck was gone and so were the guns, he would know he got away.

Every couple of days Buck checked the route over the mountains he needed to take into Canada. Even as the snow melted away on the flats to the east and the low hills burst forth with green grass and wild flowers, the pass remained in deep snow and ice. Each time he rode up into the rugged pass that few men outside of his people knew about, he made it a bit further until the bay bellied out in the snow.

Buck estimated the month to be June. There was still snow in the colder spots that the sun never reached; however, he should be able to make it over the high pass now. He was packing up his gear when he heard noises outside. He stopped and listened. It was the movement of horses. His people never made that much noise so it meant only one thing.

He hunkered down and peeked out of the cabin's sole window. He could see riders moving in position around the cabin. He cursed to himself, he had been so close. He quickly pulled the bunk back and pried up the board in the floor. Wrapping the guns in buckskin he dropped them in the hole along with the Bowie. He covered the plank with dirt, packed it down, and then pushed the bed back in place covering the scratch marks made by the bunk legs.

A voice called out, "Buck Drake, this is Territorial Marshal Allen. You are surrounded by my posse. Come on out and make this easy on everyone."

Buck stayed inside and waited. He didn't trust them enough to believe he wouldn't be shot the moment he walked out.

"I know the circumstances of your charges, Buck. You will get a fair hearing. I need you to come out and go down the mountain with me."

Buck shouted out, "Am I going to take a bullet the

minute I step out, like Swift Runner did?"

"You have my word Buck, no one will harm you. Throw out your guns and walk out showing me your hands."

Several minutes of silence passed before Allen spoke again. "Major Bates is convinced you are hiding in the Teton River village. He wants to ride through it and take you out, and you know how he rides through a village. I'd be the first to say that Bates is scum, so let's not give him the excuse. I can't hold him off forever."

Buck pushed open the cabin door and looked out. The marshal was sitting on his horse looking at him. The fact that he was trusting Buck not to shoot him said a lot.

"Throw your guns out, Buck."

"I've only got the one." He threw the old Navy out.

A voice shouted out, "He's a liar. I know he's got a Henry and a good pistol in there not what he just throwed out there."

"How about it, Buck? You have a Henry in there?"

"I gave my good guns to my brother in case I got caught. I only kept that one."

"Okay, walk on out here with your hands up."

Buck put his hands up and walked out. It was either that or have Bates slaughter his family. He walked out into the sunlight and stood facing the marshal. He could see several men emerging out of the trees and bushes all pointing their guns at him.

Then, he saw Del Yarrow step forward with a grin on his face. "Got you, breed."

Buck looked up at Allen, "He knew I had been trapping up here. You just kept wandering around until you found it."

"Yes."

Yarrow ran into the cabin. "I know he's got other guns in there."

Yarrow came back out empty handed. "Where's the

guns, breed?"

"I told you I gave them to my brother."

"You're a liar."

"Yarrow!" Marshal Allen's voice snapped like a whip. "Shut your stupid mouth and get back. I don't like you and if you give me half an excuse, I'll blow your head off. I don't want to hear another word out of you for the rest of this trip. Am I clear?"

Yarrow glared at him and walked away.

A man came from the back of the cabin leading the saddled bay. "This is the only horse back there, Marshal."

Allen looked at Buck and spoke in a low voice, "I don't blame you for what happened, but I have my job to do."

Buck looked at him, "I understand."

"If you give me your word to come along without problems, I won't bring you down the mountain shackled like an animal."

"You would take the word of a half breed?"

"I would take the word of a man if you give it to me."

"You have my word."

"Mount up and let's get going."

Yarrow yelled out, "You ain't gonna tie him up?"

Allen pulled his revolver, cocked the hammer and pointed it at Yarrow. "What did I say?"

Yarrow's eyes widened as he clamped his mouth shut.

"You're a belly crawling snake and a yellow livered coyote Yarrow, and I'd like nothing better than to gut shoot you, so give me an excuse. Please."

Yarrow turned on his heels and angrily mounted his horse.

Buck watched Allen as he holstered his revolver. He glanced at Buck, "I hate that man."

"Then, why is he with you?"

"He said he knew where to find you. We were well on our way before I figured out what he was."

"So, you were stuck with him."

"Unfortunately."

They moved on down the mountain with Allen riding beside Buck. Three men rode behind them and two, including Yarrow, rode in front. Allen wanted Yarrow where he could keep an eye on him.

Badger stood back in the trees watching them go. He would have jumped in and helped his brother, but if he did they would have had to kill the marshal and the men with him. That would not have helped Buck's situation and it would have given the army an excuse to kill the rest of them.

He waited a long while and then went into the cabin and dug up the guns. He came back out of the cabin with the knife and Remington buckled on and the Henry in his hands. He looked around and decided to ride for Fort Benton to see if there was anything Prater or Jim Twist could do for his brother.

Chapter Twenty-Four

Buck sat in a cell in Marshal Allen's Helena office awaiting his trial. Allen had told him that the judge would be up from Virginia City in a few days. The trial would be civilian rather than military since Buck was a civilian working for the army, but not military himself.

Jim Twist had ridden down to see him and said he would stick around and speak up for him at the trial. He said that Yarrow was going around telling everyone how Buck was going to hang and if the judge didn't hang him, there were people who would.

Allen explained to Buck that the days of the vigilantes were at an end. Territorial Governor Potts had put his foot down on the practice and the last men who drug someone out and hung him were tried for murder and in turn hung. Yarrow was just making noise.

Buck sat in the cell with Allen sitting outside the bars. "What will the judge do with me?" Buck asked.

"Well, there's not enough evidence to charge you with murder and hang you, so you can stop worrying about that. Depending on how the judge feels about the witness testimony, he could charge you with manslaughter and sentence you to prison for a few years. If he sees it as self-defense, he could let you go altogether."

"That's not going to happen and you and I both know that. It's my word against Del Yarrow's and he's a lying snake, but he's white and I'm a half breed. It will be Jim Twist's story against Clarke's and Jim's a half breed, too, and Clarke's an army officer, so guess who will be believed there."

Allen looked at Buck, "It isn't fair, I know."

"If it was fair, Bates would be on trial for mass murder and Yarrow would be in here for the murder of Swift Runner. Instead, they have been painted as heroes killing over two hundred vicious warriors in a *fierce battle.*"

Allen could only sit and look at Buck as there was nothing he could say to that. He knew Buck was right and he was powerless to make it different. He had performed his duty and for the first time it had not set well with him.

"So, tell me exactly what did happen, how you came to kill those men."

"I admit I went after them. I was going to beat them to within an inch of their lives for what they had done. I was going to turn Jones over to Shelton as a deserter. When I found them they were hiding and drunk.

"Del Yarrow came at me with a knife. Jones and Abe Yarrow pulled guns and I shot them before they could shoot me. That's the whole story. Jim and a Gros Ventre scout came on it right after, they didn't see the actual shooting though. Shelton and Clarke have already called Jim a liar for saying it was self-defense and that he's only trying to cover for me."

"Do you want a lawyer?'

Buck laughed with thick cynicism. "Do you really think any lawyer would want to destroy his place in the community by representing a half breed that killed two white men?"

Allen was silent. He knew no lawyer would cut his own throat on this case. He also knew that Buck would not get a jury of his peers, because Indians, or worse in the eyes of the public, half Indians, were not allowed to participate in the legal system or even step inside a courtroom. "I don't know what to tell you, Buck."

There was a long span of silence between them and then Allen met Buck's eyes. "I wasn't trying too hard to find you. I figured those men got what was coming to them. It was when Major Bates marched into this office and told me I'd better find the murderer of his Sergeant or he would kill every Blackfoot looking for you. That's when I figured I needed to step up the effort to find you and beat him to the punch. Bates sent Yarrow to tell me about your cabin. I was between a rock and a hard place. I had to bring you in."

"Yes, for the sake of my people. I'll gladly trade my life for their protection." Buck paused a moment and then added, "I appreciate how you've treated me."

Allen nodded. "I understand you fought through the war."

"I was someone then and looked on as an important part of the fight. Now, I'm just another half breed and what I did counts for nothing."

"Heckuva thing isn't it?" Allen stood up. "I'm going for some supper. I'll bring you back a decent meal."

Two days later the judge arrived from Virginia City. The Helena courtroom was set up and a jury panel selected. Jim Twist was in the room as was Captain Clarke. Del Yarrow sat directly behind the Prosecutor. Buck sat with Marshal Allen at the Defendant's table. A noisy crowd filled the audience section of the room.

Judge McCormick walked out from a back room and sat down at the bench. He pounded his gavel on the table and told the audience to quiet down. He went on to warn the spectators that any man who disrupted the proceedings would be thrown out.

Judge McCormick then looked at Buck. "Do you have legal counsel, Mr. Drake?"

Buck stood up. "No, sir."

"Why not? Considering the charges against you, I believe it would be prudent."

"With all due respect, sir, there isn't a lawyer in this Territory who would represent a half breed."

The audience burst into laughter.

Pounding his gavel on the table McCormick shouted, "One more outburst and I will have this courtroom cleared." The room fell silent as everyone wanted to see what would happen to the accused killer.

The judge then looked at Marshal Allen, "Is that true, Marshal?"

Allen stood up. "Yes, Your Honor. I asked several lawyers if they would represent Mr. Drake and they all said no."

The judge frowned, "Fine state of affairs for the legal system. This is 1872. It's about time this Territory stepped up to the modern age." The comment drew scowls from the audience and Prosecutor.

"The Bench will ask questions on Mr. Drake's behalf." The judge leaned back in his chair. "Mr. Prosecutor, state your charges and case."

The Prosecutor stood up. He was wearing an expensive suit and bobbed his head arrogantly as he cast a sidelong disgusted glance at Buck. "The Territory of Montana charges Buck Drake with the malicious and willful murder of Abraham Yarrow and Sergeant Mervin Jones. We seek the death penalty, Your Honor."

"Call your first witness."

"I call Mr. Delbert Yarrow to the stand."

Yarrow walked with a cocky swagger up to the bench and sat down in the witness chair. The bailiff swore him in.

The Prosecutor walked up to Yarrow. "Will you tell us what transpired on the afternoon in question?"

Yarrow stared at him stupidly and whispered, "What does transpired mean?"

A smattering of stifled laughs went through the audience.

McCormick rolled his eyes back.

"What happened when the men were killed?"

"Oh. Well, the breed . . ."

McCormick cut Yarrow off, "The who?"

Yarrow looked at the judge with the same dull look and pointed at Buck, "The breed."

"The *Breed*, Mr. Yarrow, will be referred to as the

defendant or Mr. Drake. Am I clear?"

Yarrow looked at the Prosecutor, who prompted him with a silent nodded yes.

"Yes," Yarrow answered. "The dependent."

Twitters of laughter again drifted from the audience as the Prosecutor dropped his head in frustration.

McCormick glared at Yarrow, "Just tell your story." Then, he mumbled under his breath, "Idiot."

"Well, Abe and Merv and me was all in the tack room when he come walkin' in, pulled his pistol and sayin' he was gonna kill us. Naturally we pulled our weapons to defend ourselves, but he had his out already and we was too slow and he shot Abe and Merv. I tried to stop him, but he hit me with his gun and was gonna shoot me, but the Captain, he come in and saved me."

The Prosecutor asked, "By 'he' are you referring to Mr. Drake?"

"Uh huh, the dependent."

The Prosecutor clenched his jaw and then relaxed it. Using the simplest language he could he asked, "So, Mr. Drake said he was going to kill you all and then he did. Is that what you are saying?"

"Yeah."

The Prosecutor glared at him, "Yeah, *what*?"

Yarrow looked at him confused, "Yeah . . . sir?"

The Prosecutor growled, "I was referring to your statement about Mr. Drake saying he was going to kill you."

"Oh, yeah, he said he was gonna kill us and then he did."

Knowing he didn't dare have Yarrow say more he dismissed him from the stand.

"Just a moment," McCormick stopped Yarrow. "Reading this report of the case, it is mentioned that there was a partial bottle of whiskey on the floor. Had the three of you been drinking?"

"Oh, no sir. Actually, we had got together to sing hymns for the Sunday church meetin'.'."

McCormick raised an eyebrow, "Singing hymns?"

Laughter came from the audience.

"Yes, sir. We don't sing so good and was told to practice our singin' in the tack barn."

McCormick glared at the Prosecutor, "Such an articulate and *pious* witness. Do you have any more like him from the mental institution?"

The audience burst into laughter. McCormick told them to quiet down.

"Yes, Your Honor, I mean no, Your Honor. I do have Captain Clarke, who arrived on the scene shortly after the shooting."

"Call him up. Mr. Yarrow go sit down."

Yarrow walked back to his seat. Clarke stepped up to the witness chair and was sworn in.

The Prosecutor strolled up to him. "Tell us what you saw Captain Clarke."

"I heard two gunshots come from the interior of the barn. I was nearby and came on the run to see Mr. Drake galloping out of the barn on his horse. I entered the tack room and saw three men lying on the floor. The physician was summoned, he checked them and declared Sergeant Jones and Abraham Yarrow dead. Delbert Yarrow was unconscious."

McCormick looked at Clarke. "Captain, if Delbert Yarrow was unconscious how did he see you come in and *save* him?"

"He was unconscious when I came in the room, sir."

McCormick glared at the Prosecutor and then at Yarrow. "A little discrepancy in our story, Mr. Yarrow?"

Yarrow stared at him and squirmed in his chair.

The Prosecutor quickly continued, "Was anyone else in the area, Captain?"

255

"Yes, Scout Jim Twist and the two Indian scouts."

"Did you speak to them?"

"Yes, I asked them what had happened."

"What did they say?"

"The Indians said nothing. Twist said it was self-defense."

"Self-defense?" The Prosecutor feigned shock. "Why would he claim that? Did he witness the act?"

"My belief is he witnessed the murders and was covering for his friend."

McCormick broke in, "Strike that statement from the record. The charges of murder have not been established. Nor is this court interested in what you believe, Captain Clarke, only in what you know. Do you *know* for a fact Mr. Twist witnessed the act and was covering for Mr. Drake?"

Clarke stiffened in his chair, "No, sir."

"Then, keep your opinions to yourself. Did you see any weapons about the dead men?"

"I don't recall."

McCormick frowned, "Not very observant for a military officer, are you? Mr. Twist says in his report that there were weapons; however, you could not see them?"

Clarke sat in stiff silence.

"Yes, brilliant answer, Captain Clarke. Is that all you actually witnessed?"

"Yes, Your Honor. I assumed . . ."

McCormick cut him off, "Again, Captain Clarke, this court is interested in facts, not your assumptions. You heard shots, found two men dead, and Mr. Drake riding away. Did you actually witness anything other than that?"

Clarke scowled and snapped, "No, sir."

McCormick looked at the Prosecutor. "Any other witnesses?"

"No, Your Honor."

"Fine. Captain, you may step down." McCormick's

eyes followed Clarke as he sat back down. He knew a stacked deck when he saw one and didn't appreciate his courtroom being used for a kangaroo court.

"I find it interesting that there are no reports from other troopers on the scene," McCormick said as he held his eyes on Clarke. "Perhaps, Fort Shaw was closed for a holiday and no one else was there?"

Clarke stood back up. "There were no other troopers in the barn at the time, sir."

McCormick gave him a look of mock surprise, "Really. You are aware of the term *perjury* are you not Captain Clarke?" He then turned toward Jim Twist, "Mr. Twist, would you please take the stand?"

Jim Twist walked forward, was sworn in, and then sat down.

McCormick began, "Mr. Twist, yours is the only report this court received, and we received it through Marshal Allen."

"Yes sir, I didn't believe it would make it to you if I sent it through Fort Shaw. I filed my original report with Lieutenant Prater at Fort Benton. I feared it would be cut off before reaching court, so I filed the same report directly with Marshal Allen two days ago."

"And why did you fear that?"

Twist threw a glance at Clarke. "Just a feeling, sir."

McCormick followed Twist's glance to Yarrow and Clarke, "I can understand that. Please give us your story, Mr. Twist."

"I was walking into the barn with Jack and Antelope Eater, the other two scouts, when we heard shots coming from the tack room. We ran in that direction and found three men lying on the tack room floor. Two of the men had pistols in their hands and Dell Yarrow had a knife on the ground next to him."

"So, there *were* weapons in the reach of the men."

"Yes, sir."

"Was Mr. Drake there?"

"Yes, sir. He said Del Yarrow had charged him with a knife and he had knocked him down with a saddle billet, and then the other two had drawn guns and pointed them at him, and he shot first."

"A saddle billet? Mr. Yarrow said Mr. Drake struck him with a drawn pistol."

"I saw the billet on the ground next to Yarrow."

"Go on, what did Mr. Drake do then?"

"He said no one would believe it was self-defense, so he got on his horse and took off."

"Did anyone actually witness the incident?"

"Not that I am aware of, sir."

"Were there other troopers in the barn?"

"There were several who rushed in after the shooting."

"Did any of the troopers look into the tack room and see the men on the floor and the weapons?"

"Yes, sir, several did."

McCormick nodded. "Your witness, Mr. Prosecutor."

The Prosecutor came toward Twist. "Mr. Twist, did Mr. Drake have a grudge against either of the Yarrows?"

Twist looked at him, "I don't know."

"How long have you known, Mr. Drake?"

"A year or two."

"And you worked closely together as scouts, did you not?"

"Yes, for a while."

"And you never heard Mr. Drake say anything about Abraham or Delbert Yarrow?"

"Not that I recall."

The Prosecutor gestured toward Yarrow, "Do you see Mr. Yarrow's hand? His hand was as whole as yours and mine until a few years ago when Mr. Drake attacked him with a knife at Fort Benton. He also put out the eye of

Abraham Yarrow during the same attack. Oh, yes, Mr. Drake has held a long grudge against the Yarrows.

"Sergeant Jones was involved in the battle with the Blackfeet. Is there a chance Mr. Drake held him a grudge as well because he may have killed, in battle, some of his relatives?"

Jim Twist stiffened, "That was no *battle*. I was there. It was a slaughter of women and children."

"That is not what I heard and my sources are impeccable. I heard it was a difficult battle and our brave soldiers won against terrible odds."

Twist ground his teeth, "That's a lie. It was the slaughter of helpless people. Unarmed women, children and old men. Major Bates and half his officers were drunk."

The Prosecutor was now wholly playing to the jury. "My God, Mr. Twist, such an accusation against our brave men in blue who defend us day and night against the relentless abuse the white settler suffers at the hands of the Blackfeet. I am appalled, Mr. Twist."

Twist's anger was mounting. "That's a bunch of horse apples," he snapped out."

"You sound very angry, Mr. Twist. I can imagine that Mr. Drake must have been equally angry over the victory scored by our troops."

"He *was!*" At that point Twist knew he had been tricked and had said the wrong thing.

The Prosecutor smiled, "Possibly angry enough to kill. I have no more need of this witness Your Honor." He turned and walked back to his seat.

Twist knew it was nothing in itself, but it was enough for the jury to use as a basis for finding Buck guilty. He suddenly felt sick.

Judge McCormick sat in momentary silence. This was legal trickery and jury manipulation at its lowest. It was enough to sway the jury against Drake, as if they needed it, even though there was little evidence to prove the prosecution's case. "You may step down, Mr. Twist."

Twist could not look at Buck as he returned to his seat. He had been baited and he took the bait like a hungry trout.

McCormick looked at the Prosecutor. "Closing statement, Mr. Prosecutor?"

"No, Your Honor, I think our case has been made."

McCormick turned his attention to Buck. "Would you like to say anything in your defense, Mr. Drake?"

Buck shook his head.

Judge McCormick looked at the jury, "You may now deliberate your verdict."

The twelve men stood up and filed into the adjacent room.

Buck looked over at Jim Twist, smiled at him and gave him a nod that said he did not blame him for what he was tricked into saying. Twist in turn, gave him a weak smile. Marshal Allen sat stone silent, his jaw grinding as the only indication of the anger he was holding down.

The jury was out less than fifteen minutes before they filed back in. Judge McCormick gave them a disgusted look. As they sat down he asked, "What is the jury's verdict?"

The foreman stood up and looked at Buck with a smirk, "We unanimously find the defendant, Buck Drake guilty of the murders of Abraham Yarrow and Sergeant Mervin Jones."

Del Yarrow jumped up and cheered.

McCormick scowled as he turned his head and glared at Yarrow. He then looked at Marshal Allen, "Marshal, place that man under arrest for contempt of court."

Yarrow froze in mid-cheer and looked at the judge.

Allen glared at Yarrow, "Yes, sir."

Yarrow sat back down looking scared.

McCormick turned his attention to Buck. "Mr. Drake, please stand."

Buck stood up and faced the judge.

"Before I proclaim sentence Mr. Drake, is there anything you would like to say?"

Buck stood straight and looked the judge in the eye. "Only that I find it remarkable that a fine, upstanding man like Jim Twist is called a liar. That his eye witness account of the slaughter of two hundred women, children, and old men was discounted as a lie and his testimony on my behalf has no value. While at the same time, a worthless man like Del Yarrow, known to be a drunkard, thief, liar, and murderer, is held up as a symbol of truth and honesty.

"I won't stand here and lie to you, sir and treat you like a fool. Yes, I shot those men. I shot them in self-defense; they were drunk and pulled weapons on me when I came to them for an accounting of what they had done on the Marias River. Yarrow is lying, but his testimony is of more value than mine or Jim's because he is white and we are half breeds.

"I ran because I knew no one would believe me, and I was right, no one has. I look to you, sir, for justice as I feel you are an honest and decent man." Buck then sat back down.

McCormick studied Buck for a silent few seconds and then spoke. "This jury has found you guilty, requiring me to pass sentence in spite of my personal feelings on this matter. However, the charges are mine to affix to this case. How this court has interpreted the written report of Mr. Twist, and the testimony I have heard today, and the fact that the only eye witness, in this judge's opinion, is of questionable repute and intelligence, the charge is two counts of manslaughter, not murder in the first or second degree.

"The maximum sentence for manslaughter is five years for each count. Being that there is unclear proof of self-defense, nor is there sufficient proof that the act was deliberate or premeditated, this court sentences you to five years in the Territorial Prison in Deer Lodge, Montana Territory."

The men in the audience began to protest and shout angrily for hanging Buck. McCormick stood up and pounded his gavel on the bench. "*Shut up*," he shouted. The room turned quiet.

"The United States Court system is not run by a mob, to bow under to the protests of unruly men. Governor Potts has set a precedent for hanging vigilantes in this territory. Should vigilantism take place against Mr. Drake, I will personally sentence any man involved to hang. I will then instruct Governor Potts to declare Martial Law over the city, and the troopers will come from Fort Benton, not Fort Ellis, a fort that is well reputed to be under the command of a drunk."

McCormick turned his attention to Marshal Allen. "You will return Mr. Drake to jail and take Mr. Yarrow into custody. Lock up Yarrow for five days and transport Mr. Drake to the prison in Deer Lodge immediately. This court is dismissed." He slammed his gavel down on the bench.

The audience poured out of the courtroom uttering curses and angry talk. The sentencing had not gone according to their wants and demands. They also knew the judge was serious about hanging vigilantes, as it had been done already.

Jim Twist came to see Buck at the jail. He stood in front of the bars looking sick. "I'm sorry for saying the wrong thing, Buck."

"You were tricked, Jim. They had the deck stacked against me from the start. Clarke made sure of that."

"I got into it with Shelton. He decided you were a murderer and wouldn't even listen to reason. He said I was a liar when I told him about Jones. I quit and so did Jack

Spit in the Devil's Eye

and Antelope Eater."

"I thought Shelton liked me."

"Sure didn't sound like it."

Buck sat silent for a second and then looked at his friend. "Jim, I'm sorry I hit you and treated you like I did. We're friends and I didn't even give you a chance to say anything. I've felt like a dirty dog ever since."

Jim gave him a sad look, "Under the circumstances, and if I'd have been told what you were, I would have done the same thing."

"Maybe, but it was still a lousy thing for me to do."

"A lot of lousy things have been happening lately, but that wasn't one of them." He put out his hand to Buck, "See you when you get out. I'll do all I can for our people."

Buck shook his hand and watched as his friend walked out the door.

The next day Marshal Allen shook Buck's hand as he left him off with the guard at the prison in Deer Lodge. He promised to do what he could to help him.

Buck was taken inside by two gruff guards who ordered him around at every move. He was told the rules of the prison and that no nonsense or fighting would be tolerated. His clothes were taken from him and he was given a black and white striped shirt and pants and a pair of hard shoes. He was then marched down the line of cells and pushed inside one with three other men dressed in striped pants and shirts. The cell door slammed shut behind him.

One of the men walked up to him and stood nose-to-nose with him. "You get me tobacco if you want to stay alive in here."

Without a warning, Buck slammed his fist into the man's stomach, grabbed the back of his head and pulled it down as he drove up with a knee, smashing the man's nose across his face in a spurt of blood. He shoved the man back into his bunk where he lay still, looking dead as blood poured from his smashed nose. The other two men sat on

263

their bunks and looked at him unmoved by the action.

He looked at the two, "I'm a Blood, don't threaten me." With that, he sat down on the only empty bunk.

He sat there feeling like his life was ended. He was in a cage and could not see the sky. A whistle suddenly blew and the cell doors were opened by the guards who herded the prisoners into a bleak dining room. They were forced to stand in a line perfectly quiet and still until another whistle sounded and they all moved toward a long table where they were each handed a tin plate of beans with a chunk of stale bread on it. A cup of water and a spoon came with it.

Buck followed the other men and did as they did. He sat down and they all began to eat. A prisoner walked up to Buck and stood over him. Buck looked up at the man. The man was huge in stature, heavily muscled, with a bald scarred head. The guards were obviously ignoring the big man.

"You will give me your meal every day," he snarled at Buck.

"Or what?"

"Or you won't see the next day."

Buck slammed his fist into the man's groin putting every bit of power he had behind it. The man let out a squeak and fell to his knees with his head down and his jaw hanging open in pain. Buck stood up and hit the man across his loose jaw, breaking it.

He could hear running feet rushing toward him and then something hit him hard across the head. The last thing he saw were guards closing in on him as he faded off into darkness.

Del Yarrow served his five-day sentence in jail. Allen did not speak to him even when Yarrow tried to engage him in conversation. His release was not one minute early. Allen shoved him out the door telling him his horse was at the livery. He had to pay the livery the last of his money to get his horse back

Yarrow was almost to Fort Shaw when a man rode directly up to him on a lonely stretch of road. Yarrow looked at the big revolver pointed at his chest. He heard the shot at the same time he felt a horrible pain slam him backwards out of the saddle. As he lay on the ground dying, he thought he saw an Indian riding away on his brother's roan horse.

Chapter Twenty-Five

Governor Potts sat in his chair looking through a sheaf of papers while an army officer sat across the desk from him. The Governor shook his head, "Wretched business this gang. Robbery, murder, kidnapping. I want it stopped."

The officer asked, "What are they doing with the kidnapped people?"

"Running them up through Canada and shipping them out of British Columbia as slaves to Asia and other foreign markets."

"I have to apologize, Governor, but I am not familiar with this situation. My commanding officer told me to report to you and that I would be informed of my duties at that time."

"And you will be. I have gathered a task force in cooperation with the Canadian authorities to root out this gang. All those involved will be meeting here shortly."

"Who all is coming, sir?"

"Yourself, representing the army in the western Montana Territory. Officer Tracy of the Northwest Mounted Police, and a special federal investigator from Washington that I have been fortunate enough to have sent to us."

"Who would that be, sir?"

"I don't know exactly who, he wouldn't give me a name. The agency head, Colonel Parker assured me this is his top man in investigating federal crimes, in particular if they involve other countries."

A knock sounded on the closed door of the Governor's office. His Secretary would be the only one to knock during a closed meeting. "Come in," Potts called out.

The Governor's Secretary opened the door. "Governor, your special investigator from Washington is here."

"Excellent, show him right in."

With a gesture toward the open door of the office, the Secretary stepped aside to let the man walk in. The man was well dressed in a black suit that accented his neatly trimmed graying hair and short beard. He carried himself with confidence, shoulders back, indicating a man who knew his business. The Governor looked at him and saw in the man's face a hardness that said he had not lived an easy life.

The Governor stood up as did the officer. The man walked up to the Governor and extended his hand, "Pleasure to meet you Governor Potts, I have heard some very good things about you."

Potts beamed, "Well, that is always good to know. You have me at a disadvantage sir, and I must apologize for not addressing you properly; however Colonel Parker did not tell me the name of the man he was sending."

The man smiled, "He wouldn't. Renard Ravenel, Governor."

"Ah, a Frenchman."

Ravenel smiled, "So I'm told."

Potts gestured toward the officer, "Mr. Ravenel, Captain Clarke of Fort Shaw." The two men shook hands.

The Secretary stuck his head back into the office, "Sergeant Major Tracy is here."

"Very good, we are all here. Send him right in."

Sergeant Major Tracy stepped smartly into the room, his bright red tunic bearing four inverted chevrons on the right shoulder commanded attention. Under his left arm was a blue brimless cap and in that hand a black leather satchel. He stopped abruptly in front of the Governor smacking his knee-high polished brown boots solidly on the floor. "Sergeant Major Wade Tracy, sir, at your service."

Potts shook his hand and introduced him to the other two men who exchanged handshakes with him.

Potts sat down. "Let us get down to business shall we. The men took seats around the desk.

Ravenel looked around, "Is this it?"

"You were expecting someone else?" Potts asked confused.

"I have read the full file and reports concerning this gang and they have kidnapped Blackfeet girls, as well as white."

"Yes?"

"Why isn't there a representative from the Blackfeet Confederacy here?"

Clarke smiled without humor, "Surely, Mr. Ravenel, you don't expect us to have a redskin on this panel."

Tracy's eyes snapped a quick disapproving look at Clarke. "Perhaps if you treated the Indians as people, as we do, you would have less problem with them."

Potts held up his hand, "Let's not start this off with a quarrel. I will look into your request, Mr. Ravenel."

Ravenel nodded and then turned to give Clarke a hard glare. He then continued on, "We will need at least one man who can help guide us through the country where the gang is operating."

"Why is that?" Clarke asked.

Ravenel did not like Clarke. "Because, Captain Clarke, this will involve riding through the mountains of Montana and Canada, among the white populations and the Indian. I used to know this country once long ago, but I'm sure much has changed since then. We will need someone friendly with the Blackfeet who can get us into the villages. This will not be a march around the parade ground, Captain Clarke."

Clarke stiffened as he glared at Ravenel. Ravenel returned the glare with a steady eye.

Tracy opened his satchel. "Mr. Ravenel is correct, we will be working in wilderness and among the natives.

We will need interpreters and guides." He then pulled several sheets of paper out of the satchel.

"We were given information from some of the Blackfeet and white robbery victims that the leader of this gang, as well as two of the men with him, spoke with strong British accents. Therefore, we began sending inquiries to the authorities in several cities in Great Britain and we believe we have the name of the leader."

Tracy had everyone's attention as he shifted the papers.

"There was a gang of criminals based out of Liverpool, England; however, they did not limit their criminal activities to that city alone. They were pursued hard by the British authorities and then they disappeared. It is believed they left the country. We believe they entered into North America through British Columbia and eventually into the Montana Territory. The descriptions we received from England of the gang leaders match those given us from the victims. The leader is a man by the name of Jules Drake."

Ravenel stared at the paper in front of Tracy. "Jules Drake? Why do I know that name?"

Tracy looked up at him. "You know this man?"

"I've heard that name."

Clarke sniffed, "Probably related to that half breed murderer, Buck Drake."

Ravenel's head snapped around to look at Clarke. "Did you say Buck Drake?"

"Yes, some worthless half breed who murdered two men at Fort Shaw, one an army Sergeant."

"How long ago?"

Clarke gave off a careless shrug, "Three or four years ago. I testified against him at his trial. He got a mere five year sentence in the Territorial prison when the redskin coward should have been hung."

Ravenel's jaw clenched with anger, "That *worthless*

half breed coward, Captain Clarke, was awarded three medals for bravery during the war. How many did you win? He was my best friend and he saved my life and that of another man during the war. I was told he died at Chickamauga."

All eyes turned to look at Ravenel. Clarke growled with disgust.

Loud arguing voices came from outside of the office. Potts got up from his seat, stormed across the room and jerked the door open. "What is going on out here?"

The Secretary's voice sounded frustrated, "It's Marshal Allen again, about that Buck Drake business."

Ravenel jumped out of his chair and rushed out to the reception room. "What about Buck Drake?"

Marshal Allen was facing the Secretary with an angry scowl. He looked at Ravenel and took in his well-dressed appearance. "I have been trying for over three years to get Governor Potts to review the case against Buck Drake. He was sentenced on biased testimony by a biased jury and unfairly imprisoned."

"What is his charge?" Ravenel asked.

"Manslaughter, but it was self-defense."

"I'm sure it was, I know Buck."

Allen's face showed his surprise, "You do?"

"Yes. Don't worry Marshal, I will be dealing with this right now."

"Thank you, sir." Allen glowered at the Secretary and left the room.

Potts and Ravenel returned to their seats. Ravenel looked at Potts, "Buck Drake is the guide we need for this task force."

Clarke jumped from his chair and shouted, "You can't be serious! Put that murdering redskin on this panel?"

Tracy's eyes flicked from Ravenel to Clarke and back to Ravenel. "Do you think Buck Drake is the man to track down this gang?"

"Absolutely."

"*Why?*" Clarke shouted.

"I remember now why I know that name. Jules Drake is Buck's father, and Buck hates his guts. Buck knows the mountains, can go into any Blackfeet village, and he would march through hell to get his hands on that man."

Tracy nodded, "Sounds like our man."

"Well, not to me it doesn't!" Clarke shouted.

Ravenel looked at Governor Potts. "I want two things Governor, in fact I insist on them. I want Buck Drake released from prison." He then pointed at Clarke, "And I want this man off this task force."

"You can't do that," Clarke sneered.

"I second the motion," Tracy said matter-of-factly. "I also want this man off this task force. We need a man who will work with us, not a pompous ass fighting us every inch of the way."

Potts sat silently as he quickly ran this unexpected turn of events through his mind deciding on the best course of action. He was not about to go against the Washington man or the Canadian representative. In truth Captain Clarke had already worn on his nerves.

Potts looked from Tracy to Ravenel. "I do want a representative from the United States Army on this."

"Certainly," Ravenel agreed, "just not this one."

Clarke stared unbelievingly from one man to the other as the Governor considered his situation.

Potts studied Ravenel. "You are sure about this Buck Drake? He's the man for the job?"

"Yes."

Potts looked at Tracy, "And you, Sergeant Major Tracy?"

"If Mr. Ravenel feels that strongly about him, I will agree." He glanced at Clarke, "On both counts."

Potts turned his attention back to Ravenel, "I had

originally contacted Colonel Shelton about coming to this meeting and he sent Captain Clarke."

"Then, tell Colonel Shelton to get over here himself and at least understand the situation before he sends one of his subordinates."

"I agree," Tracy added. "This is Colonel Shelton's district, he needs to at least make an appearance."

Clarke clenched his fists in rage as he glared hard at Ravenel. Ravenel stepped to within inches of Clarke meeting, his eyes. "Do you have something you want to say to me or are you merely posturing for effect?"

Clarke remained silent and stepped back diverting his eyes.

Potts made his decision. "Very well." He called for his Secretary who came directly into the room.

"I want two things done immediately," Potts said. "I want a wire sent to Colonel Shelton at Fort Shaw ordering him to this office, but first I want a Governor's pardon drawn up for Buck Drake effective immediately."

The Secretary stared at the Governor his mouth open, "But, sir . . ."

"Did I say argue with me?" Potts snapped. "Or did I say immediately?"

"Yes, sir, immediately."

The man rushed out of the room.

Potts glanced at Clarke, "You may leave, Captain Clarke."

Clarke was astounded. "I don't believe this."

"Believe it, Captain. I want universal cooperation on this operation and you have proven in less than one hour that you are argumentative, uncooperative, arrogant, and a millstone around our necks, and as Sergeant Major Tracy so aptly put it, 'a pompous ass.' I want these criminals on the gallows and we certainly won't accomplish that with you dragging us down. Now, leave or I will have you removed."

Clarke's eyes burned his hatred at the two men who demanded his removal. Ravenel and Tracy both met his eyes stoically reflecting that neither was intimidated by his temper. Potts ignored him altogether. Clarke stomped out of the room.

Potts turned his attention to Ravenel, "I hope you know what you're doing."

"I do." He then added, "I want two more men on this task force."

"Not more prisoners I hope, I can only pardon so many."

"United States Marshal Kai Maddock out of Denver, and Marshal Allen."

Potts let go of the breath he was holding. "Well, I can agree with putting two lawmen on the force, but why Marshal Allen? You don't even know the man."

"Because any lawman who would work that hard to find justice for a man he arrested is a man I can trust."

The Secretary came in with the written pardon and handed it to the Governor who signed it. As the Secretary turned to leave Ravenel stopped him. "Please send a wire for me."

"Of course, sir."

Ravenel took the Governor's pen from his desk and a sheet of blank paper. He wrote, *US Marshal Maddock, Denver, Colorado. Federal order. Report to Governor's office, Virginia City Montana, immediately for mission. I found Buck. Raven.*

He handed the note to the Secretary and looked back at the Governor. "I think we should break off for right now and meet again when the Marshals and Buck can plan with us."

"Yes, we seem to have come unraveled here."

"Trust me, Governor it's for the best."

"I hope so."

Raven took the pardon from the Governor's hand.

"I'll deliver this personally."

Chapter Twenty-Six

The guard opened the door illuminating the tiny dark room. Buck sat on the floor with his back against the wall. The dim light inside the prison was still more than Buck's eyes could quickly adjust to as he put his hand over his eyes. "How am I supposed to get any sleep around here if you keep lighting the lamp?" Buck's tone was belligerent and unbending.

"You must like it in there," the guard laughed. "It's the second thirty-day stretch you've pulled in the box this year, and what is it, five times over all?"

"Six," Buck sarcastically answered. "What do you want?"

"You have a visitor."

"Go to the devil."

"You don't have a choice, Drake. Walk out or get dragged out."

"Why don't you pound on me with that stick again, you like that don't you?"

"You like to fight, Drake and we don't tolerate fighting."

Buck gave him a cynical laugh, "Unless it's from men you're all afraid of and then you let them beat up on whoever they want to. I don't let them beat on me and in your book that's bad. Are you boys still wetting your pants every time Big Earl looks at you? After I changed his singing voice to a little girl's he settled right down. Walks kind of funny though."

"Get out of the cell Drake, I don't have all day."

Buck got up and walked out. "Do I get to take a bath? I smell like the inside of a dead buffalo."

"Just stay downwind and walk. You know where the superintendent's office is."

"I should, I've been beaten up there twice. He doesn't like Indians, you know."

"Shut up and walk."

Buck walked down the hall past the cells with the guard trailing several feet behind. One of the prisoners yelled out from his cell as they passed by, "Hey, big chief, you gonna scalp the superintendent?" Several men laughed and made Indian war cry sounds. Buck thrust his arm into a cell and grabbed a jeering prisoner by the shirt front and yanked him forward smashing his face into the bars.

The guard shoved Buck hard in the back. "Move, Drake." He cast a quick look into the cell where the man sat on the floor pulling a tooth from his bleeding lips. "That oughtta shut you up."

Buck reached the superintendent's door and stopped. The guard knocked on the door and had it opened to him. He pushed Buck into the room. The superintendent stood looking at him and gestured for a guard already in the room to put Buck in a chair. Buck shook off the grabbing hand, "I can sit by myself." The guard smacked him on the shoulder with his stick.

Buck glowered at the guard and then the superintendent. "Who's my visitor?"

"A man from the Governor's office. He probably has decided to hang you."

"Go to hell." Buck slunk down in the chair and fixed his eyes on the open door.

Footsteps approached the door and then he heard a voice that was vaguely familiar say to the outside guard, "Get out of my way."

A guard's voice came on top of it, "It's okay, he has business with the superintendent."

The man walked into the room and looked at Buck slunk down in the chair. Buck's eyes began to widen. He slowly sat upright and whispered, "Raven?"

The guard jabbed Buck in the ribs with his stick. "Shut up unless you're told to speak."

Raven turned his eyes on the guard, "You touch this

man again and I'll put that stick someplace you'll need a surgeon to remove it."

The guard glanced at the superintendent who eyed the stranger suspiciously.

Raven turned his attention to the superintendent. "What kind of place are you running here? When I finish with my reports to the Governor and Washington, you'll be pushing a cart shoveling horse manure off the streets."

The superintendent swallowed nervously. This was an important man; he could see it in his clothes, as well as by his tone and presence. He obviously had big connections.

Raven looked back at Buck feeling a bit of shock at his friend's appearance. He was emaciated. His blonde hair was ragged and streaked with gray. His beard was gray. He looked like a fifty year old man rather than one in his thirties. The years had clearly been hard and him.

"They told us you were dead, Buck. Kai and I went everywhere trying to find you. We had Parker check the records and it said you had been killed at Chickamauga."

Buck could only stare at his old friend, suddenly ashamed of his place and appearance.

A guard went suddenly flying past the open doorway as if jerked by an invisible rope. A voice snarled, "Put a hand on me again and I'll blow your head off." Kai Maddock walked in the door with a badge on his shirt front.

He and Buck stared at each other. "I couldn't believe it when Raven said he had found you. We were told you had been killed."

Buck found his voice, "I looked for you after the war." He shook his head. "I thought you had both been killed at Gettysburg."

"Well, we're all here now, partner," Kai smiled at him.

Kai then looked at Raven, "Did you tell him yet?"

"Not yet." Raven grinned at Buck, "We've got a job

for you."

"I'm kind of stuck in here, Raven."

"Oh, that reminds me." Raven pulled a paper from the inside of his coat pocket and tossed it down on the superintendent's desk. "That's a Governor's pardon for Mr. Drake. He is to be released immediately."

The superintendent picked up the paper and read it. He looked at Raven, confused, "I don't understand."

"You don't need to understand. Marshal Maddock and I are walking out of this outhouse with Mr. Drake. If you have any of his property I suggest you return it immediately or face theft charges that I will personally initiate."

The superintendent gestured to the guard, "Get his things."

The guard hurried out, the sound of his running feet slapping down on the stone hallway floor diminished in the distance.

"Rest assured superintendent," Raven said in a low voice, "you are finished here and there will be changes made."

The guard came back with a cloth sack holding Buck's elkskin shirt, pants, and boots.

Buck hurriedly took off the filthy striped clothes belligerently throwing them in the guard's face who had been hitting him. He put on his own clothes that now hung on him because of all the weight he had lost.

Buck stuck his hands in his pants pockets and then he cursed.

"What's wrong, Buck?" Raven asked.

"I had a hundred dollars of my scout wages in this pocket when they brought me in here and now it's gone."

Raven fixed a furious eye on the superintendent, "*Well?*"

The superintendent in turn gave the same look to the guard, "*Well?*"

The guard held out his hands as if to say he had no idea.

Raven turned to Kai pointing at the superintendent as he did, "Marshal, arrest that man for theft."

Kai began to move toward the superintendent.

"You can't do that," the superintendent protested.

"Actually, I can," Raven responded. "I'm a Federal Investigator, I have nationwide authority. I promise you one thing superintendent, when I start turning over rocks on your little operation here, you will be the one in the striped suit. A theft charge will keep you locked up until we can add others."

"Wait!" The superintendent's shaking hands pulled his wallet from his suit coat. "I have one hundred dollars that I can give Mr. Drake." He laid the bills out on his desk. "I will find out who took the money and they will owe me instead of him."

Raven looked at Buck, "That work for you?"

"As long as I get my money back."

Raven picked the money up from the desk and handed it to Buck. "Looks like you did." He then looked at the superintendent, "There will still be an investigation. Don't think you have appeased me."

The superintendent stood silently clutching his white knuckles around the nearly empty wallet.

Raven glanced at Kai, "Let's get out of here."

The three men walked out together without another word.

They walked out the prison gate and Buck turned his face to the sun and stood still soaking it in.

"We've got a horse for you, Buck," Raven said as he watched his friend.

Buck looked at him and then at Kai, "Thanks for getting me out of there."

"Our pleasure. We both owe you a lot, it's the least we could do."

"What have you both been doing all these years?"

Raven smiled, "There's a lot to tell."

"There's time to talk it all out. Now, what?"

"We have rooms in town, got one for you too. You're probably wanting to take a bath and get a real meal."

Kai laughed, "From the looks of your clothes I'd say you could use about a month of good meals."

Buck glanced down at his clothes that once fit him now hanging loose over his skinny frame. "They feed you beans and stale bread, two meals a day."

Kai looked at Raven, "Steak and spuds, a big steak."

They walked on to where the horses were tied. A well-built blue roan was saddled for Buck. Buck looked the horse over, "Nice horse. I had a bay they gave me after the war, great horse. I lost him when they arrested me. Clarke probably has him, he favored that horse."

"Captain Clarke?"

"You've met him?"

"Yeah, had the pleasure. A real horse's butt."

"He is that."

Buck stepped into the saddle and the three men rode toward Deer Lodge.

The sign for a barber shop and bathhouse caught Buck's eye. "That's my first stop. I'll catch up with you."

Raven nodded, "Meet us at the hotel. Maybe you should get some new clothes while you're at it."

Buck laughed, "No, these will do. After all they haven't been worn in almost four years."

An hour later Buck knocked on Raven's hotel door. Raven opened the door and looked at him. "You look like a new man."

Kai moved up behind Raven. "And you smell like one too. My friend, you *were* a bit gamey."

"Like the inside of a dead buffalo?" Buck grinned.

"Very close."

"Kai and I were discussing the mission and waiting for you," Raven explained. "Now that you're here let's go get some dinner."

"Real food for our friend," Kai laughed.

"And then we'll come back here and I'll fill you in on this job," Raven added.

Sitting down in the restaurant they ordered and sat back relaxing. Buck looked across the table at Raven, "Federal investigator, huh?"

Raven nodded. "At the end of the war, Parker, who by the way is a Colonel now, told Kai and I that he was being put in command of a special department for investigating federal crimes. He wanted us to work with him. I was pushing forty years old and figured I'd better do something with this education I have, and my life, so I took him up on it."

Kai put in, "I wasn't interested in staying in the east and told him I was heading west. Parker said he had some pull and would I be interested in a U.S. Marshal's job in a western area? I said I'd do that. Two days later he told me to report to the Governor in Denver and start work as the Marshal for that district. I've been there ever since. Raven and I have kept in touch, obviously."

Buck smiled, "I'm glad for you both. So, they had me as dead did they?"

Both men nodded at the same time. "We searched for you," Raven began. "We even went to General Sherman and asked. He said he had lost track of you. Then, we asked Parker to check and he found your name in the death records, that you died at Chickamauga."

Kai said, "Well, you can bet we were pretty upset."

"We went on from there figuring you were dead," Raven finished the story.

"I can't blame you for that." Buck grinned, "I wonder how I ended up dead at Chickamauga since I was never even in that battle?"

"Mistaken identity. There wasn't much left of some men so guesses were made."

"I suppose. I looked for you two and found nothing. No one I asked had heard of Parker and I had no idea how to find him. The last I had seen of you two was when we were split up before Gettysburg. With that many dead after the battle I figured you were among them."

"Remember big Sergeant Freeman? He died at Gettysburg."

"That's too bad, I really liked him."

"We all did. It was a big loss, especially to Parker. In spite of their beliefs against it, they were close friends."

They sat in silence for a moment. Raven then changed the subject. "So, you went back home?"

"Yeah, back to the village. Trapped a couple of winters. Got on as a scout at Fort Reno and then when they abandoned the forts on the Bozeman, I went back to the Teton River. Met Jim Twist and hired on as a scout at Fort Shaw, and then Lieutenant Prater, the Indian Agent at Fort Benton, had me sent to work for him as an interpreter."

The meals came and they stopped talking until half the meal was eaten.

"What's this job you have for me?" Buck asked.

Raven shook his head slightly, "Not here, back in the room."

Buck nodded and continued eating.

Raven asked, "Do you know Colonel Shelton?"

"I knew him as Major Shelton at Fort Shaw. My friend, Jim Twist was Shelton's head scout. Jim told me Shelton went against me on the shooting and called Jim a liar when he tried to stick up for me. Jim quit over it."

"Would you work with him again?"

Buck gave Raven a suspicious look, "If I had to. Why?"

"Later."

Buck shrugged as he finished the food on his plate. They made small talk over final cups of coffee and then left for Raven's hotel room.

Kai and Buck followed Raven into his room and sat down. Raven poured whiskey into three glasses and handed them out to his friends. He sat down on the edge of the bed.

"Here's what's going on," Raven began. "There is an outlaw gang based somewhere in Canada that is operating there and down into Montana. They are robbing coaches, trains, stores, banks, you name it they're robbing it, on both sides of the border. They are responsible for several murders and likely more than have been attributed to them. The worst part of the operation is they are kidnapping young women and older girls, both white and Blackfeet, and shipping them to the Orient as slaves.

"Governor Potts contacted our office asking for help since the local authorities have been unsuccessful in catching them and the crimes cross international boundaries that affect both countries. Parker sent me to meet with the Governor. Potts also requested cooperation with the Canadian authorities in finding this gang. They were happy to work with us and sent Wade Tracy, a Northwest Mounted Police Officer, to assist on the Canadian behalf.

"We have set up a task force. Potts had originally included Captain Clarke, until he proved to be such a pain that Tracy and I both demanded that he be removed from the operation."

Buck chuckled, "How long did it take you to figure out he was a horse's butt?"

"About five minutes. The Governor sent him on his way and has ordered Colonel Shelton to show up at the meeting to represent his district. That's why I asked you about him."

"We don't like each other much."

"Is he as bad as Clarke?"

"No. I can stand to be in the same room with

Shelton. Clarke, if I was ever in the same room with him again, I'd gut him."

"That's understandable. We have Marshal Allen in the group as well. Did you know Allen has been hounding the Governor since your conviction to review your case because he was convinced you were railroaded?"

"No, I didn't, but he said he would be trying to help me."

"Well, he did because he's the one who told me about you. He came to the Governor's office while we were there."

"I'll be sure to thank him."

"You'll get the chance."

"So, I'm in this group? Is that the job you said you had for me?"

"I told Potts I wanted a guide who knew the country and to serve as interpreter as we would be dealing with the Blackfeet.

"When Allen came in arguing to be heard in regards to you, not only was I excited to learn you were alive, I knew you were the perfect man for the job." Raven grinned, "And it gave me the clout I needed to get you released."

Buck smiled, "Thanks."

"We all meet with the Governor again in two days. I suggest you get a suit for the meeting."

Buck looked at himself, "Yeah, not exactly the best for a high-powered meeting is it?"

"Sometimes you need to make an impression and clothes do that."

Buck laughed, "Your impression sure scared that superintendent into fits."

"That and the fact I can back up what I said and I fully intend to."

"Good. Lots of corruption in there, it needs a good cleaning."

"There will be one. Anyway, back to the Governor's meeting."

"Okay," Buck said. "Tell me what you know about this gang?"

"Tracy's people learned that the leaders of the gang spoke with heavy British accents. The Mounties sent letters off to all the authorities in Great Britain and learned that, previous to their inquiries, they had a similar gang operating in that country. British authorities said they were closing in on the gang when they suddenly disappeared. When the Mounties starting putting two-and-two together they figured out they had the same British gang now operating in Canada and down here."

"The gang is from Great Britain?" Buck asked.

"Yes." Raven looked directly into Buck's eyes, "There's another reason why you were perfect for this job. The leader of the gang... is Jules Drake."

Chapter Twenty-Seven

Buck followed Raven and Kai into the Governor's office. It had taken him several minutes to digest what Raven had said two nights before about Jules being the leader of the gang. Once the reality had set in that he would have a chance to even the score with his father, he set his mind to accomplishing the goal of hunting down this gang. He walked into the office with that thought in mind.

Buck made a quick scan of the room to see several men seated together. They all stood as the three of them walked it. The Mountie in the red coat he spotted first, the man next to him was dignified and had to be the Governor. He recognized Marshal Allen, and then his eyes locked with Colonel Shelton's and held for a long second with no friendliness in them.

Buck was thankful that Raven had steered him into a decent suit of clothes. His hair was cut, beard trimmed, and he was bathed and clean. The men around him were all in suits or uniforms and he would have felt like the poor share croppers he had seen down south. As it was, he felt equal to the men in the room.

Raven took the liberty of introducing Buck and Kai to those in the room. Allen shook Buck's hand and smiled, "Good to see you, Buck."

Buck smiled in return. "Thanks for your help."

"Clarke did a first rate job of railroading you. Judge McCormick even commented that you had been sold down the river and the testimony was ridiculous. He would have charged Clarke with perjury if it hadn't been such a fine line between his testimony and the vagueness of the facts." Allen did not like Clarke or Shelton and said what he did for Shelton's benefit as much as Buck's.

Tracy was next to shake Buck's hand. "I have heard good things about you, Mr. Drake."

Buck nodded, "Thank you."

The Governor extended his hand as he studied Buck carefully. "You are not what I expected, Mr. Drake."

"Depends on what you expected, sir."

"Yes, indeed. I may have been misled in the past."

"We often are, sir."

Finally, Buck faced Colonel Shelton and both held back for a moment before Shelton reluctantly put out his hand. "What is your purpose on this force?"

Buck shook his hand as a formality with no feeling behind it. "I know the leader of the gang. I know how he thinks and what he will do. I know the country and the Blackfeet."

"That could be useful."

Buck looked at him with distaste, "No doubt."

The men all sat down except for Raven.

Raven wore a broad smile. "Before we get down to business, I have a presentation to make."

The men all looked at him as Raven pulled a small black box out of the pocket of his suit coat. Kai was grinning, as he knew what was about to happen.

Raven turned his attention to Buck. "I've been carrying these around ever since the war. I guess there was always a seed of hope in me that I would find you again." He opened the box to reveal three medals neatly pinned to the satin lining. He showed them to the group. "These were awarded to Buck during the war. He never received them because he was too busy fighting his way across Georgia and then was mistakenly declared dead."

Shelton's eyes opened wide, he knew the medals were for bravery in the face of the enemy. The Governor was surprised as well. Wade Tracy stood up and extended his hand to Buck, "Bravo, Mr. Drake, congratulations."

Allen shook Buck's hand next, "Good man."

Raven handed the box to Buck. "Okay, now we can get on with the meeting."

Buck stared at the medals for a moment and then

closed the box and put it in his pocket.

Colonel Shelton was obviously rattled by the presentation. He cleared his throat with a cough and spoke, "Governor, I am honored that you selected me for this task force. I appreciate the confidence my fellows have placed in me; however, I can only serve in an advisory capacity. My duties as commander at Fort Shaw require my full attention and I am not in a position to go afield in search of these criminals. That is why I originally sent Captain Clarke in my stead." He frowned, "Clarke does have a way of being abrasive."

Potts huffed, "Abrasive is a polite way of putting it. I would use a stronger term myself. I can think of several, actually. I can understand your duties and you are free to send a man to represent you. We all felt that it was necessary for you to be present to hear firsthand what the plan for pursuing these criminals will be."

"I appreciate your understanding Governor. I have in fact brought a man with me today to represent me and the army on this task force. He is a veteran of many years and battles, and one of my most trusted cavalry Sergeants. He came to my command two years ago and a finer cavalryman never lived. He is also a man who works well with others and I believe you will approve of him."

Potts showed interest, "That would be fine, who is this man?"

"Sergeant Major Timothy Duffy."

Raven and Buck both jumped in their chairs, "Duffy?" Raven blurted out.

Potts looked at Raven with a worried expression, "Is there a problem with Sergeant Major Duffy, Mr. Ravenel?"

"Absolutely not."

Buck smiled, "I scouted for Sergeant Duffy at Fort Reno, and Raven and I knew him before that."

Buck and Raven grinned at each other sharing the

secret of how they had met Duffy.

Raven excitedly said, "Sergeant Duffy is as good a man as ever drew breath. I definitely want him on this and we're lucky to have him."

Potts gave a relieved sigh and smiled. "Well, Colonel I guess it's unanimous. How soon can Sergeant Major Duffy join us?"

"Immediately, sir. Your Secretary has him waiting in another room.

"By all means bring him in."

Shelton got up and went to the door and addressed the secretary, "Please bring Sergeant Major Duffy in."

A few seconds passed before Sergeant Duffy stepped in through the door. He looked older and grayer, yet he stood erect and proud in his spotless dress uniform bearing the inverted gold chevrons topped with rounded gold stripes.

Raven jumped to his feet and went directly to the Sergeant. The two men smiled at each other and shook hands. "Lord, Duffy, it's good to see you again."

"Aye, I've heard some fine things about you, Ravenel. You are a very important man in Washington these days." He leaned in closer to Raven, "And I recall the first time we met, and those boys having their little accident in the chow line." He winked.

Raven laughed and noted how Duffy had not lost his brogue after all these years. He concluded that he wouldn't know him if he did.

Duffy walked directly up to Buck and put out his hand, "Pleasure to see you again, Buck." They shook hands and smiled at each other. Duffy added, "I heard what happened to you, son, and I never believed a word of it. A load of mule marbles it was."

Colonel Shelton shifted nervously at Duffy's comment regarding Buck. Shelton then introduced Duffy around to the other men in the room coming to Tracy last.

Duffy looked up at the taller Tracy and shook his hand, "Sergeant Major."

Tracy bowed slightly, "Sergeant Major."

Duffy laughed, "A couple of horsemen like us ought to go by a less formal greeting don't you think? Call me Duffy."

Tracy smiled, "Wade."

The men all sat down.

Tracy and then Raven brought everyone up to date on the details regarding the gang.

At the conclusion of his explanation Raven said to Potts, "I still want a representative from the Blackfeet Confederacy on this force. Since these kidnappings involve their people, that person could be invaluable to finding these criminals as little escapes the eyes and ears of the Blackfeet."

Potts answered, "I have given that a good deal of thought and have discussed the matter with Sergeant Major Tracy. It would seem a good idea to include such a person. Who would you get? Do you have any idea who would cooperate with us?"

"My brother," Buck broke in.

Potts looked at Buck, "Please elaborate, Mr. Drake."

"My brother is one of the head Braves in The Comrades and has an ear and eye into everything that is going on in every village, including those in Canada."

Potts raised his right eyebrow, "I have never heard of The Comrades, or a Brave."

"The Comrades are the policing society for the tribes and the Braves are the police officers. My brother, Badger, has been in that society for years and knows everything that goes on. You could compare his position to Marshal Allen's."

Potts showed surprise, "The Indians have police?"

"Yes. The four tribes of the Blackfeet nation have a

government, political leaders, laws, voting, and a police society that makes arrests for violating our laws."

"I never knew that."

"Yes sir, we are more than most white men think. We're not mindless savages as the eastern press likes to make us out to be. We had a government system long before the white man ever set foot in this country."

Raven cringed inwardly at Buck's directness toward the Governor, but he knew Buck was right and it was Buck's way to speak his mind no matter to whom. Buck was not afraid to speak out, nor was he intimidated by position or power.

Potts frowned, his expression revealing his indignation at being spoken to in such a direct manner.

Tracy was quick to concur. "Mr. Drake is correct, sir. We have been negotiating with the Blackfeet Confederacy to give them a reservation that no white man can violate. They indeed have a government and order that we respect. In turn they respect ours, and as a result our talks have been positive and peaceful."

Shelton looked at Tracy, "How do you accomplish that? We have been dealing with the Indians for years and have had little success, they are completely uncooperative. The Indians in your country must be easier to deal with because they are impossible here."

Tracy's ears and neck turned red with anger, yet he maintained a cool countenance. "With all due respect, Colonel Shelton, and please do not take this as a personal attack, but I am familiar with how the United States Army *deals* with the Indians. You starve them out, readily break treaties, slaughter women and children and then cover it up by calling it a victorious battle, and then wonder why they are uncooperative with you. We are well aware of the truth of the Marias Massacre in spite of your government's official reports. The answer to your problem is quite simple, yet it seems to escape the United States Army."

The room grew tense as the two men locked eyes with each other. Shelton stifling his anger and Tracy holding cool and fearless.

Potts coughed exaggeratedly, "Shall we get down to business here, gentlemen? I think we have established that the American and Canadian ways of dealing with the Indians is different. I would like to move past that, if we may."

Potts turned his attention to Raven, "Will Mr. Drake's brother suffice for your Confederacy member?"

"Yes, sir."

"Good. I don't know that there is more to be accomplished here in this room. The next step is for you to organize your team, Mr. Ravenel, and start tracking these criminals down."

"I agree, sir. We have the men together that we need and we can get outfitted today."

Potts stood up. "Very well, good luck gentlemen. Mr. Ravenel, I would appreciate regular reports as to your progress."

"Yes sir, I will do that."

Potts walked out of the room with a release of a pent up breath. Tensions were building in the room that would have escalated if left to go on any longer. He was more than happy to pass the whole affair off to the Washington agent.

The men all stood up and looked at each other. Tracy turned to Shelton, "I apologize for my comments, Colonel, I did not mean to offend."

Shelton glanced at Tracy, "You know what your problem is, Sergeant Major?"

"I fail in diplomacy? It has been a weakness of mine."

Shelton looked the Mountie in the eyes, "Your problem is you're right. Certain events over the past few years have caused me to look with a less jaundiced and biased eye and some of what I see is disturbing. Unfortunately, it's bigger than I am." He bowed his head, "Sergeant Major." He then walked out of the room without looking at anyone else.

Tracy looked at the other men. "Diplomacy," he shook his head. "My superiors have lectured me on that point more than once. I must work on that."

Buck grinned at Tracy, "I think you and I are going to get along just fine."

"Diplomacy isn't your strong point either?" Tracy grinned. "You were rather direct with the Governor."

"If it means buckling under to people just because of who they are, then it's not."

Raven laughed, "Buck's idea of diplomacy lands somewhere between a Henry rifle and a Bowie knife."

Tracy laughed. "I was told by my Superintendent that if I caused an international incident I would be, and I quote, 'sent to the most remote, desolate, God-forsaken outpost the Hudson Bay Company has.'"

Duffy let out a flat whistle, "He sounds serious."

"I have had a few incidents where I should have been more diplomatic in the manner in which I worded something and have upset certain representatives of varying Government offices. I tend to speak my mind when someone makes me angry."

Raven grinned, "My kind of man."

"What should we do with our fancy clothes?" Buck waved his hand across the front of him.

"I have a house here in town," Allen spoke for the first time. "You are all welcome to leave your property there."

"I thought you were based out of Helena," Buck asked.

"I have an office in Helena where I hold prisoners caught up that way until the judge comes around to hear the cases. I stay in the hotel when I'm up there, but my main office and home is here in Virginia City since it's the capital."

"I serve at the pleasure of the Governor of Colorado," Kai said. "If I raised cain with him like you just did with Potts, I'd be fired."

Allen smiled, "Governor Potts is a decent fellow. He's all for law and order, he put the lid on the vigilantes. It's just hard to light a fire under him to act when it comes to something he considers mundane like reviewing criminal cases. I have a little leeway with him, if not always his ear."

Raven listened to the marshal's story. "I like you better all the time, Marshal Allen."

"Call me Ty. I have to ask you, Mr. Ravenel, why did you include me in this group? You barely know me."

"Fair question. In a nutshell, it's because of your nerve and integrity. You arrested Buck because that was your duty; however, you realized there was more to the case than what was in black and white. You pushed at the Governor to look into the case. That took nerve and sticking to your belief that something was wrong.

"This hunt is going to involve two countries and we don't know if this Jules Drake has bought himself protection from public officials so he can carry on business. The men on this hunt can't be swayed or scared off by intimidation. If we run into political roadblocks, I intend to smash right through them. I need to know the men I have beside me will be there no matter what. That's why I chose you."

"My years of experience told me that Buck's case was one of self-defense and he was being railroaded."

"I appreciate that," Buck said to Allen.

"Just glad it all worked out."

Buck looked around him, "I think since we're all going to be working closely together we should drop all the titles and ranks. Just use our names like normal people."

The men all looked at each other and agreed.

Tracy grinned, "Yes, saying Sergeant Major Tracy will get on my nerves after a bit."

"Amen," Duffy agreed.

Raven turned toward the door. "We probably shouldn't be hanging around in the Governor's office too long. Let's check out of our rooms and go with Ty to his house to change our clothes and stow our unneeded gear. We can go to the livery from there and head out."

The men all filed out of the room and left the building. Buck walked with Raven and Kai. "I'm going to need to buy a rifle," Buck said.

"They take your Henry when you were arrested?" Raven asked.

"No, I hid it with my revolver and Bowie so my brother could come and get them. I told him if I was taken, he could have them."

Ty turned his head as he walked, "I knew you had other guns, but you weren't showing hostility so I let it be."

"I had a hiding place and told my brother to come and get them if I was captured. I didn't want the likes of Yarrow to get my property."

"We'll take care of that," Ty said. "I have mine and two extra Winchester 1873's at the office. The Territory pays for them and to my way of thinking they owe you a rifle. You can have one of those."

"That's generous, thanks."

They arrived at the Marshal's office. Ty went in and explained to one of his deputies where he was going, that he would be gone for an unknown amount of time, and that he should take over until he returns. He then took two of the rifles off the rack and handed one to Buck. They walked out headed for Ty's house.

An hour later, the group was riding out of Virginia City. Wade Tracy had exchanged his red dress tunic for an older trail-worn red jacket and his dress cap for a hat with a wide brim. Duffy wore his cavalry patrol uniform and the others were dressed for the trail. Buck felt at home again in his soft buckskin shirt and battered old hat with the equally battered eagle feather stuck behind the leather string hat band. The group drew attention from curious onlookers as they left the city behind.

The party traveled light with bedrolls behind their saddles and trail food consisting of hardtack, dried beans, and jerked beef in their oversized saddlebags. They would kill what they needed along the way and find meals at the Blackfeet villages they came to, as it was customary for friends to be fed. Pack horses would slow down the pursuit of the quickly moving Jules Drake gang.

Their route led northwest to the upper Teton River and Buck's home village. It had been more than four years since he had been back to it and he wondered what changes had come about. He had not heard from Badger and hoped he was there and still alive. He also wondered about his mother and sister. So much could happen and change in four years that he rode with a feeling of apprehension as to what he would find when he got there.

The boys with the horse herds were the first to spot the group coming. They ran for the village to tell the men that soldiers and white men were coming. Few, if any, of the Montana Piegan boys had seen a red-coated soldier. They spoke excitedly about one man in a blue seizer coat and a man in a red coat with stripes on his arm like the blue coat. The old men understood the boys spoke of one of the Braves from the Rupert's Land police society.

Thirty armed Piegan warriors stood at the border of the village awaiting the oncoming group. They would not have a repeat of the Marias River killings and had met all strangers with weapons since that day. The head chief of the village made his way through the warriors and stopped in the front. "Who is coming?" he asked one of the men.

"I do not know," the warrior answered. "The boys

say a Rupert's red coat, and a seizer, and other men."

"They could not be the Jules party then."

The women had moved the children and older daughters back into the lodges and watched with curiosity mixed with apprehension. The men stood ready to fight if need be. The sound of the approaching horses drew closer.

The first to appear through the trees was Buck. The chief stared at him for several seconds before recognizing him. He called to the others, "It is Buckingham Palace."

The man beside him asked, "Why does he have soldiers with him?"

"We will find out." The chief walked up to meet Buck.

Buck pulled his horse up and smiled. "He Who Fights, how are you?"

He Who Fights smiled back, "Still alive. Once again we thought you were dead. Badger told us that you had been taken to the white man's prison."

"I was, but the friends that I have with me helped me to get out." Buck studied him. "I see you are now a chief."

"Yes, soon after you went away. I was chosen to replace Swift Runner."

The rest of the group pulled up behind Buck and eyed the armed Indians in front of them.

He Who Fights looked past Buck to the men behind him. "These are your friends?"

"Yes."

"You have a Rupert's Brave and a seizer with you, why?"

"That is what I want to talk to you about. Is Badger still in the village?"

"Yes. He has two wives now and several children. They keep him busy feeding them."

"Good. I will need his help."

"Come to my lodge we will talk. Bad things have

happened that I must tell you about." Buck dismounted to walk beside him.

He Who Fights called out to the warriors still standing at the ready. "It is Buckingham Palace and his friends. They are welcome." Everyone in the group, with the exception of Raven and Duffy, lifted a curious eyebrow at the name the chief called Buck by.

The warriors stepped aside, yet kept their eyes on Duffy, not trusting a seizer no matter who he rode with.

Buck's mother came out of their lodge and embraced her son. "Buckingham Palace, you were in the white man's prison?"

"Yes, but I am free now." He looked around, "Is Nuttah out gathering?"

Tears filled Hurit's eyes, "She has been taken, as have two other girls."

Buck's expression instantly showed alarm. "What do you mean taken?"

"Your father came back to the village with other bad men. He Who Fights and your brother were gone hunting. I told Jules he was not welcome here. He said they would be gone soon. Several of the warriors in the camp approached them and they left."

He Who Fights broke in, "That is the bad news I wanted to tell you. Your father lives. Angry All The Time was also with them. If I had been here I would have fulfilled my promise to kill him. Dirt Eater left with them. It was after they had gone that my wife found that my daughter and two other girls were missing. We believe they took them."

"How long ago was that?"

"Three suns."

Buck's face turned red with rage. "It was Dirt Eater and Angry All The Time who took Nuttah to strike back at me and Badger. They are too cowardly to fight us so they do this evil thing for revenge."

298

"And to strike at me," Hurit said, "because I told them to leave."

Buck looked at the men behind him who had dismounted and stood back silently letting Buck do the talking. "They were here three days ago and took three girls. one was my sister."

Buck turned back to He Who Fights and asked, "Did anyone see where they went?"

"They went north. We had it passed down to us from other villages that they went into Rupert's Land. None knew that they had stolen our children or they would have killed them and taken the children back."

"That is what we have come for. My friends and I are hunting Jules. He has a party of evil men that came from far away. They are killing and robbing, and stealing white and Blackfeet girls and selling them for slaves."

Hurit began to cry, "My daughter is to be a slave? I cannot bear it."

Buck embraced his mother. "We will get them back, mother. My friends are good hunters and we hunt Jules. That is why I need Badger to come with us."

Hurit stepped away from Buck. "Before you go, Nuttah made something for you." She turned and entered the lodge, a few seconds later she came out carrying something in her hand. She held it up for Buck to see. It was a bone and leather necklace with a single blue bead in the center. "Your sister made this for you to keep you safe from your enemies."

Buck bent slightly forward as his mother tied it around his neck. He straightened and looked into his mother's sad eyes. "We will bring Nuttah home."

"I will go and bring Badger to you." Hurit walked away toward Badger's lodge.

He Who Fights looked over the group. "Is that why you have a Rupert's Brave with you? To hunt Jules into his land?"

"Yes, they have had trouble with Jules as well and want him caught."

He Who Fights narrowed his eyes giving Duffy a hard look. "Why is there a seizer with you?"

"He is my friend and not like the others."

He Who Fights nodded his understanding. "Your friends can make their camp there," he pointed to a level spot a short distance behind his lodge."

"That is a good place. I must camp with my party so we can plan how to find Jules."

"You do what you must." He gestured toward a rack with strips of buffalo drying on it. "I will give you meat for your camp."

"Thank you. Have Badger come to our camp."

"I would hunt Jules with you except I have duties in this village now."

"Your duties are very important. We will find Jules and bring Nuttah back." The men then led their horses to the spot indicated for their camp.

The horses were stripped of their tack and picketed to graze. A fire was set and the buffalo meat hung over the fire to cook. By the time they were set up in the camp, Buck spotted Badger walking toward them with a bundle in his hands.

Badger shouted a greeting to his brother then stopped in front of him. "I see they did not hang you in the white man's prison. Many thought you would die at their hands."

"No, I am alive. Did you find my guns and knife?"

"I did."

Badger handed Buck the holstered Remington with the belt wrapped around it. "I will keep the rifle, you can have your white man's short gun back, I do not like it." He also handed Buck his knife, "I already have one."

"Thank you, I do like this gun and knife. Did you shoot it at all?"

Badger cast a cold eye on Duffy and then the two men with the badges on their chests. "One time."

Buck gestured toward the other men, "We are hunting for Jules."

"Mother has told me. They took Nuttah, you know."

"I know. We will get her back."

"Angry All The Time was with them. Myself and two Braves rode after them for two suns. They were too far ahead and we lost them."

"We will have help from the Rupert Braves and we will find them."

"Will you kill Jules when you find him?"

"If I can."

"He is a man who needs to be killed."

Buck looked at Badger, "I know you must care for your family, but I need you to come with us and help us with the villages that do not know me. I need you to help us find Jules and get our sister back."

Badger nodded. "I have set in plenty of meat for my family. I will go with you and help."

"Good. Stay with us for a while and meet my friends that you will hunt with."

"I see you have a blue coat seizer, can he be trusted?"

"Yes, Duffy is my friend. We fought in the same war."

"If he is your friend I will trust him."

Buck pointed toward the Mountie, "Wade."

"A Rupert's Brave, they are good men."

"Ty Allen, Kai Maddock, and Raven, they are my friends who got me out of the prison. We went into battle together. Everyone, this is my brother, Badger."

The men all gave him a greeting.

They all sat together and began to eat. Badger said between bites, "Jim Twist told me that the one named Yarrow is the one who shot down Swift Runner and lied to have you put in prison."

"That is true."

"This Yarrow is dead."

Buck looked surprised. "How do you know that?"

"Someone shot him. One time with a short gun."

Buck looked at Badger and grinned, "Only shot it one time, huh?"

Badger grinned back at him and said nothing.

The other men caught the drift of what he meant and said nothing. No tears would be shed over the death of Del Yarrow.

Wade asked, "Nuttah, how old is she?"

Buck thought for a few seconds before answering, "I would say about thirteen or fourteen now."

Wade cringed; he knew her fate would be terrible if they didn't get to her on time, as would that of the other girls. "How old are the other girls taken with her?"

Badger answered him, "The same ages. They were all friends and would go out gathering roots and berries together."

"How many were in Jules' party?" Raven asked Badger.

Badger counted in his head and held up all ten fingers. "That is how many they had when Dirt Eater left with them."

"Who are Dirt Eater and Angry All The Time?" Raven asked.

Buck answered, "Dirt Eater is a false shaman. He puts on big shows and was a friend of Jules. Angry All The Time is the one who killed the white men that caused Bates to wipe out Swift Runner's winter camp. He's a bad one. The other Piegan don't like him and blame him for the massacre. Those two would be the ones to join up with scum like Jules all right. Dirt Eater bears me a grudge and Angry All The Time bears both Badger and me one."

Badger finished eating and stood up. "I will see to

my family and meet you back here at the rising sun."

Buck stood up with him. "It will be good, us riding together again."

Badger looked at him seriously, "Angry All The Time needs to be killed for his violating our laws and causing the deaths in Swift Runner's camp. Jules, I have always hated. He is a devil, as the whites call the evil one. I will let you have his scalp though; you have more reason to hate him."

Buck shook his head, "I don't want his scalp. I only want to spit in the devil's eye and shoot him."

Chapter Twenty-Eight

The nights in the mountains remained cold in spite of the warming days. The men rolled stiff and chilled out of their bed rolls with the first rays of sunlight to find Buck and Badger sitting by the fire drinking coffee.

Buck watched Raven with a wry grin. "Getting soft Raven. You used to be a mountain man, you know."

Raven rubbed his hands over his face. "Out of practice, I guess."

"Got coffee and meat cooking."

Raven fought on his stiff, cold boots, dug a cup out of his saddlebag, and moved stiffly to the fire. He stretched out his hands to the warming flames, "Boots are half frozen. I forgot how cold nights get up here." He filled the cup.

The other men followed him to the fire and filled their cups with hot coffee. They stood around the fire soaking in the heat and letting the strong coffee wake them up.

Kai stared in his cup, "I see you haven't lost your touch, you still make the nastiest coffee in the world. I don't think it's supposed to be chewy."

"Oh, listen to you cry," Buck chided him good naturedly. "Seems I recall a lot of mornings behind Rebel lines when coffee was only a dream."

"As was food," Kai chuckled.

Wade looked at Buck from over his tin cup, "Is Buckingham Palace your actual name?"

Buck snorted, "Yeah, my old man's idea of a joke. I didn't know what it was until I met Raven and he explained it to me. He and Parker suggested I just go by Buck, which I have ever since."

Wade pondered Buck's explanation for a second, "That proves Jules is from Great Britain."

"Liverpool," Buck said. "I didn't know anything

about it at the time, I learned later. I do remember that whenever he'd get drunk he'd talk about Liverpool and brag about the villainous things he'd done there. He was a thief, murderer, and all-around scum of the earth. He would also babble something about killing mutton, whatever that meant."

"Sounds like a fine fellow," Wade said with sarcasm.

Buck snorted, "The finest human nature has to offer."

"You obviously dislike him intensely and it appears to go deeper than a name."

"It's more like I hate his guts. It's a long story involving a lot of his bad actions over many years. He tricked and lied to our grandfather, married our mother to gain a place with the tribe and then did nothing to support her or us. Later, Jules led a pack of renegades that did not follow the proper ways of war parties and fighting. He was a liar and an incredible coward who avoided armed men. He preyed on women and terrified pilgrims. He was despised by all the true warriors.

"In the stupidity of my youth, he used my pride against me and tricked me into riding with his party. They attacked a lone covered wagon that proved to be a trap. The wagon was filled with soldiers. Jules sacrificed the party to save himself. He hit me with his rifle and shoved me into the soldiers so he could escape.

"I ended up a prisoner at Fort Bridger and was given the choice to hang or go east and fight in the war. The village all thought he was dead as none of the party ever returned. I always suspected he ran away and deserted my mother. Now, I know that's exactly what he did."

All the men were listening to the story.

Duffy broke in, "I think it should be known that Buck tried to stop the attack on the wagon by shouting warnings to it. He wasn't part of it."

Buck nodded, "That's true."

"What happened to you then?" Ty asked.

"I had never been out of the village and knew nothing of how white men did things. I met a mountain man named Ravenel," he grinned at Raven, "who *educated* me about the white world I was heading into."

Raven laughed at the memory. "At the time Buck and I were in the same boat and had been given the same choice."

Ty's eyebrows rose, "Really." He looked more intensely at Raven. "Why was the army going to hang you?"

Raven laughed at Ty's surprised expression. "I was in a card game with a couple of Fort Bridger troopers. When my hand beat this one fellow's, he pulled a knife on me. I shot him. The army wasn't interested in why I shot him, only that I had."

Ty looked at Buck. "Like with you, Buck. They didn't care why you shot Jones, just that you had."

Buck nodded, "The army thinks everyone in uniform is perfect so it has to be the other man's fault. That's why so many soldiers get away with their crimes."

Duffy put in, "Aye, there are plenty of bad seeds in the army, and I have to admit, when civilians are involved the army does stick with its own. They like to keep the public image neat and tidy. Internally it's a different story. I knew that man Raven is referrin' to and he was a bad one. Put him in the guardhouse twice myself. I'd also heard plenty about Bates and Jones as well and none of it good."

"What do you think of Clarke?" Buck asked Duffy.

Duffy made a sour face. "Bein' a Christian man I shan't say what I think of him."

Buck laughed. "That says enough."

Raven grinned at Duffy, "Buck and I met Duffy at Fort Bridger. On opposite sides of the bars."

Duffy chuckled, "Aye, two of the roughest

scoundrels I ever laid eyes on."

The men all laughed.

Ty grinned, "Sorry, Buck, I can see you in that position, but I never would have guessed it from Raven."

Raven laughed. "I didn't always work for the government. I had my wild days back when I was a trapper."

Wade was smiling with the others. "You men obviously have a long history together."

Buck nodded. "Raven and me ended up in Lieutenant Parker's special unit going behind enemy lines and blowing things up. That's where we teamed up with Kai."

Kai agreed, "We made a team we did. We were separated before Gettysburg though. Buck was sent south to General Sherman as a sharpshooter. Raven and I were kept as General Hooker's sharpshooters. After the war we looked for Buck and found he was listed as dead having been killed in action."

Raven looked at Ty. "I couldn't believe it when Clarke said Buck was alive and then you roared into the office demanding to be heard in regards to him. Talk about your timing, one shot in a million."

"All of us in the right place at the right time," Ty agreed.

Buck looked from Ty to the others, "I owe you all a lot."

Raven was quick to reply, "Not as much as we owe you. Buck saved my life and Kai's during the war."

The men all looked at Buck. Buck only stared into the fire.

Raven went on, "Kai and I were captured by the Rebs and about two minutes away from being executed as spies. Buck cuts a door into the back of the tent we were being held in, steps in and shoots the two Reb officers that had us. We did some fast scrambling out of there, I'll tell you. One of those medals was for that. We wouldn't be here if not for him."

Wade smiled, "I say we have a crack outfit here then."

"Amen," Ty added.

Badger spoke for the first time as he remained hunkered in front of the fire. "My brother is a great warrior and has counted many coup against the Shoshone, Gros Ventre, and Sioux. If he had not been captured by the soldiers, he would have been a war chief."

Buck smacked the back of his hand on Badger's shoulder. "My brother is a great warrior as well, his lodge skins cannot hold all of his coups." Buck laughed, "Us great warriors should ride before our boasting makes us too puffed up to get on our horses."

Badger stood up. "Maybe for you, I am a better rider than you."

"Only if my horse has three legs."

Badger grinned, "Then, all of your horses must have three legs."

The men all broke into laughter.

After eating they saddled up and mounted.

Wade looked to the north, "Since we already know the gang went into Canada we should head directly to my home base at Fort Macleod and learn if anything new has come to light about them." He glanced at Buck and Badger and said, "If that sounds acceptable to our guides."

Buck and Badger both agreed it seemed like a reasonable first step.

Badger moved his horse forward. "I know the place."

The party progressed north over the next week stopping at Piegan and Siksika villages along the way. They were met with weapons and suspicion until Badger explained he was a Brave and Buck was the son of Hurit the Medicine Woman. Once the village men understood that they hunted the Jules Drake gang, who had stolen their children, they were welcomed into the villages.

There were those in each village who had seen the gang pass through. Some of the warriors had stopped them to see what their business was. Dirt Eater took them to task for stopping a holy journey. Afraid to upset a holy man, the warriors did not question why they had white men with them. Jules had told them that the Shaman had been sent to them by the Old Man and he was called White Eagle Messenger, leading them on a holy quest.

Badger and Buck shook their heads to show disgust over the lies and explained to the people the Shaman was a fraud named Dirt Eater. The truth brought anger to those who had been deceived.

Those who had seen the Jules party confirmed that they were a mix of white men and Piegan and they had women with them. There were five Blackfeet girls in the party and two young white women as well. Jules had told them they were the children or wives of the men. Had they known the truth, they would have killed them all and released the captives.

All those Badger asked said there were seven white men, two Piegan warriors, and the Shaman. Badger wondered who the second warrior was as he knew only of Angry All The Time. Somewhere along the line they had picked up another renegade. As they left each village, the men promised Badger that if the Jules party passed through again they would stop them.

Once the task force crossed into Canada, Wade worked with Badger as the Siksika and Kainai knew the Mounties and trusted them. Wade knew this part of the country intimately as it was his regular patrol area. Wade was able to speak enough of the native tongue to get by; however, he still relied heavily on Badger and Buck to act as intermediaries.

The seventh day brought the party onto a Canadian

plain. In the distance they could see a crude fort built on an island between the channels of a river. Wade pointed. "Fort Macleod. Not exactly the Grand Palace. We only raised it up last year and it is still undergoing renovations."

"Don't you get flooded out?" Duffy asked.

Wade looked slightly embarrassed, "Colonel Macleod thought it a picturesque and defensible position. He was right about it being picturesque. He was also right about it being defensible because the spring floods make it near to impossible to get to it. Which also goes for getting out."

"That's okay," Duffy consoled. "Our officers built forts in the same manner and suffered similar catastrophes."

The spring floods were subsiding as the party splashed across the river to the fort gates. Two red-coated guards holding rifles watched the group advance. Upon recognizing Wade the guards opened the gates to let the party ride in.

The grounds were muddy from recent rains and the buildings rough and roofed with sod. The neatly dressed Mounties were in direct contrast to the grounds. "As I said," Wade repeated, "it is not much to look at."

"That doesn't matter," Raven said. "What matters is the work you men are doing here. I have heard a lot about the Northwest Mounted Police. You came in to break up the whiskey trade and criminal activity at Fort Hamilton."

"Yes, Fort Whoop-Up they called it."

"And the outlaws fled at the very thought of you. You don't have anything to apologize for."

Wade lifted his chin, "I am not apologizing for the Northwest Mounted, I only apologize that I cannot offer you a more respectable appearance."

"I've seen mud before."

The men stopped in front of a building. "This is Superintendent Forsythe's office."

The men dismounted and followed Wade into the building. Two red-coated officers sat at tables with paperwork in front of them. They looked up at the group. One of the men with Sergeant's stripes on his sleeve grinned at Wade. "I see you made it back. Bet you a dollar Forsythe says something about your hat."

Wade grinned, "I never bet when I am sure to lose."

Hearing the voices and moving feet outside his closed office door, Superintendent Forsythe left his desk and made his way into the room. He looked the party over and then frowned at Wade. "That hat is not regulation, Sergeant Major. Where is your pith?"

Wade snapped to attention. "Misplaced it, sir."

"You used that excuse the last two times. Sergeant Major, I believe you should find a new one."

"Yes, sir, I will find a new excuse, sir."

"I meant a new *pith*."

"Yes, sir."

Forsythe glanced at the men standing behind Wade and then looked back at him. "I hope you did not cause any international situations with your flair for diplomacy."

Wade didn't answer as he shifted his weight slightly from foot-to-foot.

Forsythe groaned, "I don't even want to know. If it is bad, I will hear about it soon enough."

Forsythe looked at Raven, "My God, he is a trial, but I wish I had a hundred more just like him."

He waved his hand at Wade, "Relax Wade, and introduce me to your party."

Wade broke out of his stiff stance and introduced the group one by one. With each introduction the men shook hands with the Superintendent. He introduced Raven last. "This is Renard Ravenel, Special Investigator for the United States Government." The two shook hands.

Forsythe's expression was serious, but his eyes were laughing as he asked Raven, "Will I be receiving an angry letter demanding Wade's resignation?"

Raven smiled, "Sergeant Major Tracy was the epitome of British manners, a credit to the uniform, and didn't say anything that was not true."

Forsythe groaned again, "Oh God, it is going to be an angry letter."

"Just send it to me, sir, I'll deal with it."

"Thank you. Do you want to come and work for me? I could use that kind of talent."

Raven laughed. "I'm spoken for, sorry."

"Just my luck. Gentlemen, I am sure you are hungry and could use hot coffee and food. Come with me to the Mess. Back in more civilized surroundings we would have separate Messes for the officers and enlisted, but we are less formal here and we all eat together. You do not look to be men who are offended by lack of formality."

"We all kind of bunch together," Buck said.

Forsythe looked at him, "Buck Drake? Not related to our own Jules Drake, I suppose?"

"He's my father."

Forsythe's eye brows lifted, "Interesting. You are hunting your own father. Is that awkward for you?"

"The only awkward part will be deciding how to kill him."

"No love lost there, I take it."

"None. He is a scoundrel, murderer, and yellow-bellied coward, and I want to shoot him in the face."

"I suppose that answers my question."

The men entered the Mess building and poured cups of coffee and sat down while Forsythe spoke with the cook. He joined them at the long table. "The cook will have food for us momentarily."

Wade looked at his Superintendent. "Is there anything new on the Jules Drake gang?"

"Weaver happened onto them on his tour and they had a shootout. One of the gang was killed. The rest made it over the pass into British Columbia. Weaver did not pursue as his orders were to stay on this side of the mountains."

"I take it John is all right?"

"Of *course* he is, he is a Mountie."

"Did John say how many there were, or if they had women with them?"

"He could not get an accurate count, but estimated at least eight, and yes, they had women with them, which is why he stopped them in the first place."

Wade nodded. "They have stolen at least five Blackfeet girls and two white women. One of the Blackfeet girls is the sister to Buck and Badger."

"There have been reports of robberies to the south and west of us. Whether it is the Drake gang or not is difficult to say, there is a pattern of criminal activity following them west though. My guess would be they are headed for the coast to meet a ship and sell the kidnapped women, as they did in England."

"New Westminster, do you think?" Wade asked.

"Possibly, however, I believe New Westminster is too far up river to suit their purposes. I am thinking right on the water front. After speaking with several Hudson Bay men, I learned there is a small port at Richmond, at the mouth of the Fraser River.

"There has been a good deal of smuggling in and out of there. That would be my guess for their rendezvous, or close to it. A boat comes into the shore at night and takes the captives back to a ship anchored off shore."

"That sounds plausible," Wade agreed. "I would expect them to have a stopover place in British Columbia, perhaps halfway between here and the coast. A place to resupply and hide out for a rest."

"Yes, I agree. A cabin in the woods off the beaten path."

Forsythe turned his attention to Raven. "What do

you think, Mr. Ravenel?"

"I agree that they will head for the coast. They have to get the kidnapped girls out of North America. Shipping them out of a Pacific port would be the only way, with the Orient the most likely destination. Our agency has been aware of a white slavery market operating in the west, particularly in the Barbary Coast section of San Francisco. Reports name the Orient as a destination. It is one of our ongoing investigations. This may well involve the same people."

"Jules Drake may have the same contact as the Barbary Coast market, you mean?"

"Very likely. How far is the coast from here, a thousand miles?"

"About that."

"Then, yes they would need a halfway house to rest and resupply, maybe two. The trappers and Indians would know about something like that, they see what no one else does. I'm sure we can narrow it down by talking to them."

"Trappers are a tight-lipped lot, but if they like you they can be a wealth of information."

"If we are going that far, we'll need a pack horse and supplies," Kai said.

Forsythe looked at Kai, "I can supply that." He studied Kai for a moment, "Not meaning to be rude, and I realize this is a joint effort between our countries, but I want to make clear that the jurisdiction is presently ours."

"We have open warrants for the gang."

"In the United States."

"You are welcome to add some of your men to our party to make the arrests."

"Not necessary. We at the Northwest Mounted believe that a single Mountie should be able to handle most situations. Sergeant Major Tracy has never failed to find his man and has single handedly brought in several desperate criminals. That is why he was the man I sent when

Governor Potts asked for a representative for your task force."

Kai nodded his acceptance of the Superintendent's comment. "We will have to decide which country will try them in court since they have committed crimes in the United States and Canada."

Forsythe said firmly, "If you capture them in Canada, they will be tried here first. The Northwest Mounted is authorized to hold court hearings and carry out sentencing. Should they slip down into the Washington Territory of your country, they would be yours first. Agreed?"

"Agreed."

"There is one other solution you might not have thought of," Buck added to the discussion.

Forsythe looked at him with curiosity, "What solution would that be?"

"If they make a fight of it there might not be any left to try."

Forsythe grinned slightly, "That would definitely take the complication out of it."

Chapter Twenty-Nine

The men sat around the fire scowling and miserable. The mosquitoes plagued them unmercifully, only relenting when they sat directly in the campfire's smoke. The little bloodsuckers only added to their frustration and increased their irritability. The fatigue of the long journey bore them down like sacks of lead on their backs.

They had profited at times, and blew through it on gambling, liquor, and women. This trip had not come close to the profit realized on the previous forays even though the miles traveled were equal to those. The original members were frustrated that the free-wheeling days of their outlaw life appeared to be over. The new members were angry for they had yet to see the wealth they were promised for their efforts.

Jules Drake hunkered brooding and glowering into the flames. His shoulder-length gray hair hung down framing his face and the eyes that reflected a cruelty that only grew more intense with age. He had done well back in England robbing and kidnapping. He had not wanted to leave.

With the sea ports readily at hand, it was a simple matter to sell the captives. Street boys, who no one even knew existed, sold well to the North African slave traders, and there was a ready Oriental market for young women. It was easy to pocket large profits.

The sticky part had been that only decent women were wanted in the Orient, not street trash. There was profit in stealing the girls of working families, whose calls to the police were taken lightly as their class did not warrant a complement of police investigators. As he stared into the fire he reviewed all that had happened over the past few years trying to determine where it had gone wrong.

It was the accidental taking of a girl of noble birth, who had snuck off to a working class party, that brought the authorities out in mass, nosing around like fox hounds. When Scotland Yard got involved it become a matter of run or swing on the gallows. He had escaped to the only other place he knew.

He had bought passage on the first ship he found that was bound for California. He took with him Prich and Ed, his two best men. He had fed the rest of the gang to the police so they could escape. Competition was stiff for the slave trade in San Francisco and it was a full time job dodging the crimps. They headed north to Grays Harbor.

"Further inland," he had boasted to his men, was a wealth of furs and gold for the taking. It didn't take long to realize that things had changed greatly in the years he was gone. The British Columbia gold booms were over and furs, though still worth the taking, had lost much of their former value.

He had recruited the four new men from the whiskey traders and outlaws around Camp Whoop-Up. He painted them a picture of wealth for the taking and headed down into the Montana Territory where new gold booms promised wealth. The venture into the territory had proven successful. They had a great run of robbing stages and anything else that had money attached to it. Gold was being dug out of the mountains and killing a few miners had brought them a goodly amount of that precious mineral.

Jules growled to himself and tossed a stick of wood on the fire. He had not anticipated the vigilantes. That was the undoing of the Montana operation. There had never been retribution for crime in the old days. Now, the vigilantes simply hung men without the benefit of police or courts. When they got on his scent he led the gang back into Rupert's Land and worked their way back to the coast.

Along the way they had done well as highway robbers. The killing of some Hudson Bay men was worth a hefty pouch of gold coins in furs. He grinned slightly at the memory. They sold the furs in New Westminster and made their way to Richmond on the inside passage. They had escaped the vigilantes and were doing well enough. Then along came Colonel Smithe and his bright ideas. That was the beginning of the end. He cursed the British military man for his present troubles.

He cursed the day he had met the British officer in a Richmond dockside dive. Smithe had sought him out with a bottle and they began talking of trade. Smithe said he was stationed in Hong Kong and made it a point to regularly cross over on business. He had correctly guessed that smuggling was Smithe's business.

Smithe had deliberately mentioned that there was a good market for women, if a person knew the right connections, as well as furs and other items of value. By the end of the bottle they had struck a bargain. He would supply the women; Smithe would pay handsomely for them and arrange transport to Hong Kong. It had all sounded very promising.

Their rendezvous point was a gravel beach leading into a secluded inlet north of the Richmond port. No one would see them, no one would know. Smithe would come in with long boats at night and take the cargo back to his ship anchored in the passage. He would pay in gold. Easy money. Jules ground his teeth. What a fool he had been.

On their first transaction they kidnapped four prostitutes from the Richmond docks and tried passing them off as decent women. Smithe was smarter than he thought and rejected them. What he wanted was what they had produced in England, fresh young girls, not street whores. The Orient had a glut of those.

Wasted effort, no gold. They took the women back into the woods and killed them so they couldn't talk. Taking decent women from the populated areas would be quickly noticed, so they moved back inland.

Smithe never said the girls had to be white. The next haul was six Indian girls under fifteen years of age, easily taken. Smithe had accepted them. He especially liked Indian girls, *exotic* he called them. The gold changed hands. There had been two more transactions of that nature and the men were happy and flush with money and whiskey.

Their next undoing was when they nabbed four white girls from a lumber camp. His men had talked him into it saying that if Indians were worth so much, white women should go for double. They didn't. It was the same price, the only double was the risk.

They made the trade and then barely escaped with their lives as the loggers were riled up to catch the kidnappers. It was back to Montana, but this time they would raid their way back to Richmond, not giving the vigilantes a chance to get onto them. It seemed like a brilliant plan, picking up women over a long distance where no one knew who they were or where the women were spirited off to.

They nabbed Indian and white girls as they headed north. He had not taken into account the problems of hauling a bunch of captive women thousands of miles by horseback. It was difficult, yet they succeeded and the profit was substantial, enough to make them try it again. They had knocked around for the winter on the coast and then headed back to Montana. He should have quit while he was ahead, but his men wanted another run like the last one. He had agreed and now here they sat blaming him for the failure of the trip.

They were still in Rupert's Land when they stopped at a Blackfeet village where they were approached by Angry All The Time and his cousin. He remembered Angry as a bloodthirsty youngster. He told Angry what they were doing and the savage wanted to join them to wreak vengeance on certain people in his old village. He figured he could use a couple of savages like Angry and his cousin, so he took them along.

Angry led them into the old village. He had not expected such an unwelcome response. It was get out quickly or be killed. Angry fled the village ahead of them. When they caught up with him he had Dirt Eater with him and three of the village girls in tow. He had forgotten about Dirt Eater, but saw a use for him as their holy guide through Blackfeet country. His lip curled in a sneer at the thought of a *holy* mission.

They kidnapped two young white women and two more Blackfeet girls before reaching Canada. That's when they ran into the red-coated mounted policeman. One more problem and complication. Unlike the unarmed police in England blowing their whistles and impotently commanding you to stop in the name of the Queen, these red coats dogged you and shot with deadly accuracy. He since learned they were called Mounties.

They had laughed at the Mountie and his one to their ten, and then the bullets flew. One of his new men was killed and they barely slipped through Crowsnest Pass and into British Columbia ahead of him. Where there was one there were likely more. They lost him on the pass.

Jules' brooding mind was filled with anger at the hindrances they had encountered. He continued to glare into the fire feeling the anger and blame from the men around him. He now had a clutch of women to deal with and who knew how many red-coated policemen on his trail. He could kill the women and move more quickly, but they were worth a small fortune and if his men didn't get something for their trouble, it would be his throat being slit.

They needed to make the house on the Okanogan River where they could hide, rest, drink and get ready for the last and final push to Richmond. Smithe was due to rendezvous with them the last week of July. He was calling it quits after this one while he still had his head.

They had more than a month to make it. In the meantime they might as well pick up a few more women, furs, and whatever they could take in robberies. Some more profit, a week's rest, and several bottles of whiskey would improve the men's spirits and lessen Jules' chances of having his life ended in a woods mutiny.

Jules flicked his eyes around the fire without moving his head. Prich sat to his right, Ed to his left. These men had proven their loyalty. The three remaining Whoop-Up recruits, across the fire from him, would be the ones to turn on him given their foul mood and continual mutterings about their situation.

Angry All The Time hunkered beyond the fire with his cousin, their savage faces and wild eyes staring, unblinking, into who knew what. They had been quick to kill and quicker to scalp. He had men like them when he led his renegade Blackfeet party. Indians didn't mutiny if they could get scalps.

Directly across from him, sitting cross legged, was the gray-haired Dirt Eater. He was dirty, foul smelling, and had a face that looked like crumpled brown burlap. He sat and incessantly chanted under his breath. He had gone completely insane. He had provided them passage through the Blackfeet villages, but now, out of Blackfeet country, he had become a burden and a source of irritation with his mumblings and occasional outbursts of gibberish. He might still be useful for something though.

He needed to lighten the load back down to just him, Prich, and Ed, but not yet. He needed the extra men to watch over the growing number of female captives, and that number he intended to increase. Once they reached the coast, the number in the split was the number he intended to decrease.

Without warning, Dirt Eater suddenly drove his hands into the hot fire and threw ashes and embers into the air and shouted some nonsense in the Blackfeet tongue. The men jumped back from the flying debris, cursing the Indian.

Prich growled to Jules as they moved back up to the fire and squatted down, "We need to kill that bloody, loony redskin."

"Soon." Jules said no more.

Clancy, one of the Whoop-Up recruits, cast a glance over his shoulder at the silent Indians who had not moved during Dirt Eaters ash throwing episode. He looked back at Jules. "I don't like having them red devils sitting behind me. They give me the jitters."

Jules glanced across the fire at him. "Then move."

The two men locked eyes on each other. Clancy got up and walked away from the fire and into the surrounding darkness. They heard him roll up in his blanket and canvas cover.

Ed called to Prich, "Give me a hand feeding these women."

The two men filled plates with beans and hardtack and carried them to the trees where the women were tied together at the ankles. They handed each women a plate and said nothing to them. Being constantly threatened with death if they tried to escape, and the occasional beating with a stick, had weakened the women's will to fight. They took the food without comment.

The two returned to the fire. Prich said, "I think we should make for the Okanogan house and lay over, what say you Jules?"

"Yes. We can lay over a few days before setting out for the coast."

"And get drunk," the one named Frank muttered.

Jules glanced at him, "You can get as drunk as you like."

The man leered into the darkness where the women sat. "And have at them women." He chuckled dirtily.

"You touch one of those women and I'll split your skull," Jules said in a calm voice.

Frank sneered, "And, if I split your skull?"

"Then, Prich or Ed will split your skull or," he pointed at the Indian cousins, "they will have at you and under Blackfeet torture a man takes a long time to die."

Frank glared at Jules and worked his jaw back and forth. He wanted to kill him, but he knew the odds were against him.

Jules held the man's eyes from across the fire. "You would like to kill me, wouldn't you?"

Frank only glared at him.

"I will take that as a yes." Reaching into the dark area of his back Jules brought out a pistol, leveled it on Frank, and pulled the trigger. The bullet caught the squatting man in the chest, throwing him backwards. Jules stood up and fired a second time into the prone body.

The man sitting to Frank's left jumped out of the way. The cousins didn't move, and Dirt Eater continued to mumble, unaffected by the gunfire twelve inches to his left.

Clancy sat bolt upright in his bedroll, "What was that?"

Jules replaced the loads in his pistol. "Your split increasing. Go back to bed."

Three days later the gang stopped in the fir trees surrounding the Okanogan house. The Okanogan River flowed silently behind it. The house was a large, long log structure originally built by the Northwest Fur Company and then taken over by Hudson Bay as a fur trading post. It had been abandoned for several years before Jules and his group came across it and moved in.

The men studied the house before riding up to it. Smoke was coming from the chimney and half of a deer hung from a ridge pole.

"Someone's moved into our house," Jules spoke in a low voice. "We will serve an eviction notice." He moved his horse forward with the others following.

They pulled their horses up to the house and dismounted. Pushing the door open Jules led the way in.

Two men sat in the house eating at the table. They stopped mid-bite and stared in surprise at the gang coming in.

"It seems you have taken over my house," Jules said.

One of the men put his spoon down. "We found it empty and didn't know anyone lived in it."

The men grew nervous and knew they faced outlaws. Their Winchesters leaned on the wall near the back door too far to reach. A glance out the window and they saw the line of trail-worn women heavy with distress mounted on horses that were tail-tied together.

One of the men got up from the table. "We'll be happy to leave, let us get our gear and we'll go."

"I'm sorry," Jules shook his head, "you've seen too much to leave now."

"I didn't see anything," the man said. "Just let us go."

Jules motioned with his head toward Prich. Prich pulled out a pistol and shot the man. As he was falling, the second man dashed for the back door, grabbing his rifle as he flung the door open and burst outside. Several shots knocked chips of wood off the walls around him. The man never slowed as he ran for the surrounding woods.

Jules shouted at Angry All The Time, "Get him!"

Angry All The Time and his cousin ran out the door behind the man, following him into the trees.

The man stumbled and fell. A bullet had torn a bloody gash across the outside of his thigh. In his fear-fueled burst for escape he had not noticed it. Now, he felt the warm sticky blood soaking his pants leg. He heard the running feet and spun around on the ground aiming his rifle at the sound. As the two Indians cleared the trees he fired, dropping one of them into a face first dive. Levering in another cartridge he fired and missed the second Indian.

There was no prize to be won by facing the man's rifle. Angry All The Time retreated back down the way he had come. The man looked at his leg and found a wide rip in the pants where the bullet had torn across the flesh. He was lucky the bullet hadn't gone in. He packed a handful of damp moss into the wound, clamped his hand over it and limped into the woods heading east.

Angry All The Time returned to the house alone. Jules looked at him, "Where's your cousin? I heard shots."

"He is dead."

"Did you kill the man?"

Angry All The Time did not look at Jules. "He is dead."

Jules looked around the Indian, "Where's the scalp?"

"He died a crying woman, and I did not want his scalp."

Jules knew he was lying, as the bloodthirsty savage never passed up a scalp. "Yeah, okay." He didn't worry about the escaped man. Who was he going to tell out here in the wilderness? Besides, they would be gone soon enough.

Jules pointed at a side room. "Put the women in there." He then gestured toward the dead man on the floor. "And get that out of here."

They had been in the house four days when Clancy went out hunting for camp meat. He was coming back into the open area surrounding the house with a deer over his shoulders when he heard a thumping sound from behind and a woof, like a dog. He turned to see what had made the sound as a grizzly bear jumped on him. He fell backwards under the weight of the bear, letting out a series of blood-curdling screams that mingled with the roars of the attacking bear. He tried to roll over on his face but the deer under his shoulders prevented the move.

The men poured out of the house to see the big bear ripping into the man with teeth and claws. They all fired their guns into the giant mound of rippling fur, causing the beast to roar with fury and pain. Then, like blowing out a candle, the bear dropped dead.

The men rushed up to Clancy, who was shivering from shock and fear. Blood flowed from bite and claw wounds so numerous that it was hard to tell solid flesh from wounds. They carried him into the house and laid him on the floor in a corner. Bandages made from the torn clothes abandoned by the evicted men were wrapped around the bleeding wounds as the man lay whimpering and trembling violently in shock. They threw his blankets over him and left him.

Three days passed after the bear attack and Clancy had not improved enough to travel. Jules conferred with Prich and Ed, "This is as long as I intended to stay here. We need to be moving on for the coast." Jules motioned with his head toward the lump under the blankets that was Clancy. "We're going to leave him."

The two men nodded in agreement. Prich added, "Leave the loony redskin with him."

Jules looked at Dirt Eater sitting on the floor mumbling, oblivious to everything going on around him. "Good idea, he's dead weight."

Jules went to Angry All The Time and the last Whoop-Up man. "We're pulling out."

The latter jerked his thumb at Clancy, "What about him?"

"He's staying."

"That's not right."

"Then, you can stay with him, Oatman, and hold his hand until he croaks."

Oatman and Clancy were the last of the four men recruited from the Whoop-Up crowd. They had been strangers and no friendship existed between them. Greed and avarice were all the members of the gang shared in common, even after the year and a half together there was no loyalty.

Oatman snorted, "Fine, leave him. He's going to die anyway."

Jules went on, "We're leaving Dirt Eater too."

The man glanced at Dirt Eater. "Good. I'm sick of that red devil's mumbling."

Jules looked at Angry All The Time, "Any objections to leaving Dirt Eater behind?"

"No. I never liked him."

"Fine, pack up."

The men split up to begin preparing for the last leg of the journey to the coast. Horses were saddled and the women put on them. Jules went back into the house and looked at Clancy, who was asleep and breathing raggedly.

He then hunkered down in front of Dirt Eater who still sat on the floor, eyes closed and mumbling. "White Eagle Messenger."

The old man opened his eyes and stared at him. He stopped mumbling. "You wish a vision?"

"I wish you to stay here where it is warm and dry and pray big medicine for us. We must go on to meet our friend. We cannot succeed unless a great Shaman prays and invokes the Old Man to bless us with victory. Will you do that, wise one?"

"Yes, I will give you victory."

Jules patted him on the shoulder, "Thank you wise one. In all the world there is no greater Shaman or Medicine Man than White Eagle Messenger. We will come back for you."

"I will make medicine for you."

Jules stood up straight as Dirt Eater closed his eyes.

"One more thing, wise one."

Dirt Eater opened his eyes and rolled them up at Jules.

"If any white men come here looking to destroy our quest, you must kill them." He laid a knife by the old man.

Dirt Eater nodded, "I will." He closed his eyes and

returned to mumbling.

Jules looked at him and shook his head. He walked out of the house and joined the others. "Let's get out of here."

***

Clancy woke up and stared at the log ceiling above him. He was in pain, sick, and burning with fever, he wanted water. He listened to hear if there was anyone he could call to. He heard nothing, no movement, no talking. He had no idea what day it was or how long he had been unconscious. He turned his head and saw that the house was empty. He began to panic. He had been deserted.

Letting his eyes rove over the room, he saw the crazy old Indian lying on the floor snoring. He fought his way up on his knees and looked out the window above him. There was no one. The door stood open to the room the women had been locked in. They were gone. He began to curse the men who had deserted him and left him with the crazy redskin.

He had no idea if he would live or die, but he could do something to get his revenge even if he died. With great effort he crawled on his hands and knees to the fireplace. The ashes were long cold. They had been gone at least two days. He picked a piece of charred wood from the ashes and crawled back to his blankets. He knew someone would eventually come to this place. On the floor he scrawled with the piece of black wood, *tel polic drak takng womin to richmond coost boat end of juli.*

With a grin of satisfaction, he crawled back under the blankets and fell asleep.

Chapter Thirty

"Five days back. They had a whole string of women mounted on horses that were tail-tied together like pack horses. No bridles, just halters on the horses and them women looked sorely miserable. There was a bunch of the meanest-looking white and Indian men I ever saw riding with them. It seemed mighty odd to me and I thought to question what they were doing, but then I thought better of it. I was well outnumbered; the odds in favor of getting myself killed were too good."

Raven and Wade listened to the trapper's story.

"You made the right decision," Wade said. "They are a murderous band of outlaws and it would have cost your life to approach them."

The trapper nodded, "That's what I figured. I'm as brave as the next man, but not a fool. I figured I should tell someone though, but out here who's to tell? Then, I saw the red coat and knew you were a Mountie."

"They were staying to this trail?"

"Seemed so. It's the clearest route to the Okanagan."

Wade looked at Raven, "The Okanagan River is a two-day ride. We are closing the gap."

"Do you know that country?" Raven asked the trapper.

The man nodded, "Trapped it for five years before moving my lines this way."

"We think they might have a cabin or house somewhere that they use for a stopover place. Ever see anything that would work for that?"

The man scratched at his beard in thought. Most cabins I can think of have someone living in them." He thought further, "Maybe the old Northwest House."

"Tell us about that," Wade encouraged the trapper.

"It used to be a gathering house for the Northwest

Fur Company. They stored furs and supplies in it. When they pulled out Hudson's moved in. I ain't been back that way in a few years, but I was told Hudson's moved out of it too. The place is abandoned now I guess."

Raven and Wade glanced at each other. "It's worth a look," Raven said.

"Indeed." Wade turned his attention back to the trapper, "Where do we find it?"

"Stay on this trail until you get to the Okanagan then head upstream about a mile. It's in a clearing, big long log house."

"Thank you."

"So, what's the story on that bunch?"

"Robbers, kidnappers, thieves, slave sellers."

"Slave sellers? You mean they're selling those women?"

"Yes."

The trapper sighed with disgust, "I should have done something."

"If you had, you would be dead right now and not here telling us what you saw. By being alive you are helping those women far more."

"Yeah, I guess so. Well, good luck to you."

Wade nodded at the man as the party set off down the trail again.

That night they camped in an open area where the breeze could help blow the hordes of mosquitoes away. They were all men hardened to trail and saddle, although Raven had to admit that it took the first few days to get the stiffness out of his joints as he had not ridden much in the last few years. That opened up a long string of good-natured taunts and jibes that Buck threw at his friend. Raven took it with good nature, having to admit that his new life had softened him.

The men spooned stew out of a pot and filled their coffee cups. Settling around the fire, spoons scraping on plates made the only sounds as the hungry men ate. Raven was the last to fill his plate and cup. He settled down on the ground with a slight groan.

Buck looked at him with a wry grin. "I told you to bring a little pillow to sit on Raven, but oh no, you wanted to show that your backside was as tough as ever."

Raven gave him a level stare, "How long did you sit on a pillow after Badger shot that arrow in your butt?"

"How did you know about that?"

Raven gestured with his head toward Badger, "A badger told me."

Buck looked at his brother, "Buffalo paunch mouth."

Badger grinned at him, "You must be kept humble."

The silence between the men had resumed when the sound of clumsy footfalls emanated from out of the dark. Thinking that a moose or bear might be coming through the camp, the men jumped up and drew their guns. A voice came out of the night, "Can a wounded man get some help?"

Wade spoke quickly, "Come into the firelight so we can see you."

The man came forward leaning on a forked branch that had been fashioned into a crutch. His free hand held a rifle.

"You are injured?" Wade asked.

The man looked at the group and then saw the red coat reflecting in the firelight. "Thank the Lord, a Mountie."

Ty and Wade went to the man and helped him closer to the fire. "What happened to you?" Ty asked him.

The man looked at him and the badge on his shirt, "Who are you?"

"United States Marshal."

The man looked surprised, "Up here?"

"They are with me," Wade said. "Let me see your

wound."

They helped the man sit by the fire. Wade looked at his leg, the pants stiff with dried blood. "Remove your trousers."

The man looked at him weak and exhausted. He forced a tired grin, "I usually don't hear that from a man."

Wade glared at him, "Do you want help or not?"

Leaning on his right hand the man lifted his left, "Sorry, I've been four days without food except for a couple of rabbits and fighting this wound, I'm a little punchy." He worked his pants down revealing the jagged moss-choked groove across the width of his thigh.

"That is ugly," Wade commented.

Buck looked at the wound. "I've seen worse. You'll live."

Wade retrieved a small medical pack from his saddlebag. He knelt down next to the man and went to work cleaning the moss out of the wound. They didn't bother to ask questions as the man winced and gasped in pain while Wade scraped and dug the dirt out of the deep gash and washing it as clean as possible with water.

Wade pulled the cork on a small bottle of whiskey, "This will hurt like the devil." He poured the brown liquor into the raw wound.

The man jumped and yelped. He gasped for breath until the sting settled to a dull burn. "Can I have a pull on that?" he whispered to Wade.

"No, it is strictly medicinal for stopping infections."

"Too bad," the man grimaced.

Wade wrapped clean bandages around the wound.

Once the wound was bandaged the man pulled his pants up and lay back catching his breath and looking sick. Duffy laid a blanket over the man who looked at him and nodded his thanks.

"You want to tell us about it?" Wade asked.

"Can I have some of that coffee and grub first?"

The man sat up and shifted the blanket around to cover his shoulders. Buck handed him a filled plate and cup. He took them and eagerly devoured both within a pair of minutes. He then sighed contentedly.

He looked at Wade, "I've got something for you. A gang of mixed whites and Indians, with a bunch of women. Pretty odd if you ask me."

"Not so odd, we are chasing them."

"Stolen women, I'll wager."

"Yes, they are."

"Thought as much. I've spent time at sea, I've seen it before."

"Tell us."

"My partner and me was staying in the old Northwest House. It was abandoned so we moved in and was hunting and prospecting the river. Four days back this outfit shows up and said we had taken over their house. We offered to get out. That's when this one, who seemed like the leader, says that it was too late 'cause we had seen too much. They shot my partner and tried to shoot me. They winged me, but I got away. A couple of their Indians came after me, I shot one and the other headed for safer parts."

Kai commented, "That sounds like our boys all right."

Ty agreed. "If it took him four days in his condition we should make that house by horse in one or two at the most."

"Especially if we move quickly," Wade added.

Buck poured the man a second cup of coffee and handed it to him. "Then, we should get a move on at first light. What about him?"

Wade looked at the man, "We don't have a horse for you."

"And I'd just slow you down in catching them. Leave me some grub, matches, and a blanket, and a few extra .44 cartridges and I'll stay at this camp until I can move better. I can find a settlement and get outfitted again."

"You will have it," Wade told him.

The man put his hand out to Wade, "Mike Stone, and you've got a friend if you ever need one."

Wade shook his hand, "Sergeant Major Tracy. We can use all the friends we can get out here."

"Do me a favor Tracy. Shoot a couple of them for me, especially the leader with the long gray hair."

"That one's mine," Buck said. "We'll shoot the others for your partner."

Stone looked at Buck and lifted his cup in a salute, "Fair enough."

***

Late morning of the second day after leaving Mike Stone at the camp, they reached the Okanagan River. They sat on their horses and looked up and down stream; there was no one in sight.

Duffy moved up next to Wade. "That trapper, and Stone, both said a mile upstream from this trail. Interested in some advice from an old army man?"

"Of course."

"Send two scouts upriver to locate the place first. We have no idea where it is except a mile upstream and we could blunder right into them unless we know exactly what is there. They will bring back a report and we can plan our assault."

"I agree. Good plan."

Both men looked at Buck.

Buck hit Badger with his hand, "Come on, that's us."

The remainder of the party watched them ride up the river. "We should move back to the trees and out of sight to wait," Wade suggested.

As a group, they turned their horses back to the cover of firs and maples and dismounted to wait.

Buck and Badger moved upstream keeping to the trees for cover as much as possible. They saw no other people, although there was evidence of several old camps. Ahead, through the trees they caught a glimpse of a clearing and the unmistakable horizontal lines of aged logs. Moving cautiously to the edge of the trees, they studied the clearing and the long log structure.

"That has to be it," Buck whispered.

"I see no horses," Badger said.

"No chimney smoke either. Looks empty."

They stayed as they were for another half hour watching. In that time nothing changed or indicated occupancy. They moved through the trees slowly circling the house.

"There," Badger pointed at the ground.

Looking where Badger pointed, Buck saw a man's body. "That must be Stone's partner."

"It has been there for a time, the animals have eaten on it."

"That would fit with the timing Stone talked about."

They continued the circle until they came back to where they had started. "Leave the horses here," Buck whispered. "We'll go in on foot and get a look inside."

Dismounting, they tied their horses to trees and moved in slowly. Badger pointed at the dead bear a hundred feet from the house. Buck nodded his acknowledgement of it.

Buck crept in under a window. Rising up slowly he peeked in through the dirty glass. He could see part of the large interior. He looked at Badger and shook his head.

Going around to the opposite side of the house Buck peeked in a different window. Once again he saw an empty room. He whispered, "Looks empty."

Buck met Badger at the door. Badger pushed on the door, but it did not open. He looked at Buck with an expression asking how to open the door.

Buck pushed on the door with the same result. He peered in through the half inch gap between the door and the wall. He could see the wooden bar was down and no cord hanging on the outside to pull it up with. Sliding his knife out of the scabbard he slipped it into the gap and forced the bar up. He then pushed the door open.

Both men looked cautiously into the empty room. Seeing nothing, they stepped tentatively inside. A sudden rush of movement accompanied by a hoarse scream of fury caught Badger off balance knocking him several steps away from Buck. Buck turned his head to see a rush of brown and the flash of a blade. With his knife held low he slashed up and toward the figure. Feeling the blade hit solidly, he followed through with a dragging sensation. The brown figure fell to the floor.

Badger moved up beside Buck as they stared at the figure lying face down on the floor with a widening pool of blood spreading out from it. It was a man with long, snarled gray hair wearing worn-out buckskins. Badger squatted down and rolled the man over. He looked up at Buck, "It is Dirt Eater."

Buck's knife had ripped open Dirt Eater's stomach spilling his intestines and killing him.

"They must have left him here," Buck commented as he sniffed the air, "It stinks in here."

Badger pointed at Dirt Eater, "He stinks and his guts."

"No, something dead," Buck said as he looked around the large open room. "The far wall, there's something under those blankets."

They carefully approached where Clancy lay. Badger was about to step on the charcoal marks when Buck stopped him. "Don't move, there's a message written on the floor." Buck moved around so he could read it.

Badger stepped around the black words, pulling his knife he used the tip to turn back the blanket revealing the body under it. "This one is dead." He picked at the bloody, dried bandages with the knife. "He was attacked by the bear, see he is all torn up, that dead one out in the yard."

Buck looked at the dead man. "Yeah, that's what I smelled. Been a day or two, infection likely killed him. They deserted him, left him to die."

Badger pointed at the message, "What do the words say?"

"It says that Jules was here and they are headed for Richmond. Go get the others and bring them back here quickly. I will stay here and make sure nothing happens to the message."

Badger left the house and ran to his horse. Buck heard him gallop away as he turned to look the room over. He walked over to look down at Dirt Eater. It was then he recalled the prophecy Bighorn Chief had given him years ago: "one day you will gut Dirt Eater like a deer."

His raising among the Blackfeet had taught him to believe in the prophecies of the elders so the fulfillment of it did not come as a surprise. If this part was true, then the part about him finally confronting his father had to be true as well. He rolled the old man into his blanket that lay on the floor and dragged his skin-and-bones body out of the house.

Circling the house, he spotted several piles of horse manure. Kicking into the piles he could see they were not more than a couple of days old. They were closing the gap.

A short time passed before the party rode into the clearing with Badger in the lead. Wade quickly dismounted and hurried toward Buck who was standing in the open doorway. He looked at Dirt Eater lying in the blanket.

"That's Dirt Eater," Buck said matter-of-factly.

"Why was he here?"

Buck shrugged, "They left him, I guess. He attacked me."

Wade frowned at the body, then looked at Buck.

"There is a message inside?"

"A dead man left you a message written on the floor."

Wade entered the open door and then stepped back a step, "Oh, it smells foul."

"Dead man with rotting wounds, and fresh blood tends to smell things up." Buck was more accustomed to the sight and smell of violent death than Wade was.

Wade walked across the room and grimaced at the stiff, ravaged body in the blankets and then read the message. He hurried back outside. Buck noticed his greenish complexion and followed him.

Wade looked embarrassed. "My apologies for my weak constitution, it is the smell."

"It's okay," Buck assured him. "I've seen and smelled so much death in the war that I'm hardened to it. Hope you never do get used to it."

"Thank you for understanding."

"How about that message?"

"Wonderful. Just what we needed. We should ride without delay directly to Richmond."

Raven glanced at Wade as he approached the open door. He hesitated momentarily at the threshold, "Smells like death."

"Dead man in the corner," Buck commented.

Raven walked in and read the message on the floor. He came back out to where the others stood.

"We should bury the dead," Wade suggested.

"We'll take care of it," Raven answered.

Wade took in several deep breaths of fresh air. Raven recognized Wade's problem, but said nothing in regards to it. "That message says it all."

"Yes," Wade agreed. "I told Buck we need to ride directly to Richmond harbor and cut them off before the women are lost."

"We'll finish up here and get on it."

Wade looked out to the west across the river, "And hope we are not too late."

Chapter Thirty-One

The two teenaged sisters were busy washing clothes in a stream. They chattered excitedly between themselves, unaware of the danger that lurked behind them in the brush. Jules studied the young women, sizing them up for their potential value. They were attractive, young, and white.

"I want them," he whispered to Prich and Ed, who stood next to him.

Ed slipped back to where Oatman and Angry All The Time waited. "We're taking those two girls. Oatman watch the women, Angry come with me."

The four men snuck down toward the girls. In spite of their father's teaching to always be aware of their surroundings, the girls were oblivious to what was going on around them. With a rush the men sprang at them from different sides, grabbing the girls and clamping hands over their mouths.

The girls struggled against the men, their futile screams muted. Their eyes were wild with terror as they were quickly dragged back to the concealing brush. "Make it quick," Jules ordered. "That settlement's not far from here."

Rushing back to where the captive women sat on their horses, they tied rags around the girls' mouths. Their hands were tied in front of them and the ropes wrapped around their waists so they could not reach the gags. The girls were pushed up on two of the spare horses that had belonged to the dead men.

The girls continued to struggle until Jules growled at them, "You'd better behave or I'll let that red savage have his way with you." The girls stopped and stared wide-eyed over the gags at the vicious face and hate-filled eyes of Angry All The Time. Jules then pulled out a knife and raised the point to within an inch of the nearest girl's throat. "If you try and escape we will catch you and slit your throat *after* we let the savage have you. Do you understand? If you want to live, do what you're told."

The girls sat still with tears streaming down their faces. The other women sat silent and pitied the girls who were now facing their same fate. It had been a long ride for them, weeks filled with threats, abuse, and fear. None of them had an idea what was to become of them, their only hope was to cooperate so they could live and hopefully be rescued.

Jules turned to Angry All The Time, "Do some backtracking. Make sure we aren't followed."

The Indian slipped out and disappeared without a word.

Prich watched the Indian disappear into the trees. "Gives me the bloody shivers when that red savage vanishes like that."

"He's useful," Jules answered. "Tie his horse to the others."

"He's useful until we get to Richmond anyway." Prich grinned.

Jules gave a smirking grin in return, "Yeah." He glanced at Oatman, who was busy with the horses. "Three way split, mate."

Prich led Angry All The Time's horse and handed the reins to Oatman. "Tie him on the end."

They moved out quickly, keeping to the brush and trees as much as possible. Ed came up beside Jules, "I think that's enough women for now. It's getting hard to hide them and we're bound to run into more people as we near the coast."

Jules looked back at the string of women. "You might be right. Another three days to the coast. The trails are clearer now; we'll go by night and hide during the day."

They moved off the narrow trail and into the woods. Riding deeper into the trees, Jules called them to a stop. "We're only traveling by night from now to the coast." He then looked at Oatman, "Go up on the trail and watch for the Indian to come back and bring him in here."

Oatman frowned, but did as he was told. He had seen what happened to the others when they gave Jules backtalk. He wondered how long before they killed him too. He should ride away, except he had too much time invested in this venture now. He had gotten his cut of cash and gold before without a problem. He should get his cut of the women as well and it would be a fortune to him. He wasn't about to lose that. All he had to do was keep his mouth shut, take his cut, and get out fast.

Jules and his friends pulled the women off the horses and ordered them to sit in a group. Their hands were freed from their waists, but left tied together. The gags were pulled down so they could breathe and eat.

Jules snarled in the dirty strained faces of the women, "If any of you tries to shout I'll cut your tongue out, and don't think I won't."

The women cringed back and remained silent except for the sound of sniffling and low crying. One of the new girls asked, "Why are you doing this?"

Jules gave her an evil grin, "Money, girl."

"I don't understand."

"You don't need to. Shut up or I'll put the gag back on."

The girl stopped talking and cast a glance to either side of her at the other women. They were an even mix of white and Indian. She knew her father would come to the stream when they didn't return home. He was an expert in the woods; he would figure it out and come looking for her and her younger sister.

Her initial panic and fear had passed. She had to think and plan for her sister and the others as well. The other women looked like they had traveled a long way and rescue for them might never come. She would listen and be quiet and, if she could, she would leave signs for her father to track them by.

The girl's younger sister began to cry. She leaned into her, "Don't cry, Bridget. Pa will come for us."

"I'm afraid, Cassie."

Jules looked at the women, "What are you talking about back there?"

"I'm just comforting my sister, she's afraid."

"Well, stop it."

Cassie nodded at her sister and mouthed the words, "I will get us out."

The men cooked food and waited for Angry All The Time and Oatman to come back. Two hours passed before the sound of a man moving clumsily through the brush came to them. The men pulled their guns and watched. Angry All The Time suddenly stood at the fire like a ghost. Prich jumped and cursed.

A minute later Oatman stumbled in.

"Do you have the whole Northwest Mounted following you?" Jules snarled at Oatman. "You make enough noise for ten drunken men."

"Trying to keep up with that stinking Indian," Oatman grumbled.

"I take it no one is wise to us?" Jules directed the question at Angry All The Time.

The Indian shook his head as he shoved food into his mouth.

Oatman sat down by the fire and ate. Prich and Ed left the fire and walked to where the women sat. "We'll untie your hands so you can eat," Ed told them, "but, if you run we will hunt you down and kill you. If you get away, we will kill one of the other women in your place."

The women rubbed their raw and cut wrists as they were each handed a plate of food and a canteen of water to pass among them. Cassie knew she could probably escape, get back home and bring help. She would have to leave her sister and it would cost the life of one of the others to do it though and that was out of the question. She had overheard enough talk to know they were headed for the coast.

Her father was a trapper and had taught her how to track. They had often played tracking games in the woods and had devised a set of signs to give the other clues. One of those signs was to tie a series of knots in a thin red huckleberry branch as a directional signal.

They were sitting with a cluster of huckleberry bushes at their backs. She slowly worked her hands up and inched one of the thin green branches with the tiny green leaves down and quickly tied a big knot in it. She repeated the action with a second branch. The two knots was a sign that meant go west from there.

She then pushed the heels of her shoes into the soft dirt and made marks her father would see and know it meant to look for a sign. He would then find the knotted branches and know which way they went. He would pick up the trail from there.

When it was fully dark the men went to the women. Jules posed tauntingly in front of them. "We don't want anyone falling off a horse in the dark so we are not going to tie your hands. But, if one of you runs away we will send the savage after you, and you know what that means. We will then kill you to teach the rest a lesson. Just keep that in mind."

Cassie wondered if they actually would kill one of the women since they expected to get money for them. Then, again they were a mean lot and probably would. She would have to rely on her father and leave him signs.

The group rode out of the trees led by Angry All The Time. Oatman rode behind him. Prich led the string of horses carrying the women while Jules followed behind them. Ed brought up the rear leading the two pack horses that carried their food and furs they had stolen from trappers along the way.

***

It was still light when Zeb Adams' wife sent him down to the river to find Cassie and Bridget. She was concerned because they should have been back from washing the clothes long before. Zeb assured her they had likely gone exploring or watching some baby animal. They often got involved with something and forgot the time. He walked down the river where the girls were supposed to be.

He looked around without seeing them. Believing he was right and they had gone exploring he shook his head, he would have to have a word with them about frightening their mother. That idea instantly dissolved when he saw the abandoned clothes basket and clothes still in the water. They would never do that.

He studied the tracks and panic rose when he found men's boot tracks mingled with the girls. Scuff marks and the tangle of tracks told him there had been a struggle. He pushed down the panic and forced his mind to think clearly. He picked up the men's trail and followed it.

He tracked them into the woods where he found horse prints and those from an Indian's moccasins. Light was fading and the trail could only be followed until dark and then he would have to go back home and start up at dawn. He followed the tracks to the trail and saw that a large number of horses were lined out single file.

He returned home and told his wife, who began worrying and crying. Zeb promised her he would be on their trail at dawn. He would track them down and kill every man involved in the kidnapping of their daughters and bring the girls home.

In the morning light, Zeb saddled his horse and followed the trail left by the string of horses. He found where the party had made the previous night's camp. He studied the area around the burned out fire carefully. He identified the same boot tracks he had found at the river.

Making an ever-widening circle, he found impressions in the dirt and fir needles where several people had sat in a group for a long time. Looking closely he made out the small shoe and moccasin tracks unmistakably left by women indicating that the kidnappers held several white and Indian girls. He found the deep heel marks gouged in the dirt and knew it was one of the markers he had taught Cassie. It meant he was to look for a sign. He looked at the huckleberry bushes and saw the twin knots.

He whispered out loud, "They're heading west. Good girl, Cassie."

He mounted his horse and followed the tracks out to the trail. He was studying the hoof prints on the dirt trail when he heard horses approaching from behind him. He turned his horse crosswise on the trail and held his Spencer rifle across the saddle's pommel pointed at the oncoming horses.

He was mildly surprised when the first man he saw in the line was a red-coated Mountie. He knew the Northwest Mounted had come into the country east of British Columbia. He never expect to see one this far west though. He was further surprised when the rest of the group came into sight with a United States soldier, two men with badges on their chests, and two other men including an Indian. They came to a stop in front of him.

Wade greeted the man, "Sergeant Major Tracy, sir. We are chasing a group of criminals. They would have several women with them. Have you by chance seen them?"

"No, but it's likely the same men who stole my two girls. Took them from the river. I tracked them to here; they camped in the woods yonder. My girl left me a sign that says they were heading west."

"Yes, they are. We have word that they are heading for Richmond harbor."

"I know the place. It's at the mouth of the Fraser. Why are they going there?"

"To rendezvous with a boat. These men have been

robbing, murdering, and kidnapping woman from the Montana Territory to here. I am sorry to say, in regards to your daughters, that they are selling the women into slavery overseas."

Zeb's eyes narrowed with anger. "Then, we need to get there before they do."

"I'm sorry, Mister . . . ?"

"Zeb Adams."

"I'm sorry Mr. Adams, I cannot allow that."

Zeb glared at him as he clenched his jaws and turned a chew of tobacco in his cheek. "You can't *allow* that? Those animals took my girls and you can't *allow* me to go after them? Let me tell you something right here and now, I fully intend to get my girls back and kill the men responsible. So, there is no *allowing* me anything. I can shave a day off and get there before you, so, you can follow me or you can pick up the pieces after I'm finished with them."

Wade studied the man.

Zeb pinned Wade with a hard eye, "What would you do if it was your girls?"

Wade gave in. "Point taken. You referred to a shortcut?"

"I know a faster way to the coast that doesn't need this trail. Since you know where they're going, we can cut them off or at least get there the same time they do. I'm going now. You can come with me, or not."

Wade looked back at the group as they listened to the exchange.

"Getting those women back is our first priority," Raven said. "If Adams can give us that day we're behind, I say we go with him."

Buck added, "We need to stop this gang once and for all. If we get there ahead of them we can save the women and nail the gang."

"And hopefully catch who is on the other end of the

deal," Duffy said.

Wade looked back at Zeb, "Lead on, Mr. Adams."

"I hope you boys can ride because I don't aim to slow for nothing." Zeb turned his horse and cut off the trail in a southwest direction. The party followed and disappeared into the woods.

Chapter Thirty-Two

The sound of gently lapping water against the shore drifted up the hill where Jules sat on his horse sighting through a spy glass. He searched the channels in between the islands and out to the big island that blocked his view of the Pacific Ocean. He studied every ship that looked remotely like Smithe's.

Directly before them sprawled the wide expanse of the Fraser River spilling out into the Strait of Georgia and the fishing village of Richmond clinging to its bank. Behind them, up the river, was New Westminster. To the north was the isolated shoreline leading back into the river channel that hid the rendezvous point with Smithe's long boats. There was activity on the shore and in the harbor, but no sign of Smithe's ship.

Jules cursed under his breath. He was not late and there should be a ship anchored with a red pennant flying from the mainmast as a signal. He put the glass back in his saddlebag. They would go to the rendezvous site and wait there.

Jules reined his horse to the north and stayed above the strait overlooking the inside passage. He led the group over the point of land that jutted out into the waterway and rode directly to the rendezvous beach along the channel.

Unseen by the group were two Indian women gathering roots. The women hid in the long grass and watched the string of riders melt into the trees. They knew captives when they saw them.

The day was late as Jules ordered a camp set up in the trees. They herded the women together as they usually did at night. Jules and his two partners took turns sitting where they could see out to the expanse of water and used the glass to watch. Night fell and Jules cursed. He did not want to be stuck with these women and stolen furs any longer than necessary. At any time someone could come

349

along and see them. He had spotted several British war ships in the harbor and that made him nervous.

The morning broke with fog hanging low over the water and a fine mist soaking them. Jules hoped Smithe would use the fog as cover to send in the long boats. It was better this way than in the dead of night when he really couldn't see what Smithe was up to or what tricks he might be playing. He told Prich to go down to the shore and make a signal fire to let Smithe know they were at the rendezvous. If anyone asked he was warming himself.

As the hours passed, the men took turns keeping the fire going and watching. The light misting rain had stopped as the fog began lifting up off the water in blowing wisps. Jules was at the fire when Prich came down to relieve him. They looked out over the water, "I've got a bad feeling about this, Jules."

Jules scowled, "I know, we have never had to wait before. Something is wrong."

"I never saw that many war ships in here before."

"That's what has me worried."

Prich jerked his thumb toward the hidden camp. "How long do you want to wait with them?"

"I have to think about it."

"Don't think too bloody long or we'll be doing the gallows jig."

"If they haven't shown up by dark, we kill them all and the three of us head down to the Columbia. We can say we are fur buyers and sell the furs, at least get something out of this."

Prich scowled, "Bloody shame, those females are worth a lot too."

"Not worth a rope."

Jules turned to walk away when the subtle sound of a wooden oar turning in an oarlock and splashing water drifted out of the fog. Prich grabbed Jules by the arm, "Listen."

They listened into the diminishing fog. The sound came again, the unmistakable rhythm of oars in the water. Another five minutes and two long boats broke into view with two men oaring each one. A third man clad in black oilskins and a seaman's rain hat covering his face sat in the first boat. With a great pull on the oars the bows of the boats slid into the sand and marshy shoreline.

Prich shouted at them. "It's about time you got here."

The man in the oilskins stepped out of the boat onto the beach. Jules strode up to him and snapped, "We were about to dump the cargo, Smithe, what took you so long?"

Smithe grinned sardonically, "You are too impatient my reprobate friend. We have been under observation by the Queen's navy and had to anchor on the windward side of yonder island and post a watch for you. Then, we had to wait until there was enough cover to come in. So, here we are."

"Are we being watched now?"

Smithe answered in the same tone, "Perhaps. The longer we stand here chatting the more chance there is to be discovered. What do you have for me?"

"Nine women; five Indian, four white, all under twenty years of age."

Smithe smiled, "Excellent."

"We have furs as well."

"Even more excellent. Trot it on down here and let's get going."

Jules jerked his head for Prich to bring them down.

Prich ran back up the hill and into the trees.

Smithe watched him go and then turned his attention back to Jules. "We will have to curtail operations for a while. The navy is cracking down hard on smuggling, likening it to piracy of the last century. Smugglers are being hung from the same gallows that pirates once swung from."

Jules agreed, "It's getting hot for us as well. We were thinking about moving further south and laying low for a bit."

Prich came back down the hill leading the parade. The horses had been left in the trees and the women were herded single file, hands tied, down to the water. Ed, Oatman, and Angry All The Time brought up the rear carrying the furs.

They stopped at the water's edge as Smithe looked the women over. "Very nice, very nice indeed. He leered at Cassie, "I may purchase this one for myself."

Jules stepped between the girl and Smithe. "Let's see the money."

Smithe turned his hard steel blue eyes onto Jules'. "Have I ever cheated you before?"

"Not yet, but since this is your last trip you and your boys might have some ideas about cutting this relationship off prematurely and permanently."

"Would I do such a thing?" Smithe grinned.

"Of course you would."

Smithe laughed, "No honor among thieves is it?"

Jules simply looked at him without a reply.

"I can only take half the women in the boats at a time and some of the furs. We will have to make two trips." Smithe pulled a pouch of gold coins from his pocket. I will pay you half for this load and then the other half when we take the second load."

"Fair enough."

Smithe turned to the sailors with him, "Three women in one boat and two in my boat. Get them down on the floor and put the furs over them."

Smithe's men stepped forward and roughly seized onto five of the women and pushed them toward the long boats. The women cried, their faces reflecting fear and panic.

"Easy lads," Smithe chastised the men. "Let's not

damage the merchandise."

The women were put in the boats; Cassie was in one, Bridget the other. Bridget cried out, "Cassie, help me."

"Shut her up," Smithe snapped out.

The sailor wrapped a dirty saltwater-soaked rag over her mouth and shoved her down in the boat.

Smithe turned toward the boat. Jules tapped him on the arm, "Money?"

"Oh, yes." Smithe handed Jules the leather pouch. "Almost forgot."

Jules snatched it out of his hand. "Funny how things slip our minds isn't it?" He hefted the pouch and gave it a shake hearing the familiar sound of rattling coins.

Smithe turned toward the boats, but Jules grabbed him by the arm. "Not you."

Smithe glared at him.

"You stay here until they come back."

"What?"

"I want to make sure the rest of the deal comes to a satisfactory conclusion. Tell them to hurry, the fog is lifting."

***

Wade rode beside Zeb Adams as they broke out of the trees overlooking the strait and islands. It was close to noon. The mist held the fog over the water keeping them from seeing far.

Zeb pointed, "The river mouth and Richmond are there and the strait is in front of us."

Wade growled, "Cannot see a blasted thing."

They all stopped. Zeb turned in the saddle to look at them, "Too much business going on to the south and in front of us. They couldn't make the exchange without being seen. There is a lot of empty shoreline to the north that they might use. That's my first bet." He reined his horse to the north and kicked him into a jog.

The group followed him riding to the north for

several minutes.

The two Indian women who had been digging roots the day before were back out. Seeing Wade's red coat that they took for one of the British soldiers occupying the port area, they ran up to them. They began to chatter in their native tongue and pointing north.

Wade looked to Zeb, "Do you understand?"

Zeb shook his head, "They have dozens of different dialects over here."

Buck and Badger moved up to the women. Buck used sign language that was understood by most of the tribes he knew. He hoped it was universal. Eventually, between him and Badger they managed to get the information from the women.

Buck turned to the group. "Yesterday, men with captive women rode through here headed north."

"Let's go," Zeb shouted.

Wade waved his thanks to the women as the men broke their horses into a jog in the direction the women had indicated.

The fog began to steadily lift as the summer sun burned through. A long expanse of open shoreline was in clear view before it curved back to the east following the channel. In the distance they could make out the tiny forms of men and boats on the point of the beach where it began to curve back.

Staying back from the water and in the trees they drew closer. The thickness of the brush and long grass made it difficult to move quickly. All the same, they were closing the gap undetected.

The last of the fog blew away revealing a clear blue sky with the sun reflecting brightly off the water. They broke out of the trees onto a rise above the shore and a hundred yards from the boats. There were men and women on the beach and the boats were full to the gunwales. A man was at the oars in each of the boats and a second was outside each boat in the process of pushing it out into the water.

Buck yanked his horse to a halt. He called out, "Raven, Kai the near boat." The three men had performed this drill a hundred times in the war. Raven and Kai were to shoot the men in the near boat. They jumped off their horses grabbing their rifles as they did.

Buck snapped an order to Zeb, "The one at the oars, far boat."

The four men sat quickly in the wet grass and steadied their rifles with elbows on their knees. Within a span of a few seconds the hard reports of four shots echoed off the trees and across the open water. The two men pushing the boats fell in the sand. The oarsman in the near boat slumped over while the one taking Zeb Adams' .56 caliber Spencer round was hurled out of the boat and into the water.

Wade led the charge down the hill with the men who were still mounted riding with him. They bore down on the group. Nuttah, who still stood on the beach, recognized Badger and shouted for the remaining women to fall to the ground which they immediately did.

Prich pulled up a pistol and fired at the oncoming riders. Wade fired his revolver at a gallop hitting Prich solidly and spinning him to the marshy ground. Smithe made a clumsy run for the boat as more gunfire erupted sending Ed and Oatman to the ground.

Jules sprinted for the trees and the waiting horses that meant his safe escape. Angry All The Time was running directly behind him. Jules turned quickly, punched and tripped the Indian causing him to fall. Jules hoped they would grab the Indian giving him the extra seconds he needed to escape.

Wade charged his horse directly into the fleeing Smithe sending him somersaulting into the water alongside the boat.

Still on the rise above the water, Buck saw a man running for the trees and knew it had to be Jules making his escape at the cost of others. He swung into the saddle and drove the horse at the fleeing figure. They reached the trees at the same time. Buck hurled himself off the horse landing on Jules.

Grabbing Jules by the back of his coat he swung him around slamming him face first into a fir tree. He spun him around and drove a fist into his face, knocking him down on his back. Buck pulled the Remington, cocked the hammer, and pointed it at Jules' face.

Jules squirmed on the ground with his hands out in front of him. Bits of bark clung to his scraped face as blood trickled out of his nose. His eyes were wide in horror and recognition. "Please, Buckingham, please. Don't shoot me, please." He began to cry and whimper.

Buck stood frozen with his finger a press away from killing the man he had hated for so many years. He thought of all the reasons he hated him, why he was justified in blowing his head off. He watched the pathetic man squirming and writhing in his fear.

Jules lay on the ground crying and looking into the bore of the cocked .44. "I'm sorry for everything, Buckingham."

Through clenched teeth Buck snarled, "My name is Buck; I'm no longer your drunken joke. I am going to blow your brains into the dirt, I just want to look at your pathetic, cowardly face and remember this moment before I do. I suffered; I suffered so much because of you. I hate your guts. God, how I hate your guts."

The sound of a man's steps moved in behind Buck and stopped. "Do not do it, Buck." It was Wade's voice.

"Give me *one good* reason why not," Buck growled between clenched teeth.

"Because you are not vermin scum like he is. You are a decent man, too decent to murder this pathetic coward. You accomplished your goal; you have caught and stopped him. Wasn't that the goal, to stop him?"

"No, the goal was to kill him."

"Look at him Buck, look at what he is. He is nothing, he is less than nothing."

A second voice came from behind him, "There is no power to be gained by killing the cringing, cowardly woman, my brother." It was Badger touching the Blackfeet side of his mind. "I would not want the scalp from such as this creature or to count him as coup. Spit your contempt in his face and let Wade take him to be hung."

Still holding the cocked revolver on Jules, Buck slowly turned his head to look at the two men standing behind him. "Can you promise me he will hang?"

Wade looked directly in Buck's eyes, "With all he has done, I can promise it. A quick hearing and a quick execution."

Buck lowered the hammer on the Remington. "Take the stinking yellow dog."

Wade reached down and jerked Jules up off the ground. Jules was still crying and terrified. He looked at Buck for an instant as Wade led him away.

"Wait," Buck said.

Wade stopped as Buck walked up and put his face inches from Jules'. He stared his hate into the terrified eyes of his father and suddenly spit in Jules' face. It was the highest insult a Blood warrior could pay to an enemy too cowardly to kill.

Jules' head jerked back at the impact. He did not lift his hand to wipe his face as Wade led him away.

Badger put his hand on Buck's back, "Well done, brother."

The men returned to the water where Kai and Ty held guns on Smithe and Ed, who was wounded. Zeb, along with Raven and Duffy, had pulled the boats further up on shore and had the women all out and sitting on the ground.

The women were crying in relief and the Adams girls were clinging to their father.

Wade ordered Jules to sit down, which he quickly did.

Prich and Oatman were lying where they had fallen in the wet grass. The four dead sailors had been drug back out of the water. Nuttah jumped up from the ground and wrapped her arms around Buck, and then Badger.

Buck looked around. "Where's Angry All The Time? Wasn't he supposed to be with them?"

Badger pointed to the east, "He is there, I killed the thing. He is the one responsible for the deaths at Swift Runner's village, he killed our grandfather who we loved, and he stole our sister and made her a captive. It was my duty as a Brave."

"But, I wasn't supposed to kill Jules?"

Badger looked into Buck's eyes with all seriousness, "Yes, you had the right." He glanced toward Wade standing a ways from them over the prisoners. "He would have arrested you if you did."

Buck looked toward Wade and asked, "Why didn't he arrest you for killing Angry?"

"Because I was carrying out our law, Angry All The Time was condemned to death. It was not his place to stop me."

"I see. I don't need to go back to prison." He looked into his brother's face, "Thank you."

"I am your older brother. It is for me to keep my younger brother from causing himself too much trouble."

They all turned as several red-coated men riding in a column approached the group. The man in front of the column called them to a halt. He stepped out of the saddle and up to Wade and put out his hand. "Major Long, of Her Majesty's Service."

Wade shook his hand. "Sergeant Major Tracy, Northwest Mounted Police."

"We heard the shooting."

Wade nodded toward the battle scene and prisoners, "We stopped these men."

Long looked over the dead men and the seated prisoners. He gave a concerned look at the bedraggled women. "White slavers?"

"Precisely. We have been on their track since the Montana Territory."

Long gave a low whistle, "Quite a trek."

"It was worth it," Wade smiled.

Long looked hard at the man in the oilskins whose face was hidden under the wide brimmed hat. He narrowed his eyes, "Strip that hat and oilskin off of him."

Kai yanked the man to his feet and roughly pulled the slicker over his head taking his hat off with it to reveal the red army tunic under it.

Long beamed a smile. "Colonel Norman Smithe, fancy meeting you here. It is my distinct honor and *absolute* privilege to place you under arrest in the name of the Queen."

Smithe glared at Long and then commanded, "Major, I order you to arrest *these* men who have murdered these fellows around me. I outrank you, that is an order."

Long laughed, "*Please*. We have been onto your little smuggling ring for some time. You smuggle opium and other contraband into British Columbia, run whiskey to the Indians, and then take stolen loot back. Then, on top of that, you are a kingpin in the white slave trade. It is called piracy, Mr. Smithe, and that carries a death sentence. You have disgraced the uniform and shamed the Queen's Service; it will be my greatest joy to personally put the noose around your neck."

Long turned to his men behind him, "Sergeant Wallis, clap Mr. Smithe in irons."

The Sergeant stepped forward, took Smithe by the arm and led him back to the horses where iron restraints were locked onto his wrists and ankles. "How am I to ride?" Smithe snarled.

"You won't be," Long answered. "You will be walking as you are not fit to be mounted on one of the Queen's horses."

Long turned back to Wade. "And what else do we have here?"

Wade pointed at Jules, "He is the leader of this gang. They began their criminal rampage in British Columbia and worked their way into the Montana Territory of the United States which is why Sergeant Major Duffy and Marshals Allen and Maddock are with me. They kidnapped women, robbed, and murdered their way back to here to meet with Smithe and sell the women and goods."

Long nodded, "These must be the ones we were told to watch for."

"Major Long, I can take these two back to Fort Macleod for trial and execution, or maybe you would like to try them and hang them here?" Wade's expression and tone indicated to the Major that it would be a great help if the men were turned over to him.

Long gave Wade a slight, knowing smile. "I would not want to overstep the jurisdiction of the Northwest Mounted Police; however, we are under strict orders from the Queen herself to clean up all smuggling and the navy to sink their ships on the high seas.

"As to Smithe's ship, I will have the navy seize her and have it towed into dry dock to be taken apart plank-by-plank and nail-by-nail to find the contraband hidden within its hull. The hanging of its wretched crew will serve notice to the rest."

Wade gestured toward Jules and Ed, "These *were* connected to the smugglers so, yes, they would fall under your jurisdiction, Colonel." He smiled slightly.

"Yes, I believe they would. If you are agreeable I would be happy to take them off your hands."

Wade looked at the other men. "Is that acceptable to you?"

Buck snapped a quick reply, "I want to stay and see it. If Jules doesn't hang, I will kill him myself."

Long answered, "I can assure you, sir they will swing within the week. You are welcome to watch."

"I will agree to that," Buck said.

The others agreed to accept Long's proposal providing they were allowed to watch the hanging and assure themselves that justice had been served. Major Long extended invitations to them all to stay as his guests.

Major Long was true to his word and before leaving the men had watched Smithe, Jules, and Ed be found guilty of piracy, white slave trading, and murder. They were hung side-by-side from the gallows. Smithe's crew was taken from the ship and also hung as pirates.

Chapter Thirty-Three

Buck and Badger had been back in the Teton River village for two months. Buck was satisfied with the conclusion and Jules' punishment. The brothers had explained to the village the course of events and there was no woman willing to weep for the deaths of Jules, Dirt Eater, or Angry All The Time. It was a relief to be rid of them.

Buck sat alone staring into the fire in front of his tent set up behind He Who Fights' lodge. The events of the past several months passed through his mind. Zeb Adams had taken his daughters back home. The two white women from Montana were returned home with the help of Major Long, who got them to California, where they boarded a train to Salt Lake City. The Blackfeet girls had returned with the party. The Americans parted ways with Wade Tracy at Fort Macleod.

Buck wasn't sure what to do with his life now. The village life no longer held appeal for him as he had seen too much of what lay beyond their hunting grounds. He had no interest in scouting for the army. His parting with Raven and Kai had been difficult yet none of them let on, ending their association with barbs and jokes. Raven had returned to Washington, and Kai to Denver. He missed his friends.

His thoughts were broken at the sound of a horse walking up to him. Placing a hand over his eyes to shield them from the bright autumn sun, he looked up to see Jim Twist stepping out of the saddle. He walked up to Buck. "Not often you see a coffee pot on a Blackfeet fire."

"I'm making coffee converts," Buck grinned. "I've got another cup if you're of a mind to set."

"Never pass up coffee." Jim sat down opposite his friend. Jim took the cup from Buck and filled it. "I never got a chance to thank you for speaking up for me to the tribe. They welcomed me back in without a problem."

"You're a good friend to them and they know that. The massacre was not blood on your hands."

"You might not have heard, but Bates was transferred back east and finally got himself court martialed for being drunk on duty one too many times."

Buck smiled, "Couldn't happen to a nicer snake. You still working with Lieutenant Prater and the Bureau of Indian Affairs?"

Jim nodded. "We've been doing a lot. They will be forming a reservation for the south Piegan here pretty quick."

Buck shook his head in sadness, "It was bound to come."

"I've been sent to bring you back to Fort Benton for a meeting."

Buck gave him a suspicious look, "What kind of meeting?"

"It has to do with the reservation, that's all they told me."

"Who is *they*?"

"Prater and Shelton."

"*Shelton*," Buck spit the name out with contempt. What does he want, to have me sent back to prison?"

Jim shrugged, "I was just told to get you. They want to talk with Badger, too."

Buck studied Jim's face for several seconds. "I'll go, but only because I trust you that it's not a trap."

"It's not, but if it is I'll help you shoot your way out." The young scout smiled.

"Okay. Finish your coffee, I'll get Badger and we'll head down with you."

The three men rode into the Fort Benton grounds. The town was growing up around the fort walls as fast as the fort itself was falling into decay. Buck knew in a short time this would be its own town as the army was very close to leaving the fort. Fort Shaw was now the primary military presence in the area.

Jim led them to a building that housed the army offices. Tying their horses to the hitch rail, they went inside. Jim opened the door to the meeting room and stepped in. Buck gaped with surprise to see Raven sitting with Colonel Shelton and Lieutenant Prater. The three men stood up.

Raven grinned as he crossed the room and shook hands with Buck and then Badger. "Bet you didn't expect to see me so soon."

"No," Buck answered, "but I can't say I'm sorry." He then grinned. "Recover from your trip?"

Raven feigned embarrassment, "Shh, I don't want everyone to know I turned soft in my old age."

Buck shook hands with Prater; however, he and Shelton held back, looking into each other's eyes without moving.

Colonel Shelton took a deep breath, released it, and straightened his back. "I was wrong about you, Mr. Drake. I checked deeper into your Fort Shaw case and talked in more detail with Mr. Twist. I also spoke with the troopers who were in the barn that day. Told them to be frank, and they were. They didn't care much for the men who were killed and those that had observed the scene saw the weapons and bottle, a few had even seen the three men drinking beforehand. They unanimously believed it was self-defense on your part.

"It seems Captain Clarke had ordered them to keep quiet under threat of punishment and they were not allowed to testify or write reports. There was manipulation by Captain Clarke to condemn you and that is not how I believe justice should be carried out. I cannot return to you the years you lost in prison; however, I had your criminal record cleared up so it no longer exists."

Buck stood in surprise. "Thank you, Colonel."

"It was a matter of self-defense, I know that now.

You did not go in with intent to murder. In fact I had my doubts as to Clarke's convictions even at the time, particularly when you shot their horses when you could have easily shot the men. I should have pursued the matter with an open mind. I have no excuse for not doing so."

"I only wanted to get them off my trail, not kill them," Buck said.

Shelton willingly extended his hand. "Shall we move on from here as friends?"

Buck knew it took a lot for a proud man like Shelton to admit he was wrong and make amends. Buck quickly put his hand out. "Yes, sir, I'd like that just fine."

"Good. Since we are going to be working together we should get along." Shelton looked at Raven, "You may proceed, Mr. Ravenel."

Buck and Badger sat down, as did the others.

Raven began, "As you all are aware the Territorial capital of Montana has been moved from Virginia City to Helena. Colonel Parker has been granted permission to open one of our investigative offices in Helena. I am to head the office and Kai has agreed to come up and take the position as my assistant. We will also be working closely with Ty Allen and his office.

"Colonel Shelton has been put in charge of organizing the new Blackfeet reservation here in Montana. Aside from investigating federal crimes, we will also be working with him to ensure that the rights and property of the Blackfeet are protected."

Shelton added, "We are going to be incorporating the Canadian methods for negotiating with the Blackfeet. Maybe we will have better success for a peaceful solution than with previous tribes."

Raven continued, "Wade has been put in charge of negotiations with the Kainai, Siksika, and Piegan in his area. We will all be spending a good deal of time together, along with the tribal chiefs, to work out a fair compromise.

We want this to work for the Blackfeet and for us. The Bureau of Indian Affairs has established a permanent office here with Lieutenant Prater in charge."

Buck asked, "That sounds good, but how do Badger and I fit in to all this?"

Prater answered, "If you are agreeable you will come to work for me on the payroll of the Bureau. I need a man of your skills that the Piegan trust. Jim Twist is already on my staff. You and Jim understand better than anyone what is at stake for both sides. We do not want the kind of bloodshed that the violations of the Laramie Treaties have caused."

Shelton added, "Besides that, Sergeant Major Tracy specifically asked for you to be involved. Do you accept?"

"Yes, I accept."

All the men smiled their approval at Buck's acceptance.

"Why did you want me here?" Badger asked.

Prater focused his full attention on Badger. "Because of your position as a lead Brave in The Comrades. We will need to organize a reservation police force to enforce the laws. To make sure the tribal members obey the law and don't ride out of the reservation to steal horses and raid the other tribes or whites. The police force will just as importantly make sure the Blackfeet are protected from white intrusion, whisky runners, and other crimes against them. We want you to lead that police force."

Badger considered the idea and then nodded, "I will do that."

Buck glanced at each of the men and then finally to Shelton. "Will we have trouble from Clarke?"

Shelton shook his head. "Captain Clarke stomped into my office like a spoiled child demanding to know why we are not wiping out the Blackfeet instead of, as he put it, *coddling* them. Between that and learning of his manipulation with your trial, not to mention his behavior with Governor Potts, I decided that I had quite enough of Captain Clarke.

"I pulled a few strings and, since he hated Indians so much, I thought a stint on the Dakota plains fighting the Sioux would be good for him. He was transferred to Fort Abraham Lincoln, to the Seventh, under Lieutenant Colonel Custer's command. Their temperaments should complement each other."

"Looks like a fair deal all around," Raven commented.

Shelton stood up. "Then, gentlemen, let us get to work."

The meeting concluded and Buck walked outside with Raven. They stopped together and looked at the autumn sun setting over the rugged peaks of the Rockies. "It's all changing, isn't it?"

Raven nodded, "Everything does. Fifty years ago there were only trappers and Indians in this country. Now look at it. The Indians don't stand a chance against the push; you've seen that yourself from recent history.

"If we start now, we can prevent a war with the Blackfeet, a people accustomed to fighting and taking no steps back from anyone. If pushed too hard, they'll fight, blood will flow, and they will lose. What's left of them will get shipped off to some God-forsaken hell hole in the southern desert and this beautiful country of theirs will go to the highest bidder. It's not a perfect solution, but it's the best one we have to protect them and keep the peace."

Buck sighed, "Yeah, I guess so."

They stood silent for a minute before Buck said, "We've come a long ways together, you and me."

"And, we've got a lot further to go, and much to accomplish."

"Well, we sure have the right people for it."

Raven chuckled, "Remember that kid throwing

down the tent and saying he did not want it?"

Buck looked at the ground and smiled, "That was a long time ago." Buck then looked up at Raven, "Back before you got soft and wore blisters on your butt from a little ride."

"I did not get blisters on my butt."

Buck pulled the reins to his horse loose from the rail. He stepped up beside the horse and grinned at Raven, "Your secret is safe with me."

"I should have left you with that tent and minded my own business."

Badger walked out and looked at each of them. "Are you children arguing?"

Buck stepped into the saddle and called out to Badger, "Come on, we have to start talks with He Who Fights and the other chiefs about what we're doing."

Badger mounted up and moved alongside Buck. Buck looked at Raven, "You left your little red pillow on your chair in there."

Raven looked at Badger, "Will you get your baby brother out of here?"

"Do you want me to shoot him with an arrow?"

"That would be nice," Raven answered.

Buck laughed. "It's good to have you back, partner."

"Get out of here."

Buck turned his horse with a laugh as he and Badger rode out of the compound.

Raven watched as the two brothers rode out of the fort gate. He smiled to himself and spoke in a low voice, "I'm sure glad they didn't hang that kid." He turned and walked away across the compound. There was a lot of work to do.

About the Author

Mountain men, Voyageurs, pioneers, and explorers make up the branches of Dave's family tree. His mother's side was from Canada where the men plied the fur trade in the Canadian wilderness. Others moved down into the wilds of Northern Minnesota and established trading posts among the Chippewa.

On his father's side, his grandfather, born in the 1800's, was Kainai Blackfoot from Montana. He was a hunter and horseman who brought a great deal of Old West influence into the Fisher family.

As a lifelong Westerner Dave inherited that pioneer blood and followed in the footsteps of his ancestors. Originally from Oregon, he worked cattle and rode saddle broncs in rodeos. His adventures have taken him across the wilds of Alaska as a horsepacker and hunting guide, through the Rocky Mountains of Montana, Wyoming, and Colorado where he wrangled, guided and packed for a variety of outfitters.

Dave weaves his experience into each story. His writing, steeped in historical accuracy and drawing on extensive research, draws his readers into the story by their realism and Dave's personal knowledge of the West, its people, and character.

He has near to 500 fiction and non-fiction works published. Included are 19 western and adventure novels and short story collections, 70 short stories, and inclusion in 18 anthologies. He is the first, and currently the only, writer to win the *Will Rogers Medallion Award* three times. In 2008 for Best Western Fiction, in 2013 for Best Western Humor, and 2014 for Best Western Novel. Nine of his short stories have earned Reader's Choice Awards.

You can learn more about Dave's background and writing at his website: www.davepfisher.com